MERCHANT PRINCE OF ARCADIA

Rob Preece

BooksForABuck.com
2009

Merchant Prince of Arcadia

Rob Preece

BooksForABuck.com
2009
ISBN: 978-1-60215-017-1

Chapter 1

"Where is that worthless sniveling pile of bat dung? I swear, this time he's gone too far. I'll rip off his head and stuff it--"

"We're almost there, Captain."

Jake Borenski heard the commotion in the hall vaguely. He hunched over his computer, watched the latest rumor swirl onto the display, and nodded. Commodity markets had topped. Time to sell--everything.

His finger stabbed at the confirm button feeling the tiny prick as the computer sampled his DNA for identity confirmation.

Are you sure you wish to proceed with this transaction? Since lost prehistory, computers had stupidly asked this question rather than simply obeying instructions.

Jake glanced to see that he hadn't made any mistakes, bent to send the final confirmation--and was sent flying into the corner of his room. "Uh--"

"I told you to have the cargo holds ready yesterday." Captain Trabert's face had turned a rather attractive shade of violet. Jake wondered if there was some way to capture the color and start a new fashion statement back home.

He tried to pull his full attention from the commodity corner he'd discovered and to his job. "Uh, I'm sorry. What did you say?"

"I said you cost me twenty million com-credits worth of silk tapestries. They're ruined because you didn't do your job." The captain picked him up and shook him. "Guess what? I'm taking it out of your hide."

Jake's computer beeped, signaling that it was still waiting for confirmation. Uh-oh.

He took a deep breath and tuned down the adrenalin running through his system. Twenty million would take a bite out of his profits, but it would leave plenty more. "Just let me finish on the computer and I'll pay you back, I swear it."

"Ha, ha, ha." Trabert didn't have much of a sense of humor on the best of days. Today was a long shot from Trabert's best day. "You'll pay me back with what? Your salary?" The older man grasped Jake's ear and twisted.

"I've made a little money on commodities on the hyperboards. Let me close out my position and I'll pay you."

From the darkening shade of Trabert's face, Jake guessed he hadn't found the right answer. "You let my rugs rot while you played the commodities boards--on my time. Get out."

The old man's command didn't make a lot of sense on an enclosed space freighter, but now didn't seem to be the time to point that out. Jake stood, then reached for his computer.

Trabert slapped his hand away. "Leave that."

Jake barely resisted the ingrained reflex to block the slap and counter. From the look of the ship's guard glaring at him from behind the captain, that was a quick way to get himself shot. "But it's mine."

"It's evidence." Trabert shoved the computer into an insulating pouch cutting it off from the ship's network.

Trabert was a bully and terrible captain but Jake had never seen him go this far. A small bubble of panic accumulated in his stomach and climbed up his throat. "I've *got* to close out my positions, sir. You know what the Commodity Police are like." Appeal to the shared interest, he thought. Once he'd covered his shorts, he would have enough to buy this bathtub of a space freighter and put Trabert out to permanent pasture. Never mind the twenty million.

"You'll do what I tell you. And I'm telling you to get the hell off my ship. If the Commodity Police are after you, I suggest hiding."

Jake's panic grew. "You can't dump me off on New Earth #47. It's a Class 5 restricted. That's totally against regulations."

"Tell that to the Traders' Board." This time, Trabert's laugh sounded genuine.

There was no Traders' Board on #47 and, scheduled and certified ships barely made it there every year or so. If Trabert was serious, and despite his grin he appeared to be, Jake would be marooned. Of course, being marooned on some god-forsaken planet might be the best place for him if he couldn't undo his shorts in a hurry.

Jake gave Trabert his most engaging smile. "I'll admit I got distracted and fell short on my job this one time. Over all, though, I've been getting superior evaluations. I'd really appreciate a second chance." A chance to jump ship somewhere civilized, that was.

"Shoot him."

"But--"

Blackness descended.

* * * *

Jake Borenski felt like he'd swallowed a mule--a mule that insisted on continuing to kick from the inside of his head.

He groaned, forced his eyes open despite the gluey mess keeping them closed, and looked around. Dirt floor? Wooden walls? Stench of organics? Where was he?

An elbow smashed into the back of his head. "Oi yonna ti gornam."

"Huh?" Jake turned to look at a hugely overweight man with arms the size of liquid oxygen cylinders.

The man's words blurred into something comprehensible as his translator kicked in. Just as well Jake had his implant programmed for all of their stops before he had left home. He'd certainly been too busy since. Not to mention, this was the first time he'd been allowed off the ship.

"Your friends said you're paying. It's one crown, six shields."

Jake suspected his *friends* were Trabert's ship guards. After they'd stunned him, they'd come here for drinks, dumped him, and left him to pay for his own abandonment.

He pulled up local currency information and calculated. One crown, six shields was more money than the average local would make in a month. What had they been drinking?

"They weren't my friends." He tried to push himself to a sitting position but failed. Gravity here on #47 was brutal, especially after a couple of months on a low gravity cargo ship.

The fat man shrugged with a complete lack of concern. "Should have thought of that when you were offering to pay."

"But I was unconscious."

"Enough beer will do that. Now do you have the money or don't you?"

Jake felt through his pouches. A letter from his mother, a Dear John from his girlfriend in MBA school, and, at the bottom of the last pouch, a fat roll of ship script.

"What conversion are you running?" He pulled out the roll and slapped it on the table.

"Is that for the John Gault? She's left. Left a lot of folks holding the bag too. Guess you were one of them."

"It's all the money I have."

That rated a truly nasty growl. "Do you know what happens to men who refuse to pay their debts?"

If he'd been connected to the hypernet, he could have pulled up all the information on #47 ever assembled. As it was, he only had the limited amount he'd fed into his implant. Which wasn't much. He had the translation program, of course. That was standard. His comm. Was worthless without FTL. Even more worthless were a couple of his last semester's testbooks, *The Catcher in the Rye*, and a fantasy novel entitled *The Arena of Otranto* that used #47 as its supposed location were almost its entire contents.

In the fantasy novels he read, castaways always had more equipment or at least special knowledge. Why couldn't he have majored in chemistry rather than ancient literature and business? "You don't have a friendly bankruptcy system, then?"

The bartender just stared at him for a moment, his mouth halfway open. Finally he pulled himself together. "If that's a funny way of saying you've got no cash, I'm not amused. Here in Otranto City we're real civilized. We don't execute our debtors the way they do in the provinces. You pay what you owe, or we sell you into slavery and use the proceeds to pay off any debts. A big guy like you should be worth at least four gold."

Jake reached into his pouches again and pulled out everything he could find. "How much would you give me for this lot?"

The bartender fingered the letter from Jake's mother, then jumped back when his touch activated the letter and Mary began talking.

"It isn't magic," Jake was quick to comfort.

The bartender rolled his eyes. "Just what I need, a joker. Magic." He looked more closely at the letter. "She's a pretty little thing, isn't she?"

His mother? Jake had never thought about her in that way. He wasn't sure he wanted the bartender to think that way either but that was the only thing he'd seemed remotely interested in.

"It'll last forever," he wheedled. "How about I give it to you and we call it even."

The bartender grinned and, for a brief instant, Jake though he was in the clear.

"I don't suppose the wife would appreciate that much," the fat man told him.

"How about the uniform?" Jake suggested. "It's thermally controlled so you can wear it in virtually any weather conditions. It should be. He'd bought it himself when he realized what junk the John Gault supplied.

"You think I'd be caught dead in something that makes me look like a spacer? Besides, you've got ten centimeters on me and I've got a good fifty kilos on you."

"You could sell it. I paid a bundle for this uniform."

The fat man held up a hand. "Give it up. You don't have anything I want."

Trabert's joke hadn't been very funny in the first place. Now it was appearing completely grim.

"I wouldn't make a very good slave," Jake suggested.

"Slavers have ways of fixing that. Are you a good worker?"

This sounded promising, sort of. "You mean as a hired laborer?"

"That's it."

"I pull my weight."

"Yeah, but can you pull my weight?" The fat man's laughter sounded a lot more genuine than Trabert's had. Unfortunately, in both cases, the joke was on Jake.

Maybe he could put his MBA to work.

"How about a deal? I'll put together a marketing plan for you. You'll get enough new business to pay off my debt in no time."

"I've got all the business this city can support."

Jake looked around. He was the only one in the bar. On the other hand, it appeared to be first thing in the morning, local time. The huge yellow sun still hung low to the horizon and, outside, the noise and stench levels were still under control. From what he knew about cities on Class 5 worlds, things were likely to get far worse by the afternoon.

"Uh, do you make your own alcoholic beverages, or do you purchase these from a supplier?"

"Sometimes you talk like a priest, you know. I make most of the beer and mead in the city. The tavern is a sort of sideline."

Jake rubbed his hands together. "Great. How about I give you a complete audit of your operation here. I'll review the manufacturing process, suggest means for improving the quality of the product, and look for ways reduce transportation and labor costs." What a fabulous opportunity. When this was over, he would write a book on how the modern MBA program contributed to business success on #47.

"Are you saying there's something wrong with my beer?"

"Oh, no. It's just that there's always room for improvement."

"And some pipsqueek is going to come in and tell me how to do it, right? Have you ever brewed even a liter of beer?"

Jake did a quick search through his textbooks. He'd planned on an eventual career in business consulting or in commodity trading but he'd taken all the required classes in the more boring aspects of business--like manufacturing.

"I haven't actually brewed beer, but I know a lot about modern process engineering."

The big man didn't echo Jake's enthusiastic smile. "Uh, process engineering refers to--"

"I know what it refers to. It's a fancy name for what I do."

"Great. Well, if you don't want me in the operations side, I can take over your accounts. You'd be surprised how much a good accountant can save in costs and in prevention of bad debt."

"Bad debt is what we're talking about, but that's the first thing you've said that made any sense at all." The fat man grasped Jake's arm and lifted him from the table. "I'm going to give you one chance. You do whatever I tell you to do and I'll apply the standard apprentice pay toward what you owe me."

It didn't sound like a great deal but it did sound better than being sold into slavery. "What does a standard apprentice make around here?"

"Two bits a day."

At that rate, he would be working for half a year before he paid for what the guards had drunk.

"Eight bits, plus room and board."

"Three."

"Five or I'll take my chance with slavery from someone who values his workforce."

"Done." His new boss spat on his hand and stuck it out. "Hardly anybody wants to work any more. I'll see if you spacers are any better. My name is Manny Delphonte. You can call me Sir."

* * * *

"Right, uh, sir. I'm Jake Borinski. Uh, do you know when the next ship will be calling here?" Sitting on a planet with rampant disease, where the average lifespan was probably less than a hundred, and where mule-drawn carts constituted high technology didn't seem like a great use of his talents. Not to mention he had about two weeks to close out his positions, even at a loss, or his name would be mud with the Commodity Police and he'd never be able to leave.

Manny laughed again. He seemed to find a lot of humor in Jake which didn't fill Jake with any great confidence. "There won't be any more ships here."

Up until then, Jake had been doing his best to roll with the punches. Trabert had been a jerk, but there were always opportunities for men who were willing to work and didn't ask too many questions. For the first time, real panic reared up.

"That's impossible. Your planet isn't a huge consumer, but those handcrafted textiles have big markets in some of the core worlds. Most of the ships aren't registered, but I'd guess you get one or two a month."

Manny nodded. "I don't mean that they won't come to the planet. They just won't be coming to Otranto City." He turned and spat on the floor. "We've been dying for a few hundred years already; you spacers just put one more nail in the coffin lid."

The fantasy novel on #47 actually did cover this. Jake pulled its contents into frontal memory lobes and scanned the content before responding. If the book was at all accurate, and Jake hadn't seen any three-headed men yet so he didn't have complete confidence in it, space trade was about the only thing propping up ancient Otranto's economy. Without it, it would become just another faded city with pretensions to glory. Well, at least that wasn't his problem. "So, exactly where will the next ships be landing?"

Manny shrugged his massive shoulders. "The way our luck is going, probably somewhere in the Granger Khanate. Maybe a few will go to the eastern Barbarians, although what they'd want from that lot, I have no idea."

"Woolens," Jake told him. "The big planets don't have room for animals to run around and grow fur. It's considered very exotic and just a little kinky to wear something that was originally part of a living animal. It's even kinkier if you can say that human hands actually created the material."

Manny stood and wiped down the table next to where Jake still sat. It was a largely ineffective exercise since the rag he cleaned with had to be at least as dirty as the table.

After a full minute of silence, Manny turned and whirled toward Jake, thrusting a huge fist under his nose. "I've always said you spacers were strange, but that's the strangest thing yet. The barbarians barely have working looms. Their product is pathetic. I could make better textiles in my brewery."

Jake knew better than to argue. He also knew the market for hand-loomed sheep wool back on Vega 2 and Jutland. Twenty thousand kilograms of finished fabric could set a man for life. If he could just go east and somehow corner the market, he could leverage that into a trip back to civilization. Of course the Commodity Police would still be an issue. "Well, that's what they're looking for."

Manny pulled himself a foaming beer. "The Eastern Barbarians haven't even figured out how to handle second fermentation. Pathetic."

Jake stared at the dark beer so thick with sediment that it looked like a soup rather than the clear brew he was used to. To his surprise, he was tempted. Going native was considered one of the great sins of the restored human civilization, but Jake would forgive himself just one slip.

"Mind if I join you with one of those?"

Manny looked at him like he'd grown horns. "Why am I letting you waste my time? There's work to do. You'll eat when it's done."

Jake stood, then collapsed back to his seat. The combination of #47's 138% of Earth-standard gravity and his being recently stunned conspired against him.

"You sick?"

Jake wasn't about to try to explain differential gravity, nor the aftereffects of a stunner. "No."

"You look sick." Manny patted him on the back almost driving him through the rough boards that formed the floor under the bar. "Forget about the hair of the dog trick. Just learn your limit and stop when you get there. If you can't hold it, no point in putting it in."

"I didn't drink. I was shot."

"Don't see any bullet holes. No arrows sticking out."

He'd known better than to explain and he'd tried to do it anyway. Jake pushed his hands against the table and forced himself to his feet.

His head swam and his knees felt like rubber but he didn't immediately collapse. The longer he could keep going, the faster he'd get the residual damage from the stunner out of his system.

"So what did you have in mind for me to do today?"

Manny put one of his oversized paw-like hands on Jake's shoulder and twisted him around until he was facing the door. The sun's bright glare nearly blinded him.

"Don't even think about running away," Manny told him, tightening his grip.

"Where would I run?" He would head out the moment he heard about a ship landing, debt paid or not.

"Actually run? Nowhere. You could _try_ to run any number of places. The problem is, you'd never get there and you wouldn't like it if you did. Trust me, be an apprentice, learn a good trade like brewing, and the world will be your oyster."

Did they even have oysters on #47 or was this just his translator acting up?

"Lead on, Sir."

"That's the attitude. Let's see how many of these barrels you can get clean before noon."

* * * *

Jake looked at the huge barrels, each easily two meters deep and nearly that wide. "What the heck are those?"

Manny looked offended. "Beer barrels. Don't tell me you don't even know where beer comes from. You spacers are strange people."

Jake had concentrated on commodity arbitrage, not manufacturing. Still, he knew that beer was brewed in huge syntho-ceramic tanks that were sealed against any atmospheric contamination. "You just put the beer juice in there and let it ferment?"

Manny raised another fist. "You're too old to beat, but too stupid to treat like an adult. Try to listen. It's called wort, not beer juice. And no, we don't just put it in and leave it. What we do with it is my job. Your job is to clean them out. Maybe in a year, you'll know enough to help me with the beer making."

Jake rolled his eyes. He didn't intend to spend anything close to a year being a beer maker's flunky. He'd find some way to put his MBA to use and show Manny that he could contribute much more as a partner than a gofer. Then he'd start figuring out how to amass the credits he'd need to pay off the Commodity Police. A handful of coppers a day would pay off his fines in about ten thousand years. Even if he managed to improve his medical implant, Jake didn't figure he had that long.

"Make sure you scrub the entire barrel," Manny told him, pulling Jake's mind back to the present. "Then rinse it down with the chemicals from the smaller barrel near the spring."

"Yeah, I know. You're worried about wild yeast contamination, right?"

Manny shook his head. "Keep things clean to keep flavor good. I never even heard of wild yeast. What would it do, make the bubbles go sideways?"

Jake rubbed his eyes. So much for the benefits of a classical education. Wild yeast had been a problem back in ancient Earth. He'd just assumed it would be a problem in a similarly primitive planet. But the ancient terraformers wouldn't have brought in that kind of contaminant.

"With no wild yeast, your beer should last a long time."

"Gets drunk right away," Manny confided.

"I see." But Jake's mind was already boiling with opportunities. If beer didn't spoil, maybe the market could be bigger than this one city. And maybe Jake could help create #47's largest beverage enterprise.

"But those barrels still need to be cleaned," Manny growled. "And talking isn't getting it done."

Manny shoved Jake toward the first of twenty huge barrels lolling in the sun.

As a child on poverty-stricken Wayward, Jake had dreamed of being out in the newly discovered planets where a man could carve out a kingdom and marry a princess. In his dreams, he'd always arrived with a powerful weapon the locals would mistake for awesome magic. Well, he was here. So far, the closest he'd seen to a princess was a hundred and fifty kilogram man with a belly the size of a beachball. Of course the closest thing he had to a weapon was the scrub brush that Manny thrust into his hands.

Manny took a deep swallow from his beer mug. "There's lye in the chemical barrel so be careful."

10

This whole adventure fell into the category of being careful what he wished for. Jake surreptitiously pinched himself to make double-sure he wasn't dreaming. No such luck.

"Right. Twenty barrels. Coming up."

"You should be able to finish those by noon. Then we'll carry out last night's set."

If Manny went through that kind of beer in one night, no wonder he wasn't much interested in Jake's marketing expertise. Otranto might be the largest city on the planet, but it couldn't have over a couple hundred thousand people. Even if there were only a few brewers, that had to add up to some serious beer drinking. He pulled up his implant and calculated that each barrel had to hold about 4.7 cubic meters of beer. The twenty barrels translated to 94,000 liters. Better than a third of a liter for each resident every day.

Either Otranto drank a lot of beer, Manny was exaggerating his daily volume, or this was one of the biggest operations in town.

"Uh, how many of us are working on this?"

Manny grasped for his ear again but Jake had learned that lesson. He ducked away. "Counting you, zero, so far. I'm starting to think that the slave market was a good idea after all."

"Never mind, I'm going to work."

Jake walked to the first barrel. Every muscle complained at the higher gravity #47 inflicted on him. At least he hadn't shifted his cabin to zero gravity the way some career spacers did. Still, he also hadn't trained for anything like this.

He stared into the first barrel.

A yellow, froglike amphibian stared back. "Reek."

Jake wrinkled his nose. "You're right about that, fellow. Stinks to the high heavens. You'd better move out before I start scrubbing."

"Reek."

#47 had no intelligent native life so he didn't have to worry about training his translator to understand frog.

"Let's move, little guy." He reached in and grasped the yellow amphibian.

The thing was slippery and cold. It wiggled in his hand and then, with a suddenly exposed set of sharp teeth, bit through the webbing between Jake's thumb and forefinger.

"Ouch." He threw the frog into the field on the other side of the stream and put his injured member in his mouth. *The Arena of Otranto* hadn't mentioned poisoned amphibians. He wondered whether the author had ever actually been to the planet.

"That wasn't very smart."

He whirled around.

A pre-pubescent boy sat on the fence that surrounded the used barrels.

"What?"

"Letting the gar-frog bite you."

His blood circulation alarm confirmed the kid's message. "Poisonous, huh?"

"Usually people don't die. You'll be sick for a week, though."

He scanned his functions, cranked up the toxins filter, and toned down the filter on steroids. If he was going to be here for a while, he'd have to build up the muscles to deal with the increased gravity.

"I'll be fine. I just wonder what other surprises are going to be waiting for me."

"More gar-frogs. They like beer. But you should know that."

"I don't know much about frogs or beer."

The boy stepped down from the fence, approached Jake, and grabbed his hand. "Should be more swollen."

"You mean like this?" Jake let the toxins take full effect for a moment, then clamped back down. The bite responded instantly. Those gar-frogs would make a nice little surprise if Captain Tragert ever decided to visit.

The kid wrinkled his forehead. "That isn't possible."

"What the hell is going on out here?" Manny's deep voice cut through the youth's chatter.

"Your new apprentice got bit by a gar-frog."

"I swear, I am going to sell you," Manny shouted. "Nobody should be stupid enough to get dumped by his shipmates and bit by a gar-frog in the same day. The only way they'll ever bite is if you pick them up. Even a baby knows enough not to do that." He grabbed Jake's injured hand out of the youth's grasp. "I see the tooth marks, but you aren't swelling."

"I'm toning down the toxins," Jake admitted. "I guess its technology that hasn't reached New Earth #47."

"Our world is called Arcadia," Manny growled.

"You didn't tell me he was a spacer," the kid babbled. "How come he's working for you? I thought they were all rich."

"We got ourselves a cull," Manny replied. "And saying he's working for me pushes the definition of work a long ways. Now don't you have studies to do?"

"Eric went to the library to get some new scrolls. I decided to stay and check out the new guy."

"Right. Well, don't distract him. He needs to get those barrels cleaned or he won't eat tonight and we won't have any beer for our customers in a couple of weeks."

"That your son?" Jake asked.

"Daughter. And don't you be looking at her that way."

As if. The idea that he'd ever find a woman from one of the primitive planets attractive was pretty funny, let alone a child that he hadn't even been able to guess was female. "Don't worry about that."

The child under discussion pulled back an arm and swung it in an open-handed slap.

It had been a bad day for Jake. If he'd been on the ball, he would have taken it. How hard could a little kid hit anyway. Instead, his reflexes clicked in.

Even slowed by half-again as much gravity as he was used to, Jake slipped into a fighting stance, blocked the slap, then grasped the girl's arm and twisted.

"Ouch." The girl twisted back, fighting with a strength far beyond what Jake would have guessed possible. The gravity effect again, he thought. Why was it that in the fantasy books he'd enjoyed in his ancient lit classes, the hero always ends up on a planet with less gravity than he's used to?

He let go and stepped back. Not a brilliant idea.

The girl waded in, throwing punches and kicks as fast as he could block, until she leaned forward half a step too far and stumbled into him.

Even with the higher gravity, he could have avoided her. A quick glance behind him said that wouldn't be a good idea. Sending the boss's daughter headfirst into a pile of pig dung would not give him high marks.

Instead he caught the child, grasping both arms so she couldn't start swinging elbows and do any real damage.

Something yielded under the girl's jacket and he raised his mental age estimate by five years. She might be a kid, but she was in the process of turning into a woman. She probably wasn't too much younger than he was.

"Interesting," Manny offered.

Jake was too busy holding onto forty kilograms of fighting female to ask just what Manny found so interesting. If he let her go, she'd just start in again. If he held her, Manny would probably have him arrested for fondling his daughter. It was interesting all right, but not in any useful way.

Finally he shoved the girl away.

She planted her feet at the last minute and he ended up doing most of the moving himself. He had to skip to miss the pig dung.

Manny grasped his daughter's ear in much the same way he'd held Jake's earlier.

She calmed down after a minute. "Let me go. I want to learn to fight like a spacer."

Jake looked at Manny imploringly. "Can you keep her away from me? I've got barrels to wash."

"About time you realize that. Castile will help you. Looks like you can use it."

"Dad." It sounded like Castile wanted to help as much as Jake wanted the assistance.

"And no more fighting."

Chapter 2

Jake stared at the long row of barrels, then glanced at the female who'd been assigned to help him.

"I'll haul them down to the stream and you can scrub," he offered.

"You must have done something terrible to get dumped here," Castile observed. "Should I trust a criminal like you?" She lowered her eyes slightly. Just enough to leave Jake wondering if she was flirting with him.

"I'm especially dangerous to those who don't do their share of the work," he growled. He walked up to the first barrel, grasped it on both sides, and heaved.

The empty barrel had to weigh close to a hundred kilograms. He only managed to pick up one edge of it.

"You're pretty weak, aren't you?" Castile sounded like she was reconsidering her earlier flirtation.

Jake glared at the heavy barrel. Having Castile think he was a wimp wouldn't help. "I'm used to low grav. I'll get over it. In the meantime, do you have a cart you carry these with?"

"My father can lift an empty without any trouble. The full ones are hard, of course."

Yeah, a few cubic meters of beer could be heavy. "Well, I'm not your father. And guess what. Neither are you. So what do you suggest?" It galled him to ask, but Castile had been here longer than he had. His training didn't let him ignore experienced help.

* * * *

"I could lift and you could wash."

He gave Castile a closer look. She wore a shapeless gray tunic that looked like silk, wooden clogs, and a cap that hid her hair completely. The tunic exposed slender arms and legs that showed hints of muscle. Not enough, he thought, to pick up this kind of weight.

"Maybe we'd better work together."

"You don't think I could do it, do you?"

He didn't, but arguing about it wouldn't help matters. In one of his summer intern jobs, he'd made the mistake of antagonizing his boss's son. The rest of the summer had been absolute hell. "It would be easier if we worked together. Let's dump it over on the side and roll it."

"Dad always carries them."

"Your dad isn't here." He grasped the top of the barrel and put his weight into it. Slowly, the heavy wooden container shifted.

Then, without warning, it accelerated, crashing to the ground as he barely jumped out of the way.

Castile nodded to him. "I guess this will work. 'Course if you break them, they'll come out of your pay."

New planet, same story. Between the fines and outrageous charges for necessities like daily showers, he'd fallen into debt on the John Gault. Which was part of the reason he'd started playing the commodity boards in the first place.

He leaned into the barrel and managed to get it swaying back and forth about two centimeters.

"My mother always says how important it is to exercise," Castile told him as she manhandled the barrel over the small rock that blocked Jake's path. "I guess your mother forgot to mention that to you."

Jake could barely remember his mother. Like most women on modern planets, she'd dropped him off at school when he'd been five and gotten on with her life. He could have explained why this was proven better, but he thought he could guess the look of pity and condemnation he'd get from Castile. Instead he simply nodded, then leaned his shoulder into the barrel. Once it was moving, he could keep it going--until it ran into another rock, at least.

He should have hit the weights more during those long boring stretches between planets.

Jake closed his eyes, gritted his teeth, and shoved, putting all of his weight behind the blasted barrel. To his surprise and delight, it started rolling down toward the stream, finally smashing into the stony streambed with a satisfying boom.

"Hey, careful," Castile called. "I wasn't kidding. Those barrels will break."

He wiped his eyes and examined the massive container. "I don't see how."

Castile brushed her hand across the iron bands that held the barrels together. It was, Jake thought incongruously, an oddly sensuous gesture. "We could re-use the iron, of course," she told him. "The iron is the expensive part." She offered a sponge to him. "Climb inside. I'll pass you the chemicals."

Jake thought about arguing but this was his job. For his own pride if nothing else, he decided he would show Manny Delphonte that he could put in a fair day's work--even if that meant letting Castile boss him around.

He gripped the iron band that held the barrel staves in place stepped into the icy water that had flooded the barrel and took the sponge from Castile.

"Hey, this is one of my hoops."

Jake concentrated on his scrubbing trying to ignore the way that the beer fumes reacted to the stunner-induced headache his implant hadn't dealt with yet.

"You wouldn't think I'd be strong enough to swing the hammer, would you?" Castile went on as if he'd given her some encouragement. "But it's really all about using the weight of the hammer rather than the strength of the arm. I started with horseshoes, of course. I guess everybody does. But then I moved up to barrel hoops. Eric says he'll let me make a matchlock next. Fun."

The girl had an odd sense of fun, Jake decided. She also had a mouth on her that wouldn't stop. At first, he found that a little annoying. On the overcrowded surface of Wayward and on the John Gault, artificial privacy barriers kept conversation to a work-related minimum. After a few minutes, though, Jake realized that he couldn't shut her up and that he might actually learn something. While Castile might be a child, she had lived in Otranto City all her life. Since he was stuck here, he might as well learn what he could. Besides, her constant chatter did seem to make the morning go faster.

Jake suspected that he would smell beer in his dreams--or rather, nightmares. He clambered out of the last barrel, threw the sponge on the ground, and collapsed next to it.

"You're getting muddy," Castile warned him.

"Tough."

"My mother won't like it."

"You're not the one getting muddy."

"Yeah. But you're the one who's going to have to show up at dinner looking like that."

A sharp gurgle in Jake's stomach let him know that *dinner* was one of those magic words. "When?"

Castile looked at the sun. "Uh, now."

Jake was covered with mud, old beer, sweat, and the chemicals he'd used to clean the barrels. Even if Castile's mother wasn't a bear for personal hygiene, he wouldn't be a popular seatmate.

He looked at the stream they'd used to clean the barrels. "Is that safe?"

"Going to pick up any more gar frogs?"

He shook his head.

"Then it's safe." She paused. "Can I watch?"

"Sure." He plunged in fully clothed, sputtered to the surface, and climbed out.

"Is that it?"

"All clean," he announced. It was about time he did something right in Castile's mind--even if all he'd done was take advantage of a modern suit's ion-based ability to self-clean. He shook himself off, shedding the water that had briefly clung to the parts of his body not covered by the suit. "I'm starved. Let's eat."

* * * *

Any preconceptions Jake had about Castile's mother were shattered by her appearance. Where he'd expected an earthy barmaid, he saw a fairy princess, blonde to Manny's nearly blue-black hair, slender to his bulk, yet with an imperious glance that took in everything and seemed impressed by no one.

Unlike the dirt-floored bar, the meal room was floored with a mosaic that would have been in a museum on any of the civilized planets, and was spotlessly clean with whitewashed walls.

The woman presided over one long table while Manny crowned the other. All of the other places were taken by boys and men ranging in age from about five to fifty-five. In all, there had to be close to forty of them. By pre-industrial standards, Manny ran a major operation.

"She looks like a princess," Jake whispered out loud.

"Maybe because she is," Castile suggested. "Not that there aren't a whole lot of Otranto princesses these days."

Manny stood when Castile and Jake tried to slip into the room, mussed Castile's hair, and clasped Jake on the shoulder almost driving him to the floor in his enthusiasm.

"Boys, I've hired us a spacer. At least 'til he pays off his bar debt. This here's Jake something. Can't remember his family name but guess it doesn't matter since he ain't got no family within a few billion kilometers." Manny rattled off the names of the apprentice, journeyman, and master brewers he'd gathered, then pushed Jake to the only empty seat, only two spaces down from his wife. "Eat up. This time, the beer's on me."

After hours breathing the odor of stale beer, the last thing Jake would have asked for was more beer. Still, when he sat, one of his neighbors forced a tall tankard on him and he could hardly refuse a swallow.

The souring mash in the barrels he'd been washing couldn't compare to the strong, cool, yet refreshing sensation. "Good beer."

"You like it?" The man who'd forced it on him looked a little like Manny in his beer gut and bear-like arms.

"Like it? It's the best beer I've ever had." Which it was. Could the civilized world's obsession for the primitive extend to handcrafted beer? Jake shook his head. Even the jaded tastes of civilization wouldn't go that far. Carrying heavy loads of beer between planets wasn't going to pay.

The neighbor to Jake's left rolled his eyes. "If this is as good as you've tasted, you must have had some real swill." This man was short, but looked like a body builder with no noticeable body fat at all. "Theo's got a long wait before he gets his mastery. Now this is some real beer." He shoved another stein into Jake's hand.

Jake took a swallow of the second beer. This was a dark beer with a head so thick it made the legendary Guinness foam seem fragile. "Wow."

"Don't let Angert fool you," Theo argued. "He makes it strong, but it has no finesse. That's why he's still working here when he's been a master for five years. Nobody else will take him."

Angert laughed, but even Jake could tell his heart wasn't in it. "I suppose the sheep piss you peddle as beer is going to let you do better. I'm here because Manny pays well and because he has about the only business that's hiring in the whole city. Unless you want to be a priest, that is."

"Sheep piss? Let me tell you--"

Angert casually pulled a knife from his belt and cut off a cuticle. "If you ever make master, which I doubt since I've drunk your beer, then you can tell me whatever you want. Until then, talk to the kid."

He had been tossed into the middle of an ongoing rivalry, Jake realized. Still, one thing Angert had said stood out. Why was Manny able to thrive when everyone else in the city, or for that matter the entire country, suffered a continual decline?

Jake put up a hand. "It looks like I'm going to be here for a while so I'll have time to sample everyone's work." Which was, he realized, the point. This dinner meal was also the time when they compared new brews, determined new strategies to distribute their massive production, and rewarded anyone who had made a new discovery.

Jake ate quietly, drinking from the two mugs that had been shoved at him and listening to the bragging, shop-talk, and gossip that swirled around him.

Whatever Manny might think now, the fact that his brewery was a mass production business meant that Jake's MBA process training should be able to pay off.

Except, nobody had re-introduced mass production to Arcadia. The Trader's Guild frowned on people spreading technology without being licensed. So where had Manny come up with this idea in the first place?

* * * *

"My husband tells me you were cast out from your ship. I would love to hear your story." The voice was soft, low, and would have been worth millions if she ever made it into the tri-Vs.

Jake realized he was still eating after most of the men had vanished. He looked up into the deepest purple eyes he'd ever seen. Except maybe on Castile, which didn't count at all. "I would be honored, of course, Mrs. Delphonte."

"We don't stand on formalities here. You may call me Marie."

His stored copy of Arena of Otranto clicked again letting him know how unusual was any type of informality in the highly structured and socially conscious Otranto society. "Thank you."

"Follow me, then."

He followed, trying not to notice the gentle sway in her hips as she walked in front of him. The narrow silk dress she wore fit her like a second skin and emphasized rather than diminishing what it covered. Manny was a lucky man.

If the dining room had been medieval-institutional, Marie's chamber was a fantasy. Genuine wood floors glowed with hand-applied wax. Tapestries, that Jake suspected were genuine hand-made articles, depicted country scenes with bizarre animals and strange trees.

Marie gestured to a heavy wood chair, took another one herself, then clapped her hands.

One of the servants who'd carried in the plates and pitchers of beer appeared, put a plate of cheeses and bread between them, and vanished.

Marie looked around. "I know you're hiding here somewhere, Castile. Come out."

Jake would have sworn that Castile had still been in the dining room when they'd left. He certainly didn't see her here.

Castile scowled at him as she stepped out from a shadow beneath a large hanging plant. "I'm stuck doing most of his work so it's only fair that I hear his story too."

"Would you mind, Jake?"

It didn't take a genius to know the right answer to that question. Of course he'd rather sit and lap up the presence of a beautiful woman alone. He'd also rather not be snapped in two by the woman's husband: a man who could pick up hundred kilogram barrels as easily as Jake could pick up a computer. A chaperone was an excellent idea.

"I don't have any secrets."

"Really." Marie's eyes danced. "That is a pity. But then again, you haven't been in Otranto very long."

Was she flirting with him? He supposed spacers did have a bit of a reputation on some of the more sedate worlds. After spending a few months in a ship, crews were wont to get out, get drunk, and find a willing partner for some desperate lovemaking. Still, although Jake was as prone to fantasies as the next guy, he didn't think Marie was looking for that kind of action.

He ran through the story of his brief space trading career, his discoveries of manipulation on the commodity boards and his increasing fascination with the chance to make big bucks, leading up to his abrupt dismissal from his position. Even to his own ears, he hardly sounded like a hero.

"You deserved it," Castile told him when he'd finished. So much for his hope that he'd sounded less like an idiot to the locals.

"From what you've said, your colleagues aren't likely to return for you."

Jake hesitated for just a moment. Was she trying to find out exactly how vulnerable he was? Then he took a deep breath. He was alone in a huge and dangerous world. He would have to trust someone. So far, Manny and Marie had been straight with him. "It is possible that the Commodity Police will eventually track me down. They don't take kindly to traders who don't close out their short positions."

"That will be in weeks? Months?"

"Years, if ever." And probably never. Banishment to a pre-technology world was worse than any punishment they were allowed to meet out.

Marie nodded. "What about other traders?"

"Manny told me that they won't be coming to Otranto City any more. None would go out of their way just to pick me up, even if they did know I was here."

"I have heard that you spacers have some way of communicating amongst yourselves, even over long distances."

He nodded, took a bite of bread and cheese, then a sip from the cup Castile had poured him.

He coughed. "This isn't beer."

"It's mead. A kind of beer we make from honey," Marie told him.

He'd heard of it but never tasted it. "It's good."

Castile grinned, then clapped her hands. "I told you."

Marie smiled. "I know. But he's never tried mead before, so he doesn't have a standard for comparison. You may want to find a more qualified judge before you submit it for your masterwork."

Castile's joy faded. "But--"

"Were you going to answer my question, Mr. Borinski?"

His stomach fell at her use of his full name. What had happened to the informality of a few moments before?

Technology is a trade good. The exchange of technology, or even the information that a technology exists, is considered the property of the Trader's Guild. Individual spacers who exchanged technology freelance would face the wrath of the Guild--and they would be willing to track him down if they found out about it.

On the other hand, the Trader's Guild was a long way away and Marie Delphonte was quite close.

"Just about everyone has a computer implant with comm capabilities. They run off the body's electri--" he realized he'd just jumped out of his translator into Galactic System. "uh, power. Unfortunately, they have a limited transmission range."

"I see." Marie stood and walked to a bookcase, removing a large, leather-bound book. "Do you know what this is?" She held it in his direction.

His translator blurred the unfamiliar characters and then communicated their meaning. It was *The Arena of Otranto*.

"I'm vaguely familiar with the novel." He hesitated, wondering whether he would offend her if he told her what he thought. "It's the only book about Arcadia I found in the library but it isn't really very good."

Marie's laugh was warm, almost fruity, inviting the listener to join in its pure joy. "You are certainly the master of understatement, aren't you? It is, in fact, the single worst book I've ever read."

Jake was sure this conversation had a point. He was also sure he was clueless on what it was. "It looks like a beautiful edition, though. I assume it's a local translation."

She nodded. "We sometimes get spacers who want to hunt. We had one who planned to take trophies from each of the animals mentioned. He commissioned a translation so he could show his guides what animals he wanted. I was able to secure a copy." Marie paused a beat. "At considerable cost."

"But why? We've already agreed that it's a literary disaster."

"Listen to this." Marie carefully opened the tome, slowly paging through before finding the passage. "Braker grimaced as he quaffed the flat, vinegary brew. Yet with poor sanitation, zero refrigeration, and no ability to hold pressure, this was the best his planet had to offer."

Jake couldn't hold back a chuckle. "Quaffed? I can't believe it made it through even the worst editor in New New York. I don't suppose you really have people named Braken here, do you?"

"Not that I've heard of. Look around you, Jake."

Jake checked out the elegant room. "What?"

"Everything here came from that passage." She held up a hand to forestall Jake's objection. "Manny experimented with sanitation, cooling, and pressurization until he was able to brew a beer even spacers could enjoy."

"I see." If one line from a cheap adventure novel could create the biggest business in the biggest city in Arcadia, what could the complete knowledge of a galaxy's science do? A man who knew the formula for smokeless powder could revolutionize warfare and end up Emperor of an entire world.

Too bad he'd been an Ancient Literature major before pursuing business administration. He didn't see how the works of Shakespeare or Marlow could come in handy here. Maybe Machiavelli.

Marie leaned forward, exposing, either through design or accident, a generous view of her cleavage. "I know spacers aren't supposed to reveal any of their science, but we need it. Otranto has been whittled away from both west and east. What do you think will happen when we fall? Because we are falling, Jake. The spacers' decision to abandon us and go directly to the barbarians will hasten the end."

"You can bet they'll put dad out of business too," Castile added. She'd sunk into the shadows again and her sudden re-emergence was almost as big a shock to Jake as her initial appearance had been.

Marie smiled at her daughter but pulled back, eliminating the view she'd just shared with Jake. "She's right, Jake. Depending on who gets here first, either the Granger will enslave us all, or the barbarians will simply loot and burn. It isn't much of a choice."

She was playing hardball, but Jake didn't think she was exaggerating. Not by much, anyway.

He shook his head slowly. "I really can't help you."

"You mean you won't," Castile corrected. "You probably think you'll do better when the barbarians get here."

"Castile," her mother admonished. "You have to respect a man's principles."

"That's not it," Jake corrected. "Most spacers are engineers. They could come in and develop new weapons and show you brilliant tactics and win the wars. Sort of like the Boss in *Connecticut Yankee in King Arthur's Court*."

"Who?" Castile wanted to know.

"That's the point. I majored in Ancient English. I know old books. Mostly books written thousands of years ago when all humans lived on Earth and the technology level was about what you have now." He shrugged his shoulders. "I don't know any of those things."

"But even something small like that quote on brewing," Marie objected. "Look what it did. You may not realize what you may know without even thinking about it."

That much was true. If scientists knew where to look, they were more likely to find something. "How long did it take Manny to work out the details after he'd read that section?"

"Maybe twenty years."

"And how long before the invasions?"

Marie shrugged fetchingly, her breasts moving just slightly to keep pace with her shoulders. "Maybe two years, if we're lucky."

He put his face in his hands. "There's no possible way."

* * * *

Jake's body groaned as he stretched out on the thin pad he'd been given. Every muscle ached although he'd put his implant to work pumping up the endorphins and accelerating deployment of natural steroids.

"Get up, you bum. It's late." Castile's voice was joined by her sharp-toed shoe, which jammed him in the ribs.

It wasn't late. In fact, his implant told him it was only five in the morning, local time. The sun should barely be above the horizon.

"Go away."

"Uh-un. It's a new day. You've got twenty more barrels to wash and my tutor is back." Castile made a face. "If you want my help, you'd better move."

He thought about telling her he didn't need any help, but then he moved his arms and almost screamed. He was sore in muscles he hadn't even known he had.

"We didn't start yesterday until after ten."

"That's when Eric gets here."

"Oh." He stood, wondering why he'd drunk so much beer. "Did you really make that mead?"

Castile grinned. She had her father's hair and strong jaw, but Jake could see flashes of the pure femininity that Castile's mother exuded peaking from underneath that. "You liked it, didn't you?"

"It was good."

"I've been experimenting with different wine yeasts. That and the flowers the bees used for their honey are what make for the big taste differences. You can't just use beer yeast."

"No?"

"Huh-un. 'Cause barley makes maltos and honey doesn't have that much maltos. I've been experimenting with different yeasts for the last two years."

Jake rubbed his eyes, instructed his medical implant to give him a shot of whatever natural substitute existed for caffeine, and stood. "So you're into this beermaking stuff too, are you?"

Castile put her hands on her hips. "This isn't just about beer. We have some of the old books, you know. Those that got copied before the old readers lost their power. Dad's beermaking is the beginning of industrialization. That's why I'm studying mead *and* blacksmithing."

"Always assuming that Otranto is still here by the time you grow up," Jake reminded her.

"Like you're such an adult," Castile answered. "Besides, that's why I'm helping you. You're going to teach me those spacer fighting moves you used yesterday."

Jake started to shrug, then stopped abruptly as the muscle aches cut in. He cranked up the pain avoidance in his implant although he knew he would end up more banged up without the warnings that pain provided.

"Besides," Castile continued, giggling. "Mead is more fun than beer. Honey has more sugar and so you get a higher alcohol content. A couple of glasses and look out world."

How much had he drunk the previous evening? Jake didn't have a clue but he instructed his implant to do its best with whatever remained of alcohol toxins still floating around in his system. As soon as he got off this planet, Jake promised himself he'd upgrade to a full pharm kit rather than the basic medical system he'd bought.

"Well, your mead was good," he said, trying to placate Castile. "I don't suppose there's a chance of breakfast before we start working."

"How fast can you eat?"

He looked at her, completely suspicious. "Why."

"Breakfast is about over. Better move that cute little tush of yours."

Castile gave him a swat as he headed past her toward the dining room. He was completely in control of his reflexes this time and didn't even come close to breaking her arm. He might be weak by Arcadia standards, but that didn't mean he was completely helpless.

Breakfast was a great deal like dinner except there was less talking. Manny was finishing up last minute instructions on the mix of beers they would start that day, the supplies available for journeyman projects, and the break they'd require when the teamsters arrived for their daily loads.

"Do you load those whole barrels on carts?" Jake asked Angert who had been frowning at him since he'd sat down.

"Those big barrels are for primary fermentation only. For secondary, we decant to smaller barrels. Those are the ones we ship."

"Why don't you use bottles? That's the way beer is served in the civilized planets."

"We know that, idiot. Why do you think the boss and the boss's lady wanted your help. If you know how to make cheap glass, we could double our business."

Glass was made out of sand. That, unfortunately, summed up everything Jake knew about it. He checked his computer implant without much hope and came up empty there. "Sorry."

"Yeah, me too. Well, at least keep the barrels clean and you've earned your keep."

"For as long as we're still here," Theo added.

"Aren't you finished yet? I've never seen anyone eat as much as you." Castile had finished and was obviously in a hurry.

Jake grabbed half a loaf of bread off the table and followed Castile out to the cleaning area. Twenty barrels, looking almost identical to the ones they'd washed the previous day, stood waiting.

A growing realization that he could be in for a long spell hit Jake.

"What?"

"I was thinking I might spend the rest of my life rolling these barrels into the stream."

"Nah. If you keep eating the way you do, you'll either be able to carry them or you won't be able to waddle."

He grasped the first barrel and pushed. It moved a little more than it had the previous day. Progress. "I'm trying to get used to the higher gravity."

"I've heard about gravity but I don't really understand how it works," Castile told him.

This was another opportunity to look smart. Unfortunately, Jake's full understanding of gravity could be summed up with the fact that it made apples fall on scientists' heads. Not particularly useful.

Chapter 3

"Get your lazy butt outside and help me load the wagons." Manny's sweat had soaked through the hard leather of his apron and his gut seemed to have shrunken visibly during the past hours.

"But dad, you know how weak he is."

With supporters like Castile, Jake would almost rather stick with his detractors. He pulled himself from the barrel he'd been washing. "I'm on my way, boss."

"You may not have noticed, but after a month of good food, your weak little plaything has put on some muscle," Manny instructed his daughter. "You'd better watch out for him now." He laughed loudly, smashing his fist against his thigh.

During his month on the job, Jake could think of exactly two suggestions he'd made that had actually helped Manny's business. He'd made no progress at all on getting off the planet.

Even his two suggestions--offering some of the master brewers' special blends at a premium price, and plumbing up a system to speed barrel washing-- were hardly world-altering insights. He had toyed with the idea of a logo and slogan, but Manny had put his foot down when Jake had suggested hiring an artist. *They'd drink enough to bankrupt me,* had been Manny's exact response.

As Manny said, all Jake had to show for the month was some added muscle and a deeper understanding of primitive beermaking. Neither made him unique on Arcadia nor would they help him if he ever got back to space. Time was wasting and helping load carts was an even bigger waste.

Four of Manny's beefiest assistants stood around a huge wagon pulled by the six biggest horses Jake had ever seen. Of course he hadn't ever seen a horse before coming to Arcadia, but he'd seen plenty since. The remains of a shattered barrel and an expanding pool of beer lay next to the wagon. One of the horses sucked at the puddle.

"What's the problem?" Jake asked.

"Are all you spacers slow, or is it just you?"

"Probably all of us," Jake answered. "'Course I've got it better than most."

"I'll bet." Manny mopped his sweating forehead with a rag that already dripped, then pointed an accusing finger at the teamster who seemed to be encouraging his animals to take advantage of the free treat.

"Arnie there built his cart just a little higher than everyone else."

"Keeps me away from the mud," Arnie announced. He spit into the beer pond.

"Right. So loading his vehicle creates a problem," Manny continued. "I thought we'd use some of that new muscle I've been paying for."

"You want me to pick up a thousand kilograms of beer?" He did a quick body scan. Sure enough, he had increased his body mass and increased his strength by a good thirty percent over the past month. That didn't make him anything to write home about.

"Actually, I thought you'd help the rest of us. Unless you've got a spacer trick." This last was somewhere between a sarcastic comment and a serious question.

Jake decided to take it as a question. "We could rig up a block and tackle." They still loaded shuttles that way, although no people actually tugged on ropes back in civilization.

"Yeah, and we could increase the height of the ramp too, if we had time. Any other brilliant ideas?"

Jake shook his head. He was still low man on the guild totem pole. He should have kept his mouth shut.

"Are you going to help us, Arnie?" The words were a question, but Manny's tone made it a command.

"Somebody's got to mind the horses. Wouldn't want them to take off next time a beer barrel smashes next to their faces."

"Great. Castile has been looking for something to do."

Castile stepped out of a shadow.

"Oh, all right. I'm already late. I don't suppose it would hurt any to give your men a hand." Arnie's eyes never left Castile, though. His whole body seemed to twitch with each step she took.

"Your daughter is growing up," he commented. "I've always liked my women young."

Arnie's words were followed by complete silence. The whisper of one journeyman talking to another, Castile's small words of comfort to the horse as she dissuaded him from further attempts on the still expanding lake of beer, even the omnipresent cicadas seemed struck dumb.

Manny's face went from red to white. He opened his mouth, shut it, then opened it again. "You've been tempting fate for a long time, Arnie, but now you've crossed the line. Do you really think working for the Granger ambassador gives you that much protection? I probably killed a hundred Granger when I was a mercenary. You think I'd be afraid to add another to the list?"

In a month working for the man, Jake thought he'd seen every side of him. Manny's ice-cold voice and hard stare were something completely new.

Manny was a large and powerful man. Arnie was a monster.

Moving at a speed that shouldn't have been possible on a high-gravity planet like Arcadia, Arnie whipped out a knife and closed the distance to the waiting Manny who hadn't even taken his hands from his hips.

It was none of his business, Jake reminded himself. Sure Manny had fed him, but he'd also paid him a pittance and treated him like he was a foolish child.

By the time he'd reasoned that through, he'd reached Arnie's knife arm, grasped it, and swung the oversized giant over his hip in as sweet a throw as he could remember.

Arnie landed hard but bounced back fast. This time he swung his knife hand in an arch designed to fool Jake's eyes and nullify his hands. Arnie wasn't just big, and quick. He also knew something about knife fighting.

"Meet my pet spacer," Manny said. "'Course he's the runt of the litter. Jake, you back off and let me handle Arnie."

Arnie's gaze flickered between the two men. "Pet spacer? IImm--I heard you'd taken on a new apprentice. You know the rules, Delphonte. An apprentice strikes a master, he loses that hand."

"I didn't see any striking," Castile called out. "Looked to me like you were trying to knife my dad and fell over poor Jake."

"Yeah. Well, you're a woman. Otranto may be a pathetic has-been, but at least we don't listen to women in our courts. So let go of my horses. Delphonte, if you want to load my wagon, you'll do it with no help from me."

He jerked the reins suddenly, sending Castile sprawling.

Manny grasped Jake's arm. "He won't hurt her and he has powerful allies."

"But he was trying to kill you," Jake whispered.

Manny shrugged. "When he isn't doing deliveries, he does a little killing for his boss. In this case, I don't know if it's personal or Arnie doing his job.

"If Emperor Fernis wasn't such a weakling, he'd kick the Granger out of Otranto City and send an army to keep them out."

* * * *

Jake nodded but he understood Fernis's position too. If your army were made up of mercenaries who already knew they were fighting a losing battle, you wouldn't risk it more often than you had to. That meant taking a certain amount of abuse from more powerful enemies. It made sense that the Granger would take every opportunity to disrupt any attempt to revive the Otranto economy. Which Manny's brewery certainly was.

Jake barely controlled himself as Arnie swung a fist in Castile's direction--a blow she neatly avoided.

"He looks serious."

"Injuring up a Master's daughter would cost him five gold and cause problems for his boss. He might risk the fine but the ambassador tries to cultivate the Otranto masses."

Sure enough, Arnie flipped his knife in the air, caught it by the hilt, and deposited it back to his belt. "Load up the ambassador's beer."

Manny looked at the smashed barrel. "We wouldn't want another terrible accident, would we? Let's block the wheels so they don't slip."

From Arnie's scowl, Jake guessed he'd planned to move the cart just as the men lifted the tons of beer onto it. Even a small lurch could result in a big fall-- as the now evaporating puddle of beer testified.

Once the blocks had been set, Manny positioned his men around the next barrel. Together, they lifted the heavy container. The timbers of Arnie's wagon creaked under the load but held.

"One more," Arnie commanded. "Careful not to strain yourself, boys."

Jake was shocked at the amount of weight his monitors said he had been able to shoulder. Even when he'd played shortstop for his college baseball team, he'd been lucky to deadweight lift eighty kilograms. Now he was lifting more than twice that.

The second barrel proved no more difficult, although one of Arnie's horses, the one that had drunk all the beer, didn't look very happy about the load.

"I'll be back with the Metropolis," Arnie snarled as he left. "They'll take care of that supposed apprentice and that perjuring daughter of yours."

Manny's hand clasped Jake's shoulder. "Maybe it's time we tried out a couple of your marketing ideas. Outside of town."

* * * *

Jake stared at the mismatched mules pulling his wagon, one yellow and barely larger than a pony, the other a huge animal that looked like the result of a breeding between a donkey and a Shire. A second pair followed docilely pulling the second cart in their makeshift caravan.

"I'm hungry." Since they'd left Otranto City, Castile had alternated between sitting next to him on the wagon bench, driving the second team, and skipping ahead of the mules on the stone-paved road. Now she swung up onto the seat beside him.

"We just ate."

"I'm hungry again."

He was too and it was a problem. His habits, formed by twenty-one mostly sedentary years in much lower gravity, led him to prepare small meals. His new appetite, created by a high-gravity planet and plenty of exercise, demanded that he more than double his normal calorie count. During the two days they'd been traveling, food had been the most frequent topic of conversation.

"Would the Metropolitan Guard really have listened to Arnie rather than to you and your dad?" he asked, trying to keep his mind off of food for at least a minute. Later, when they stopped, he'd cook up a huge batch of the beans and rice Marie had sent with them. If they stopped now, built a fire and cooked, it would be near dark by the time they were ready to hit the road again. Fast food was a concept Arcadia had lost. He wondered if he'd be doing the planet any favors if he reintroduced that invention.

"Half of the Guard are in the Daniel, the Granger Ambassador's pay," Castile told him. Apparently she'd made her food protest and was ready to let him distract her.

"Literally half? Or are you exaggerating?" The only reason for such widespread corruption was that the Granger were planning on moving soon-- probably within the year.

"At least half. With the Emperor paying them brass washed with silver, Granger gold looks awful attractive."

Jake shook his head. He still planned on laying low, building up a stock of trading goods that the civilized worlds would be interested in, and getting out of here. Increasingly, though, it looked like the tired remnants of the Otranto Empire wouldn't be around long enough to meet his plans. From what he'd read about ancient warfare, a start-up merchant wouldn't have much chance in a war zone.

"Maybe your father had an ulterior motive on sending us on this trip, then," Jake said.

Castile gave him a suspicious look. "Of course he had an ulterior motive. He used to be a general."

"Oh." Castile was definitely not the kind of girl who'd ooh and ah over male discoveries. "So you think he wants us to scout out someplace where he could relocate if Otranto City falls to the Granger?"

Castile's glare spoke of contempt. "He's sending us to scout the territory. Also, if we really can find some new markets for our beer and mead, so much the better."

Jake spotted a wooded area a couple of kilometers ahead and shook the mules' reins to get them moving a little faster than the slow trudge. If Castile was right, it was up to him to figure out a way to save the Delphonte family, and Manny wasn't going to do anything to help him.

"This wasn't the first time the Granger tried to shut Dad down." Castile hopped from the wagon and walked alongside picking wildflowers and twining them through her hair.

Jake nodded. "Countries with dynamic economies are a lot harder to conquer. But I'd think your father would be relatively safe from overt attack. Since he makes most of the beer in Otranto City, the people would probably riot if the Granger move too obviously."

Castile's laugh was bright but had a fruity tone--the laughter of a woman rather than a child. "Dad's a barbarian. As far as the mob is concerned, they're as bad as the Granger, no matter that they've been fighting our wars for us for the past two hundred years. Besides, he's put a lot of other brewers out of business. Those who don't work for him hate him."

Jake's studies of ancient literature should have prepared him for this type of irrational economics, but he was still surprised. He was also surprised that a barbarian like Manny had been able to marry an Otranto princess. What if Jake could--he cut off that train of thought. He might be a barbarian by Otranto standards, but Castile had already told him that Manny had been a general. The market for ancient literature majors with newly minted MBA degrees was likely to be a lot less attractive.

"How'd your dad become so successful, then?"

Castile nodded soberly. "He was a mercenary. Won a couple of battles. So there was nothing they could do but marry him to a princess and let him do whatever he wants as long as he stays far away from politics."

"Staying away from politics sounds like a good idea." Offhand, Jake couldn't think of anyone who'd gone into politics and come out a happier person. Richer, maybe. Happier, no.

"It was a good idea as long as Emperor Julian lived. He was a soldier like dad. Now he's dead and Emperor Fernis is in charge. He's only interested in two things. Keeping the mob happy and keeping the Granger happy. And Dad gets in the way of both of those goals."

Maybe so, but Manny was still in business. "Let me guess. Your father stays out of politics, but your mother keeps her finger in the pot?"

Castile grinned at him as if he was a slightly slow student who'd finally learned an important lesson. "Right the first time. There's got to be some advantage to being married to an Otranto princess."

Jake managed not to smile. To Castile, Marie was probably just impossibly old. Jake though, could think of a lot of advantages to being married to a princess who looked like Marie, even if she didn't dabble in politics.

"Hey. It looks like there's a village behind those trees," he said changing the subject to avoid saying anything really stupid.

Castile hopped back on the wagon and stretched. "If there's an Inn, I get the bed. Let's see if we can sell them some mead at the tavern and make some money on this trip."

Jake had no doubt that they'd like Castile's mead: they'd be insane not to. Now that he'd experienced a couple of days on the road, he wasn't convinced that even a vibrant market could justify the costs of hauling heavy barrels of beer and mead across the countryside. And from what he could see of the village they were approaching, the words vibrant market weren't jumping to his lips.

As they crossed the outskirts of the town, Jake realized that it had once been far larger. Sheep stared at them from the open atriums of abandoned villas. Beautiful mosaic tiles depicted allegorical subjects and were now overgrown by some of the same nature they'd celebrated.

Closer to the ancient center of the town, most of the buildings had been pulled down. The building material had obviously gone into construction of a rough wall that seemed equally composed of dirt and ancient statues that would fetch tens of thousands of credits back home.

"What happened here?" Jake whispered.

Castile looked around. "What do you mean?"

"I mean, this used to be a good sized town. Now it's a wreck.

"Looks pretty normal to me." She glanced around, indifferent to the gradual decline of a once beautiful village. "Come on and let's find that tavern before dark."

The town's gates hung open, with one of them slipped from one hinge and drooping down like an old man too tired to pick himself up yet unable to surrender.

Jake shivered at the image and at Castile's indifference. Otranto seemed caught by a wasting disease. This village was simply another example.

Jake pulled their wagons next to a tavern marked with a large sign proclaiming it to be the Ax and Shoe, then unloaded a small flask of Castile's mead.

Castile stepped behind him onto the wagon and pulled the canvas covers closed. "I'll only be a minute."

Whatever else Castile might be, she was a female. He would believe she could dress in a minute when he saw it.

It was, according to his implant, exactly sixty-five seconds later when Castile emerged. Somehow, during that period, she had transformed herself from the androgynous child who skipped in front of the wagon to a younger version of a Marie in her merchant princess guise.

"Will I do, sir?" she asked.

He realized his eyes must be bugging out. He nodded. "That is an excellent plan. They'll value the mead more if it seems to come from an aristocrat."

"Well that too." Castile giggled, transforming from beautiful woman to child in that moment, then abruptly transmuting back. "Let's go. I'm hungry."

* * * *

The barkeep reminded Jake of Manny although, later, when he pointed out the resemblance to Castile, she'd hit him. Unlike Manny, this man was short and scrawny and he squinted when he looked at anything. Squint or not, he looked around his domain with complete confidence, as if he planned on taking care of himself no matter what else happened.

"I'm Lucer, your host" he said. "I've got lamb stew in the pot and bread in the oven. Are there others coming?"

"Uh, no," Jake started.

"I'll talk to him." Castile walked imperiously to the bar.

"We don't get a lot of aristocrats in here," Lucer said. He spat into a small spittoon near the bar. "No great loss."

"Perhaps that is because they abhor the taste of your brew."

"Perhaps that's because they won't leave Otranto City when the empire is collapsing around them."

"Oh? I suppose you think you're doing a great deal for the empire sitting in the middle of a dying town brewing a swill that probably poisons anyone who comes in contact with it."

"I was a soldier for thirty years. I guess I've done my share. 'Course I wouldn't expect either you or your servant would understand that."

Castile might look like a princess but she'd certainly missed something when it came to sales technique.

"I'm sure we all do what we can," Jake remonstrated. "By way of apology for any insult, why don't we share a drop of mead?"

"I serve ale here," Lucer answered. His eyes were narrowed and he half-reached for a sword that wasn't there.

"And we'll have a sample of that as well."

"If your mistress insults me any more, I'm putting you out on the street, aristocrat or no."

"Castile won't insult you."

"Don't talk about me like I'm not here. And my mead is for sale, not for free samples."

"We have to sample before we can sell," Jake reminded her. "You have to understand the artistic temperament," he told Lucer.

Lucer's face went through an amazing transformation, from anger, to hostility, to pure disbelief. "You want to sell me something and you come in here like you've just come from the capital itself?"

"We did come from the capital."

Lucer shook his head. "You're expecting me to believe that they make something in Otranto City besides taxes? I wasn't born yesterday. And even if they did, they'd never send it out to the sticks like this. They'd give it to the barbarians or the infidels to keep them from attacking for another day."

"You haven't heard of Manny Delphonte's brewery?"

"Big man. Voice like an elephant."

"That would be Castile's father."

Another facial transformation. Lucer spun around, grasped Castile by the arms, and pulled her to him, kissing her on both cheeks. "So the General finally got his wish. The mother must be a knockout if a man as ugly as Manny could give rise to this."

"My mother is a princess."

"And therefore genetically beautiful, of course." He shook his head. Delphonte was my first Sergeant. Even then, he was moving up, though. And now he has a brewery?"

"He has the largest brewery in Ortranto."

Lucer slammed a fist into the solid oaken bar. "Excellent. I hope he puts their entire guild out of business. There has never been such a band of thieves in the world. Soldiers used to fear Ortranto City because of the price of its beer and because it killed as often as did an enemy's sword."

"Would you like to try the mead, then?" Jake asked. He seized the flask from Castile and pulled the cork allowing the rich aroma to fill the air.

"I should have a couple of glasses here somewhere." Lucer vanished behind his bar and began rattling deep in a cupboard. The idea that a bar might be nearly glass-free surprised Jake. For the second time in a week, he cursed the choice of reading materials stored in his implant. If he had any clue how to manufacture glass, he could get rich.

Finally Lucer emerged, triumphantly holding a small glass the size of a shot-glass, a cracked earthenware mug, and what looked like a Ming teacup.

"What is this?" Jake demanded, gingerly inspecting the paper-thin ceramic.

Lucer shrugged. "One of the villages nearby makes them. Some crazy man from way off in Shara moved in, built a kiln and started experimenting with glazes and clays. The church burned him at the stake after a couple of years but some of the villagers kept what he learned and continued his art. According to the man who sold this to me, this cup is an original. Made by Master Kwong himself." He smiled. "Not likely, of course."

"It's beautiful," Castile observed. "But not very practical."

It could be practical for a space trader, Jake realized. Old-Earth Ming porcelain existed only in museums or in the homes of a few of the truly ancient trading families. Although molecular reproductions were common, handmade new creations of quality comparable to the ancient Chinese works could be worth thousands. A hold full of artworks like this could be the ticket to the upper echelon within the galactic plutocracy.

"Are you going to pour, or are you just going to stare at my crockery?" Lucer demanded.

Jake poured.

Lucer took the shot glass and Castile the Ming teacup leaving Jake the cracked mug. He didn't mind. He wanted to buy the monopoly on the porcelain, not drink from a single piece of it.

"You know you're wasting your time here, don't you?" Lucer demanded, the glass halfway to his mouth.

"Why do you say that?"

"Look at the village." Lucer waved his arm in a way to take in the surrounding huts and decaying villas. "It's dying. We pay taxes to Otranto, then we pay taxes again to the Granger. We are left with too little for more than life's necessities."

"Yet you are still here," Castile remarked. "I think there must be more to the story than you are telling."

"I was warning you not to expect anything when I try this. Since you won't take my warning, I've certainly done what I could to repay what I owe your father."

Lucer opened his mouth, poured in the entire contents of the shotglass, and smiled.

"Ah. Quite nice. I'll have another if you don't mind."

Jake ignored Castile's gesture, the universal rubbing together of thumb and forefinger meaning 'get the money.'

"Do the tax collectors come to you, or do you send your taxes to them?" Jake asked as he poured the refill.

"They come here, of course. Do you think we are mad enough to send money to people without the swords to back it up?"

"And do they visit your inn?"

"Sometimes." He paused. "Well, always. Not like there's another inn in a day's travel."

That didn't sound encouraging. In the few hours when they'd hastily packed, Manny had told Jake of dozens of towns and villages within a couple of days journey from the capitol. From what they'd seen, situations had deteriorated in the years since Manny had retired from fighting to become a full-time brewer.

"These tax collectors. Do you serve them what everyone else eats, at the same price?"

"I try to gouge them a little."

Otranto had a lot to learn about tourism. "A little? You've got to do more if you want to get your money back from them."

Lucer downed his second glass of mead and held out the shotglass for another sample. "Like what?"

"Like cook something special, and offer them something that only they can afford. Something, perhaps, like Castile's mead. You could charge perhaps three silver shields for a cup like this." He pointed to Castile's small coffee cup.

Lucer looked at him, then began to snicker. "Three shields. You've spent too long in the capitol. Nobody here has that kind of money."

"The tax collectors do," Jake argued. "Then there must be merchants who come through."

Lucer shook his head. "Long ago. I haven't seen a merchant caravan since I returned from the wars fifteen years ago."

"All right, just the tax collectors, then. And perhaps for a wedding." A thought hit him. "Do you have priests nearby?"

"Everyone has priests nearby. They are like maggots that gather on the bodies of the dying."

You couldn't be an ancient literature major without studying history. "The church always has money. You could get some back."

Lucer shrugged. "They have their own breweries. The priests are even less anxious to share their wealth with the poor than are the tax collectors. An irony, is it not."

Jake poured a fourth glass for Lucer and watched him swallow it down. "Between special occasions for the villagers, the two sets of tax collectors, an occasional merchant, and frequent visits from priests, once word gets around that you have something special, I'd guess that you'll need about fifty liters a year."

"Fifty liters a year?" Both Lucer and Castile gave indignant squawks.

"Your servant is a madman," Lucer told Castile.

"Fifty liters a year is nearly my entire production," Castile added. "I would be insane to give it all to you."

"*Your* entire production?"

"I have to search for the right mix of honey, blend it in just the right proportions, siphon it to leave the silt behind. I couldn't possibly offer you more than, uh, five liters a year."

Lucer eased to the seat beside Castile. "My son will be wanting to take over this inn now that he's nearly grown."

Jake didn't like the sound of that although he couldn't explain why. "And?"

34

"And I have been married to the same woman for twenty years."

Jake was now officially clueless on where this conversation was headed. He'd thought he had Lucer right where he wanted him. Castile's offer of five liters a year had been perfect. Lucer should be arguing for more, not telling them the story of his life.

"Tax collectors and priests visit many villages," Lucer continued.

"Too true," Jake agreed. Tax collectors were a universal. Even if he got off this cesspool of a planet, found a way to lose the Commodity Police, and caught a new attempt to manipulate the commodity markets, he'd still end up owing ninety percent of his take to the Revenue Service.

Lucer narrowed his eyes. "If you are traveling through the countryside, you aren't back in Otranto City brewing this wonderful mead."

Lucer held out his hand again. This time, Jake filled Lucer's glass only halfway. The hook was set. Now they had to learn what they'd caught.

"Our business is certainly expensive," Jake agreed. "Still, you will achieve a good margin when you buy by the liter and sell by the glass."

"But if a trader could take your mead and share it among the villages and cities of lesser Otranto, you could stay in the capitol, enjoy the culture of that fine city, and make more mead."

"Didn't you just tell us that no such traders exist?" Castile asked.

Lucer shrugged. "What would they have to sell when each village works to become self-sufficient? Already, you have shown me two things that I could sell. The mead and the porcelain from Ancor. Different towns will have their own distinctive commodities. A smart trader could do well." He held a finger to his nose. "A trader who was experienced enough in battle to dissuade the thieves who roam the roads in search of easy loot."

"If other villages are as poor as yours, what would you sell for?" Jake asked.

"Even the poor need some luxuries in their lives. As you said, there are always aristocrats, tax collectors, and priests." Lucer's face took on a pathetic look. "I'll probably go bankrupt, of course. The expenses of merchandising are high."

"Don't try to bargain too hard. We haven't said we want a factor," Castile said.

"You sell your mead to me, I sell it to others. We all benefit."

Jake had a sneaking suspicion that Lucer might just drink up his profits, but the idea had a distinct appeal.

"My son," Lucer continued, "will buy three liters."

"That'll hardly--"

Lucer interrupted Jake before he could really get started. "Later I will sell him more, at a price agreeable between father and son."

Chapter 4

Jake looked behind him but the sight hadn't improved. At least ten riders were bearing down on them. He toyed with the idea that they were desperate merchants hoping to buy some of Castile's mead before it was gone. The idea was too ridiculous to maintain. Their attire, their riding style, and their weapons spoke of bandit.

"Castile, go right. I'll take the left." Lucer spurred his mule off the road and into the woods. Castile slipped off the seat next to Jake and faded into the underbrush.

Jake hadn't liked the odds before. Now, deserted by his supposed friends, he liked them even less. Could Lucer have set them up?

He briefly considered whipping the mules into something like a trot but rejected the idea almost as soon as he'd had it. He couldn't outrun the freshly mounted bandits no matter what he did. And killing his mules, even assuming mules would run until they died, wouldn't delay the inevitable more than a few minutes.

He could also abandon the carts and all of their property like Castile and Manny had done. But where would he go if he did? Returning to Manny without daughter or wagons would ensure that he was sold into slavery--if he was lucky. The bandits couldn't be worse than Manny on a rampage. Jake shrugged his shoulders. Who knew, maybe they'd settle for a beer.

Five minutes later, the bandits surrounded him, forcing him to pull his mules to a stop.

"Good afternoon," Jake began. "I hope that you're interested in a mug of fine ale from the Delphonte breweries." He lowered his voice as if including the bandits in a conspiracy. I was able to buy several of the master brews.'"

"I wouldn't mind a brew myself," the bandit leader said. He was a short and slender man but his muscles bulged and his cold gray eyes seemed to cut through Jake like a blade through Castile's mead.

"I can offer you a special price, then," Jake effused. "Just because I want to lighten my load before I climb the Erlang hills, I will sell you an entire cask for two silver shields. If you're going my way, I'll throw in another cask when we reach Erlang itself as payment for helping defend the cart against bandits."

"But--"

The leader held up a hand before his man could pop out with the fact that they were, themselves, bandits.

"We'll take our cask now. If it's any good, we'll bodyguard you all right."

Jake no more believed that than he believed that Trabert would send a shuttle to pick him up. He did believe the bandits would keep him alive at least long enough to drive the wagons until they'd gotten him to wherever they were going. They'd probably slit his throat when they got there, but keeping alive until then would be worth something. Maybe the time would give him a chance to turn this to his advantage.

"Well," he looked at the bandits. "You look like a strong group and I have heard about the problems merchants have been having. I guess that's a fair deal."

Castile had suggested equipping one of the casks with poisoned beer. Jake had refused. In a society where even the children drink beer, it would be too easy for an innocent accident to lead to death. Right now, he wished he'd been a little less noble.

He reached back for a cask of one of the less spectacular master brews and pulled it out.

The leader watched him carefully, his hand on the hilt of his weapon. Three of his fellow bandits were archers. All had strung their bows and were now pointing arrows at Jake.

Jake pretended not to see them and knocked out the bung. If he survived this mess, he'd deserve an Oscar.

"Pour me the first cup," the leader ordered.

"But I spotted them, Harold," one of his flunkies whined.

Harold silenced his whining colleague with a quick glare. "Pour the first beer for me."

Swearing that, from then on, he'd listen to Castile and carry poisoned beer, Jake nodded. He took out the pewter mug which Marie had given him and filled it with the foaming brew. Manny had introduced the idea of pressure and second fermentation so Jake hadn't even been able to suggest that.

"What's that on top?" the Harold demanded.

"It's beer. That's its head," Jake answered. "Trust me, you're going to like this. Delphonte knows how to brew beer."

Harold took the cup, inspected it, and handed it back. "Now you drink it down."

Jake looked at Harold, then at the beer mug. Maybe poisoned beer wasn't such a great idea after all. If Harold could figure that out, Jake suspected that just about any bandit would.

"You want me to drink my own beer?"

"Why? There isn't anything wrong with it, is there?"

Thanking his fates that there wasn't anything wrong with the beer, Jake shook his head. "Mighty generous of you, then. Mud in your eye." He downed the mug with an overly expressive 'aah,' and much wiping of the foam from his face. "Nobody like Delphonte when it comes to superior brews. Mind if I have another?"

Harold's lip barely turned up. "I think one was sufficient." He took the cask from the wagon where Jake had laid it and sniffed the bunghole.

Harold turned to one of his archers. "Did he put anything in there?"

"Just poured it and drank it."

"Right. So I suggest we do the same."

Two of Harold's men and Harold himself had mugs. The rest of the men held out iron caps. Harold administered the beer generously, pouring the dregs of the brew onto the ground and then storing the empty cask in the wagon.

"We'll have another cask when we stop for the night," he shouted.

That brought more cheers than Jake would have guessed. Apparently this group of bandits had been a while without adequate beer. Of course this entire planet had been a while without truly adequate beer.

"But the bargain we made." Jake felt compelled to protest to keep up any semblance that he didn't know what was going on. "You said one cask now and another when we reach Erlang. We aren't even close."

"Don't worry about it, boy-o." Harold gave Jake a gape-toothed smile. "We'll settle up with you once we reach our destination."

"Well all right. But this is special beer. It costs me two silvers a cask and I can hardly sell it for less." Jake had once played an obsequious British servant in an ancient play from pre-space days so he felt comfortable in this role. As one of his martial arts teachers had instructed him, *appear weak so you can be strong.* He wasn't at all sure about being strong, but he had the appearing weak down to a science.

* * * *

Darkness fell with a thump as drunken thieves dropped from their horses. Unfortunately, Harold hadn't imbibed with the rest, limiting himself to that single mug of ale he'd taken hours before when they'd waylaid Jake.

"You know, just last night I prayed for a godsend," Harold told him as he dragged Jake off the wagon. "Without drink, this band of, uh, guards isn't worth spit." He spat to show his emphasis. "Then you came along. I'd say you were the answer to a poor man's prayers except everyone knows no deity would listen to me."

Jake could play at stupid and at obsequious, but he had reached the limits of believability. Stupid or not, it would be easier for Harold to kill him now than it would be to tie him up and risk letting him slit all of their throats during the night. Jake had been certain he would find an opportunity to escape before now, but Harold had watched him too carefully.

"I prayed that I would make it through the forest without running into thieves," Jake admitted. "I guess only one of us got our wish."

Harold laughed, then clasped him on the shoulder. "Isn't that the way of the faith. Granting one man's wish means another does without."

Harold's arm felt like a steel mace. Jake had noticed the muscles. He hadn't realized how strong Harold was. Maybe he should have taken the chance to run when he'd had it. At least a lifetime of slavery was a lifetime. Getting his throat slit wasn't anything at all.

"Once, I dreamed of becoming a bandit," Jake mused aloud. "Of charging out and stealing from the rich, only to share with the poor. If I return to Otranto without my merchandise and cart, I'll be sold into slavery. Right now, that dream of becoming a bandit sounds good."

Harold laughed, then shouted so his men could hear. "So you think you could be a bandit, do you? With the land filled with unpaid soldiers, how could a failed merchant hope to hold his head high?"

Several of the bandits echoed Harold's laughter. "You tell him, boss."

"A merchant learns to defend what is his own. How different is that from a soldier who attacks to take what belongs to others?"

"The difference is that between a man who rides a cart to market and one who rides a chariot in the races. Just because both have wheels doesn't make them the same."

Jake looked around, trying to put contempt in his gaze. "There isn't a man here who I'd be afraid to fight. Bare handed, or with a stick against their sword."

"Why should we fight you when we could simply kill you?" Harold seemed genuinely interested, willing to calculate slim probability that this merchant might have something to offer beyond beer and mead.

"If you kill me, you'll never know how much assistance I could offer a group of bandits living off the land, waiting to be hunted down when the emperor finally has enough and decides to launch a strike."

That got more laughter from all the men. "When good Emperor Fernis gets around to dealing with the bandits, he'll finally have to pay his mercenaries to do it. So we'll go in and clean ourselves out. Then, when Fernis's gold runs out, we'll be back in the forests."

Jake could understand the benefits of a mercenary army. Until low-cost muskets became available, an urban civilian drafted into the armed forces could take months to train to a barely marginal level. Professional soldiers, who spent their lives training, were a far more cost-effective approach to battle. Unfortunately, they were a terrible choice for the nation as they alternately bled it dry with their demands for more money, deserted when the enemy looked overwhelming, or simply ravaged the countryside for anything they might find of use. This wasn't their country, after all. What did they care that they were destroying it?

Jake laughed loudly although he wasn't sure anyone would be convinced by his laughter. "These men, mercenaries? Even Fernis has better taste than to hire a bedraggled lot like them."

"He hasn't been too proud yet," Harold snapped.

"He's not supposed to be too bright. Maybe it took him a while to see that he was throwing away his money."

"Bastard. I'll fight you." The largest of the bandits spat into his huge hand, then clamped it down into a fist. He repeated the exercise on the other side.

Jake decided jokes about chemical warfare would go over this crowd's head. "Barehanded, is it?"

"If you beat him, you can use your stick against Clovis with a sword." Harold gestured to a bone-thin man who towered even over Jake. And Jake was tall for this high gravity and nutritionally backward planet.

"I said I'd fight either, not both."

"Don't worry. There won't be anything left for Clovis to slice," his giant shouted.

"Form a ring," Harold ordered. "Archers, keep your arrows pointed for the merchant's gut. If he tries to escape, shoot him."

"Any rules?" Jake asked the giant who was rapidly closing in on him.

"Yeah, the rule is you die," the giant shouted. He shot a heavy but slow fist toward Jake's head.

Jake automatically upped his heartrate and set a surge of adrenalin through his system.

Blocking the punch was obvious. It was almost Jake's final decision.

Jake's block was perfectly executed, bringing the hardness of his forearm against the softness of the giant's muscle. He planned to follow with an elbow break, then maybe a knee to the midsection.

The giant's fist kept coming, brushing past Jake's guard as if he'd been a yellow belt who didn't quite have the technique down yet.

Jake spun out of the way, reeling from a blow that just glanced off his ribs-- despite his block and everything he could put into it.

"Pretty little tricks work in the gymnasium, but on the battlefield they are worthless," Harold intoned, sounding for all the world like one of Jake's business strategy instructors.

Pressing his advantage, the giant followed his first punch with a second and third. Jake was able to avoid the second and nearly avoided the third, but dodging a killing strike is a long way from victory.

Jake skipped back, throwing a low snap kick as the giant lumbered into range.

It barely missed the knee, his target, but a miss was as good as a mile. The giant staggered for a moment, then let out a horrible roar. "He kicked."

"You said no rules." Harold didn't seem especially concerned. He was, however, taking notes on a thin vellum pad using a space-provided ballpoint pen. One of the billions manufactured to spread around the galaxy like so much popcorn. "The fight goes on."

"Bah. Only children kick." To Jake's ears, the giant's voice didn't sound labored at all. It shouldn't be possible to carry that much weight without feeling it, especially in a high gravity planet. Apparently his opponent made a habit out of the impossible.

"Beat him, Norbert," the swordsman Clovis shouted.

"I'll beat him all right." Norbert glanced down at the ground, then suddenly kicked a clod of dirt at Jake's head.

Jake had seen Norbert's glance and was ready for the ploy. He ducked, but then grabbed at his face pretending that he'd been blinded.

Norbert charged in, ready to end the fight. He also dropped his guard.

Jake smashed a spinning inside crescent kick into Norbert's throat, followed with an elbow just below the ribs, then danced away with a clearing front kick.

In all of his years of martial arts training, Jake had never actually fought against a human. The training robots knew enough to hold their punches when they were at the point of breaking bone. Jake didn't suspect that Norbert had any similar limitations.

"Fancy stuff," Harold shouted out. "Looks like he has your number, Norbert."

Norbert laughed. "When I catch him, I hurt him. When he catches me, he can do nothing. I think that means I win."

Jake thought so too. That kick and elbow combination should have Norbert on the ground puking out his guts, not exchanging notes with his boss.

Norbert slipped into a classic boxing stance, his hands up to protect his face and his body angled away from Jake. Obviously he'd learned a little caution. Equally obviously, he had at least some skill to go with his huge size and gravity-enhanced strength.

A hundred and fifty kilograms of Norbert danced in, flashing jabs at Jake's head.

Jake ducked one, actually managed to block the second, and spun away from the third. He stopped his spin just in time to pile a mule kick into Norbert's crotch.

Norbert grasped the damaged area, squeaked the word "foul," then collapsed.

"Must I kill him?" Jake asked Harold. He was surprised his voice didn't squeak like Norbert's had.

"Let him live. He yields."

"But he fouled me." Already Norbert had regained some part of his breath and was scrambling to regain his footing as well.

"Norbert was a prize fighter in the arenas of Otranto for a while. He forgets that he is a soldier now, not a circus performer."

"I thought you were bandits."

Harold laughed. "Bandits, soldiers. You make it sound like there is a difference."

"I see." As long as Jake was talking, he wasn't dying.

According to Machiavelli, mercenaries are always bad--if capable, their ambitions will destroy you; if incapable, they are worthless. From what Jake could see of Harold and his gang, old Mac had a point. But Otranto city's overfed bureaucrats and sending them out against desert-hardened Granger warriors didn't have any appeal either.

A citizen militia could defend a walled city. Certainly that had to be a large part of the explanation of why Otranto had taken so long to fall. The city itself was a hard target. But no militia could be effective against mounted raiders. Otranto needed a professional army, but its professional army threatened to destroy it.

Jake shook his head. Otranto's survival had nothing to do with him. He was a spacer with interests that went far beyond the fate of a single nation on an obscure planet no one had ever heard of.

"That last kick was fairly obvious," Harold said, breaking into Jake's reverie. He peered at his notes. "The one where you jumped into the air and kicked Norbert in the throat, can you explain it to me?"

How to explain a lifetime of martial arts? Except that Harold had his own lifetime of training. "If I joined your group, I could teach all of you a few tricks."

Harold's face darkened. "Perhaps I was too polite with my question. I'll rephrase. Show me how to do that kick or I'll kill you now."

Jake nodded. "Help yourself to another keg of ale," he shouted out to Harold's men. "We'll be a few minutes before I have my chance against Clovis." He paused at Harold's angry stare. "With your permission, of course."

Harold was their leader, but this was a mob rather than a chain-of-command military organization. He could no more tell them to leave the beer alone than he could order them to stop breathing.

Jake took Harold through the mechanics of the crescent kick before adding the pivot and jump that made it such an effective weapon. By the time he'd finished, the men had broached yet another keg of beer and were feeling no pain. Even Norbert had joined in the drinking and the three archers had unstrung their bows and caught up with the rest of the drinkers.

Unfortunately, neither Harold nor Clovis had touched a drop.

"Can I take him now, boss?" Clovis demanded when Harold had successfully completed the spinning jump crescent kick for the third time in a row.

Harold narrowed his eyes. "I'd like to see what tricks he has against the sword, yes."

"Against my sword, he won't have anything." Clovis spoke with the conviction of a man who truly believes that he is a master swordsman. Well, Jake had been defeated before. It was completely possible that he would be again now.

"I'll need a stick." If he could sneak away now, he could come back in a couple of hours and steal back what was left of his cargo.

"There's a pile of wood near the fire." Harold grinned at him. "You don't seriously expect that I'd let you wander away into the night, do you?"

Harold wasn't the most brilliant soldier Jake had ever met--not a competitive field. Still, he seemed able to guess each of Jake's plans before Jake had the chance to execute them. Jake walked to the woodpile and selected a strong straight branch about six feet long.

"You're going to use a quarterstaff against a sword?" Clovis turned to Harold. "I thought he was a merchant, not a peasant."

"It will be interesting to see how he proposes to defend against your weapon," Harold admitted. "I have never seen a peasant with a staff who could stand against a trained soldier."

If he'd been a bystander, Jake would have put money on the swordsman too. Still, the tree branch was close enough to the bo's with which he'd trained to give him a fighting chance. He'd barely begun his sword training before he'd left the dojo and started on his short career as a space merchant, but he'd gotten his first bo when he'd been seven.

Clovis stared at him, then swept his sword across his body in a faint salute.

Jake bowed, then spun his stick around and switched hands.

"See, he does know some tricks." Harold seemed almost ecstatic.

"So do I." Clovis spoke softly. His calm voice seemed far more threatening than Norbert's bluster.

The man stepped into a fencing stance, extended, then lunged with textbook form, except with twice the speed that Jake's neuro-training textbooks had indicated was common.

Jake knew enough about the sword to know that premature commitment universally leads to problems. He forced himself to wait as that sword point headed straight for his right eye.

At the last fractional second, Clovis's wrist flipped and the sword was pointing for his heart.

Jake parried, then riposted, sending the opposite tip of his staff plunging at Clovis's head.

Clovis shrugged, bringing up the sword to block the staff, then sliding the edge of the blade along the grain of the wood in an attempt to slice off Jake's fingers.

"Nice stickwork," Harold said. "It appears to me that you've met your match, though, friend Jake."

Jake thought so too. Clovis used some fencing techniques, but his zen-like oneness with the sword made him appear more like the ancient Samurai from earth's past than any collegiate fencing team member.

A few more passages left Jake with a somewhat shaved staff and a bleeding slice down his ribs.

"I'll remember that trick with the end of the staff," Clovis promised. "Maybe next time I need to train some peasants to die in war, I'll show that to them. Who knows? It may keep one or two of them alive."

It wasn't going to keep Jake alive, though.

He tried to press the attack, but it was instantly clear that this left him even more exposed to Clovis's quick ripostes. Finally, he backed away panting, and ordered his internal systems to flush out the poisons, close off the bleeding wound, and prepare to die.

As his system obeyed him and shut down the capillaries that supplied his wound with its blood supply, he realized he could try something completely desperate--something that only an implant-equipped spacer could even consider. He could impale himself on Clovis's sword, finish the swordsman off while his weapon was unavailable, and then rely on his internal systems to repair him before he died.

It was a terrible plan, but it was the only one he could think of.

"Well if it isn't my old friend, Clovis."

Clovis whirled around at the sound of an unexpected voice. Jake recognized Lucer's intonations instantly, and took advantage of Clovis's momentary distraction by clouting the swordsman on the back of the head.

At least he aimed for the back of Clovis's head. Although Jake moved silently, Clovis must have sensed his movement and spun around, his sword coming up in a guard.

Ignoring technique, Jake put every ounce of his muscle into the strike, smashed through Clovis's guard, and rammed his staff into Clovis's head.

"I thought I saw someone else on the wagon," Harold said as Lucer stepped out from behind a tree. "Maybe it will be worth our while to pay a visit to the slave merchants in Erlang."

Lucer carried a heavy sword but was otherwise unarmed and unarmored. Harold had his sword, his men, admittedly mostly drunk, and a small arsenal he carried over a chain mail shirt.

"I came to get my wagon and my partner," Lucer said. "If you insist on visiting the slave markets, I guess we can oblige."

"It's Sergeant Lucer," one of the older bandits announced. "Nobody's ever beaten him in a fair fight."

Harold's eyes widened. "Marc, Brian, circle around behind him. Fred, Cannal, get your bows ready for god's sake."

One of the men, either Fred or Cannal, reached for his bow, then stopped. An arrow penetrated his wrist, pinning it to the tree where he'd leaned his weapon.

"He's got somebody with him," the bandit who'd recognized Lucer announced. "I'm out of here." He turned and crashed through the woods in the opposite direction from where the arrow had come.

"An arrow can't penetrate armor," Harold announced. He ignored the crashing sound as several of the other bandits followed the deserter who'd first recognized Lucer.

"Too true." Lucer swung his sword almost as fast as Clovis had swung his own, then suddenly shifted his grip and caught Harold with the sword's flat.

Harold collapsed into a heap.

"The rest of you get out of here. If you stay anywhere around, the posse will hunt you down like dogs."

"Posse?" This was the first Jake had heard of any civil organization intended to protect innocent merchants and pilgrims from attack.

"Posse, the fat man is moving too slowly."

An arrow flashed out, creasing the pants to Norbert's leg.

That was enough for all of the bandits except Clovis and Harold. Those two slumbered on.

Lucer looked around, waited until the last sounds of running feet faded away, then called "coast is clear. Come on, posse."

Castile stepped out from behind a tree. A thin bow, set with another arrow ready to launch, was in her hands.

"Anybody else?" Jake asked. Maybe Otranto could save herself if people would show this type of concern for strangers.

Lucer spit on the ground. "We're it. Now how much of the beer do we have left?"

Lucer may have been a soldier once, but he was a merchant now. His first concern was for the wasted beer.

They did a quick inventory, learning that they'd only lost the three barrels of ale and none of Castile's unique mead.

"Well, tie these two up and throw them in one of the wagons," Lucer ordered. "I'm thinking that we can find a use for them."

Jake complied while Castile covered him with her bow, watching for any evidence that either of the two men might be conscious.

He heaved Harold's body into the wagon on top of Clovis's, then took the reins.

"I think we should get out of here."

Lucer nodded. "Your bandits will be back soon. They left too much here to just walk away."

"Should we burn everything they left, then?" Castile asked, her voice filled with an almost sensuous anticipation.

"They'd just rob from poor villagers until they replace it," Lucer said.

Lucer had recently been one of those villagers, Jake knew. How often had bandits come into his life, taken what they wanted, and then ridden away?

"Are we really going to sell these two in the slave markets in Erlang?" Castile sounded happy about that idea too. This was, Jake reminded himself, a primitive planet.

Chapter 5

Harold sputtered back to consciousness after they'd gone about four miles. "Aurgh."

Castile slapped a lead sap against her palm. "Should I hit him again?"

The bandit raid had showed Jake another side of Castile--a side rich with practical skills and just a touch of sadism. He hadn't even realized she carried that weapon. Had she been prepared for bandits? Perhaps, her mother had armed her against him?

"We can't just go on knocking him unconscious," Jake answered. It could do permanent brain damage.

"And I'm supposed to care?"

It was a legitimate question. They would have been within their rights as Otranto merchants to kill Harold and Clovis while they lay unconscious. They hadn't, though, and now Jake couldn't see killing them in cold blood after dragging him all this way.

"Let's see what he has to offer," Jake temporized. "We can always kill him later. Or, we could just sell him into the Erlang slave markets."

That got a shudder. Horrible a reputation as the Otranto City slave markets had, Erlang was worse. The mines that supplied the city with so much of its wealth demanded a steady stream of able-bodied slaves. A stream that was quickly transformed into broken and maimed men set free to rot on Erlang's streets.

* * * *

"Are you complete fools?" Harold demanded. "Cut me loose at once before my men sweep down and kill all of you."

"Would they now?" Lucer asked. "It's my guess they'd go after easier prey, if they don't fall apart completely as a band."

"Ridiculous." Harold sounded like he needed to convince himself. "They know they can't live without me. If they break up, they'll be hunted down like wolves."

Clovis grinned from the bottom of the wagon where he still lay. "Just like you told them so often."

Jake had thought Clovis still unconscious but he'd obviously been following the conversation for some time.

"Don't you know how they resented that?" the bandit continued.

"But--"

"A clever man like you might just be able to talk himself into a better job in the mines," Lucer interrupted. "There are worse things than slavery. I was a slave once myself."

Jake wondered if that was true. Lucer seemed to have depths he hadn't guessed at.

"And you survived?" Harold sounded amazed.

"Not in Erlang, of course."

Harold's face dropped, but only for a moment. "Perhaps there is some other solution."

Castile tapped her sap significantly. "We could use him for target practice, or just turn him in at the next village we pass. We wouldn't get the money for selling him, but we wouldn't have to listen to him either. 'Course some of the villages are pretty poor--they might just eat him."

"A merchant always needs guards," Clovis interrupted. "I think we proved that. You could hire us as your guards. That way we live, you have a better chance of living, and nobody has to get hung."

Jake looked at Lucer, saw the man was actually considering the idea, and blew up. "Are you crazy? They're bandits. They'd sell us to the next lot of bandits before you could count your missing fingers."

"That is a concern," Lucer agreed. "You do not appear to be men with a great deal of moral backbone."

Harold surged up with an angry look in his face, then grasped his head and sank back down. "What did you hit me with?"

Lucer grinned at Jake. "Sometimes I miss the old days of adventuring."

Castile stowed her sap, hopped off the wagon, and ran ahead, laughing as she picked a wildflower from beside the path. She tucked it into her hair.

Her laugh and her coltlike run reminded Jake again of how young she was. Once she had arranged the flower in her hair, she stared at him with a look that was as adult as any he could remember.

"Clovis can be a guard. Harold will come back with us to Otranto City." Her voice sounded as imperious as her mother's ever had.

"But--" all four men started at the same time.

"Clovis and Lucer are enough to scare off a small band. One more man wouldn't help with a larger band. Besides, we need someone clever back in Otranto City. Someone with the morals of a weasel. Someone who can talk to the mercenaries as an equal."

"He'll just fade into the woodwork once we're there," Jake protested. "We might as well let him go here."

Harold brightened for a moment, then shook his head. "The only time I was in Otranto City, I marched in a triumph. It was beautiful. All the streets decked out in white silk, beautiful women throwing flowers at us as we passed." His eyes misted with the reminiscence.

"What had you done?" Castile demanded.

Harold shrugged. "Not much, really. We'd beaten off a Granger attack on some nameless village, but the Emperor was there and wanted to take credit for the victory. While we were in Otranto City celebrating our triumph, the Granger attacked again and the town fell for good."

"So you wouldn't want to go to Otranto City again?" Jake asked. This sounded hopeful.

"Are you kidding? It's the center of the universe. When I was growing up, my mother used to beat me with a wooden sword if I didn't practice. She'd tell me I could never get to Otranto City if I didn't always do my best. I'd kill to go there."

He probably had killed dozens of times, Jake realized.

"It's settled, then," Castile announced, still using that voice of her mother's that expected and commanded obedience. "We'll turn around in Erlang, head back to Otranto City, load up Lucer and Clovis with beer and mead, then start working on Otranto City."

"What sort of work?" Jake demanded. It hadn't been too many days before when he and Castile had been forced to flee Otranto City and now she was talking like she would come back as some sort of conqueror. He didn't see himself and Harold as any kind of conquering army.

"Weren't you listening to my mother? Don't you realize that Otranto is on the verge of falling to the pagans? We've got to save it."

Jake ticked off his fingers. "First, Otranto has been fighting the pagans, as you call them, for over a thousand years. Second, you said yourself that we'd be arrested if we go back to Otranto City too soon. And third, look at us. Even assuming that we could trust these two, we'd have two bandits, one barkeep, a girl, and a complete foreigner. Besides, are these pagans really so bad?" He scanned *The Arena of Otranto* quickly for any mention of the western pagans and came up only with references to their fierce pride, their literary tradition, and their arts. Could that be so much worse than a slave owning and decadent culture like Otranto?

Lucer gave him a funny look. "I suggest a slight change of plans. First we go to Erlang, then we take a big swing through Granger territory. That'll give Otranto City a little more time to cool down for you two. We'll still end up back at Otranto City. If young Harold here doesn't behave, we can sell him into any of the slave markets along the way."

"Not the Grangers." Harold's face turned a pale green.

"I do hear that castration can cause complications," Lucer agreed. "Still, it's up to you to convince us that you're worth more to us as a colleague than you are as merchandise."

If word ever got back to the Trader's Guild that Jake had traded in human slaves, he could kiss his chances for full guild membership goodbye forever. So far, though, he'd only heard threats. He hadn't been involved in any transfers. From the Trader's Guild perspective, he'd just been negotiating. Shrewd negotiators were always respected.

"The Granger are our enemies," Castile announced.

"You should always know your enemies," Lucer told her. "Besides, Otranto isn't exactly at war with them right now."

Otranto wasn't at war because they'd paid some huge bribe to be left alone. Until the bribe money was spent, they would be at peace. That also meant, Jake realized, that the Granger Empire was where most of Otranto's money was. It just might make sense to extend their trade expedition into an area where people had some money.

* * * *

The remaining two days of the trip to Erlang was largely uneventful. One group of bandits had spotted them and charged, but had broken off when Clovis and Castile had launched arrows.

Castile had let Clovis keep his bow after the attack although she did insist that he keep it unstrung. Jake kept the man's sword stored on the bottom of the back wagon. Clovis was just too skillful to be left alone with that weapon.

"Now that's a city," Clovis announced when they rolled over the last hill and Erlang came into sight.

High white sandstone walls surrounded a city that stretched along black beaches on a huge inland sea. Much of the trading from the silk routes to the west arrived at Erlang in huge caravans before being loaded on ships and sent to Otranto City for eventual distribution to the world. At least they had once. Like many of the villages they'd passed, Erlang City seemed a shadow of itself and the sailing ships bypassed Otranto City to dock in nearby barbarian-controlled Tantalus.

As they came closer, they could see cracks that ran through the once formidable walls surrounding Erlang. The city gates were guarded, but by men who looked more interested in contraband than in preventing an invasion.

"They aren't exactly ready for an attack, are they?" Jake observed.

Harold gave him a scornful glance. "Who would attack Erlang? What other port would the Grangers use to convert their merchandise into gold?"

Jake could have cited a thousand cities on fifty worlds that had been similarly harmless, yet were still invaded, raped, and destroyed. He decided to hold his tongue.

"Maybe their taxes will be low," Lucer grunted, "if they don't have to worry about invasion."

Jake let Lucer enjoy his fantasy. In his experience, taxes had little to do with financial need and more to do with ability to collect. Erlang knew how to collect.

The first inn they approached claimed a tax of a golden crown for a room on top of an already outrageous rent. Even the second, which obviously appealed more to farmers coming to town with their merchandise than it did to the major trading houses, demanded five silver shields. Both taverns blamed their prices on the Erlang government's incessant demand for more revenue.

Worse, none of the tavern keepers would even taste the mead and ale that they carried. "We'll be executed if they find unlicensed drink in our establishment," one innkeeper finally explained. "Without a tax stamp, I shouldn't even be talking to you."

By the time they returned to their overpriced rooms, they were hot, hungry, and unhappy.

"Perhaps we should contact the government," Jake suggested after they'd consumed several loaves of a light fluffy bread that could be had, amazingly in this overpriced city, for practically nothing. "Even after we paid the taxes, there'd still be room for some decent margin. Maybe the government would even take over the distribution for us. That way we'd actually get something for our tax shields."

"Something for your tax shields. Are you crazy?" Harold demanded.

"Tax crowns is more like it," Lucer grumbled. "Delphonte makes it, I ship it, and other people drink it. What possible claim does the government have on our beer?"

"This whole thing doesn't make sense," Castile complained. "Erlang is part of Otranto. The government you're talking about is our government. Since we have valid Otranto tax seals, we shouldn't have to pay again."

Clovis looked at Castile for a moment, then laughed. "Erlang part of Otranto? Maybe that's what the Emperor in Otranto believes. But if he's gotten a single silver shield in taxes from them over the past fifty years, I'd be surprised. The richest Erlang merchant families have ruled the city for generations. Over the past twenty years, they've paid the Granger for protection." He spat on the reeds on the floor.

Jake shot Clovis a dirty look and was pleased to see Castile giving him another. Someone was going to have to sleep on those reeds.

"Wipe that up." Castile gave orders like she expected to be obeyed and Clovis followed her instructions before he could even think about it. How long Harold and Clovis would continue to obey Castile was another question.

Castile nodded briefly, then grasped her loaf of bread and twisted, her face a study in anger and frustration. She took a large bite, chewed, then swallowed. "How is Otranto supposed to defend itself if one of our largest cities ignores our laws and relies on our enemy for protection?"

Jake couldn't tell her that Otranto was past protecting. Erlang was just another nail in a coffin already more than adequately sealed. If even spacers who touched down every five or ten years could see what was happening, the situation was hopeless. "We'll try the government offices tomorrow," he announced.

"Tell them you brought only a quarter of what you actually have," Clovis urged.

"Why?"

"Because they are likely to steal it from you. This way, at least you'll have something to sell when we leave Erlang."

* * * *

The next morning, Jack and Lucer carried two small casks of mead from their inn to the keep in the middle of the city.

Its huge black stone walls glared down at the whitewashed adobe homes that surrounded it.

"Who lives there now?" Jake asked.

"Lives?" Lucer seemed surprised by the question. "Nobody lives in the keep. It is the treasury. It's where we will need to go to find if we can sell our goods in this city."

They were stopped at the gate to the keep. This gate, at least, appeared well oiled and fully operational. While Erlang might be confident about the external protection they'd arranged from the Granger, its government was less confident about its own citizens and its visitors.

Three guardsmen crashed halberds on the floor. Looking at the two men, they evidently decided that Lucer was the man in charge.

One of the men appeared to be their sergeant. He glared at the casks. "Where are your papers?"

"We are merchants from Otranto," Lucer explained. "We are seeking permission to exchange our mead and fine ale for the goods of Erlang."

"Trading in alcoholic beverages is subject to tax and license from the bureau of alcohol," the sergeant announced. "Unfortunately, their meeting was held last night. They won't meet again for a month."

"That's ridiculous," Jake started. "How can they expect--"

"Forgive my excitable partner," Lucer interrupted. "We understand that it might be inconvenient for the bureau to meet outside its usual hours. Still, given the quality of this product, I feel certain that they would wish to do so."

The sergeant sneered. "What merchant doesn't claim to offer the best merchandise. Yet few do. Talk is cheap and, in Erlang, cheap doesn't take you far."

Lucer nodded sagely. "It is as you say. Too many of my fellow merchants are willing to stretch the truth to the point where its own father would not recognize it. Still, in this case, the quality is easy enough to prove."

He stepped closer to the Sergeant, lowering his voice in a conspiratorial fashion. "I assume that an important guard like you would have the ear of the gentlemen of the Bureau of Alcohol. With a word from you, they would meet earlier, is that not so?"

"Perhaps," the sergeant blustered. "But their meetings are expensive. They--"

"Think how pleased their families would be if they had the opportunity to receive early samples of the best mead and ale in all of Otranto."

Jake had studied negotiating skills in business school. Now he was getting a firsthand lesson in the fine art of graft. Neither Lucer nor the Sergeant could come right out and say that the take was on--even Erlang had some limits on its corruption.

Lucer deftly filled three small pewter glasses with mead, handed one to Jake, the second to the Sergeant, and sipped from the third. "You can taste the nectar from the blackberry flowers in this one, Sergeant. Imagine taking a vial home to your wife. At her next dinner party, she would be the envy of the entire guard corps." He nudged the burly Sergeant in the stomach. "Shouldn't doubt that she'd want to reward you in important ways, eh, Sergeant?"

Jake wasn't sure he could taste the blackberry nectar himself, but the mead was excellent. The sergeant's eyes widened as he sipped from his cup, then took another swallow.

"Alas, my wife invites dozens to her parties. A single vial would make me appear cheap. Sadly, I must do without."

Lucer snapped the pewter cup back from the Sergeant. "I had thought we were men of discretion here. At two gold the vial, I assure you, the vial would make you seem rich rather than the contrary."

He turned on his heel and stalked away from the dumbfounded sergeant. "Come, Jake. I told you that Erlang would be a waste of our time. They have stepped too far from culture here. We must go to the courts of the Granger to find gentlemen of taste."

"For two vials of the mead, I would arrange a meeting of the Bureau, say in two weeks time," the Sergeant sputtered.

"Today," Lucer thundered. "And nothing if the result is not completely favorable."

"It will have to be taxed," the sergeant protested.

"It has been taxed in Otranto City."

The sergeant shook his head. "You could offer me fifty vials and I still couldn't change that. Anything sold in Erlang is taxed here."

While Lucer and the Sergeant bickered over the exact tax rate, Jake inspected the keep where they were meeting.

Although the building must be hundreds of years old, the mortar holding together the heavy granite stones appeared sturdy. The silk tapestries were much the worse for years or decades of hanging in a room lit only by smoky oil lamps, yet even Jake's relatively untrained eyes could see that they would be worth thousands if only they could be cleaned and taken to a galactic trading center.

He narrowed his eyes, taking advantage of the computerized enhancements he'd paid for and rarely used. Under magnification, the tapestry depicted a victorious naval battle between the forces of Erlang and Otranto against the Granger. However old the tapestry was, the battle itself must have been far older. From what he'd been able to learn, Otranto hadn't had a navy in generations. Instead, the eastern barbarians carried trade from the west, bypassing Otranto but enriching the Granger. Although the barbarians supposedly shared a religion with Otranto, their merchants never passed up an opportunity to weaken the great empire, even ferrying Granger troops to flank the Otranto lines from time to time.

He recovered from his reverie as Lucer completed his transaction.

"I'll expect to hear from you, then. Come, Jake." Lucer poured three more glasses of mead to celebrate an agreement.

* * * *

The following day, with full government approval, Lucer held a tasting and auction in the common room of the inn. Barnoff, the innkeeper, had contacted the other masters of his guild to bid on the ale. Lucer's sergeant, evidently concerned about collecting his two vials, had mobilized the wine stewards from the aristocratic homes of Erlang. The mixed crowd muttered, formed into small cliques, and pushed at the bar where Jake and Castile poured thimble-sized glasses of mead for tasting.

Jake had decided he could trust Clovis and Harold, at least where they could be watched. Those two were assigned to ensure that no one snuck into the inn looking only for free drink. Only the truly committed were welcome.

After nearly an hour of sampling, chatting, and catty remarks between innkeepers and wine stewards, Lucer stepped up on a table. "You have heard of the famous Delphonte ales that all Otranto swears by. Well--"

"Those Delphonte ales put every brewer and most of the innkeepers in Otranto out of business," a man shouted. He was wearing the brewers' guild key on his silk shirt.

Lucer held up a hand to quell the angry murmur. "Indeed, and those innkeepers in Erlang who hope to keep their custom when the next Delphonte journeyman arrives in Erlang had best be aware of it. You have tasted the mead that will let you hold your heads high knowing that there is no other place in all Arcadia where a better drink can be had."

"Three silvers a barrel," the silk-shirted master shouted. "Let's get on with it."

Lucer shook his head and smiled sadly. "For Erlang, we have allotted a total of two hundred liters a year. Shall we begin the bidding at one gold Crown per half-liter."

From the angry roar that brought up, Jake thought Clovis and Harold would find their hands full.

Lucer held up a hand again for silence. "Mead like this requires a delicate touch. I assure you, besides Otranto City itself, and the Granger capitol Bathsheeba, Erlang is receiving a larger allotment than any other city in the world. The barbarian cities get nothing, unless, of course, Erlang decides they wish to trade some of their allotment to the east."

That perked up a few ears.

This was, Jake realized, a different type of trading than he was used to. In the galactic commodity boards, trading was done through computers with no personal engagement whatsoever. On Arcadia, by way of contrast, everything was personal and close. Rather than an investigation by the commodity police, an overly unscrupulous trader could expect a knife in the gut.

He wasn't sure he was up to it. Accomplished traders like Lucer, for all that he had spent his life as a soldier and innkeeper, could run circles around Jake.

The bidding started in earnest then, yet Jake hardly paid attention. The hopelessness of his position had once more been brutally thrust in his face. He couldn't outsmart and out-trade the Arcadians. He couldn't out-muscle them. He might know of large numbers of inventions that had changed galactic society, yet he knew none of the details necessary to create, say, a modern antigravity tank.

"Drink another cup and don't look so grim," Castile hissed in his ear. "People are starting to look at you."

He pasted on a smile, took another sip of the fine mead, and nodded. What possible difference did it make that he could never amount to much here? He wasn't a native. He'd make his way to Bathsheeba and catch the next flight home.

"Lucer is good, isn't he," he observed to Castile.

"He'd better be. We already agreed on a price. Everything over that price, he keeps."

As opposed to Jake who was making almost nothing to pay off his debts. He'd been pushed out of Otranto City so fast he hadn't even thought to renegotiate his apprentice wages. At the rate he'd been earning, he might not even have Manny Delphonte paid off when Arcadia's bad medical technology caught up with him and he died of premature old age.

As Lucer auctioned one lot after the next, he stressed that each allotment would go to the current bidders. They were not just buying a half-liter of fine wine. They were buying a unique right--a continuing option to buy Erlang's limited annual allotment. It was something that they could sell as an asset if they ever needed quick cash, or wished to escape the lot as barkeep or wine steward.

Jake saw some raised eyebrows over that. If a wine steward purchased a half liter of mead for his master, the mead itself certainly belonged to the master. But what of the right to receive additional mead at the same price? Wouldn't a steward with that right be able to name his price if ever he tired of his current master?

Bidding zoomed.

Two hours later, Harold and Clovis heaved out the last drunk barkeep and stared at the table. A substantial pile of golden coins were stacked in neat rows as Lucer scurried to note who had purchased what and for how much.

Jake's eidetic memory proved to be helpful. Without even needing to pay close attention, he had stored every detail of the bidding process and could identify who had bid what for each of the numbered lots.

"We'll deposit most of the gold at one of the Erlang banks, then head on to Bathsheeba," Lucer said. He turned abruptly and kissed Castile on the lips. "You are going to make me rich, my sweet. And you," he grasped Jake by the hand, pumping it repeatedly. "If it hadn't been for you, I would have sat in my little village with my little inn and my uh, large wife, and waited to die. I owe it all to you."

So Jake had been doing some good for someone, at least. He made Lucer rich and he'd helped Castile get away from her father. Now, if there was only something he could do for himself.

"The Granger are our enemy," Castile stated. "Why would we want to offer them our goods?"

"We are at peace now," Lucer protested. "And remember, they have all the money."

"Money they've looted from Otranto cities," Castile argued.

A glimmer of an idea tried to make its way into Jake's forebrain but, although he could tell it was there, it evaded his attempts to bring it out. It didn't matter. He wanted to go to Bathseeba sooner or later. If they had an ongoing merchant relationship with the Granger, he would be able to get there more easily when the next spacer ship landed.

"So if we sell them your mead, we'll be getting some of our own money back," he argued. "Encouraging our enemies to drink and taking their gold has got to be worth something when it comes time to fight them."

Castile's face darkened. "Are you saying there's something wrong with my mead?"

"Nothing that's not wrong with your entire culture," Harold said.

Four heads whirled to see him as Harold hadn't said anything that entire day. "What?" Castile gasped.

"You are more interested in comfort than in strength. Why do you think that the Granger have defeated you so often? Perhaps, you say, because they are more numerous than you. It is true now, but it was not always so. Once Otranto spanned the continent. And even putting aside the idolaters, what of the barbarians to the east. They lack your fine armor and weapons, yet still grasp huge hunks from the once mighty Otranto empire."

"It sounds like you've been giving this some thought," Jake said. He'd been having many of the same thoughts. Like countless societies in the Galactic past, Otranto had lost its will to thrive.

"How could I not when my father chose to become a mercenary for Otranto? Each year, my family moved closer to Otranto City, yet we were always at the border. Castile's wine is sweet, easy on the tongue, and provides a pleasant buzz. Yet it weakens rather than strengthens those who drink it."

Castile stomped her booted foot. "Ridiculous. Look at my father. There is no man stronger than him in Otranto City."

"He is not a native of the city, then?"

"Of course not. He was a mercenary, like your father, until he helped Julian gain the throne."

Harold nodded, as if that explained everything. "Perhaps, when we go to Bathsheeba, you will see why Otranto is losing its wars. Who knows? You might even learn something that could slow the fall of our Empire. Give us a few more years to live under our own government before we are swept into the arms of the barbarians or the idolaters."

It was not, Jake thought, a happy note. Of course, he was getting off the planet as soon as he could. Why should he care?

Chapter 6

The border crossing was a hut on the side of a small river. An aging soldier poked his head out, looked at Jake's small company, and shook his head. "You fleeing from arrest?"

"We're merchants," Castile explained.

The soldier glared at Castile for a moment, then spat. He deliberately looked away from Castile and spoke directly to Jake. "Six silver per Orthodox slave you sell to the Granger. Is she the only one you've got?"

Jake was surprised to feel his nails clamping into his palms as his fists formed involuntarily. "We don't trade slaves."

The soldier shook his head and spat again. "Thought you said you were traders. That's about the only merchandise I've seen traded through here. Guess I'll just tax you for the slave girl and you can decide what to do."

"Omkar, you lazy slug," Clovis shouted. "Are you looking to have your head removed and fitted with a working brain? Just nod your head and let us get on with our business."

The old soldier squinted, then grinned. "Is it really you, Clovis, lad? I had heard you fell at the defeat in Tullock."

"And I heard you died at the rout in Bartlett," Clovis returned. "Looks like we were both wrong."

"Bartlett was a damn near thing for me," Omkar muttered. "Laid me up for months." He squinted at Clovis, then glared at Castile again. "Just because we fought together doesn't mean that you don't have to pay the taxes Otranto so badly needs."

Clovis laughed. "Otranto may need them, but they'll never see what you collect, Omkar. These men and woman saved my life when I was taken by bandits. How could I repay them by letting a bandit like you steal their goods?"

Clovis had, Jake thought, an interesting way of retelling their story.

"So you're finally giving up on the Empire and looking for work with the Granger," the old soldier asked. "I'd never go that way myself, but I can't say as I blame you. The way Fernis manages to find money for his concubines but none for his army is criminal. 'Course that would be all right if he'd share the concubines with us but I haven't seen one lately."

Clovis shook his head. "The Granger treat mercenaries like dirt anyway. You of all people should know that."

"Yeah. They got some crazy idea that they should do their own fighting. Makes them real men." Omkar shook his head at the foolishness.

"Anyway, I've got a new job as a caravan guard," Clovis explained.

Omkar laughed again, then lowered his voice to what he probably thought of as a soft whisper. To Jake, it seemed something of a modulated roar. Digitally enhanced hearing wasn't always a blessing.

"Didn't tell them that the Granger keep their roads clear of bandits, huh?" he announced in what might have passed for a whisper in a hurricane. "Good on you, boy. Make a little from the rich merchants is my motto."

"Touching as this reunion is, we've got to be getting on," Jake said.

Omkar grumbled but let Clovis mollify him with a small cask of ale. "Just ride straight ahead," Omkar shouted after him. "But you know the way, Clovis, lad. We was driven out of that country only a few years ago. Remember the fight we gave them at Arinapole? We nearly had them that time."

They splashed across the narrow creek that marked the temporary boundary between the shrinking Otranto Empire and the expanding Granger. Clovis insisted that they fill their water bottles and empty casks. The next watering hole was several days journey away.

To Jake's surprise, Clovis seemed to have adopted Castile as his personal princess. While he treated Jake and Lucer with respect, he insisted on instructing Castile on the practical aspects of weapon care and construction and gave her considerable advice on leading mercenary forces. Advice that Jake eavesdropped on shamelessly, committing everything Clovis said to long-term storage. Clovis also insisted on setting aside an hour after they pitched camp to work with Castile on her archery, which improved dramatically.

"The lass is a natural," he insisted each time he put up his bow.

Jake had little experience with subplanetary borders and, at first, it seemed that the Granger countryside was identical to that on the Otranto side of the river. Scrawny peasants scratched narrow furrows in the ground and carried water for irrigation. Even their language was much the same, a heavily accented version of the tongue spoken in Otranto City.

As they traveled farther from the river, Jake noticed tumbled-down constructions that followed the path of the road and even spanned the dry ravines that filled the increasingly desert landscape.

"What are these?" he asked Clovis.

The ex-mercenary shrugged. "Don't guess they've always been ruins, but they were that by the time I fought here. Land was fought over a few times before we lost it for good. Funny place to put walls, though. Out here in the middle of nowhere."

Harold, who had been silent almost since they announced their decision to venture into Granger lands, glared at Clovis. "What looks like walls was part of the irrigation system." He gestured widely. "This desert you're looking at was the richest farmland in Otranto for hundreds of years."

The sheer scale of the construction project staggered Jake. Without modern construction equipment, it would have taken years and thousands of workers to build the aqueducts whose remnants he could see. If the entire desert had once been irrigated, the project would have been monumental, spanning generations. "What happened to them?" he asked.

"Granger are herders, not farmers. They tore them down so they'd have room for their sheep."

"So where are the sheep?" They hadn't passed a single animal since they'd moved beyond the thin layer of settlement along the boundary creek.

Harold laughed. "Stupid Granger didn't realize it took water to grow the grass their sheep need. The sheep starved. Same as the farmers they displaced." The bleached skeleton of a herbivore on the side of the road punctuated Harold's commentary.

"So they just pulled back?"

"Not their army. They're here," Harold warned. "Just because they don't have an old broken-down soldier on the side of the road doesn't mean they aren't watching."

They may have been watching, but they certainly weren't using the land they'd fought so hard for. On overcrowded Wayward, any plot of bare land would have been seized and built upon instantly. Viewing the crumbling cities of Otranto shocked him. This vast emptiness that had once held hundreds of thousands of souls felt like a knife twisting in his gut and made him feel more alien and out of place than he could remember. It was, he decided, a good reminder that he was the alien here, that he needed to return to the civilized planets.

"Why would they want to displace working farms with sheep?" Jake demanded. "Or didn't they have the population to support intensive agriculture?"

Harold reached into his hair, scratched vigorously and came up with a flea, which he crunched between two strong nails. "What do you mean, population to farm? Weren't nothing wrong with the farmers that lived there at the time."

"But they were from Otranto."

Harold gave him a look that should have been reserved for a particularly slow second grader. "Who do you think lives in Granger land? You don't think they farm themselves? Or raise their own sheep? That would be a laugh."

Jake mulled that. Before he could ask anything else, Harold grasped his sword and Castile did her disappearing trick. Watching carefully, Jake actually saw her climbing under the wagon where, he guessed, she would hold onto the axles until she judged it safe to emerge.

"What--"

Lucer shushed him and gestured at a distant dust cloud, a cloud that was moving against the wind and directly toward their wagon.

"Like Harold told you, they watch their borders."

Clovis removed the string from his bow and set the wooden device in the wagon. He caught Jake's eyes watching him and gave Jake a grimace. "Wear a sword and that's all right. They'll stay out of your reach and maybe you can talk to them. Carry a bow and six will get you twelve, they'll split you before you have a chance to use it."

The dust cloud separated into a band of about twenty blond warriors who laughed as they raced their horses toward Jake's short caravan.

"Not much of an invasion army," the youngest one said to a one-armed man who appeared to be the leader of the band. Jake's translator clicked in, instantly finding a reference to the Granger language and allowing Jake to understand. "They look little better than peasants." His face brightened. "Could we use them for target practice, Alton?"

"They might be spies."

"Not very sneaky for spies."

"We're merchants," Jake explained, his translator instantly converting his words to the Granger tongue.

Every one of the warriors pulled back. Two strung short bows in a jerky motion that looked, for all of its awkwardness, to be practiced and deadly.

"You know the language of the warriors?" Alton demanded, speaking this time in a roughly accented Otranto dialect.

Lucer shook his head in a barely detectable denial.

"Only the word for merchant," Jake lied, speaking in Otranto. "I was not aware that you spoke the language of your enemy."

"The Granger have no enemies, only slaves. All men of the Granger speak the slave tongue. How else would we communicate our orders?"

That question didn't seem to need an answer.

"Are you, perhaps, guarding the roads, keeping them free of bandits for merchants such as myself?" Jake asked.

Alton's face reddened. "We are warriors, not mule guards. The word of the great Khan is enough to keep the roads safe. We search for Otranto spies who, unfortunately, are less wont to follow the orders of the mighty one."

It was, Jake decided, the most patently foolish thing he'd ever heard. First, from what he'd heard of the idiot Emperor, Fernis probably didn't have enough in his treasury to hire worthwhile spies. Second, no spy would be stupid enough to sulk across the border without a proper cover story, especially when Otranto had a large embassy in Bathsheeba. And third, he couldn't imagine what Otranto would want to spy on. From what Marie Delphonte had told him, Otranto hadn't mounted a real offensive for close to two hundred years and any incursion they did make would surely be limited to an area recently controlled by Otranto and at least as well known to Otranto soldiers as the Granger.

"Fortunately, we are not spies," Jake told the officer. "Instead, we are merchants looking to enrich both the Granger and ourselves."

"It is my experience that few spies admit to being spies," the officer told Jake. "Only a spy would speak the language of the warriors."

Lucer made a point of slowly drawing his dagger and testing it against his thumb. The much-stropped blade left a thin line of blood behind it.

Jake took that as a warning and cranked even more adrenaline into his system. Four men and a young girl against a trained military squad of twenty seemed like suicide but sitting still and being slaughtered was an even worse option.

"Show me your merchandise," Alton ordered suddenly.

"Of course. We are humble merchants of ale and mead." Jake began his pitch as he pulled back the tarp over the lead wagon exposing the barrels and casks that made up what was left of their cargo. "What you see here is intended as samples only, of course. We hope to find other merchants or factors who will purchase enough to let us send caravans."

"Caravans from Otranto would be filled with spies."

"I am certain that the great Khan would take steps to control any spies. With the taxes he gained on the trade, he could increase the number of soldier patrolling the border."

He almost added the obvious corollary--that any officer already commanding a border unit could expect to move up in the ranks but decided, at the last possible moment, to let the officer draw his own conclusions.

Alton nodded shortly, apparently taking the point. "Few Granger indulge in the weakness of alcohol. Our slaves make all the beer and mead that we can drink. What possible use do we have for more of this swill brought all the way from Otranto?"

Jake consulted *The Arena of Otranto* for just the right analogy and came up with one he felt sure would appeal to the officer. "Just as a man might receive love from one woman, yet enjoy adding another to his harem, so might a man who has the local brew enjoy sampling something more refined and elegant from time to time."

To Jake's surprise, Alton smiled and two of his men laughed. "Ha, that's what I like about you decadent Otrantos. You'll be bringing slave girls with your ale, will you?"

Jake shrugged. Perhaps metaphor was a little sophisticated for these Granger soldiers. "First we must see what the factors and merchants of Spoleta wish to buy." They had agreed on the nearby city as a compromise when Jake had learned how long the trip to Bathsheeba would take.

"Spoleta?" The officer looked scornful. "That handful of mud dwellers offer nothing."

The Arena of Otranto called Spoleta a garden city of half a million inhabitants. Could Alton be lying?

Jake's doubt must have shown because Alton drew his sword and held the point to Jake's throat. "You believe I would soil my word for the sake of a mere merchant?"

Alton had moved more quickly than Jake would have believed possible. In his years of martial arts training, he had met and sparred with some of the best black belts in Wayward but none of them, even on that low-gravity planet, had moved with such devastating speed. Alton glared at Jake, his eyes filled with the desire and inclination to put a permanent end to the conversation.

"Uh, no," Jake gasped. A hint of moisture, either sweat or blood, trickled down his neck. "I had heard of the beauty and grandeur of Spoleta. If that wealth has passed, our journey must be longer. I am, of course, grateful for your warning. An unnecessary journey to a dying city would hardly add to our profits."

"Bah, that is why Otranto will fall to the Granger," Alton told him. "You think of profits and losses. We think of armies. You build wealth. We come and take it."

Jake had heard talk like that on the streets of Wayward growing up. It might work for street gangs, but no great society could support itself simply by taking from others. There had to be a productive core to the Granger Khanate. If there wasn't, he reminded himself, the current trickle of galactic trading visits would shrink to an occasional anthropology vessel and one Jake Borinski would be a permanent Arcadian.

"If Spoleda is unworkable, what great cities are near?" Jake asked.

"Talking is parching work in the desert heat," Alton said.

"You understand that we carry only samples of our merchandise and a few casks for our own consumption?"

Alton nodded greedily. "I am sure that my men would appreciate a cask of ale."

Jake considered refusing but the sword's point hadn't wavered from his throat.

"We would be happy to share one of our casks with you," he offered.

"Make it so."

Jake gestured for Lucer to breach one of the more mediocre casks of beer and serve Alton's squad. Even warm, Jake was certain it would be better than anything that could be produced in this desert or, unless the Granger had somehow discovered refrigeration, in the warmer southern latitudes that made up the bulk of the Granger Khanate.

"But that's the good stuff," Lucer whined in a voice that Jake didn't even recognize. "Surely they'll be just as happy with the swills."

"We'll take that," Alton insisted. His blade nicked Jake as he pointed it at the small cask Lucer was holding.

"We must not hold back from our new friends," Jake said hoping that he didn't sound completely condescending. "In the future, we will be sure our caravans bring ample ale for the expanded armies of Alton the general."

Alton puffed up his chest and supervised the pouring even, to Jake's surprise, allowing Lucer to pour mugs for himself, Jake, Harold, and Clovis. Castile remained out of sight.

Alton drained his mug, then handed it back for a refill. "Refreshing, perhaps," he conceded. "I have had better, but of course I am an officer and a nobleman of the Granger court."

If Alton was a nobleman, Jake would eat his boots, but he merely nodded politely. "We hope that many will find it pleasant, so that we can bring caravans of beer and other goods to your rich lands."

"So we can tax the Otranto peasants to buy it. It is a most humorous joke," Alton insisted.

* * * *

The Granger soldiers passed the heavy cask around as if it was a canteen, and handed it back empty.

"My cousin serves in the garrison at Epheses," Alton said. "It is not much farther than Spoleta and has at least some pretense of culture." He belched loudly after the word culture although Jake wasn't certain whether it was an editorial comment or simply the beer doing its work.

"You recommend we go to Epheses, then?" Jake asked.

"I do not *recommend*." Alton glared at Jake. "I order you to proceed to Epheses and report to my cousin there. If you fail to do so, my band will hunt you down, drink your beer from your skulls, and enjoy that little girl hiding beneath your wagon."

Alton called for a light and wax and placed his seal on Jake's wagon. "Show this to my cousin Mikael. It should keep you alive long enough to get to him."

Laughing, he mounted and rode off. In seconds, only the cloud of dust from his troop remained.

Castile climbed from under the wagon. "He saw me."

"Now you begin to see why we always lose," Clovis said. "They notice everything. When you outnumber them, they disappear. When they outnumber you, they hunt you down like wolves after an elk.

"They must have seen you before you hid," Jake comforted Castile. "They were probably watching us ever since we crossed the border."

"Almost certainly they were watching us before we crossed the border," Lucer corrected. "Their patrols have little respect for boundaries."

"Wonderful. So just how far is Epheses?"

During the next week, the small band drank a significant part of their inventory, hunted occasional edible lizards and a couple of rabbits, and celebrated with every water hole they found.

Jake caught Harold shaking his head as they gathered around their evening fire.

"What?"

"Have you given any thought to our wood?"

"There seems to be plenty. We just pick it up as we go."

"There is plenty. But there aren't any trees. So where did it come from?"

Jake's experience in camping came from a one-week scouting trip more than a decade before. He shook his head in frustration over how much he was missing. "You have a theory?"

"I'm thinking we're burning old farmhouses, old orchards." Harold shrugged, "Hell, I'm no philosopher but this used to be something and now it's a desert."

Jake repeated his mantra that this was none of his business--Arcadia wasn't his planet. Alien or not, it was getting more difficult. Could he really stand by and do nothing in the face of the destruction that the Granger brought? He paused to examine the fragment of wood he had been about to add to the fire. The weathered wood still bore the likeness of a beautiful woman carved into the fine-grained material.

Clovis speared a lizard on a long stick and held it over the fire. "Otranto has been losing for hundreds of years. You and I thought we could do something and we joined up." He turned the lizard and glanced pensively at Harold. "Look where it got us. Shorted on our wages when Fernis took over, that's what." He gestured so emphatically that the lizard fell off his stick and into the fire. "Damn."

"But if Otranto had spacer weapons," Harold argued, "we could march right back through here. Hell, we could rebuild the Otranto of five hundred years ago." He waved his hand expansively. "This could be farmland again."

"Jake doesn't have spacer weapons," Castile said. She had developed the habit of fading into the background even within their small group and surprised them every time she spoke.

"All right. Well, nobody expected him to bring 'em by the ton. But there are abandoned factories in Otranto city where they used to build ships. So why can't we build spacer weapons. They'd come in handy right there, in fact. We could get rid of Fernis and put in a real fighting Emperor before we attack the Granger."

"I have no clue how to build any space weapon," Jake said firmly. "I couldn't even tell you how to build the type of cannons you already have."

"Leave the man alone," Lucer said. "Your job is to protect the wagon, not to get Jake involved in some romantic crusade to save a dying nation."

"Not just a nation," Castile argued, putting on the full court press. "We're talking about the end of civilization." She waved her hands at the desert. "The countryside around Otranto City depends on irrigation as much as this land did. The Granger will bring the desert with them."

Jake stood and stomped away from the fire. These were his friends and he could do nothing to help them. It didn't seem fair. In all of the books he'd read about spacers being set down on de-civilized worlds, the hero would parlay his knowledge of smokeless powder, or plastique explosives, or matter-antimatter energy generation to create powerful weapons, arm the small but militant armies of the oppressed kingdom, marry the princess, introduce space flight, and then bring the newly united planet into the galactic mercantile republic. Unfortunately, none of these novels had ever detailed the technology involved in making plastique explosives, matter-antimatter energy generators, or even smokeless power so Jake was stuck with a sense of frustration.

"Maybe you're thinking about this wrong." Castile's voice jolted Jake out of his momentary funk.

"Thinking about what?"

"About Otranto and the Granger. Just because you don't know how to make weapons doesn't mean you can't help us. You've been all over the universe. Surely you learned something out there. Something that no one here knows."

Castile might have been a sort of princess but Jake certainly wasn't going to marry a teenager. Still, he wished that he could be a little more of a hero to her. He decided to abandon that losing battle and shook his head. "Arcadia is only the fifth world I've ever been on. My spacer career lasted about six months. During that time, I updated the computer program that handled the ship's storage optimization and speculated in the commodity futures market which is basically a huge gambling organization. If you wanted me to tell you how to pack your closet, or even the wagon, I might be able to help. I just don't see that saving Otranto."

"I know you'll think of something." So quickly that he was never certain that it had ever happened, Castile brushed her hand against his lips and disappeared.

The pisser was, now that he'd seen what the Granger did to the land they conquered, he actually wanted to do something.

* * * *

The following day, they began a gradual descent. Almost imperceptibly, sand and stone were replaced by tufts of grass and substantial flocks of sheep. Red dirt blew across the old stone Otranto highway that they followed. Barely curious shepherd boys glared at them as they passed.

To Jake, the looked like neither the blond Granger nor the dark-haired natives of Otranto he'd seen. "Are they mixed blood?" he asked Harold.

Harold laughed. "No such thing as mixed blood to the Granger. You're either Granger or you're dirt. Doesn't stop them from drafting you into the army if you're not Granger, though. Just keeps you from ever becoming an officer."

That confirmed Jake's understanding of the Granger military which seemed based on some combination of a warrior class and a feudal muster, unlike the wholly professional force that Otranto fielded, if *force* was any word to describe Otranto's troops.

"Well, these boys don't look like they're Granger."

Harold shook his head. "They're Ebron. Surely you've heard of them."

Jake did a quick search of Arena of Otranto and came up with only a couple of cryptic references. "Should I have?"

"Hell, yes. They practically destroyed Otranto a couple of centuries ago. Captured the entire southern half of the Empire is what they did. Bunch of pagans, of course. Then they taught the Granger their pagan religion and that was that for the Ebron. If you think the Granger have been bad for Otranto, they were a hundred times worse for the Ebron. 'Course maybe the Ebron don't mind since they're all part of the same pagan faith."

Jake might not be an expert in psychology, but he thought it would take more than a shared religion to keep a conquered people happy.

Perhaps the solution the Granger problem could be found in Granger land among the people they had conquered rather than in the militarily hopeless and non-spacer armed forces of Otranto.

"So they let them serve in the Granger military."

Harold hawked and spat. "They'll take spearcatchers from anywhere. From the stories I've told, they were pretty effective soldiers once, but that's been a couple of hundred years."

Well, it was something to keep in mind, anyway.

Over the next several days, the landscape transformed gradually to grasslands, then to irrigated farms. These, Jake noticed, were worked by peasants who spoke the language of Otranto.

"You know this isn't going to work, don't you," Castile told him as he perched on the wagon bench urging the mules on toward what was finally beginning to look like a city.

For once, she didn't surprise him. He'd gotten used to her appearing from nowhere. "What isn't going to work?"

"Trading beer with the Granger."

"I don't see why not. It's obvious they don't have anything as good. Besides, it takes cooler climes to make good beer. That's why your dad brews his in the cellars."

"I'm sure you'll get a good price for the beer. Think about the costs, though. One or two wagons could get through that desert without any problems, but a caravan would have to carry its own forage. Probably their own water as well. We wouldn't be able to bring enough beer to build brand identity so each caravan would have to start all over developing the market."

Jake almost fell off his seat. He'd discussed brand identity and marketing concepts exactly once since he'd been on Arcadia and that, he had been certain, had been when he and Manny had been alone. How could Castile have picked up either the vocabulary or the understanding?

"What are you talking about?" he demanded.

"I heard you using those words and I did a little research."

He toned down the adrenalin spurt. "What sort of research."

"Otranto has a library, you know. Most of it was burned when the barbarians occupied the city a couple of centuries ago, but it's not completely gone. There were some books on marketing. So I read them. It seemed to me that I should know what you know so you don't cheat us."

Jake put his head in his hands. The one advantage he'd counted on was his MBA. If anyone in Otranto could go to the library and pick up everything he'd learned, he might as well have let Manny sell him into slavery that first day and have done with it.

"So?" Castile demanded.

"So, you're right." Beer was a bulky and relatively low value commodity. Unlike gems, fine textiles, and spices, which could be transported across or even among worlds, beer tended to be a local product. In terms of manpower, it would cost more to bring beer from Otranto to Epheses than it would to bring it from one of the trader worlds.

"All right, then. So why are we here? And don't tell me it's to keep me safe. There's nothing safe about being an Otranto princess in the middle of the Granger Khanate."

There wasn't any particularly good answer to Castile's questions. They'd entered the Granger Khanate with the idea of heading for Spoleta. Since Spoleta was on the seacoast, he'd planned on transporting production quantities of beer to Erlang by wagon, then from Erlang to Spoleta by water. Since they'd been redirected away from Spoleta, he'd pretty much been running on autopilot, afraid that if he turned around, Alton, or another Granger captain, would decide they really were spies.

"There's got to be something they need and want to pay for," he argued. "Your father's manufacturing methods can be applied to a lot of things other than beer. We'll find what they want and ship it to them."

Castile cocked her head as she looked at him and, for a brief moment, he imagined he saw her mother's wisdom looking out her eyes rather than a young girl. "Maybe you really are a spy after all."

He shook his head violently and looked around to see if she'd been overheard. If Alton was typical of the Granger military, it wouldn't take more than Castile's hint to send Jake to the headman or whatever other primitive execution method they used here. Perhaps as a concession to modern sensibilities, *Arena of Otranto* had avoided any mention of the local judicial system.

"Looking for markets isn't spying." He lowered his voice until even he could barely hear it

Chapter 7

A heavy pall of smoke assailed them before they even passed the ancient and disrepaired city walls of Epheses. Jake pointed the mules toward what remained of a gateway, the actual gate having fallen by the side of the road.

"Doesn't look like they fear attack," he observed. "Must have a lot of confidence in their military."

Harold nodded grimly. "Who'd attack them? The real reason they tore down the gate is to prevent Epheses from rebelling again."

This was the first Jake had heard of any rebellions against the Granger overlords. "Epheses revolted?"

"If you want to call it that. The Granger raised taxes, the local Otrantos refused to pay and took to the walls." He spat. "The border was closer then and we were supposed to bring a relief force. A few of us thought we'd actually recapture a bit of territory."

"So what happened?"

"Our general decided he wanted to be emperor and marched on Otranto City instead. The Epheses garrison pulled themselves together, marched out, and slaughtered a few thousand Otrantos. The usual. Otranto has done a great job making sure no one looks to it for help. Speaking of the garrison, looks like we have company."

An armored soldier waved Jake off the stone road and demanded Jake's business.

He was, Jake soon realized, reluctant to allow them to enter Epheses, but his reluctance had nothing to do with whether they were spies.

"Is there trouble in the city?" Jake finally demanded. "We are peaceful merchants and a Granger officer suggested that we trade here."

The words *Granger Officer* got more attention than had ten minutes of explanations of their business. "What officer?"

"His name was Alton. I don't know his family name but he said he had a cousin Mikael here in the Ephesis garrison."

The Granger guard nodded. "I will summon Mikael. Wait here."

He turned and stepped into the city gates.

Jake turned to Harold. "Surely they could have let us water our mules and get a bite to eat while we waited."

"Granger don't think of their own comfort and they certainly don't care about anyone else's comfort. Sooner or later, they will come back and let us know what to do."

In the meantime, Jake and Castile unharnessed their mules and let them crop the stunted grass that grew around the Epheses walls.

It was an hour later when the guard returned, accompanied by a blond giant of a man. The giant wore dented armor that showed signs of scorching and what looked like a new blood stain.

"Which of you is the leader here?" the giant demanded.

Jake stood. "We are merchants from Otranto and the Granger officer Alton suggested that we would find good trading here in Epheses."

"What my cousin knows about trading, he could fit between his horse and saddle without fear of blistering." The giant looked at the bedraggled party. "Well, since you're here, you might as well come in and see if you can find anything to trade."

Jake waved his hand in the direction of the billowing smoke. "Is it safe? Do you need help fighting the fires?"

Mikael shrugged. "The men setting the fires are likely to take a dim view of such behavior."

"Setting fires? Who would set fire to their own city?"

Mikael glared at him. "Are you completely ignorant of the world? Men burn their city because it is there, because they are fools, and because our government protects its rule by turning the slave populations against each other." He waved off Jake's attempt to interrupt. "I believe this current riot was started when an Otranto lad had the effrontery to send flowers to an Ebron girl. What else could the Ebron do but riot, burn, and kill?"

Jake thought that Mikael spoke ironically, but he wasn't absolutely certain. "But why?"

"What else can they do? Otranto and Ebron blame one another for all of their problems. It suits the Granger well enough."

If it suited the Granger so well, why did Mikael seem so distressed? Jake tagged that in his memory as well. But would a reformist movement among the Granger give the locals anything like independence, or would it merely strengthen the Granger economy?

"Is it safe for us to enter the city?"

Mikael shook his head slowly. "The Otranto districts are filled with armed mobs. Taking a wagon filled with ale into those narrow streets would be foolhardy at best. Fatal at worst."

No one had asked Jake what cargo he carried, nor had any of the garrison inspected his wagon. The Granger must, Jake realized, have an effective intelligence and communications system. Perhaps that was why they were so concerned about Otranto spying. They were doing it themselves.

"What do your recommend?"

"Return to Otranto. Epheses makes its own ale and has no need of anything else."

"Any other suggestions?"

"Yes. I don't have resources to give you an escort so you're on your own. If you go into the Otranto quarters, you'll almost certainly lose your wagon and probably your life. If you insist on going in, stay in the Ebron districts and make sure everyone knows you are a foreigner."

Mikael inspected the seal Alton had left on the barrel. "Alton sees spies everywhere but he must have liked you. For now, that will be good enough for your passport. Welcome to Epheses." Mikael turned before Jake could express his thanks, drew his sword, and headed back toward where the smoke billowed most aggressively.

"Is he protecting the Otrantos or helping slaughter them?" Jake wondered out loud.

"Neither," Clovis said. "He's trying to protect Granger property. Neither Otranto nor Ebron lives are worth saving."

The attitude didn't make economic sense to Jake. People were resources. They paid taxes, supplied labor, and were consumers for the wealth that poured out from galactic trading factories. Letting such valuable resources simply slaughter themselves made as much sense to Jake as taking a sledgehammer to Manny's beer-making equipment.

"So what do we do?" He halfway wanted someone to suggest going to the rescue of the Otrantos living in Epheses.

"You want to make a difference, just going in and slapping heads isn't going to do it," Lucer reminded him. "There are lots of Otrantos here. Trust me, if they want to fight, they can do a fine job on their own."

Jake sighed and unclenched the fists he hadn't even realized he'd made. "Right. So let's find some customers. Before they all kill each other."

* * * *

The fourth bar in the Ebron quarter of Epheses allowed them to enter. The previous three had taken one look at them and slammed their doors. Jake tried to assimilate the idea of turning away business: tried and failed.

They sampled the local brew, found it severely wanting, and tried to interest the innkeeper in something of higher quality.

For their pains, they were tossed from that bar, too.

"We don't need any of your fancy Otranto ales," one of the bar's customers shouted. He hefted an iron bar and swung it easily. "Ebrons take care of Ebrons."

"But--"

"Come on, Jake. Let's keep looking." Lucer patted him on the shoulder. "I know I thought this was a good idea, but I'm starting to believe we're wasting our time."

When they finally found another inn to let them enter, they faked enjoyment of an even more vile local beer and kept their mouths shut about their cargo.

Jake and the men were shunned, left in a corner of the bar and grudgingly served when one of the barkeeps found the time. Jake wasn't surprised when Castile vanished but he was surprised when she showed up again, dressed in an Ebron boy's tunic, her long hair caught under a leather cap.

She moved among the crowd passing out mugs of ale, collecting the local coins, and generally fitting into the bar as if she'd lived there all of her life.

"You've got a good little spy there," Lucer murmured into Jake's ear. "She'll learn everything that's going on and whether there are any richer pickings available."

Jake knew the value of business intelligence. He also had a pretty good idea what would happen to Castile if any of the Ebron figured out who she was.

After eating, they headed out to the stable, filled with spicy Ebron food that Jake found a welcome relief after weeks of bland Otranto fare. In contrast, Lucer, Harold, and Clovis looked green around the gills.

Jake leaned against a stack of hay, letting his eyes adjust to the dark. He'd almost nodded off when a sharp tug pulled him off balance sending his face to a meeting with a large horse turd.

"Eugh," he sputtered.

"Quiet." Castile's voice could be as commanding as her mother's.

Jake wiped off his face. "What?"

"Let's go."

"Where?"

But Castile hadn't waited for an answer.

Shaking his head, Jake followed her. She was going to get him killed in a battle that wasn't his and he wouldn't even know which side got him. It didn't seem fair, but he wouldn't let her go out there alone. She was, after all, just a kid.

Twenty minutes later, he was prepared to adjust his estimation. Castile might be a kid, but she wasn't *just* anything. Weeks of hard work on high gravity Arcadia had strengthened him, given him an endurance that would have been considered freakish back on Wayward. Compared to Castile, though, he was still a clumsy male, stumbling over upturned cobblestones that she neatly avoided.

Now that the sun had set, Jake could see that the flames of hundreds of fires bathed the city in a reddish glow. Most fires were confined to a single house or church, but a few overwhelmed whole city blocks.

From nowhere, a black-clad youth joined them, his face blackened by soot, his jet-black hair marking him as an Otranto. He must have said something to Castile because she nodded and changed direction to follow him.

The youth led them underground into the sewers which might once have flowed with the filth of a huge city, but which had been washed clean by decades of disuse. Occasional oil lamps cast a golden glow making the limestone walls glisten as if this was a palace rather than a waste treatment facility.

Minutes later, they emerged into a huge cathedral, still majestic despite the holes left where mosaics had been pried from the floors and where statues had been pulled from their ancient niches.

An aged man wearing the gray robe of a priest of the Otranto religion gestured to a low granite bench that ran near the wall of the church, then nodded to the youth who vanished as completely as Castile so often did.

Although he dressed as a priest, there was nothing holy about the huge sword that hung, unscabbarded, from a wide belt at his waist. While his head was bald, his shoulders looked broad enough still to swing the sword if he needed to. The notch eight inches from the pommel made Jake suspect he'd recently done just that.

"Are you truly from Otranto City?" the man demanded.

"We are, your, uh--" how was he supposed to address this man?

"My name is Father John."

"But only the militant monks fight," Castile objected. "Not ordinary priests."

"A shepherd fights for his flock when the wolves attack," Father John replied. "You saw our city. The Granger stand over it like vultures while the Ebron wolves do their dirty work."

"I see. Well, to answer your question, we have come from Otranto City as you suspected."

"And how fares the mother church?"

Jake nodded to Castile to pick up the conversation. All he knew about the Otranto religion was that it appeared to have a rigid hierarchy.

"The Patriarch and the Emperor continue to bicker over taxes, they've begun building a new church outside the city walls to celebrate the breaking of the siege twenty years ago, and more and more monks are arriving from all over the world to retreat to the Isle of Corinth south of the city."

Father John sighed heavily. "When I was young, I thought I might become a monk and visit that sacred island. Instead, the Granger overran my city and I was left to keep alive the true faith in a land ruled by pagans."

"Yet you stay? Why not flee the Granger and come to Otranto proper?" Jake asked. "Everywhere we went, there were empty farms just waiting for someone to come and take them over."

Father John grasped his sword, half pulling it from his belt. "This is our home. You saw the city as you came here, filled with flames and murder. While we were ruled by Otranto City, this city was sacked five times, first by Ebron armies and then by Granger until Otranto abandoned us to our fate. That doesn't count the time unpaid Imperial soldiers rioted." He gestured to the bare walls. "It was Otranto soldiers who looted this church, not the Granger."

"But you are Otranto." Castile spoke softly, but Jake could hear the hint of her mother's passion in her voice. "Surely you dream of the day when you can be reunited with the great empire."

"I dream of many things." Father John laughed harshly. "None of my dreams have ever come true. That one will be no different."

"Then why did you summon us?" Castile demanded. "Or did you simply want to enter an early bid for our merchandise."

"I wanted to look at the people who wanted to recreate the days of the Otranto merchant princes. I would rather see Otranto merchants getting rich under Granger rule than free Otranto cities being ravaged by whatever pagans happen to invade."

"But--"

"Otranto is a dream now. A lost dream of the holy nation. Those who follow the true faith do better to remember it for what it was, not for what it has become. When the city and the last of the empire fall at last, perhaps a year from now, perhaps a decade, it will not matter to those of the faith because the real Otranto lives in our hearts."

"You still haven't told us why you wanted to meet with us," Jake said. "Or are we supposed to be your prophets, taking your message of despair back to the people of Otranto."

Father John laughed again. "Despair reached Otranto City long before I did. When I was younger than you, even younger than the girl, I traveled to Otranto City and found that despair already had made its home there. There is no hope for that city. No hope for the ancient and dying empire of Otranto. There is only the true faith and hope for an eternal empire that cannot fall to foreign invaders."

The man was obviously either a religious nut or a saint. Jake didn't think he would make much of a business partner in either case. "We'd better get back to the men," he told Castile. "I didn't like the way that Innkeeper kept looking at our wagons."

Father John put his finger to the side of his nose. "Forget about the wagons. The Granger will take them and call it taxes. Or the Ebron will take it and not bother with any excuse at all. What is important is that you escape this city alive."

"But not so we can tell the rest of Otranto to give up," Jake added.

"Actually, I had a favor to ask."

After hearing what Father John had to say about Otranto, Jake wasn't particularly in the mood for granting favors. Still, the handful of monks in the decaying sanctuary looked tough enough that Jake decided to hear the priest out. "What favor?"

"A friend of mine needs to escape from this city. He dreams of returning to his studies in Otranto City. I had hoped that you would let him join you."

"Why should we?"

Father John shrugged and smiled. "It is written that man is blessed by what he does for others. Who among us is so fortunate that he could not use divine blessings?"

Jake couldn't argue with that. "Is he here with your priests?"

Father John shook his head. "It would be dangerous for him to come here now. He will join you outside the gates of the city when you leave."

"Why not bring him to us?"

Father John shook his head. "I am busy. Tonight, the Ebron attack reaches its climax and by tomorrow, it will seem like a hangover, except that half the Otranto in the city will be homeless and the other half slaughtered in the streets. I'm needed to save those whom I can and perhaps to strike a blow to make the Ebron a little more cautious next time they decide to take their failure out on the helpless Otranto."

He drew his sword and marched out the church door followed by the other monks.

The youth who'd led them through the sewers reappeared wiping a tear from his eyes. "I'm supposed to guide you again. It's really a trick to keep me out of the fight, but I've got to do it."

"Do you need help?" Jake couldn't stop himself from asking.

"Do you have an army handy? Perhaps three or four thousand heavily armed cavalry could scatter the Ebron."

"We don't have an army."

"Well then, just stay out of the way."

* * * *

Father John's warning was fully borne out when they returned to the Ebron inn. Clovis lay nursing a lump on his head. From his uneven pupils, Jake guessed he'd suffered a concussion. Harold had managed to bandage up his left arm, but blood still seeped from a dozen smaller wounds on his chest and legs. Lucer looked uninjured, but even more green around the gills.

"They brought us some Otranto food and we were hungry," Lucer explained. "It must have been drugged. I was unconscious when they came."

"Who?" Jake felt himself sinking into depression. He should have stopped Castile, not followed her like a puppy. Could the whole meeting with Father John have been a setup to get him away from the wagons?

"Some of the servants from the inn," Lucer answered.

"There were a lot of Ebron when they came, not just from the inn. They knew what they were doing too. They rolled the barrels off and wheeled the wagons out in no time. I'd say some of them were brewers the way they handled those big barrels."

The *big barrels* Lucer was talking about were much smaller than the huge vats Manny used to brew his beer, but even they must have been fairly large for the local brewing industry.

"What about the mules," he asked. With mounts, they could ride home and at least claim that they'd found Lucer as a factor for their wares.

"Gone," Harold admitted. "They didn't hitch them up to the wagon, though. They rode them out."

Then they were truly gone. The men might have abandoned the wagons once they'd finished the beer but they wouldn't leave mules behind.

Jake sank to the floor of the stable, put his hand in another horse turd, and bounded to his feet. "We've got to do something?"

"I don't see any army." Clovis spoke for the first time and he sounded like even those few words took all the energy he could spare.

"But--"

"The beer will be gone by now," Lucer told him. "Every drop."

"Not quite every drop." Harold dug through the mound of stinking straw that had served as fodder for their mules when they'd still had mules. With a triumphant laugh, he pulled out two small casks and a chinking bag.

"I thought they looked suspicious when they brought the food so I decided to hide a little something."

Jake's fingers were trembling when he reached out to touch the purse. "How much?"

"I left about a third of the money on the wagon. I thought it would be too obvious if we didn't have anything."

"Smart thinking." He couldn't help wondering if Harold had originally intended to keep the gold himself. Still, the mercenary had come clean. Right now that was a lot.

"What are we going to do, then," Castile asked. "Are you ready to decide we can't trade with the Granger cities? Because if we can't, we are in trouble. Otranto needs money coming in, not just money moving around."

Jake was pretty sure his economics texts would disagree with Castile's logic. Of course, the economics texts hadn't been written to deal with an economy whose main function seemed to be generating enough cash flow to bribe the Granger and pay for mercenaries.

So much for his fantasy about returning to Otranto with an outpouring of wealth reflecting his brilliant trading--although the Erlang sales represented a significant potential. "Well, we don't have anything left to sell. I think we should head for home."

"What about us?" Harold asked. He still held the two casks of beer or mead.

Jake rubbed his eyes and instructed his medical system to increase his endorphin count. "What about you?"

"I mean, you hired us to guard the wagons. We obviously didn't do such a hot job guarding them. So, are you going to leave us here?"

And head back across a hundred miles of unfriendly territory alone with an old man and a nubile girl? Jake hardly thought so.

Time to do a little cheerleading. "There will be other wagons. We're going to figure a way to make Otranto a trading power." He paused for a moment calling up Father John's exact words. Were there really Otranto merchant princes in the old days?"

Clovis shrugged. "The old stories say that we were all spacers once, two or five thousand years ago. Maybe there were Otranto merchant princes then too. Who knows? But if you think Emperor Fernis is going to let any merchant get power in Otranto, you've got another think coming."

Becoming a merchant prince had been a ridiculous notion anyway. Jake needed to get off-planet. Maybe he could throw himself on the mercy of the commodity police and get out of jail in a couple of decades. If he listened to Castile and Marie, he would get sucked into a battle where his so-called allies were his biggest problems. Besides, from what he'd shown so far, Jake was a pretty weak reed on which to build a new Otranto.

"Anyway, we're all going back together and you and Clovis are going to get paid. Now, who has any brilliant ideas about getting out of here?

Clovis looked at Harold, who looked at Lucer, who looked at Castile. Castile looked at him. "Whatever it is, we'd better do it soon."

Chapter 8

Two hours before dawn, Jake and his companions crept out of the stable and headed out of town.

After his meeting with Father John, Jake was uncertain whether he could trust any Otranto they ran into and he was absolutely certain he couldn't trust the Ebron. Where the Granger fit into the equation, he was clueless.

The city glowed a dusky red from the flames that burned both in the Otranto quarters, but also scattered through the rest of the town.

"Were there Otranto shops scattered through the city?" he asked Lucer.

Lucer gave him a grin showing a hole where one of his teeth had been. "They don't mix much."

"Then--"

"Ours wasn't the only beer they found, lad. Some of the fires are probably where a foolish innkeeper tried to protect his property. Others may be where drunks got careless."

"And some," Castile added, "are where the Otranto are fighting back."

Clovis spat. "Everyone knows the Otranto can't fight. That's why they hire mercenaries in the first place."

"Otranto soldiers created the greatest empire this world has ever known," Castile argued. "What other kingdom has lasted more than a few generations? Otranto has survived for over a thousand years."

"Yeah. And if it's lucky, it'll stand for another ten."

"I'm sorry I asked." Jake honed in on the GPS navigational satellites left behind by the spacers. His implant couldn't transmit far but it could at least pick up the signals. "Turn right here."

"This isn't the way we came," Castile told him.

"Shh. Don't you hear it?"

She wrinkled her nose. "What?"

He yanked her arm, pulling her out into the narrow alleyway he'd selected. "People. Ebron."

Clovis and Harold had reacted as soon as he'd spoken, ducking into the alley and vanishing as quickly as if they'd been taking lessons from Castile. Lucer tried, but he had lost some of his soldier's quickness during his years as an innkeep.

"There's someone down there." The shout was followed by an angry growl.

Jake opened his mouth to shout something about just being fellow Ebron, but Harold's hand clamped over his mouth. "You'd just give away our position, lad," the bandit hissed in his ear.

Unfortunately, their position was no great secret. A dozen torches flared in the street they'd just stepped off.

Jake swallowed the bile that rose in his throat. He couldn't panic. Not with all of their lives depending on what he did. "What are we going to do?"

"Have any idea where your alley is going?" Harold asked. He was limping. Why hadn't Jake noticed that earlier?

"It runs parallel to that next street. Don't know how far it goes."

"Well then you'd better hope it's not a dead end. Let's go."

Limping or not, Harold set a good pace once he got going and Castile, Jake, Clovis and Lucer hurried after him.

A small group moves faster than a crowd and they soon widened the distance between themselves and the torches.

Harold fell back beside him and grasped his arms. "We'd better prepare a little lesson."

"But we're moving faster than the mob. We're getting away." The alley had bent slightly and the torches were completely out of sight now.

"Don't you think they know that? Even a drunk mob is smart enough to send fast runners ahead. We'll need to blunt their interest."

Harold drew his sword, then glared at the unarmed Jake. "If you want to be a merchant, you'd better learn to use a sword."

Jake had spent some time in a weapons dojo, so he wasn't completely unfamiliar with the art. There was a considerable difference, though, between the skills he'd acquired as a sport and the effortless competence a man like Harold showed.

"I'll do my share."

"Throw rocks at them and distract them while I slice them. They won't be carrying more than knives and staves."

Jake wasn't very encouraged. Both knives or clubs could be thoroughly fatal on a backward planet like Arcadia.

Harold brought his blade to his lips, kissed it, then nodded. "Now."

He launched himself into the panting Ebron, his sword flickering as he batted away a club, sliced away a hand that had held a knife, and lunged, piercing the largest of the young men now screaming for their blood.

Jake's panic grew when he saw Harold try to tug the sword from the Ebron's body. The blade snapped off at the hilt leaving Harold with little more than a set of brass knuckles. Harold threw the hilt at one of the Ebron, but the man ducked.

Harold pulled his fists into a defensive posture and spun to face the remaining six opponents with his bare hands. His limp was obvious now and he was slowing down.

Jake threw one of the grapefruit-sized paving stones he'd gathered at the man nearest Harold, but the rock panged off his helmet. Cursing furiously, Jake threw his second rock, slamming it into the back of the man's neck. This time he fell like a rock.

"Only five left," Harold laughed. "They shouldn't have sent girls to do a man's work."

All of their assailants were male, but Harold's taunt had its effect. The five remaining Ebron tensed, their fists tightening around staves, knives and, despite Harold's assurances, one long curved sword.

Jake scooped up the long stave Harold had knocked loose, then stepped from his hiding place, joining Harold.

"I thought I told you to throw rocks."

"I ran out."

"Well you should have run away. I can hold them off for long enough to let you get a lead."

That a bandit and mercenary soldier like Harold would willingly offer to sacrifice his life to help others should have given Jake a great insight into human nature. Apparently, though, he'd already drained his day's worth of insights so Jake decided he'd have to keep Harold alive instead.

"Why don't we just finish these five off and we'll both catch up."

Harold laughed shortly. "Because there are five of them and I don't have a weapon."

The Ebron circled around them, still tense from Harold's taunt, but cautious after the quick loss of three of their comrads and Jake's sudden appearance.

Jake caught the eye of the swordsman and winked. "We'll let *you* go as special thanks to your mother," he said in Ebron. "She was so, uh, accommodating."

"Bastard." The swordsman launched himself at Jake in a feeble imitation of Harold's original attack.

Jake deflected the sword's single edge, then spun the weapon out of the man's hands, tossing it toward Harold who was already beset with two more Ebron. "Catch."

"You can't--"

What the Ebron ex-swordsman intended to tell Jake he couldn't do, Jake would never know. He brought the point of his staff into the Ebron's stomach, then reversed it, smashing it down on his head.

The Ebron dropped like felled tree.

Jake whirled around, caught a knife on his staff just before it sliced into his back, then landed a crescent kick on the man's ear.

"Well that's that," Harold said. "Keep that stick away from me."

The Ebron lay in mounds, one or two moaning, one still holding the stump which had once been his hand. The remainder were perfectly still.

"Are they dead?" Jake felt sick again, this time not in panic but in pure guilt. Death had always been an abstract concept to him, not something he would actively participate in.

Harold spat on one of the writhing bodies. "Some. But none of them are likely to do any more chasing today. Let's rejoin the others."

Harold took off at as fast a jog as his injury allowed and Jake followed him.

"What about the rest of the mob?" he asked after they'd been running for a few minutes. "Won't they send out more runners?"

Harold's grin showed strong, even teeth. "If they were an army, they would. I think a mob will have a hard time finding volunteers. Likely they'll take the easy way and go burn someone who doesn't fight back too hard."

Jake ran in silence for a few more minutes trying to understand what had happened.

Finally he exploded. "None of this makes sense. The Granger conquered both Ebron and Otranto natives. You'd think they would join together. You know, the enemy of my enemy is my friend."

Harold shook his head. "I don't know where you heard that, but it isn't the way life works. The Granger are like a force of nature. Neither the Ebron nor the local Otranto can imagine fighting them successfully. Yet they have to fight someone. Blaming the other is the easiest way out."

So much for any fantasies about uniting the conquered people to rise up. Not that anyone here would trust the Otranto government to actually march to their assistance even if the Ebron and Otranto natives did somehow manage to patch up their differences.

They emerged from the end of the alley into an open courtyard. Fountains depicted winged angels battling diminutive demons and bearded prophets holding stone tablets. The fountains' water reflected dying flickers of fire. Of living humans, he and Harold were the only representatives.

"Where is everyone?" Jake was gasping although they'd only run for about ten minutes. He had finally adjusted to the high gravity but even so he couldn't do what he could do back home on Wayward. Partially, too, his sensors assured him, what he was feeling was the sensation of adrenalin being washed from his system.

"We're here." Castile did her normal appear-from-nowhere act. Lucer and Clovis stepped out from a roofless building--a building that didn't look like it had been rebuilt since the last time Epheses had convulsed into riot and fire.

"I thought you'd be out of the city by now." Harold grasped Clovis by the collar and yanked him close until the two men stood chest-to-chest. "What were you thinking?"

Despite Harold's gruffness, the mercenary had a point. The man had willingly gone to sacrifice his life to let the rest of them escape and they hadn't bothered to do so.

"They've reinforced the city guard." Clovis's voice was a little strained from Harold's choke, but he was trying to give his report. "We're close enough to the Granger guard that we figured we'd be safe from the mob. Castile wouldn't let us give up on you. Besides, if we left without you and then you showed up, the Granger would think all of us were spies."

It made a lot of sense to Jake and he told Harold that.

"Pah. Clovis thinks he is my mother," Harold said. "Still, we are all together now. Perhaps we can finally leave this god-forsaken city."

* * * *

Getting out of Epheses was far more difficult than getting in had been. One of the officers had wanted to execute them on the spot for being Otranto spies.

After spending more than half their remaining money in bribes, Jake and his crew were literally shoved out of the city.

The road back looked far worse on foot than it had on muleback or on wagon.

Jake led them to a clearing about a mile from town and collapsed. "I'm going to sleep until I wake up," he declared.

"You have to take your turn at sentry," Castile reminded him.

Castile came and talked to him when he was on sentry duty as none of the ex-soldiers trusted Castile to watch over them by herself. He tried to be polite, but had a hard time with it.

"Let him go, darling." Harold grasped Castile by the arm, holding her effortlessly despite her attempt to escape. "He killed his first man tonight. He'll need to be alone for a while. It isn't an easy thing."

"Did he really kill someone?" Castile asked. Her brown eyes widened.

"For sure the man he beaned with a rock? Crushed his spine."

"Oh." Castile smiled at him.

Jake felt even worse.

* * * *

"We've got company." Jake's ribs hurt and he guessed he'd been awakened by a swift kick.

"Ugh." None of his questions made it out past the hand pressed over his mouth.

"Ebron. I've only spotted one so far, but if they've followed, there'll be more."

Jake scrambled to his feet, his hand reaching for the staff he'd taken the previous night. It made a nice weapon while appearing to be nothing more than a walking stick. Besides, he'd trained more with the bo than with any edged weapon.

"Where is he?" Jake kept his voice a whisper.

"On the road coming this way."

Harold was right. One Ebron, by himself, walking down the middle of the road, didn't make sense no matter how he looked at it.

"I'll stop him," Jake decided. "You and Clovis fan out and see who else is planning to join the party. Castile and Lucer, you're our reserve. Help out with whoever calls for help.

Castile made a face but, for once, didn't argue. Harold and Clovis vanished into the trees at the edge of the clearing. Lucer held his ancient short sword and nodded grimly. "I thought we had gotten away too easily."

Since Lucer's definition of *too easily* consisted of losing almost everything they owned, Jake didn't completely agree. Now wasn't the time for quibbling, though.

"Stay alert."

He tried to stay alert himself, wiping the sleep from his eyes and turning up his hearing sensitivity to detect possible footsteps following the lone Ebron.

"So you escaped Epheses. My congratulations." The Ebron squatted in the middle of the road looking directly at Jake although he would have sworn that he'd approached in dead silence. Oddly, he spoke in Otranto.

"And you thought that wasn't good enough?" Jake asked. If this Ebron led a large party, he was in trouble but at least the others might be able to get away. That notion wasn't as reassuring as he'd hoped it would be. Hero material, he was not.

The Ebron stayed squatting, a faint smile playing across his white teeth. "It tells me that you are more than you appear to be."

Which wouldn't be hard. They appeared to be a small group of penniless and horseless men fleeing from an unfriendly city.

Jake walked closer, his staff resting gently in both hands. "Everyone seems to think we are spying for Otranto. It happens not to be the case."

The Ebron shook his head. "The Granger worry about Otranto spies. I don't know why. Otranto is thick with both Granger and Ebron who have fallen out of favor with the Khan and who would willingly supply all the information Otranto needs for a few pieces of gold."

"There's no one else with him." Harold's voice sounded hoarse, unnatural.

Jake responded automatically, stepping back and whipping his staff into ready position.

"Does it frighten you that I came alone?"

Jake slowly relaxed. Harold's odd tone of voice had been intended to confuse direction and not, as he'd first guessed, been a sign of compulsion.

"I am always concerned when men act irrationally. What possible reason would an Ebron have for confronting an armed band by himself?"

"The most obvious. You are going to Otranto. I wish to go to Otranto. I propose joining your party, at least until we reach the border."

"Why should we take you?" Castile demanded.

The Ebron shrugged. "I can use a weapon. Perhaps that would help. Then again, Father John said he would ask it as a favor."

"You're the one Father John asked us to take?" Jake hadn't imagined it would be an Ebron.

"The priest likes to be seen as a simple man of faith, but he is something of a philosopher. He and I spent many evenings together discussing the writings of the ancients and the meaning of the world."

Castile nodded. "It would be bad luck to refuse Father John's request. We've got to take him."

* * * *

Clovis stepped behind the Ebron's shoulder, his sword naked and glistening as the first light stole over the horizon. "Well, I don't trust him."

The Ebron stood. He easily towered over Jake and dwarfed the other men of his party. "If I meant to kill you, I would have come with a group of warriors. Instead, I came alone."

"And you're delaying us enough so any Ebron gang from the city will be able to catch us," Jake added. "You may as well join us, at least as far as the border." At the border, they could easily turn him over to the Otranto military who would, as the Ebron himself had suggested, be overjoyed to have a native of the Granger lands to ply with their questions.

The Ebron looked at the dawning sky, then bent and picked a small pack from the side of the road where it had laid, invisible even to Jake's augmented vision. "Unless they come after you with horses, I think you are well away."

"And will they come on horseback?" Jake couldn't help from asking.

The Ebron laughed. "My fellow Ebron? If they had horses, they would have better things to do than attack Otranto people. The Granger keep a monopoly on horses. Ebron and Otranto are allowed mules, donkeys, and oxen."

"They stole our mules. They could probably steal horses too."

"Perhaps. Yet how many and how would they get them through the city gates? The Granger guards will let men through for a bribe, but they would never let an armed Ebron out on horseback."

"They let us into the city and we aren't Granger."

The Ebron nodded. "In is not out, and mules are hardly a warlike steed."

As they'd talked, they had also walked. After a few moments, Lucer, and finally Harold joined them.

"What is your name, Ebron?" Castile demanded.

"You may call me Mark," the Ebron answered.

"Do you have a true name?"

"Of course." Mark showed his teeth. "You know that there is only one time when an Ebron may offer his true name to a woman. Are you asking me to marry you?"

Clovis brought the pommel of his sword against Mark's back, shoving the Ebron to a stumble. Jake noticed that Mark recovered after only one misstep. "Show some respect, Ebron."

"I answered the questions I was asked," Mark replied.

Clovis had his sword out of his sheath before Jake could do more than gape.

Mark fell back, laughing. "What, are you asking for my secret name as well? What an amorous group you are."

"Hold it." Jake raised his voice, roaring like a wounded elephant. "Clovis, you're being an idiot. Mark wasn't one of the ones who attacked us and you shouldn't take out your anger on him. And Mark, you're not going to stay if you cause dissention."

Mark looked like he was trying to stifle a grin. Trying unsuccessfully. "That is what the Granger say as well."

"What?"

"That I am a troublemaker, always stirring up dissension and argument. The captain of the Epheses guard told me that my health might be improved by a change of clime. Since guard captains in three cities had already expressed a similar sentiment, I decided to move beyond Granger territory."

Wonderful. All they needed was a troublemaker to make their journey even more painful. All Otranto needed was more dissent.

"So you cause problems? Do you have any useful skills for the road, or do you expect us to merely form the butt of your jokes and trouble making?"

"Skills? I have camped out at night, but am happier in the cities. I speak Ebron as well as Otranto, but I know that you do the same."

A twinge of suspicion coursed down Jake's spine. "You know that how?"

"Because we have been slipping from Ebron to Otranto since this conversation began, of course. Although anyone who heard you were Otranto merchants would suspect you were spies."

"Because the Granger Khanate is at war with the Otranto?"

Mark laughed. "Hardly. Trade does not depend on the winds of politics. It is simply that there haven't been real Otranto merchants for hundreds of years. Not since the Emperor Hadrian sold the trading concessions to the barbarians in exchange for an army or a navy or some such. The army is long gone, but the concessions remain."

Talk about jumping out of the frying pan into a fire. "You mean we're violating an Otranto law by trading?"

"Of course." Mark waved a hand. "That is the secret to Otranto, however. Everything is forbidden and everyone does that which is outlawed. When the Emperor wishes to rid himself of a troublesome subject, there is no end of crimes to be listed."

A rich Otranto prince might be able to flout the law. Jake didn't think that he and Manny would be able to do so. At least not enough to create the huge trading caravans it would take to make a real difference in the Otranto economy. For that matter, between losing everything on this journey and the law against Otranto merchants, Jake was more likely to find himself sold into slavery than welcomed as a merchant prince.

"You seem to know a lot about Otranto." Clovis's voice hadn't lost a bit of suspicion.

"Once, when the Ebron ruled the west, we sent vast caravans of silk and spices into Otranto City," Mark answered. "My family ran such a caravan and has passed the stories down from generation to generation. Then too, I had the opportunity to study in the school of philosophy in Otranto City itself."

Jake couldn't put any of this in the context of what little he knew of Arcadia's history. "Are you saying that the Ebron and Otranto lived in peace?"

Mark shook his head slowly. "Hardly. We were always at war until the Otranto paid the Granger to raid south from their icy wilderness and destroy the Ebron civilization."

If that was true, it had been an act which, if it was remembered at all by the Otranto, had probably been seen as a brilliant stroke for a generation, and as a horrible blunder by every generation since.

"Let's get this straight," Harold cut in. "We've picked up this Ebron who has no practical skills, and who wants to cut in and share what little food we were able to rescue from the disaster in Epheses?"

Mark nodded, then swallowed. "You have food? I haven't eaten for two days."

* * * *

Mark ate enough for two men, depleting most of the thin stack of travel bread that Harold had hidden from the Ebron thieves.

Jake insisted that they keep moving, just in case Mark had lied about them being followed and because they had suffered one disaster after another since entering Granger territory. The sooner they left, the happier he would be.

After finally filling the pit he called a stomach, Mark stepped closer to Jake and pulled a small harmonica from his pocket. He blew tentatively at first, then swung into a samba beat that had Castile's feet dancing as she walked.

"Stop that," Jake commanded.

Mark frowned. "It makes the miles go more quickly."

Even Castile looked disappointed.

"It tells the world we're here," Jake answered. "Don't you see? We're in danger. With your noise-making, bandits could be upon us before we heard them."

"Bandits? There are no bandits in the Granger Khanate. None, that is, except the Granger themselves. I already told you that they don't allow the native peoples here to practice weapons or riding. Do you fear an untrained man on an ox?"

"What about Granger bandits, then? Even assuming that you're telling the truth."

"All Granger are bandits." Mark clenched his fists until his knuckles turned white. "But those who want to survive within the Khanate do their banditry for the army. Or leave to become mercenaries. Granger mercenaries make up much of the Otranto cavalry, you know."

Mark might not have many useful skills but he did seem to have a big picture view of the world Jake found himself in. He wasn't sure how he could use any of this, but surely knowing more about the geopolitical realities could be helpful.

"And what were the Ebron before they were conquered?" he asked.

Mark waved his hands at the desert that surrounded him. "The stories we tell are numbered as grains of sand in the desert. In all of them, the Ebron are the great heroes. The prophet himself was an Ebron. Ebron merchants carried silks from Otranto and spices and jewels from the mythical west. Our armies besieged Otranto City at least three times. The legend says twenty, but you know how legends go."

"And all of that was eliminated by Granger conquest?"

Mark shrugged. "A few Ebron still trade. Although we are not allowed horses, we have camels that travel the vast deserts to the south and ships that travel the oceans. Yet, a successful trader faces taxes that destroy much of his profit. Generation by generation, the great trading families face bankruptcy and ruin."

Everything Jake heard about the Granger made them sound insane, yet he suspected that was far from the case. Still, if he could do anything to help Castile's family, he owned that to them. "Surely the Ebron resent the Granger for their part in this."

Mark nodded. "Although the Granger have adopted the words of the prophet, they do not follow the true teachings. Few indeed would shed tears if the Granger were struck by a plague and vanished from human history."

"But would they rebel? Take an active role in throwing off the Granger?"

Mark shook his head. "For fifty years after the Granger attacked, the Ebron fought. Hundreds of our cities were burned to the ground, the men slaughtered and the women and children sold into slavery. That was a time when the Ebron had armies, men trained in the ways of war and weapons, and when the Granger still held the lands weakly, with numbers too few to garrison each city. Then we had horses and powerful cavalry units so numerous that their dust darkened the sun. Now, we have mobs with sticks and knifes and rusty swords. To rebel is to die."

For an instant, Jake felt an intense disappointment. He tried to analyze his feelings but couldn't understand. Sure the Otranto and Ebron had a tough time of it. But all through the galaxy, some civilizations rose while others fell. Why was this his business?

"And if the Otranto rebelled?"

"Then the Ebron would gather their sticks and knives and kill all of the Otranto they could. Do you know what would happen to them if the Otranto Empire returned? They would all be killed to make way for Otranto farmers. The Granger don't want the land, they only want what it makes. The Otranto and the Ebron value the land itself. Both would rather have the Granger in control than risk losing everything."

Jake felt a headache coming on and nothing in his implant's bag of tricks seemed to do any good stopping it.

Chapter 9

They'd been on the road for three days when Clovis pointed out the distant pillar of dust. "Horsemen."

"Odd," Mark said. "Normally they stop parties who try to enter their country, not those leaving. Especially those who have lost everything."

Jake gathered his small band around him. "In the desert, we bought them off with ale. To escape Epheses, we bought them off with gold. Here we have neither."

"I wonder if they are after me," Mark continued. "While I am hardly a major annoyance, the Granger sometimes prefer to keep their enemies under their thumbs. It might be better for you if you left me."

Jake was momentarily tempted. After all, he didn't owe Mark anything. The man had been foisted on him by a crazy priest whose only favor to Jake was to distract him when the Ebron stole his wagons.

He shook his head firmly, resisting that temptation. "We are a team. We stick together. Besides, they are as likely to be after the rest of us."

"So we fight," Clovis said. He loosened his sword in his scabbard and gave Castile an evil grin. "Pay them in steel."

"You're being an idiot again," Castile told him. Her voice sounded fond, almost as if she were a woman speaking to a much younger brother, rather than a girl speaking to a grown man.

Harold nodded. "Castile is right. We can't fight them. They'd ride in, launch a few flights of arrows, and then circle around looking for another shot. Now if they would only attack head-on."

"Which they won't do," Lucer said.

Jake's common sense warred with his hormones until he used his implant to crank down the testosterone. "We'll wait and see what they want. They have little to gain by killing us, after all."

"They're always looking for target practice," Clovis argued. He didn't, however, argue too hard. Even he could see the futility in fighting.

As the horsemen approached, Jake was surprised to see that it was Alton's troop. The gods of coincidence might be riding high. There might be precious few Granger troops patrolling the frontier. Or maybe Alton had taken a special interest in his group. Possibly all of the above.

Alton led half his horsemen directly toward the walkers while the remainder deployed around them bows drawn and arrows ready.

"Traders?" Alton's voice was soft but didn't hide an angry edge. "Where are your wagons now?"

Jake couldn't see anything to gain by lying. "Following your advice, we traveled to Epheses where, unfortunately, our wagons and mules were stolen."

"Stolen? More likely unloaded and turned into caissons. Epheses had been pacified for years. When you arrived, it broke out into rebellion. Do you seriously expect me to believe that this is coincidence?"

"It was no rebellion," Jake explained. "It was a race riot between the Ebron and Otranto. The Granger, including your cousin, did nothing but stand by and watch the slaughter."

Alton narrowed his eyes. "No more of your lies. I know who you are. Marie Delphonte is a well known member of the war party and you work for her." He jabbed Jake in the chest with his fist. "First you attempted to start a fight with the Granger Ambassador's servant. Now you arrive to start a rebellion in Epheses. I was right to think you a spy."

Jake shook his head. "We are simple merchants."

Alton pulled a long knife from a sheath at his side and polished it with the sleeve from his silk robe. "No matter how good your ale, it could never pay to caravan it across this desert. Besides, you didn't even try to sell it to the Granger."

Jake had asked himself some of the same questions. Now that he thought about it, he realized that this trip into the Granger territories had less to do with making money for Manny Delphonte and more to do with Jake's wish to escape Arcadia and return to civilization. Explaining that to Alton wasn't going to be easy.

"I guess I'm not a very good merchant." Short, succinct, and unfortunately true.

"Perhaps." Alton glanced at the knife in his hand as if seeing it for the first time. He pushed it halfway down his sheath, then yanked it out again and pointed at Mark. "And perhaps this Ebron isn't the one the soldiers in Epheses have been looking for. You are playing me for a fool, *Spacer*."

Obviously Granger spies were efficient. Alton knew about both Jake and Mark although Jake suspected that the Otranto government knew about neither.

Jake bit his tongue to hold back any comment about what it would take to make a fool of Alton. He wanted to talk his way out of trouble, not to talk himself into more.

Instead, he forced a laugh. It sounded completely unconvincing to him but he hoped Alton wasn't as discerning. "Mark is just a scholar returning to the University at Otranto City."

Alton tugged on his long blond ponytail, then slammed his dagger back into its sheath.

"Shall we kill them?" one of his troopers shouted in Granger. Alton's group, Jake noticed, hadn't unstrung their bows when Alton had sheathed his knife.

Alton shook his head. "I'm going to send you to the spymasters in Bathsheeba. You and the Ebron you call Mark. As for the rest, the girl may have her uses. The others may live as long as you give me no reason to kill them.

With ten bows pointed at him and twenty enemy swords hanging within reach, Jake was in no position to argue. Still, he didn't like the leer that Alton sent Castile's way.

"Bring up six of the mount changes," Alton ordered.

"But sir. They are not--"

"Are you the new captain here?" Alton's eyes flashed a deadly shade of blue.

"No captain. Of course. Six spare mounts."

Before he'd arrived on Arcadia, everything Jake had known about horses, he'd learned from the ancient literature he'd studied. He'd seen the way Clovis and Harold had admired the Granger horses without really understanding. Now, as Alton handed him the reins to a huge white animal marked with large black spots, he found himself somewhere between panic and elation.

"I can't ride," he admitted. Were there even horses on Wayward? He didn't think so.

Alton's smile was anything but friendly. "Then you will learn, my friend. And you will learn quickly."

Castile, Clovis, Harold, and even Lucer mounted their horses with both confidence and some semblance of joy to be off their feet. Mark and Jake looked at each other, whether for reassurance or for direction, Jake never knew.

"I suspect that if we don't get up on these animals, we'll be left behind," Jake said.

Alton laughed again. "All but your heads. I'll take those to the Great Khan so he can add them to the pyramid of his enemies."

Jake scrambled aboard. Fortunately, one of the Granger had saddled the horse and he was able to grasp the saddle horn before falling off the other side.

Mark followed his example, looking almost as unsteady on his animal as Jake felt on his.

"There is one thing you can leave behind," Alton added when Jake's party had finally climbed onto their oversized animals.

This didn't sound good.

"What?" Jake demanded.

"A couple of you seem to have swords. He--" pointing at Clovis, "carries a bow. Why don't you throw all of these weapons onto the ground so you won't be foolishly tempted to use them?"

Reluctantly, Jake nodded at his men. "Leave your weapons." He watched to make sure no one tried anything stupid but held onto his own staff. He was quite certain that Lucer, Clovis, and Harold had knives and other weapons hidden about their persons. Unfortunately, the weapons they left on the side of the ancient Otranto road were the largest and the most effective against a large number of attackers--like Alton's Granger troop.

* * * *

Alton set what, to Jake, was a killing pace, yet the Granger didn't even seem to notice.

After an absolutely miserable five minutes bounding up and down on the horse, Jake finally caught onto how the Granger rode, using their legs to support some of their weight and to serve as shock protectors. He remembered reading some novel about a time traveler who'd changed his world when he introduced stirrups. Unfortunately for Jake's invention career if luckily for his more sensitive areas, the Arcadians hadn't lost that innovation.

The sun was setting as Alton finally led them into a tumbled down fortress set on a hill that overlooked a huge expanse of the desert. His soldiers had surrounded Jake and the others the entire ride, eliminating any chance for escape.

Now that they'd apparently ended their journey, Jake didn't think their captors looked a great deal less wary.

"Dismount and care for your horses," Alton growled.

When Jake stood, holding his horse's reins, his legs quivering from using some of the few muscles his weeks on this heavy-gravity planet hadn't hardened, Alton glared at him. "That horse bore you. So care for her. Remove the saddle, rub her down, give her water."

The horse nudged Jake with her huge head. Only his martial arts training kept him from losing his balance and collapsing to the ground.

"Of course," he said. While he'd never ridden before, he had helped take care of their mules during their journey to Epheses.

The saddle confounded him completely. The leather straps wrapped through brass rings, looped around themselves, and seemed to vanish into the saddle itself without leaving any free ends.

Finally Jake conceded defeat. All of his men had long before completed their work and had led their horses to the stone well from which Alton had promised to draw water untainted by the desert's usual mineral tastes. Only Castile remained and Jake was reluctant to confess his ignorance to her.

"You really don't know how that saddle works?" Pity seemed prominent in Castile's voice. "You spacers don't know much, do you?"

"Can you just help me without calling me an idiot?"

She smiled but shook her head. "The one is the price for the other."

"Just show me how this thing attaches, will you?"

Castile flipped up a leather flap that Jake had thought was part of the saddle, and unveiled the end to the leather girth that had eluded Jake. "It isn't very tricky."

"Now that I know where to look." He started to tug on the hard leather, loosening the strap.

Castile put one of her small hands over his. "I am concerned about this Granger."

Jake was concerned about more than one Granger but he tried to keep his voice neutral. "What do you mean?"

"Why do you think he brought us here, so far from the road? I have seen maps. This is not the way to Bathsheeba."

Jake nodded slowly. "They've decided we're spies. I suspect Alton will get more credit for bringing us in with confessions than just sending us in as suspects. And he probably wants to get away from any superior officers who might be tempted to take the credit." From Alton's hungry gaze in Castile's direction, Jake was fairly certain that wasn't the end of it.

"So we've got to escape, right? Maybe late tonight when they're all asleep."

Jake shook his head. He and the others could never escape on foot. Stealing Granger horses and trying to make it out before the Granger discovered their loss was an even dumber idea. "It'll never work."

"Maybe I could distract them while the rest of you escaped."

He had to give her credit, Castile had a vivid imagination. Next time a ship reached Arcadia, Jake just might see if he could find her a job creating stories for the simu-nets. Perhaps this one would be *Beautiful Princess sacrifices her innocence to help her friends escape*. At any rate, it wouldn't work. No matter how good a distraction Castile could be, and Jake really didn't want to think about a sixteen year-old girl distracting anyone, they would be caught before they'd even left the camp.

"We're a team," he reminded her. "We'll all leave together."

"All together dead," she fired back.

Jake led his horse over to a large bucket filled with water, let the animal drink her fill, and rubbed her down with some tufts of dry grass he found near the well. The animal was sweaty, but solid muscles lined her body. Now that Jake got a closer look, she didn't seem quite the giant he'd thought her at first. In fact, she would probably have been only an average sized horse back on ancient Earth. Arcadia's greater gravity had conspired to produce a race of stronger but stockier equines.

"Don't let her drink too much," Alton advised. "Horses are stupid that way."

Unlike people who were stupid in so many unique ways, Jake thought. Instead of commenting, he nodded and yanked the poor animal away from the water pail.

His horse gave an annoyed snort, jerked the reins from Jake's hands, spun around to face away from him, and kicked at Jake with both rear feet.

Jake dove to the ground, turning his dive into a roll to increase the distance from the angry animal.

The ground hit him hard, not at all like the padded mats in low-gravity Wayward. Still, he was on his feet again, his body reflexively turning in a combat stance.

"Interesting," Alton observed. "You say you are a merchant."

"What else?"

"You move like a warrior."

Jake laughed. "Put a sword in my hands. You definitely wouldn't think so then."

"Perhaps." Alton reached in and snatched the horse's reins without the slightest hesitation. When the horse tried to kick at him, Alton kneed the poor animal in the stomach. The fight went out of the horse in a hurry.

"Any merchant who expects to stay alive has to learn some tricks," Jake observed, trying for some semblance of credibility. "Even a bad merchant like myself."

"Perhaps." Alton led Jake's horse away, removing her bridle before loosening her in a makeshift stable that had once, Jake could see, been some sort of a human dwelling place with an open atrium. Now the roof had collapsed but much of the outer walls remained with makeshift barriers where doors and windows had once opened the home to air and light. So many windows that Jake had to believe that the home had once been located hundreds of miles from the borders, safe in the very heart of the Otranto Empire. Over the years, the border had come to this home, then passed it.

He couldn't hold back a shiver when he wondered what had happened to the family that had once called this area home. Had they fled to Otranto City, or had they, like the peasants who'd farmed so much of what was now desert, simply been killed or starved when the Granger came?

His horse kicked away a steaming new turd left by one of her fellow equines and exposed a fraction of an ornate mosaic built into the floor of what had once been a house.

Jake had fought against any sense of belonging, any excuse to take sides in this lost battle, but now he felt a terrible sense of loss. Once, Otranto Civilization had been strong. More to the point for a merchant, once Otranto had created great works of art--art so plentiful that it could spare an artist's work to be the floor in a merely well-to-do landowner's home. Whether through internal rot or Ebron and Granger attacks, it had lost some of that. Perhaps, if the Ebron had been allowed to conquer the Otranto without disturbance, they would have been able to preserve the best of Otranto culture and given it a new, hybrid life. Certainly what Mark had told him showed that the Ebron shared an artistic and literary sensibility that the Granger lacked.

The introduction of the Granger into the equation had destroyed that possibility. Alton's indifference to the beautiful mosaic was typical of what he had seen and learned about the Granger insensitivity to art. It was on a level with their insensitivity to the thousands of peasants they let starve as they transformed farmlands into desert.

* * * *

Two hours later, the sun had set and the Granger had embarked on a major drinking bout. Significantly, Jake thought, Castile was the only one of their prisoners they attempted to persuade to join them.

"Your cousin seemed well," Jake remarked to Alton. He felt the need to reestablish the human connection between the two of them.

"Yeah? Well, he should. He's got it easy sitting in Epheses where there are girls running around everywhere you look. Out here you know what we get? A couple of scrawny Otranto peasant women every few weeks. Mostly they run away when we come." He paused, took a deep swallow from his beer mug, then thrust it toward Castile. "Drink, little wench."

Castile choked on the bitter brew and Jake found himself at her side, patting her on the back.

"Move away from the girl." Alton's voice was ice-cold and sober. "You've had your chance with her on the road and now it's ours."

"You'll hardly get rich caravans coming through if you waylay them like bandits," Jake reminded Alton. "Let us go and we'll send you a couple of barrels of Otranto's best ales and a cask of Castile's famous mead."

"Rich caravans? Such a joke." Alton swallowed deeply from his mug, his Adam's apple bobbing up and down. "You came here with two wagons and now have none. Do I look dumb enough to believe that these profits will lead to whole caravans?"

"A temporary setback." Jake waved the objection away. "The Granger Khanate is rich with trading opportunities." Which ought to have been the case. Mark had told Jake about caravans of thousands of camel-like animals, loaded with spices, silk, and fine weapons crossing the deserts between the ancient cities in the Ebron oases, Erlang, on the coast of the inner sea, and the fabled lands of Shara in the distant west. Granger indifference and shortsighted unwillingness to invest, and lack of Granger laws protecting merchant property had all but eliminated this trade.

"I believed your story once," Alton said, "and look where it got me."

"It got you a cask of the best ale you've ever tasted."

"It nearly got me executed. Now be quiet before I have you gagged."

Alton took another drink from his mug, then cast the leather mug into the fire. "Enough of this. Time to determine the truth."

His hand hardly seemed to move. One moment it rested by his side, a fraction of a second later, it had caught Castile's dark hair.

"Such a pretty little thing. It's a pity that you chose to consort with spies."

"Save some for us," one of Alton's soldiers urged.

"That is up to our friends. If they tell us the truth quickly enough, the girl will live. If not." He drew a long knife from his belt. "Well, if not, we'll have to make do."

Alton brought his knife to Castile's neck. The blade seemed merely to brush against her skin, but a black-red line of blood trickled from the hollow of her neck down her chest.

"Why did you come here?" Alton demanded.

"I told you, we were looking for trading opportunities," Jake answered.

"That is your last lie. The next time you answer untruthfully, your little friend loses a finger." Alton reached for Castile's hand.

Jake fought panic. He could admit to being a spy, but even that wouldn't keep Castile safe. Telling the truth was even less likely to result in anything positive.

Castile jerked away from Alton's grasp, tearing her top and exposing a shoulder and a portion of a breast. For a fraction of a second, Alton's attention, and the attention of all of his men, focused on the girl.

There wasn't going to be a better opportunity to fight.

Jake deliberately toned down his adrenalin and forced himself to relax into a martial arts trance.

Before Alton could react, Jake slapped the knife away with a crescent kick, then followed up with a side thrust kick to Alton's ribs.

Arcadia-hardened muscles gave Jake added strength and Alton's rib bones cracked as Jake connected.

Castile sprawled to the ground and scrambled away from the Granger captain.

Jake sensed rather than saw the Granger soldier behind him and rolled away, grasping a sharp-edged rock as he hit the ground and ending his roll by shoving the rock between the eyes of the Granger who'd asked Alton to save a piece of Castile for him.

The Granger behind him bulled forward and Jake connected with a back kick to the groin.

The man fell heavily to the ground before Jake could follow up and Jake spun around to see why. His kick hadn't been that deadly.

Castile grinned at him, Alton's knife shining redly in her hand. She'd neatly hamstrung the Granger when he'd rebounded from Jake's kick.

The sound of weapon against weapon indicated that Clovis, Harold, Lucer, and even Mark had gotten into the fight.

"Stay close to me," Jake told Castile. He swept up his staff and went hunting Granger.

"Men," Castile sighed. "You can be such idiots."

Jake ducked a Granger's sword swing, rapped the swordsman's fingers, then drove the tip of his staff into the man's sternum, then followed with an ax kick to the top of the Granger's rapidly descending head. Another one down. That left how many? Maybe fifteen against the five men in Jake's band.

Castile scooped up the fallen man's sword. "See you," she called over her shoulder as she headed away from the campfire.

He started to follow, but was interrupted by three Granger intent on carving new orifices into his body.

They were clumsier than Jake would have imagined, and seemed to wield their weapons awkwardly. Jake wasn't impressed. Then he remembered that they were horse archers with limited experience fighting with swords and less with fighting on foot. His dojo training on Wayward had prepared him for this type of combat even more than their vastly longer but much more specialized military experience.

Although they seemed awkward, the Granger were obviously used to working together. They spread out in a broad triangle, ensuring that Jake could only face one of them at a time.

"Told you they were spies," the man at the center of the triangle told the others, speaking in Granger. "Otranto merchants couldn't fight like this. Besides, they wouldn't have picked up an Ebron, either."

"Yeah, so what?"

"So, when I say three, you feint and Enry can throw a knife in his back. I'll finish him off."

"I guess that's a plan."

"Darn right. Three."

Jake pretended to be drawn into the feint then spun and spanked Enry's dagger from the air, aiming it toward the point man.

His college scholarship in baseball came in as handy as his martial arts training for once. The knife sailed neatly into the point man's waiting throat.

"Well that didn't work too well," Enry said, reaching for another knife.

Jake laughed. "That's what your mother said when she had you." He spoke in the Granger warrior language.

Enry froze, obviously confused to hear their secret language coming from a foreigner. Jake took advantage of the moment, landing a solid staff-strike on Enry's helmetless head.

The third Granger came in more cautiously, but he did come forward despite the loss of his two colleagues.

"So you understood poor Enry," he said. He held his sword before him in a relaxed guard. This man, Jake realized, knew what he was doing.

"He was an idiot," Jake replied.

"Of course." The soldier beat at Jake's staff, then lunged, feinting first at Jake's eyes, then his groin, then finally trying for a his heart.

Jake barely beat the sword away. A staff can be a fine weapon, but a trained swordsman has the advantage. Of the Granger he'd faced so far, only this man could truly claim to be a trained swordsman.

Jake's carefully controlled pulses of adrenalin had let him ignore Arcadia's strong gravity. Now, as he realized he was in a fight with a superior opponent armed with a superior weapon, the gravity, hours of riding an unfamiliar animal, and pure exhaustion from being too long on the road, and too long running from one trouble to the next, crashed down on him.

"With Alton dead, you don't need to worry about your little girl," the soldier told him. "Surrender and I'll send her back to Otranto territory."

"What about my men? They're just caravan guards and merchants I hired."

The soldier shrugged. "I can't do anything for them."

He was honest. He could have promised to set the men free as well. It made Jake think he might mean to keep his word about Castile.

From the crash of metal against metal, it sounded like Harold and the others had run out of momentum.

The soldier might have been reading Jake's mind. "Your men are tiring and still outnumbered."

"Better to die in battle than in torture," Clovis shouted at Jake.

Better for himself and his men, but not better for Castile.

"I--"

A scream interrupted him.

As he watched, Clovis sank to the ground, a Granger sword emerging from his back.

"Better this way," Clovis said, biting off his scream.

The Granger soldier took advantage of Jake's momentary distraction to press in, launching a series of attacks that Jake barely managed to block. Jake was tiring fast while the soldier appeared as fresh as when the battle had begun.

"The staff is a peasant weapon," the soldier observed, "but my first sergeant told me we'd often fight peasants. He made sure I learned how to handle them."

He attacked again, finally binding Jake's staff.

That had to be a mistake as it pitted his one hand against both of Jake's.

Jake threw himself forward, wrenching at the soldier's balance and sword.

For an instant, it appeared that he would win, then the soldier twisted his body and both weapons sailed into the darkness.

The soldier unmasked a dagger he held in his left hand. "Goodbye, spy."

A stricken look came over his face, then blood gushed from his mouth and he fell forward at Jake's feet, an arrow protruding from his back.

Chapter 10

With Castile shooting at them with her bow and Jake charging at them with his recovered staff, the remaining Granger scattered into the darkness.

"Good hunting, Castile," Clovis groaned.

Lucer whooped, then threw a stone to catch the last Granger on the back. The man fell, but scrambled into the darkness before Castile could get off another shot.

"We've got to head out of here before they return," Jake said. He hated to break the moment of celebration, but once the Granger found their horses and their bows, they would hunt down Jake and his party without a lot of problem. Castile had already depleted the quiver of arrows she'd found somewhere so they wouldn't be able to fight back.

"If we're leaving, we'd better steal the horses," Harold observed. "We can put some distance between us and make sure they don't have a chance to warn any other Granger units before we cross the border."

Clovis moaned softly. He lay in a pool of his own blood, the Granger sword still protruding from his body. "I can't make it. One of you needs to finish me off."

Jake shook his head in denial. "Hang in there, Clovis. I've seen men with worse wounds recover."

"Spacers, maybe," Clovis spat, black in the darkness. "A mercenary learns to recognize death. It's coming for me now."

Jake felt a cold hand gripping his heart. He wasn't playing commodity boards any more. Here, his decisions could kill real people. People who, like Clovis, had become his friends. He'd never had many friends on Wayward and never made any on the John Gault, so he couldn't afford to lose any, especially through his mistakes. "Come on, Clovis. We're almost home."

Clovis shook his head, a faint smile playing on his lips. "I'm almost home. The rest of you still have a long trip and you'd better get started while you still can."

"We'll get you mounted and find you some healers."

Clovis started to talk, then coughed out another dark spurt of blood. He closed his eyes and his face calmed. For a moment, Jake feared that he had died. Finally, though, he gasped for another breath. "Take good care of little Castile, now, friend," he whispered.

Jake took the dying man in his arms. "Come on, Clovis. We've been through too much together."

Clovis's smile didn't even reach his lips. "You're going to have to do the rest without me, Jake. I surely wish I could be there to see it when you whip the Granger back to the deserts they came from."

He looked so confident, certain that Jake would succeed in this impossible task that Jake was momentarily struck speechless. What possible response could he offer? A promise would be trite, not to mention vainglorious and lying. Yet could he really look Clovis in the eye and tell him that he was planning on getting off this wretched planet as soon as he could?

Lucer took Jake by the elbow. "We've got to get out of here, Jake. If you try to take Clovis with us, none of us will make it."

Jake hated the burning in his eyes, but he couldn't help it. He wasn't a soldier. He wasn't supposed to have to make this kind of decision.

"Get me one of their bows," Clovis said. "With any luck, I might get a couple of them when they come back."

"Take this one," Castile said handing him her bow and the half dozen arrows she'd scavenged. She bent and pressed her lips to his. "We'll remember you, Clovis."

Clovis opened his mouth to answer, but only blood came out.

"He won't be stopping any more Granger tonight," Harold observed. "He stopped plenty in his time. He was a good man."

He couldn't be dead. Jake knelt and felt for Clovis's pulse. Nothing.

He fought down an irrational danger to hunt down the Grangers who had run. Clovis deserved a funeral entourage. The urge was natural, but it was selfish. Killing a few more Granger wouldn't bring Clovis back. Trying would, as Harold had indicated, get the rest of his friends killed.

"Let's go," Castile urged. "It's what Clovis wanted and he was right."

Next time they got in a fight, Jake decided he'd take advice from Castile rather than giving it to her. Of all of them, she had been the one to make the decisive blow.

"All right. Gather up those miserable horses and let's get out of here," he said.

Harold grasped his arm. "We need to slit their throats first."

"We'll take all the horses."

"I meant the Grangers, not the animals. The ones lying around unconscious after the fight."

Jake looked at the scattered bodies, then at Clovis. They were soldiers and Jake could sort of justify violence in a battle for survival. Killing in cold blood was something else. "I couldn't do that."

"Then I'll do it. We don't want them coming after us."

Harold was right. The Granger had kidnapped them and threatened them with torture and rape. He had no illusions as to their fate should the Granger recapture them. Sparing a few Granger lives wasn't going to make any difference. Besides, the Granger had killed Clovis. It didn't matter, though.

"If we do that, we'll be as bad as they are," he said. "Leave them. Without horses, they won't be able to do anything."

"This trip," Lucer said.

"Somehow, I don't see the Granger letting us back into their Khanate without an army at our backs."

"But--" Harold caught Jake's glare and subsided. "All right, then we'd better hurry."

Harold trussed up the Granger bodies with bowstrings but, as far as Jake could tell, he didn't slit any throats.

Hurrying was easier said than done. The Granger saddles used different sets of rings and ties than Lucer and Castile were used to and they had trouble figuring them out in the darkness. Jake and Mark were completely hopeless and Castile finally ordered them to just hold the horses' reins and keep their mouths shut.

Dawn was breaking by the time they finally headed out, each armed with a bow and leading a string of eight horses.

"With all of these spare horses, we'll be able to make good time," Lucer observed. "Even if those Granger who got away last night raise an alarm, we should be able to outrun it."

Jake nodded glumly. His legs still ached from the ride the previous day and it looked like things were going to get a lot worse. The idea of riding faster, switching from horse to horse when the animals fatigued, was about as tempting as walking back home to Wayward without a vacuum suit.

"Somehow I doubt that we'll outrun that warning," Harold observed, gesturing back to the hills they'd come out of. A couple of miles back, near the Granger campsite, a thick cloud of smoke rose to the sky.

Jake pressed his heels into his horse's side and rode up level with Harold. "How much information can that signal contain?"

Harold looked at him as if he'd been speaking Greek. "Huh?"

"You know, can they tell which direction we're heading, or whether we're a small band or a huge war party?

"How could they signal any of that? It's just a warning."

There were a lot of ways to signal more than that. The Granger weren't a naval power, however, and maybe they'd never developed the sophisticated long-distance signaling that every navy in the galaxy had independently come up with.

"If all they have is a warning, we may still have a chance. They'll be expecting us to head straight for Otranto. So where else can we go to get away from them?"

"We could go to Erlang again," Harold said. "Except I don't think that would surprise anyone."

"Erlang would turn us over to the Granger before we could get off our horses," Lucer said. "They know how fragile their independence is."

"How about if we head due north," Mark suggested. "Nobody would expect that."

Jake's mind-battered copy of Arena of Otranto explained why that was. "Nobody lives there but nomads and wild beasts," he said. "At least that's what I've heard. And the nomads are Granger relatives."

"The Tiflis may be related, but they're not Granger," Mark said. "When Otranto hired the Granger to destroy us Ebron, they picked the biggest tribe but ignored the rest. Those who still live in the desert don't have much reason to love the Granger who got all the loot and have settled down in cities rather than staying on the steppes."

"How do they feel about Otranto?"

Mark laughed. "How does anyone feel about Otranto. Five hundred years ago, maybe even two hundred years ago, people worshiped Otranto and feared it. Now, everyone knows it's just a rich prize waiting to be plundered."

All in all, that wasn't a very strong recommendation. Not to mention, Jake had little interest in mingling with people even more barbaric than the Granger. Unfortunately, no one came up with a credible alternative.

Jake swung his horse's head to the north.

* * * *

They had ridden for several hours when they reached a small stream. Jake stepped off his horse and promptly collapsed when his legs failed to hold him up.

"Let's water the horses and let them graze for a little while," Jake said. "We aren't going to make it anywhere if we kill the animals."

"That is logical," Harold said. His tone made it clear that there was another shoe about to drop.

"What?"

"Remember how we saw the Granger dust cloud before they reached us?"

"Yeah?"

"Well, now we're the ones leaving the dust cloud. Between the fire and the dust, any Granger units out here will be able to figure out what's going on."

"So turning north was a mistake?"

Harold shrugged. "I never thought I'd trust an Ebron, but in this case, I don't think Mark was trying to trick us. We'd be leaving a cloud no matter what direction we went. But we're not going to get away if we don't figure out a way to disappear."

Jake stared at the turquoise-blue sky. Their own dust trail, only partially dissipated although it had been ten minutes since they'd stepped onto the riverbank and stopped kicking up new dust, stood out clearly against it. "There is one good thing," he said.

"We need some good news."

"We'll be able to see them too. Right now, I don't see any other dust clouds out there." Although, even with the extra horses, Jake didn't count on outrunning Granger warriors once they did come into sight.

"So maybe we'd better keep moving," Harold said.

Jake nodded. "That and one other thing."

"Spread out and make more dust?" Castile guessed.

"That's it. If they know we're out here and they know where we are, we might as well make them believe there are a lot of us."

"We'll be just as dead when they catch us," Harold argued.

Jake shook his head. "If they think we're a larger group, they'll need to concentrate their forces. That'll make them slower and keep them from sending out a real dragnet. Also, it could keep any small group who might be ahead of us from getting too close without reinforcements. If we look like an army, they may stay clear until they have an army too. By that time, with a whole lot of luck, we'll be outside their borders." And hopping from the frying pan onto the fire, most likely.

"Doesn't seem right," Harold argued. "Sneaky tactics are for Granger, not for Otranto."

Jake didn't figure that the Otranto Empire was built on that theory, but it just might be falling by it. Growing empires tended to be practical. And sneaky.

"Of the five of us, exactly one is native Otranto, and even Castile is half-barbarian. So let's be sneaky and not worry about it."

Harold grumbled back to his horses, but when he mounted, he moved to be a few meters to the right of Lucer and a dozen meters behind his last horse.

Jake signaled for Mark to go next, then Lucer and Castile. He brought up the rear despite a sudden fear that this would be the perfect way to get left behind.

* * * *

An hour before noon the following day, Castile reined in next to Jake. "Over there."

On the eastern horizon, in the direction of Otranto, a dust cloud similar to their own smudged the solid blue of the desert sky.

"Good thing we didn't keep going that way," Jake said.

There was no way to tell whether the Granger party was converging, or simply running parallel.

Jake spurred up to Mark, letting Castile take over the rear guard position.

"I see it," Mark told him.

"I'm not that worried about one group, especially not one coming from the east. They won't have had a chance to learn anything from Alton's survivors. What I am worried about is running into an ambush party and getting held up with that bunch coming in behind us."

Mark nodded. "Sounds like something we should all worry about."

"Hey," Harold said. "Heading north was your idea. So what do you suggest we do next?"

Mark frowned. "I've never been this far north. Ebron aren't encouraged to move around a lot in the Granger Khanate. It just seemed to me that we were dead if we tried to head straight east and the further south we went, the less likely we'd ever be able to turn around and make it to Otranto."

"Cool down, Harold," Jake said.

For a moment, Harold looked like he was fighting back tears. He swallowed hard. "Sorry. I'm not myself."

Jake thought he knew where this was coming from. "Clovis's death has hit us all hard."

"Yeah, except you've known him for a couple of weeks. I was the idiot who persuaded him to become a soldier. I trained him from a farm boy who didn't know how to walk in a line, let alone hold a sword. I should have been able to do something."

Harold's words echoed the feeling Jake had been wrestling with that entire day but knowing that didn't help. "You're a soldier, Harold. Haven't you lost dozens of friends over the years?"

Harold balled his fists. "You think that makes it easier? For me, it's worse. The first time I lost a friend, I told myself I could make more. That I had lots of friends in the regiment and that Farrel was old anyway." He forced his hands open, then shrugged his shoulders. "He was younger when he died than I am now. That's why men like Lucer quit. You don't think there are a hundred regiments who would take him, as is, if they had half a chance? But, now, every death is worse because I'm afraid to make new friends. You start to realize that your friendship is a curse, for you and your friends."

Jake nodded. "I told myself that I would toughen up, that this one would be the worst but I suspected that was a lie."

"Yeah. But sometimes lying to yourself is the only way to stay sane."

They rode in silence for a while, watching the smudge of dust on the horizon, wondering if it was getting closer.

Castile rode up in a swirl of horses and dirt. "We're too bunched up. If you two are done crying in your beer, why doesn't Harold ride on ahead and give Lucer a break? And Mark, head off about kilometer east. Don't go too far, but see if they head toward us or away when they see you heading that direction."

Castile was right, but Jake shouldn't have had to wait for her suggestions to act. Clovis had given his life for the others. They owed it to him to stay alive.

"Right," he said. He widened the distance between himself and Harold and signaled to the others to spread out.

Castile gazed at the widening dust cloud, then nodded. "Some day, when all of this is over, the bards will say that this is the first time you made an army from nothing."

An icy chill descended on Jake. "What are you talking about?"

"Clovis was right," Castile answered. "The Granger are killing machines. They've got to be stopped. Otranto can't do it with the armies that we have now. So it's up to you to figure out how we're going to do it. Maybe this is the beginning. The moment when history changes and when Otranto's fortunes change."

"Do you really think Otranto can be saved?" Jake demanded. "It's been failing for centuries. Nobody can remember the last time they actually won a real battle. Hell, nobody can remember the last time they fielded an army that had more than a smattering of Otranto soldiers. From what Harold tells me, half of their army is disaffected Granger and the other half is barbarians from the east."

Castile raised an eyebrow. "So?"

"So? A country can't survive if it doesn't defend itself."

"Otranto doesn't make good soldiers," Castile agreed. "But there are more books in my mother's library than in the entire Granger Khanate. How many Granger can even read? There are ten thousand priests alone in Otranto City who can read at least three languages. Besides," she rode closer, putting her hand on his bare arm for emphasis, "what do you think will happen to my mother if Otranto City falls? What will happen to my father? What will happen to me? Do you know what they did when Spoleta fell? Ask Harold about that some time."

He wanted to push her away, to run into the desert in some direction where no one could follow, but he couldn't. Castile was right. Harold was right. Most of all, Clovis had been right. He had made friends and now he was stuck. Although he couldn't think of anything he could do that would make a nickel's worth of difference when war next came between Granger and Otranto, he could no longer simply walk away.

"Damn."

"Tell me about it," Castile said. "And the Granger would be idiots not to attack Otranto soon. We've got to hope that the city is still there when we get back."

If they got back.

Jake hadn't seen any signs of mobilization on their trip through the eastern-most section of the Granger Khanate, but he realized he wouldn't. The Granger army was primarily filled with true Grangers with only skirmishers and support troops from their subject populations. The entire Granger population could have mobilized and it would make precious little difference to the way the average subject's day-to-day business was carried on.

"Why do you think it will be soon?"

"Because they'll never face an emperor less competent than Fernis."

He nodded. It made sense, of course. And if he'd had a degree in weapons technology and had a reference library of great military strategies in his adjunct, maybe he could make a difference.

The sound of horses' hooves pounding the ground broke into Jake's reverie.

"That cloud of dust to the east--it's getting closer." Sweat streamed off of Mark's face and he looked about as tired as Jake felt. It had been a good thirty-eight hours since any of them had slept and the only way that would change soon would be to join Clovis. Jake was depressed, but he wasn't ready for that option.

"Head toward them," he said. "All of us."

"Are you in a hurry to die? We should run. " Castile argued. "Why don't you leave me here to fill them full of arrows?"

"Because I don't want to tell your mother how I got you killed," Jake answered. It wasn't his most diplomatic answer, but he didn't have time to play games.

Castile pushed out her lower lip. She still was a child despite moments when she seemed far more mature than Jake did. "Come on, Castile. We all need to work on our dust cloud."

They swung toward the east. It seemed to Jake that their group raised more dust than the Granger unit they were approaching, but that could have been a result of distance. This wasn't anything he'd experimented with before. A long-buried formula for a trigonometric calculation for the size of the cloud popped into his brain from god-knew what stale memory circuit in his adjunct. He made a note to reformat the thing next time he had the chance.

"I'd say they're within eight kilometers," Harold shouted at him. They had changed horses and were moving at higher speed now. "Are you sure we don't want to run?"

Jake looked at the sun but no miracle had occurred. They still had hours before sunset when they had a vague chance to move across the desert without being detected. Of course they'd have a dramatically less vague chance to fall into one of the narrow ravines that cut through the desert floor if they blundered around the desert by starlight.

"This is our only chance."

"I don't think they're going to run."

"Then we have to make them change their minds."

He held up his hand to signal a halt and had them switch horses again although they'd ridden barely ten kilometers on this change.

"Any halfway decent general would send out a scouting party before he ran headlong into an enemy unit of undetermined size," he said. "Wouldn't they?"

"I would," Harold answered. "But I'm no general and I'm not a Granger either."

"But you've fought them before. They couldn't have conquered walled cities if they didn't have competent generals."

"All right, let's say they send out a scouting party," Lucer agreed. "How does that help us?"

"And if we were a unit as large as our dust cloud indicated we are, we'd do the same thing. Feel out the enemy and make sure he isn't sandbagging."

He realized he'd translated the standard expression literally and got a confused look from Castile, but the others seemed to follow.

"So if we send out a big group, they'll assume that we have a bigger group behind," Mark guessed. "We make a big show and they decide we weren't kidding so this time they really run."

Put that bluntly, it sounded like the dumbest thing Jake could imagine. He nodded. "Yeah."

When no one responded, he added "I was hoping that they would have turned around and run before now."

"We'll need to shoot them up a little," Castile said. "A scouting party that turned around and ran away wouldn't be that scary no matter how big it was, and the biggest we can be is the five of us."

"Four," Jake said. "You're going to stay here with the rest of the horses and stir up dust to indicate the rest of the army is coming."

Castile shook her head. "With Clovis gone, I'm the best archer here. They'll need me. Besides, if anything happens to the scouting party, do you think I have a chance on my own? The only person who doesn't have to be on the scouting party is you."

* * * *

Jake spotted the stallion and four mares making a break for it and rode at them whooping and shouting at the top of his rather tired lungs. Tying all of the animals together in a long line hadn't worked. He simply couldn't get them to walk that way. Finally, he'd remembered memories of ancient 2-D films he'd seen in one of his history classes and decided to do a roundup. After all, if a few horses got away, it wouldn't be the end of the world. On the other hand, if he couldn't continue looking like a small army, Castile, Mark, Lucer, and Harold would be ground up like so much hamburger.

He was heading north again. He'd hoped the Granger force would see his turn as a flanking move and adopt a defensive posture. Instead, they'd adjusted, aiming for an interception that would take place in a couple of hours.

Increasingly, it looked like he would have been better off continuing north, or even running to the west, when he'd first seen the enemy's dust cloud.

Now, though, he was committed, or at least he would be if he could just get those horses moving.

He flapped a spare shirt he'd pulled from a Granger saddlebag, trying to coerce some cooperation when the stallion turned, rearing up on his hind legs.

Jake's gelding froze, obviously terrified by the larger animal.

He dug his heels into its side. "Come on, you miserable animal."

Sensing his animal's fear, the stallion closed the distance, running straight at Jake.

Jake jerked hard on his reins. If his horse bolted, there was no way he was going to be able to hold on. And that stallion looked angry enough, and intelligent enough, to run him down if Jake fell from his horse.

His horse's breath foamed and the poor animal trembled like someone was walking on his grave, but it remained frozen in place.

Jake drew on his martial arts training, stretching time, trying to make every moment seem an eternity, each fractional second enough to accomplish anything.

At what he judged to be the last possible moment, he brought his staff around, lowering it on the attacking stallion's head like a crane dumping a load in a spaceship.

The weight of the staff, enhanced by Arcadia's strong gravity, smacked into the stallion with more force than Jake had planned--more than he would have allowed himself despite the danger he was in.

The stallion stopped in his tracks, glared at Jake, then turned and headed away toward the north.

"Well that went well," Jake muttered to himself.

He dug his heels into his gelding, but the animal remained frozen.

"Or maybe not."

Two minutes of cajoling and screaming at the paranoid animal did nothing but frighten away the rest of their horses.

Drawing on his memory banks for every swear word in every language he knew, Jake dismounted, removed the saddle, and headed after his rapidly vanishing herd. At least they were heading toward the north.

The bad news was, they were heading that way faster than he could walk.

If he got lucky, he'd be stranded out in the desert, separated from his friends, and in the middle of hostile territory. If he wasn't extremely lucky, things would be much worse.

The Granger dust cloud was now much closer to his horses.

He'd lost track of his friends when they'd headed out. To maximize Jake's deception, they hadn't taken any spare mounts. Shortly after they'd left him, the Granger cloud had budded, creating its own scouting group.

He'd watched the clouds converge. Looking now, there hadn't been any separation. Could his friends have been taken captive? At any rate, the single scouting cloud that remained was converging with the Granger cloud.

Jake looked at the distant horses, then shrugged and turned back toward the east. If Castile or any of the men had survived, they would eventually make their way toward Otranto. If they'd been captured, he could at least tell Manny to start raising money for a ransom. At any rate, following his horses would only lead him toward the enemy. His chances of fighting it out alone were not good.

He reached a dry streambed and clambered down.

Some memory of the moisture that had once flowed through the channel kept it cooler than the superheated desert air and sustained a deep mass of golden grass.

He pulled his hat over his eyes, leaned against the tree, and sank to the ground surrounding himself by the grass.

Alone and on foot, the only chance he had of heading for Otranto was to travel at night. The best thing he could do now as sleep.

He had nearly dozed off when a hum, sounding like an angry bee, interrupted him.

An arrow trembled in the tree trunk less than a foot above his head.

Chapter 11

Jake stared at the arrow. It still vibrated, stuck perhaps three inches deep into the more or less solid wood of the aging tree trunk where he had, inadequately, hidden.

He hadn't pissed himself yet, but the evening was still early. Fight or flight went right out the window. He put his hands up, over his head.

"Ha. I told you he would be surprised." It was Harold's whisper.

"Can you believe his face?" Castile was trying to whisper but not being very successful. "I swear it's as white as my mother's petticoat."

Jake lowered his hand and stood. His panic was fading into plain old anger. "You shot at me? You could have killed me."

"Oh, give it a rest," Castile answered. "I don't miss what I shoot at from that distance."

Once in a while, hell, most of the time, Castile talked and acted so incredibly adult that Jake would forget she was still a kid. Then something like this would come along and shove it back into his face. "I take it you defeated the Granger scouts."

"That group, yes," Lucer answered. "There were only five of them and we saw them first. None made it back to warn the rest of the Granger. So then we checked up on the remainder of their army. And it is an army. There have to be five hundred men there."

"Five hundred. Why would they have that kind of force out here?" In Arcadia, logistics would be a huge problem, especially out here in the middle of the desert. Five hundred men, with a thousand mounts or more, would require tons of water, food, and forage every day. Yet they had come from the direction of Otranto.

"Before you ask," Lucer said, "they are definitely Granger. Probably a raiding party out to round up a few slaves, but possibly the beginning of the next invasion Castile was talking about. It has been seven years since the last major Otranto defeat. It's time."

"So we may have pulled the teeth out of a Granger invasion? I wonder what kind of reward that will be worth if we ever make it back to Otranto." There had to be some way to make some money out of this and, with the complete loss of their trading goods, Jake needed to come up with something before Manny sold him to debt servitude.

"It would probably earn us our heads cut off," Harold said. "You don't really think Emperor Fernis is going to thank anyone for telling him that he's in trouble, do you?"

"Besides," Lucer added, "weak as Otranto is, the Granger aren't going to invade with only five hundred men. If they're not just raiding for slaves, this group has to be part of a larger army. An army we haven't found yet and that we may be about to walk into."

"Not to mention, our chances of making it back to Otranto aren't especially good right now," Castile added. "So if you'll just pass me my arrow, we need to get back on the road."

Jake yanked on Castile's arrow. It stuck at first, then came out so abruptly he almost fell over. He handed the shaft to Castile. The point remained deeply stuck in the tree trunk.

"Just what I wanted."

"Hey, you asked for it."

"That was before I knew you were going to break it." Castile shoved the offending object in his face.

"Sorry."

"Yeah, me too. If that lot is only a part of the Granger force, we'll need every arrow we can get."

As if it was his fault she'd shot into his tree. It didn't seem to matter whether he was on a poverty-stricken world with a population of half a trillion like Wayward, a sophisticated planet like Eon, where he'd gone to college, or someplace as backward as Arcadia. Women remained a perpetual mystery, even juvenile women like Castile whom he should have been able to think circles around.

He wondered briefly if women found men as mysterious as men found women, then dismissed the question as ridiculous. Men might be irrational from time to time, but they certainly weren't mysterious.

"Well come on," Castile urged. "It's dark enough that they won't be able to see our dust trail. So get on your horse and let's go."

"I lost my horse," he admitted.

Castile rubbed her eyes. "It figures. What else can go wrong?"

Jake winced. "I lost the herd too. I think the Granger army's found them by now."

"Forget I asked. I don't want to hear anything else."

"We picked up a couple of extra horses from the Granger we ambushed," Lucer said. "So let's mount up and get going."

Jake's thighs burned when he stepped into the stirrup, then burned hotter when he pulled himself onto the animal's back.

"Which way, boss?" Mark asked.

Jake glared at the Ebron. He didn't want to be the boss. He wasn't trained to be the boss. Back in the civilized galaxy, he had probably a hundred years more training before he'd be ready to be boss of anything more serious than a couple of loading robots. So how come he was the one who had to make the decisions?

"North," he said.

"We're a lot closer to Otranto now," Castile argued. "If we ride through the night, we'll be so far ahead of the Granger army that we'll be able to outrun them to the border."

Jake shook his head. He pointed one finger into the air. "First of all, I don't think we'll be able to outrun them. And the dust trail seven or eight horses lay down isn't going to frighten them much." He added a second finger. "Second, if Lucer is right, this is just a part of the Granger army. Where do you think the rest is? My bet is that they're somewhere between this group and the Otranto border. So, we'll get chased right into the welcoming arms of thousands of Granger."

"When you put it that way, it doesn't sound especially brilliant," Castile admitted. "North it is."

* * * *

They had barely moved twenty-five kilometers when the sky began to gray and the stars started winking out. Their horses were stumbling and Jake felt as if he was going to collapse. He'd thought he had been sleepy before, but this was an entirely different experience. It had to be even worse for his friends who couldn't use their implants to clean up the worst of the poisons sleeplessness generated.

"We have to stop." His voice sounded like an old machine with its solenoids worn out and clicking.

"Good idea." Jake could see Lucer's face now as he nodded grimly. "We've made it far enough that they aren't likely to stumble across us and if we stop now, our dust will have settled before the sun actually comes up."

If only Jake had planned it that way rather than simply collapsing under his fatigue.

He slid off his horse, felt his legs buckle underneath him, and sank to the desert sand, suddenly unable to stand, move about, or do anything but fight to keep his eyes from closing right there.

"I don't see any shelter," Castile objected. "We'll cook if we just stand out, especially once the sun gets high and hot."

Jake looked around. From his vantage point, he saw mostly horses' rear ends, but what wasn't obstructed by the equines was more of the same. Flat sandy desert, the odd desert shrub, and an occasional remnant of a stone wall that had once, Jake guessed, marked the boundary between one farm and the next. Back in the days when Otranto farmers actually scratched out a living in what was now a killer desert.

"Over there," Mark said. He pointed toward one of the stone walls.

"Walls like that have snakes," Harold warned. Even without seeing him rub his thigh, Jake could tell he spoke from personal experience.

"Perhaps. But it is a bit of shelter and shade." Mark seemed unconcerned with the idea of snakes.

Jake did a quick search on his *Arena of Otranto* text and came up with a number of references to snakes, some of them measuring almost eight meters in length. Interestingly, all of the references made note of their deadly poisons. On Arcadia, it seemed that every snake was deadly.

As they approached the stack of stones, Jake saw that Mark was leading them to the remains not a wall but what had once been some sort of hunting blind or possibly a shelter where shepherds could rest and watch their flocks. The roof had tumbled years before, but there was still a bit of an overhang.

"Horses first," Mark urged.

Sharing a three by four meter room with five other people didn't attract Jake much, especially since none of them had bathed in days and the Arcadians didn't have the benefit of the medical implant that controlled body odor. Sharing that same space with five people and six horses sounded even less attractive.

"We'll sleep until it gets dark and we can move again," Mark said. "We're getting used to riding in the dark and we'll be rested. We should be able to make better time tomorrow night."

Harold laughed. "We'll be lucky if we make any time at all tomorrow. Take a look at these horses. They're not going to survive the night if we don't get them something to drink. And even if we keep them alive, they won't be worth much if we can't feed them. I think we're shafted."

It wasn't an attitude Jake would want to encourage but he could certainly understand it--and had a hard time not sharing it. Adding to his discouragement, the odor in their shelter was already completely ripe--even with the outside air blowing in from the open roof.

"I'll go out and see if I can find some water," Jake offered.

"I'll come with you," Castile said.

"Are you sure you'll know a water hole if it bites you?" Harold asked. His voice sounded more curious than critical.

Jake shrugged. "If I don't find anything, I'll let you come out show me how."

"We'll find something," Castile said. "Remember, my mother told your fortune. You're supposed to do something important, which you certainly haven't done yet. That must mean you're going to survive this mess."

Although the men looked a little reassured, Jake wasn't. He didn't subscribe to fortune-telling mumbo-jumbo and Clovis had been fatal proof that, even if Jake lived, nobody with him was safe. Of course he wasn't especially happy with Castile's bland assurance he hadn't done anything significant with his life. He had, briefly, cornered the market on lessen hides and made a short-lived theoretical fortune on the galactic commodity markets. Wasn't that something?

From the look on Castile's face, he decided not to push the point. If he *had* already accomplished something, then maybe they were all doomed.

"There are some shrubs over there," Castile said when they emerged from the shed. "I think we should check them out."

Like the men, Castile was dirty. The trickle of blood that had dried on her face must have come from a bowstring striking her ear. Black soot smudges showed on the thighs of her pants from where Alton had tried to burn her. Still, she seemed to have more energy than the rest of them put together.

She wasn't that much younger than he was, he reminded himself. In a society where spacers typically live to be three or even four hundred, what the gap between her sixteen and his twenty-one seemed insignificant. He should still have that kind of energy.

He tried to put a little more pep into his step and promptly tripped over a large stone.

"Find any water?" Castile asked.

He realized he'd stayed down, his mind so sluggish from lack of sleep that he had simply failed to get back up. "Uh, no. Sorry."

"Then come on."

He struggled back to his feet mentally cursing Arcadia's excessive gravity. No wonder he was so tired.

He tightened his focus on the tall weeds that Castile had spotted. Could that be a bit of an ancient well hanging off of a couple of stones?

He took a step forward, then stopped and narrowed his focus even more tightly.

"Turn and walk back to the shelter," he hissed under his breath. "Try to make it look like you forgot something. When you get back, break out the bows and arrows."

"What?"

He glanced again at the unmoving bit of desert. The camouflage was almost perfect. Almost, except the desert wasn't made of a thin cotton weave. "I may have spotted the missing Granger army."

He tried to whistle as he neared the camouflage, but his lips were too dry and the faint wheezing that came out wouldn't have convinced a sophisticated two-year old.

Instead, he muttered something to himself about finding gold. Who knew? On a world where even basic line of sight wavelength communications were unknown, whatever Granger units were here might just think they were a band of prospectors.

The Granger strike force blended almost perfectly with the desert but now that he knew what to look for, he was able to spot them. One by one, they came into focus. He revised his retinal programming, using false color identification to keep each man he spotted in view.

He reached the remnants of the well and looked down.

The hole seemed to drop straight down into the center of the earth. He couldn't see any water, but that didn't mean anything with this deep a well.

He bent, picked up a rock, and dropped it into the well. Dropped and waited.

And waited. For three seconds, he heard nothing, then a faint thud sounded. It might be mud. It certainly wasn't water.

So, they were surrounded by Granger, had found a dry well that was too deep to use even if it did have water, and were stuck in the middle of a desert. Things were not going well.

He was feeling so sorry for himself he almost didn't hear the faint whisk of human flesh against camouflage.

Almost.

Reacting instinctively, he spun, leading with his staff, and knocked the glittering long knife from his assailant's fist.

The hooded man reeled back, grasping his sore wrist in his left hand.

Jake kept his staff between them, watching shivers of movement under the camouflage that surrounded them.

"You aren't a Granger." The man's Otranto was strangely accented, but understandable.

"I'm a merchant."

The man waved his good hand, dropping his injured arm to do so. "I see no caravans, nor is this the usual route."

"We lost our goods and were heading back to Otranto to get more."

"And yet you march due north all night long while Otranto is to the east."

From the corner of his eyes, Jake watched the other desert warriors emerge from their camouflage. They seemed wary of him, as if they really thought he and his staff actually had a chance against a dozen or twenty armed men.

The odds weren't good, even if Castile had made it back to the shelter.

"I guess we got lost."

The man shook his head angrily. "Impossible. Why would you run from the Granger army if you are simply traders?"

The man knew more than he should. Jake toyed with the idea of taking his chances, killing this man and maybe one or two more before they shot him down. It wasn't the dumbest idea he'd ever had; after all, it would improve the odds for friends. But not enough to make any real difference. When all else fails, he reminded himself, tell the truth. "We were running from the Granger."

"Enough." The warrior pulled back his hood showing the typical blond Granger braid and piercing blue eyes. "Tell your friends to come out of that shelter and have them lower their bows."

"I--"

"You think you left the Granger behind, but you are badly mistaken. They can follow your tracks in the desert as easily as you can follow your nose to an alehouse. It took them a few hours to determine what happened to their scouting party, but they're on your trail now. Do you really want to sit here and wait for them?"

From the way he'd used the word Granger, it sounded like he didn't think of himself as one of that nomad race. So who was he? Jake decided he had to take that chance.

"I'm open to suggestions."

"Wise. Tell your friends they have five seconds to come out with their bows unstrung. Otherwise we simply leave you for the Granger."

Jake hesitated. The man could be lying and Castile and the others might have a chance against twenty warriors if there were no others. Except these men looked at home in the desert. They would know the water situation and could afford to wait for the desert to do its work.

"Unstring your bows," he shouted. "These men are going to help us."

"Help?" The man laughed. "We help our friends, not strangers in the desert. But bring your horses out. I can hear their suffering."

Jake hadn't heard anything and his cybernetically enhanced ears should be better than anything the natives could field, but he didn't doubt this man's word.

"I'm Jake Borinski," he told the other.

"You may call me Njia. These are my cousin-band."

Jake's quick search of *Arena of Otranto* didn't turn up any mention of cousin-bands, but he'd been on Arcadia long enough to know that *Arena of Otranto* wasn't a comprehensive reference.

"My fellow merchants Lucer, Mark, Harold, and Castile." Jake completed the introductions, pointing to each one. "Njia tells me that the Granger are on our heels."

"I've got to sleep," Mark said. "We've been on the go for two days now."

"An Ebron traveling with the Otranto." Njia's brow furrowed. "We live in a strange world."

"You think a bunch of sort-of-Granger who want to help us get away from the Granger army isn't strange?" Jake raised one eyebrow.

"Once we make our escape, perhaps we can all sit around a fire and share each others' stories," Njia observed. "Now, unless you have a special wish to die, I suggest you gather your packs from that ruin and let's set off."

While Mark and Lucer brought out their few belongings, Njia started signaling with his hands. Jake could practically feel his translator grind into action but there wasn't enough context for him to pick up the meaning. It could be that they had the Otranto where they wanted them and attack now, or it could be something completely different.

It was something completely different. Another twenty of the sort-of-Granger appeared from nowhere--Jake's camouflage detecting program had missed a lot. Within minutes, they were surrounded by mounted warriors including several with heavy looking breech-loading pistols.

"We worked our horses too hard last night," Harold said. "The Granger will catch us before the hour is up. He pointed at the sky where the Granger dust cloud cut a dirty streak through the sky. They couldn't have been more than a couple of kilometers behind."

"Fortunately, we have more horses," Njia said.

In minutes, Jake and his party were mounted on hairy horses so short that Jake's feet trailed on the ground.

"We Tiflis value our horses. Treat them gently," Njia advised.

Tiflis? Well, that explained things. According to Mark, the Tiflis were the nomads who lived just north of the Granger Khanate. They were also, quite obviously, ethnically identical to the Granger and spoke the Granger language amongst themselves.

Jake looked at his horses. They sweat in the already brutal morning sunshine, salt crusting to their flanks and nostrils.

"You can't just leave our animals," Jake said. While he would never be a natural rider, it seemed to him that he owed something to the poor things.

"Leave them for the Granger? Hardly." Njia gave a few more hand signals and three of his men circled around the seven horses Jake had brought, leading them off to the west. "We'll lead them on a chase, then lose them."

Jake nodded. This whole thing seemed less than half-cocked, but then that could very well describe everything he'd done since landing in Otranto.

The Tiflis' ponies picked their way across the desert with a pace even slower than Jake and his party had traveled the previous night. Njia glanced at him from time to time, but spent most of his time signaling other riders, sending out one party or another, and integrating new groups into his band.

Gradually, Jake's translator picked up enough data and the hand signals started to make sense.

"Why don't the Granger just follow us?" Jake asked. "We're the biggest party out here." Yet the evidence of the dust indicated that the Granger had veered off in the direction Njia had sent their horses.

Njia took a long drink from his canteen, then handed it to Jake.

He hadn't realized how thirsty he was until he felt the water on his lips. Suddenly, he started swallowing gulp after overflowing gulp, unable to get enough water to replace what he had lost. Castile and the others sipped at their own water bottles.

"If you don't stop, you will be sick," Njia said calmly.

Jake monitored his internal systems. "I'll be fine."

"Then you are different from any other man I know."

"He's a spacer," Castile said.

Njia reined in, grasped Jake's chin in his strong hand, and glared into his eyes. "Is he? I wonder if I would have bothered rescuing him if I had known."

* * * *

Jake shuddered as Njia dropped his hand from Jake's chin, then rode to the front of the single line of warriors he led to the north.

He shook his reins, following closely behind. "I am a spacer, but I have nothing to do with whatever you find so hateful. Can you tell me what it is?"

At first it appeared that Njia would ignore his plea. The man looked straight ahead, his eyes focused on the horizon. Then he nodded.

"Not all who appear to be Granger are. Perhaps not all who are spacers are also evil."

"Evil? We're traders. In every exchange, everyone wins. Otherwise there is no exchange." That was the first axiom of the trader civilization that had reclaimed the stars from the millennia of chaos. Jake might have problems with some of the rules, but he believed in the theory implicitly.

"Is that so? For centuries, the Tiflis have traded iron to Erlang and Otranto. Then the spacers come. Otranto can buy what they need from the spacers and Tiflis gets nothing."

"But--"

"Then the spacers trade with the Granger. Where do you think the Granger got those huge horses? They roll over our little ponies like a wave crushing a child's sand castle."

So much for any fantasy about mobilizing the Tiflis to help in any war against the Granger.

"But--"

"But perhaps you, yourself, did not do these things. Perhaps you, yourself, are not responsible for my father's death, my mother's capture into slavery."

Jake shook his head. The textbook answer was that improving the local breeding stock would benefit the entire planet over time. Some cities, some countries, might benefit first, but the benefits would spread. On Arcadia, at first appeared to be lasting for centuries.

"So the Granger are doing to you what they are doing to the Otranto?"

Njia laughed. "There is no comparison. The Otranto scrabble for the gold to hire others to battle for them. The Tiflis battle for their own homes. The Otranto hold wealth that drives the Granger mad with desire. The Tiflis have nothing but some flocks of sheep, women, and a single small city. Anyone would want to have what the Otranto hold but cannot use. The Granger attack the Tiflis because they scorn the idea of anyone but themselves having anything."

Jake shook his head again. Their circumstances varied as Njia had said, yet Otranto and the Tiflis were both on the verge of defeat to a common enemy. Still, since the Granger were already on the attack against both, how could either offer any help to the other?

He looked at the sky. Already the sun was halfway to the western horizon although he had no sense of time passing. Perhaps he had simply entered into a zone, resting his brain while not fully asleep.

He stared around. Surely, slow as they had traveled, the Granger should be on top of them by now. Instead, the Granger dust cloud rose a good twenty kilometers to the west. Or rather, the peak of the cloud stood there. The base had vanished.

"They have stopped. That is why you don't see any more dust," Njia explained.

"Great. Except where is the cloud left by our horses and the men you sent out with them? Don't tell me they got caught."

Ngia laughed. "You yourself caught a band of Granger *scouts*."

He spoke the last word with so much contempt, Jake looked at him in surprise.

"My men track the Granger armies. Even if they appear to be aimed for Otranto, many Granger generals have headed north to bloody their troops and give them a taste of real fighting." Njia flashed a broad smile, his teeth startlingly white against the dark tan of his face. "We always oblige."

Raiding their northern cousins for female slaves had probably helped account for the high percentage of Granger who retained that blond blue-eyed look despite ruling a nation of dark-haired Ebron and Otranto, Jake realized. Or perhaps their bastard sons and daughters simply faded into the mass of the subject people. When he had time, he'd ask Mark.

"How could you have gotten so close in this?" Jake waved his hand at the desert sand. "They would have seen your dust cloud and investigated you too."

"Do you see any dust clouds?"

Jake looked around. Njia must have sent out ten scouting parties over the course of the day, yet only the Granger army left any mark across the sky.

"Our ponies move slowly, but they are desert animals. How long do you think a desert animal would survive if it marked its trail in the sky?"

That explained why the the Tiflis had survived as long as they had against the overwhelmingly powerful Granger. As long as they could keep to the desert, the Tiflis would have an advantage, at least when they were running. Of course, that also meant that the Tiflis were at a terrible disadvantage anywhere beyond the desert, or when they stopped to fight.

"Will the Granger catch up with the men who went with our horses?"

Njia frowned. "Among the Tiflis, horse thieves are honored. The three men I sent off with your horses have stolen hundreds from the Granger. I have to believe that they were not caught. After leading the Granger away from us, they will erase any trail that the Granger could follow, then vanish into a streambed or rocky area where the dust does not billow. One group would have gone on the original route, dragging branches to make it look like the horses had continued. After several miles, they pick up the branches and," Njia made an explosive gesture, "then they are gone, vanished into the desert. It is most amusing."

"So the Tiflis are horse thieves, shepherds, and scouts," Jake said. It didn't sound much like a victorious army.

Njia spat into the ground. "We are weak, I cannot deny that. The Granger steal what they can from us and burn what they cannot steal. Yet we are warriors. Once, the Granger were a Tiflis clan. One clan, among many, although, they were the largest. They conquered the Ebron and the Otranto using only their little ponies." He shook his head slowly. "There were more of us in those days."

Jake knew from history that people and even whole societies could survive in desert climes, but how could they do so when under constant attack? He couldn't imagine, so he asked.

"Also, we are merchants," Njia told him. "Just as you claim to be. We trade for what we cannot grow ourselves."

That stunned Jake. "I've never heard of a nomadic tribe being merchants. It takes financial strength, education, access to markets in order to succeed."

Njia nodded. "It is difficult. As I said, we have only a single small city. Yet, with our little ponies, we range all the way to Shara. Our little boats travel to Erlang each spring. Being nomadic, as you say, prepares us to travel long distances and to judge our routes by the stars whether we travel the seas or the steppes where the wild Krang live.

Jake knew he should be thinking of armies, of military technologies and spacer weapons. Of tactics and strategies. He should be, but he knew virtually nothing about any of those things. What he did know was business. "So, are you interested in adding to your trading portfolio?"

Njia nodded slowly. "I thought you would never ask."

Chapter 12

"You want us to be beer merchants?" Njia himself looked uncomprehending, but one of his lieutenants had to run from Njia's tent when the bitter desert tea the nomads favored threatened to come up his nose.

"It's really excellent beer," Jake answered.

They sat in a large cotton tent, avoiding the heat of the day as they trekked toward Umbar, the only Tiflis-controlled city on Arcadia. Thick carpets protected their bodies from the searing sand of the desert. Njia and the other Tiflis drank copious quantities of their steaming hot, strong black tea insisting that the drink's temperature protected them from the desert heat.

Castile had tried the tea, made a face, and added almost as much honey as tea to her cup. Lucer, Mark, and Harold didn't even try, contenting themselves with the warm water the Tiflis carried in sheepskin flasks. Jake drank the tea straight. It wasn't any more bitter than coffee and he'd been missing that since he'd left the John Gault. The caffeine gave his internal systems something to work with.

Njia worked through his initial puzzlement. He was better at restraining his humor than his lieutenant had been, but his smile was too broad to be mistaken for anything else. "The Tiflis don't drink beer so our credibility as merchants might be questioned. I suspect that is why Bart found your idea so outlandish. But that isn't the worst of it. You have seen our caravans. No matter what the quality of your product, beer is too heavy and bulky for us to ship at a profit."

Jake nodded. Back in civilization, planetary transportation costs were insignificant, but the costs of space travel were still so high that intergalactic trade was limited largely to luxury goods, artwork, intellectual property, biologicals, and the few trace elements that could not economically be created in the vast fusion reactors that circled every civilized star.

"Otranto beer is a luxury good. It will be sought after by the richest customers." A vague memory reminded him that wine, at least, had been a major trade good even in the near-mythical days of medieval Europe, back when all humanity lived on a single world and transportation costs would have been as outlandish as they were now on Arcadia. Although even then, they had used ships, hadn't they?

At any rate, Njia simply shrugged. "Perhaps it is as you say. Perhaps we, a race of abstainers, could even convince foreign merchants that we have identified a special and wonderful brew. Even so, a few dozen casks a year would hardly be worth our while and certainly not make a difference to Otranto."

Jake's ideas of a trading empire popped like a soap bubble hung out too long to dry.

"There must be something we can trade," Castile said.

Njia nodded. "That was my thought. A spacer like yourself has traveled among the stars and has learned many lessons that our people have forgotten in the thousand years since we were spacers ourselves. Surely there must be something."

Jake scratched his head. It seemed to keep coming back to his unique experiences as a spacer. In a way, that made sense. What else would he have to offer? Most of the time, though, this was sheer frustration. He'd spent his youth as a student, but nothing he'd learned seemed relevant. He could program a computer, set up accounts, navigate a starship, troubleshoot the ship's environmental system, or calculate cargo stressloads with the best of them, and it meant nothing here.

"All right," Jake said, backing away from his suggestion that the Tiflis engage in the beer business. "Let's assume we find something to trade. How do we get it to you? Could you send your pony caravans all the way to Otranto?"

Njia shook his head. "We can sneak across the border and steal horses. But the Granger still have some memories of the desert and are not completely stupid. Too, many of our young men go to join them seeking their fortunes. One caravan, perhaps, might make it through. Establishing a permanent trade route," he pursed his lips together, "that would be impossible."

"But you have a plan." At least Jake hoped he did.

"Of course. We may have but one city, Umbar. But it is a natural seaport and on the coast of the Tiflis Sea."

Jake's confusion must have been painfully evident.

"You may know this as the Erlang Sea," Njia added.

"Ah." His mental map snapped into place, now with a mark for Umbar vaguely situated on the large Erlang Sea that formed Otranto's northern border.

"A few days of sail would put us in Erlang. Perhaps a week longer would put us in Otranto City itself. Since the Granger have no ships to speak of, they wouldn't threaten us."

"Interesting." Jake's mind started to sort through the possibilities.

"The barbarians, of course, are a problem."

"And there is one additional problem," Castile observed.

"Exactly," Njia said.

"Do you want to share it with me, or is it a secret?"

"The Granger aren't the only ones with no ships. The Tiflis boats are small and carry little cargo. And Otranto lost its last merchant ships in the Battle of Ringos a hundred and fifty years ago."

Jake did a hopeless search of his databanks for information on primitive shipbuilding. As he'd expected, no miracles occurred. No plans for sophisticated sailing ships or simple steam engines turned up. "What about the Ebron?" he asked. "Mark, didn't you say something about being great sailors?"

Mark shrugged. "Before the Granger. The Granger don't like our caravans but they allow them as long as we use donkeys or mules. Ships are forbidden."

"So what does this leave us? Somebody has to have ships." Although, now that he thought about it, he hadn't seen anything larger than a fishing boat in Otranto's wonderful harbor.

Lucer took a sip of water from the sheepskin watersack and shuddered. The man lived on beer. Without it, he was slowly deteriorating. "The barbarians won the trading monopoly from the Otranto over a century ago. They guard it jealously. If you had the money, you could hire them to transport your beer, or whatever goods you wish, between Otranto City and Umbar. If you tried to sail your own ships, they would stop you, sink you."

"It is worse than that," Njia said. "The barbarians do business with the Granger. They have little interest in working with us, or in changing their relationship with Otranto.

"All of this opens up one huge question," Jake said.

"Only one?" Harold barked the question out in laughter.

"Only one." Jake didn't smile. "How are we going to get home?"

* * * *

The long dugout canoe barely had room for Jake's party and the two merchants Njia had sent. Dusting off childhood memories he didn't know he still possessed, Jake had managed to rig a pair of lee-boards, a rudder, and a single triangular sail. The canoe sailed like a camel, barely able to point into the wind and splashed full of water in even the smallest swells. At six meters long by less than a meter wide, it was the largest vessel the Tiflis possessed. Until Jake's retrofit, it had been propelled by paddles.

The Tiflis who'd traveled with them had insisted on being shown how to sail. Jake had tried to reconstruct his limited sailing experience and explained the principles of tacking to the wind, as well as the practical applications of trimming the sail, coming about, and bailing. Bailing was something that all of them got to practice.

Every evening, and whenever the winds picked up above about twelve kilometers per hour, Jake would head his unfortunate ship to shore and the entire crew would climb out and feel human for the first time that day. Each morning, they would reluctantly put out their fires, swallow their last cup of hot tea, and sail back to the monotony of the Erlang Sea.

"I thought it was only supposed to take three days to reach Erlang," Harold complained early on the sixth day of their journey. "This is slower than riding a horse."

Jake tried again to explain the value of water transport. The ability to haul huge weights with relatively little effort, the ability to sail all night without having to rest animals, and the power that control of the sea gave any nation that possessed it. No matter what words he used, Harold didn't get it. He kept trying to apply Jake's words to this pathetic canoe. What he saw was an unstable conveyance with no more cargo space than a reputable wagon, no ability to sail at night, and certainly no ability to rule the waves.

"I'm trying to take your word for it, but I'm getting less confident instead of more," Harold admitted.

Ancient wind-powered ships blurred together in Jake's mind but he had spent some time on a sailing crew when he'd been working on his MBA and finally living on a world that was sparsely enough populated that it could actually use its oceans for something other than planetary-scale waste treatment plants. The twenty-meter ship he'd crewed would have been completely impractical for merchant use, but even it could carry tons of supplies and sail for weeks out of sight of land. Although now that he thought of it, they had used satellites for both communications and navigation. Once he managed to make a ship, he'd either have to sail it himself, or rediscover ancient navigational skills.

"A real ship would run circles around this sow," Jake said confidently. "It could carry enough weapons to defend itself from pirates, tens of tons of cargo, and easily travel the distance we've gone in six days during a single twenty-four hour period.

"A real ship like that one." Harold pointed at a distant white spot on the horizon.

Jake tried to remember everything he'd heard of the eastern barbarians. Even dismissing the obviously biased accounts that they smashed babies' heads into their shields and had all sold their souls to the devil, Jake had heard enough to worry him.

"Put in toward land, Bart."

"I'm Wart," the man at the tiller said.

"You're going to be dead if you don't move." In the few seconds of their discussion, the distant white blur had gotten appreciably larger.

Jake zoomed his eyesight to try for a more detailed look at the approaching ship.

Although the ship's hull was still beneath the horizon, Jake made out a number of figures swarming over the masts and yards. As he watched, another set of sails exploded, gathering wind and accelerating the ships path toward their canoe.

"I don't suppose there's any chance of fighting," he asked Harold.

Harold stared. "I'll fight before I surrender. Those barbarians like to convert you. If you don't resist for a while, they assume you don't mean it and insist on converting you longer."

That didn't sound so bad to Jake. He'd dealt with door to door and 3-D proselytizers all his life.

Harold must have seen Jake's obvious unconcern. "They convert you with heated iron rods that they put into parts of your body where you really don't want any hot iron. I've never heard of anyone who got converted without losing at least a couple of toes and fingers. Trust me, you don't want to get converted."

"They slaughter any Ebron they capture," Mark added. "Their religion requires it."

"So sail toward the shore," Jake bellowed. "Come on, Wart."

Wart put a finger to the wind, then shifted the bow of their canoe slightly. "Maybe we shouldn't have tried this shortcut," he said. "But we're about eight kilometers from shore. It's odd that they happened to catch us when we were farthest from land."

Jake suspected there had been no luck at all involved there. The barbarians probably had some sort of deal going with the local inhabitants and had worked out a signal. A silver mirror or even a polished copper disk could send a message beyond the horizon if the weather conditions were right.

The boom of a cannon started Jake. He knew Arcadia hadn't lost gunpowder but he hadn't had any real experience with it since arriving. Evidently the barbarians were going to cure that deficiency for him too.

"Are they shooting at us or demanding that we heave to?" he asked.

"Do spacers shoot their guns when they don't want to hit?" Castile asked. "The barbarians don't."

"But what could they possibly want with us? We aren't pirate bait."

"I'm sure they'll be disappointed to find that out after they kill all of us," Harold said. He dug around in his pack and pulled out a short compound reflex bow he'd gotten from the Tiflis. "You do know how to use this?"

Mark nodded grimly. "If they come within range."

The wind gave a sigh, then petered out, their single large sail flopping without much determination.

The barbarian ship didn't seem affected. If its lower sails had lost wind, the upper sails continued to draw strongly. The barbarians crept closer.

A second ranging shot rang out. This time, the sound was a retort rather than a distant rumble. And this time, Jake had been watching. The cannon ball splashed down about two kilometers short, skipped three times across the still waters of the Erlang Sea, then sank.

"They must have powder to burn," Harold sighed. "If we'd had enough powder in the last battle against the Granger, it might have made a difference. 'Course it might not have either. Once your men start to run, no amount of gunpowder is going to help you."

"It takes them a while to load," Jake said. He didn't have time to consider Harold's comment now. Maybe later, if he ever made it back to Otranto, he'd worry about whether there was a cheaper way to manufacture gunpowder. Saltpeter, carbon, and sulfer, right. But even that knowledge was far from unique here. Before then, he needed to figure a way to stay alive.

None was coming to him in any great hurry.

"If we lower the sail, we'll be a less obvious target," Castile suggested. "It isn't helping us anyway."

It was a good idea. They stepped the mast, Jake almost tumbling into the water. Finally, thought, they had the mast and sail neatly packed into its case at the side of the canoe.

"Now what?" Mark demanded.

"Now we row."

* * * *

They rowed directly into what little wind they could detect. Although this meant they were taking an indirect route toward the shoreline, Jake was counting on the square-rigged barbarian ship having difficulties pointing to the wind and hoping for something nasty to happen when they tacked.

So far, his plan hadn't been working very well.

The barbarian ship had finally lost more of its wind and was barely moving, but even a breath of air could move them faster than the crude paddles could move Jake's canoe. If they survived this, Jake decided he'd have oarlocks and sweeps put in. Their crude paddles just didn't give them the speed they needed to outrange their pursuer.

After a few more shots, the barbarians had stopped shooting. Possibly they'd blown a bombard. The last miss had angled off into nowhere. Still, the ship was full of barbarians and it was still overhauling them.

"Can everyone swim?" Jake asked.

"Not faster than I can row," Lucer answered. Harold only grunted, but Mark, Wart, and Bart shook their heads despondently.

"We are people of the desert," Bart said. "Although our great skill with this ship may have confused you, we are not accustomed to open water. If we swim, we drown."

Swimming for shore wasn't much of an idea anyway. As Lucer had pointed out, swimming was slower than paddling and the barbarians could run them down just as easily in the water as in the canoe.

"Any other good ideas?" he asked.

"Is the man standing near that large wooden wheel their steersman?" Mark asked.

Jake zoomed in. It never pays to make assumptions but, in this case at least, the normal assumptions were valid. "Looks like it."

"And if something happened to him?"

"They will have plenty of replacement helmsmen. It isn't that hard to learn. But it couldn't hurt."

"I would like to learn to steer a ship like that," Wart commented. "It makes this canoe look like a pig at a dance."

Castile perked up. "Do the Tiflis dance?"

"Later," Jake insisted. He looked to Mark. "See what you can do about the helmsman."

Mark nodded, then notched an arrow to his bowstring. "You'll have to stop rowing for a moment."

Jake signaled the others to lay off and Mark stood, balancing perfectly in the narrow canoe. He might not be used to the water, but he'd learned to shoot on something moving. If they managed to survive this, Jake intended to have a detailed conversation with Mark. Hadn't he claimed that he was a poor student?

Standing on their little boat's gunnels, he looked more like a Zen-Samurai warrior from old Earth's past.

Mark's muscles rippled as he drew the bowstring all the way back to his ear, pushing on the bow to extend it rather than pulling on the string. He muttered calculations to himself, adjusted the angle of his aim, and loosed.

Several of the barbarians had been watching, laughing as Mark lined up his shot. A few had shot back but the arrows had fallen short and the musket balls had splashed aimlessly until one of the barbarian captains had told his men to stop wasting powder.

Mark's arrow flashed through the air in a huge arc, descending to split the helmsman in the middle of his chest.

As the man fell, he held onto the heavy wheel and the barbarian ship swung away from the wind.

"She's going to jibe." Jake could hardly make himself breath.

"What's that mean?" Bart demanded.

Before Jake could answer, the barbarian ship did the job for him. Its sails billowed away from the ship, then its booms swung wildly across the ship smashing anything that got in the way. With a loud snap, one of the stays parted and the foremast sagged slightly.

"I guess that answers my question." Bart's voice was solemn.

"It's a perfectly legitimate sailing maneuver," Jake explained, "but you have to be prepared. An accidental jibe can be very bad news."

"Not bad enough," Lucer said.

Barbarian sailors swarmed to the injured foremast stripping off sails to relieve the mast's pressure but they were already rigging a new stay. Mark's arrow had merely bought them a few minutes.

"So let's stop resting and see how far we can get before they come after us again," Jake demanded. "I have a feeling they aren't going to be very happy with us."

A puff of wind signified that their troubles might just be getting worse. "Steep the mast, again" Jake urged. "Hurry."

The mast was half-again as long as their canoe. Because the Tiflis deserts lacked anything resembling a tall pine, Jake had settled for a composite construction similar to that of the bow that Mark had used to shoot the barbarian helmsman. Jake wasn't sure exactly how much the mast weighed, but it was massive.

Mark, Jake, and Harold grunted to lift the heavy mast from its rack down the middle of the craft and butted it into the well used to hold it in place while Bart and Wart tightened stays, trying to keep the mast balanced despite the increasing chop on the inland sea.

Castile, sitting at the back, held onto the tiller for dear life although their canoe had largely lost steerage way. They had drilled on this exercise and it was important to keep the canoe heading directly into the wind.

A cannon shot skipped along the surface of the sea until it plunged into a larger wave only a dozen meters from their canoe.

Whether it was the surprise of the cannon shot or the wave, Jake would never know. Whichever it was, either Wart or Bart panicked, letting go of his stay to grasp both hands for the canoe.

The wave tilted the mast just slightly but it was enough. With all their straining, Mark, Jake, and Harold could do nothing to stop the mast's collapse.

It fell, ripping the mast well from the canoe's thwart and, in the process, tearing a huge hole in the bottom.

Black water poured into the canoe and all forward motion instantly stopped.

Wart and Bart looked at Jake for sailing advice. Jake merely shrugged his shoulders. "Grab what you absolutely need and hold onto something that will float. We're going to have to swim for it."

They were closer to the shore than Jake had thought but the kilometer or so remaining would give the barbarian ship plenty of time to hunt them down, assuming that they were still interested now that they had sunk the canoe. He grasped his pack and jumped into the water.

Castile hesitated for a moment, then took one of their empty water casks and joined him in the water.

"Cold."

He agreed, but didn't do so out loud. None of the men looked like they were interested in going anywhere.

"You'll be harder to shoot if you're in the water," he urged. "Come on, they're getting close."

The next cannon shot barely missed, its splash halfway swamping the sinking canoe. That, far more than Jake's words, convinced the men to hit the water.

Bart and Wart had ignored Jake's order to grab something and now floundered in the water in convincing portrayal of drowning.

"Head for shore," he told Castile and the others. "I'll work with these two. And try not to splash."

That was easier said than done. Mark had grabbed his bow, which provided a bare minimum of flotation. He hardly looked like he had much confidence in it to keep him afloat, or in himself to keep on kicking toward the shore. Jake didn't think the bow would do them any good even if they made it to shore. Unlike even the most ancient synthetic materials, with all of that water the laminated wood and bone would warp and, unless they were very lucky, split into its constituent pieces.

"Castile, show them how," he urged. Wart was going down and Jake didn't think he'd be coming back up unless Jake did something about it.

He shucked off the heavy jacket he'd need if they made it to shore and dove after Wart.

The man might be drowning, but he was fighting for all he was worth. When Jake reached him, Wart grabbed him in a death grasp, his hands groping around Jake's neck.

This wasn't good. Jake could swim but he didn't think any human learned lifeguard skills any more. That was what robots were for. Unfortunately, there were no robots within a few million kilometers.

He felt for Wart's thumb, clamped down on the pressure point, and twisted.

Twisting without something to stand on didn't work very well. It did, at least, get Wart's fingers off his throat.

He took hold of Wart's long blond hair and dragged him to the surface.

Wart was climbing up his own hair by the time they surfaced.

Jake took a quick breath and looked around for some kind of flotation device just as Wart reached him and pressed his head under water.

Wart was, Jake knew, simply trying to keep himself afloat. It was an understandable reaction, but a reaction that was going to get both of them killed.

He reached for Wart's groin and twisted again.

This time the twisting worked better. Wart let go in a hurry.

Jake swam under water until he was a couple of meters away from Wart, then surfaced under a broken section of the boom. Holding onto one end, he thrust the other at Wart. "Take it."

Wart grabbed it, pulling himself halfway out of the water. He was coughing and vomiting which Jake decided to take as a good sign. He wouldn't be doing that if he wasn't breathing.

"Where's your brother?" Jake demanded.

"Huh?" Wart looked around as if seeing the Erlang Sea for the first time. "Bart?"

Jake's sharper eyes had already inspected the surface. Castile and the other men were moving nicely toward the distant shore. The barbarian ship was only a couple of hundred meters away. Bart was nowhere to be seen.

"Damn." Jake dove, deeper than he'd gone when he'd gone after Wart. His enhanced sight adjusted to the underwater view, partially compensating for the effect of water but doing nothing to penetrate the darkness.

He swam deeper, driving himself toward the distant bottom of the sea. Bart had to be down here somewhere. The unaided human brain could survive for ten minutes without oxygen. Bart wouldn't be completely dead yet. Not if Jake could find him at once.

The sense of failure that had come over him when he'd lost Clovis was back now, pushing him toward depression.

He resisted it. He'd been happy to save a few thousand credits by neglecting the psych pack when he'd had himself medically enhanced. Well, Arcadia was full of people with more reason to be depressed than he--and they didn't have even the implants that he did. He could conquer a little depression--and make the barbarians kill him rather than doing it to himself.

Jake's lungs ached. His gravity-strengthened muscles burned more oxygen than he was used to. Already, his body was scavenging for more.

He was at the verge of giving up when he caught a faint glimpse of movement.

Bart wasn't moving himself. He looked dead, eyes open at the bottom of the sea. His long hair swayed with the small movements of the sea.

Jake grabbed Bart's body under the armpits and pushed off hard from the bottom of the sea.

Halfway to the surface, a dark shape cut off the growing sunlight.

He looked up. He was directly under the barbarian ship.

He kicked hard. If they were like most people, their attention would be centered on the swimmers heading for shore. They might just be blind if he emerged on the other side of their ship, the side facing the open sea. What he'd do if he got there, he'd have to play by ear.

He broke the surface, gasping for air despite the need for quiet.

Bart hung loosely in his arms. Open air wasn't enough for him. He was going to need help.

Fortunately, every spacer is trained in basic first aid.

A section of the ruined canoe floated by and Jake dragged Bart up on it.

He felt for a pulse. Nothing.

"Bart?"

How long had it been? He had to get oxygen back into Bart's system quickly.

"Forget him, lad. He's gone." The Otranto sounded strange. A different accent.

Jake stole a quick look. A huge red-haired man stood on a large rowboat obviously launched from the barbarian ship. Eight rowers glared at Jake, knives either in their belts or between their teeth.

"I'm going to save him."

"His heart has stopped. He has crossed the river."

Jake shook his head and forced back the tears that wanted to come.

"I can do this." He pushed hard on Bart's chest, then released, his CPR training coming back to him as he went through the steps.

The red haired man grasped him, but let him go when Jake ignored him.

"He can't hurt the dead man so let him work his magic."

"It's blasphemous," one of the rowers said.

"They're all heretics anyway."

Jake pressed again feeling one of Bart's ribs give way. That was one of the consequences of CPR.

Could that have been the hint of a pulse in the big artery on Bart's neck?

He put his lips to Bart's, exhaling into the Tiflis's lungs.

Nothing.

Again.

In the background, distantly, he heard retching noises. What he was doing was clearly alien to the barbarian mores. Well tough. It worked.

Bart coughed, then vomited all over Jake.

Jake had never felt better in his life.

Chapter 13

Jake felt the hard press of wood against his back and smelled the strong odor of tar and human sweat. Arcadia's sun glared in his eyes until he increased his polarization to the maximum. Carefully he glanced around the ship.

"What are these?" The red-haired barbarian captain glared at Jake and Bart. His unfastened vest barely covered a huge barrel of a chest that sat over a comfortably large stomach. His sword dragged rather than simply hanging from his back-mounted scabbard. The thing had to be five feet long. Jewels hung from his ears and decorated the sword's hilt.

The barbarians who had fished Jake and Bart out shuffled their feet, eyes downcast.

Bart, who was naturally pale, looked a tad green, but he was breathing.

"Slit their throats and toss them overboard," the captain announced into the silence. "I haven't got time to waste with schismatic Otranto scum who can't even honor their treaty obligations."

"But Pierre, this one looks like a Granger." The speaker, a younger version of the huge captain, also wore a two-handed sword, but lacked the jeweled splendor of the other.

The captain threw a casual backfist at his lieutenant. The man, obviously used to that kind of behavior, ducked out of the way.

"Probably Granger by-blow," Captain Pierre said. "No concern of ours."

The only thing Jake had to go on was Njia's mention that the barbarians dealt with the Granger directly and the lieutenant's comment about Granger. He decided to run with that.

"Our little canoe was no merchant ship," he intoned in a voice he hoped would be appropriate for a Granger slave. "My master and his party were simply traveling along the coast."

Pierre glared at him. "You speak Anglic. How?"

Once again, Jake's translator had gotten him in trouble. Well this time he'd brazen it out. Pierre had already decided to have Jake's throat be cut so how much more trouble could he get into?

"I travel widely on my master's business."

"Indeed?" Pierre looked doubtful. "Or perhaps you are a deserter from an Anglic ship."

Jake laughed. "If I was a sailor, would I travel on a piece of junk like that canoe?"

Pierre scowled. "A slave travels where his master wills. If you are a slave and if he is your master."

Pierre might not look like a genius but Jake certainly wasn't running away with this conversation. "I--"

Bart interrupted, in Otranto, before Jake could make a complete fool of himself. "By what right do you threaten the life of a prince of the Granger people? Those of my servants who escaped your unprovoked attack will, even now, be reporting your description to the local emir." He made a slicing motion at his throat. "Do you believe you can run far enough to escape the reach of the Lassas?"

Pierre and the crew members holding Jake recoiled. Although Jake didn't know who or what a Lassa might be, the captain and his crew certainly did.

Pierre recovered quickly, smiling broadly if unconvincingly. Shifting to Otranto himself, he gave Bart a shallow bow and proceeded to ignore Jake completely, which was just fine to Jake's way of thinking.

"As it happens," Pierre said with a smirk, "we are sailing now for the Granger city of Spoleta. You shall be our guest until we arrive. If you are a Granger prince, you shall be released and given gifts to compensate for any harm to your servants. If you are lying, I shall enjoy tearing out your tongue and eating it raw."

Bart drew himself up. "I suggest that you save your threats. Truly, they shall come back and haunt you. As for your offer of Danegeld, one of my travel-mates was a Granger nobleman, something of a distant cousin. I doubt all the barbarians in the world could raise his price."

The captain glared at Bart, trying to persuade himself that this was a hoax. Still, Bart sounded arrogant enough, and the blond hair hanging nearly to his waist made him appear the perfect Granger. "I do not believe any aboard your canoe were killed."

Bart nodded. Jake thought he could detect more than a hint of relief.

"Sail on, then, Captain. We have a journey to complete." Bart stood, then walked over to the side of the boat and signaled Jake to follow him.

"Don't try to escape," the captain growled.

Bart wrinkled his nose as if smelling something unpleasant. "Escape. Why should we wish to escape when you are taking us toward our destination?"

"Nice work," Jake told him, speaking in the accented Granger that the Tiflis used.

Bart nodded. "Among the Tiflis, to be called a prince of the Granger is an insult. The Granger are a lazy and degenerate clan who have abandoned all that is good of our society. Alas, I have often been called a prince of the Granger."

Jake nodded. "But what are we going to do when we reach Spoleta?"

Bart shrugged. "It shall be as the great one wishes. If we are still on board when this ship reaches Spoleta, there will be a battle between our captain here and the Granger garrison to determine who can execute us first. I predict that they will quarter our bodies and divide the quarters between the two forces."

"So we had better not make it to Spoleta."

Bart gave Jake a grin so wide it nearly blinded him. "Amazing. Even a spacer can learn." He clasped Jake on the shoulder and lowered his voice although they were still speaking in Granger. "So, how are you going to get us out of here?"

For just a moment, Jake had been able to relax, to trust that Bart had a clue what he was up to. Now Jake was being forced into the role of leader again.

He cast his gaze around looking for anything to give him an idea. The barbarian ship was kilometers from land, traveling in water far deeper and rougher than they had dared attempt in the canoe. If they jumped overboard, they would be riddled with arrows before they could make it twenty meters.

Jake looked over their captors. Even more than the Granger, the barbarians stank of stale sweat, rotting meat, and the sweet smell of partially distilled alcohol. As he watched, a young Anglic sailor passed among the crew, sharing from a leather cask. From the smell, Jake guessed it was a sort of whiskey or even rum. Compared to what he smelled, Manny's beers would be ambrosia of the gods.

"It won't work," Bart said.

"What?"

"Promising them better beer if they take you to Otranto. They drink their rotgut because their water is so bad that it'll make them sick."

Tiflis and high-caste Granger did not drink alcohol and Jake needed to get closer to shore. It wasn't much of a plan, but Jake hadn't had much of a plan since the John Gault had orbited Arcadia.

"Hey, Pierre."

Pierre stomped over, his hand on his sword hilt ready to draw. "On my ship, you will address me as Captain."

"You know Granger don't drink distilled alcohol. Do you have any water that the prince can drink?"

"I've drunk my share of Granger under the table," the captain replied.

"Granger scum, perhaps," Jake admitted superciliously. He was trying to appear like a complete wimp. "True Granger keep the customs of their fathers of the desert."

"Is this true?" Pierre demanded of Bart.

"It is even as my servant says."

"Water." Pierre used the word with disgust. "Andre, bring the Granger a dipper of water." He stomped away leaving Jake and Bart alone.

The young sailor who'd been passing the beer cask nodded, then ran into the ship's hold. He returned moments later carrying a moss-covered wooden dipper dripping a positively green liquid.

"It's water," Andre said. "Although I don't know why anyone would want to *drink* it."

Bart took the dipper, stared into it, then poured it onto the deck. "Do you dare poison me?"

"You mix it with whiskey," Andre explained. "The alcohol kills the demons that live in the water."

Jake nodded. Like everyone, he'd studied civilization regression. The introduction of superstition to explain scientific fact was completely typical of the field. "As I have already told you, the prince cannot drink alcohol. And your water would poison him.

"But..." Andre wavered between trying to swagger his way out of the dilemma and escalating it to his captain. Caution won for once. From the little Jake had seen of the barbarians, they were lucky they'd run into a young one.

"Drink water or drink whiskey," Pierre said when he'd been summoned. "I am not an inn that caters to the tastes of its guests."

Jake frowned. "For myself, I would like nothing better than to share your whiskey." Could he remember enough to distill a quality product? Whiskey, at least, travels better than beer. Unfortunately, all he could remember about the whiskey business was that the whiskey needed to age for years in oak barrels. Or was it elm barrels? At any rate, he didn't have years and didn't think he would recognize oak if it reached over and bit him in the leg. He needed to do something now, and keep on doing things if he was going to keep himself and his friends alive.

The notion that Harold, Lucer, Castile, and Mark were friends penetrated his mind with a pent-up force like a hurricane. Before Arcadia, Jake had never had time for friends. Oddly enough, even though having friends meant that he couldn't simply run for the nearest barbarian city and wait for the spacers to finally return, he wouldn't have traded it for the world.

"So there is no problem," Pierre shouted. "Drink the whiskey, drink the water. It is good." He supported his proposition by pouring a generous hit of whiskey into the water and swallowing the entire mix in one huge draught.

"Truly the prophet warns against the consumption of alcohol," Bart said. "It is written that the drunkard may never achieve his place in heaven."

"Pagan savage," Pierre muttered in his own language.

"If you could put into shore, I am sure we could find a spring with pure water for the prince to drink. The prince could make sure none of the local Granger bothered us," Jake said. "Perhaps your men would be happy with fresh water as well."

"And perhaps they wouldn't," Pierre shouted. "Do you think I am stupid enough to land you on shore?"

"You could send men with us to make sure we return quickly," Jake suggested. If the ship got close enough to shore, maybe they could slip off the side and he could tow Bart in.

"Was that your whole plan?" Bart emphasized his accent making it impossible for anyone but a native speaker, or someone with translator enhancements, to follow.

"What is he saying?" Pierre demanded.

"He tells me that he feels faint from thirst. When I rescued him from your attack, he lost a great deal of liquid."

Pierre glared at them. "Tell him to speak Otranto or Anglic."

"As he grows weaker, I fear he is losing his skill in languages," Jake answered. "Are you certain that you could not put in to shore? From the shape of that foliage, there must be a spring nearby." Jake pointed at the distant shoreline.

"Perhaps." Pierre scratched his head and pulled on one of his jeweled earrings. "If you try to escape, I will kill you myself, prince or no prince."

"Of course."

Pierre stomped away. Moments later, the ship turned, heading for the distant shoreline.

"I can't believe that poor excuse for a plan worked," Bart whispered.

"Thanks, I guess."

"Now what?"

Jake didn't have a clue and said as much.

"You'll think of something." Bart found a shady spot on the deck of their ship, kicked Andre out of the way, and laid down, closing his eyes. Moments later, a gentle snoring sound emerged from his body.

Bart's confidence made Jake feel worse instead of better. None of his plans had worked since he'd come to this backwater hellhole of a planet and this didn't look to be the exception. Now that he thought about it, not many of his plans had worked back on Wayward either.

Jake gritted his teeth. He'd come up with something.

"Excuse me, sir." Andre pressed a knuckle to his cap in a distant reflection of a salute.

"Yes, boy."

Andre grimaced at the word *boy*, but didn't react as strongly as Jake had hoped he would. Now that they were close to shore, they needed some sort of distraction.

"Is it true that Bathsheeba is the richest city in the universe? That rivers of molten gold flow through the city sewers to burn away the filth? Is it true that every man can have five women who live only to serve him?"

Maybe Andre wasn't such a child after all. Just talking about five women was getting him excited.

Jake nodded. "The Granger have looted a thousand cities and brought back the treasure to their capitol. It is not true that Bathsheeba runs with rivers of molten gold, but it is true that it is fabulously rich. I am surprised that a merchant like your Captain Pierre has not traveled there. Compared to it, the wealth of the other cities of the Granger Khanate are like fleas surrounding a stag."

"Bathsheeba is inland so our ship does not reach it," Andre murmured. "Yet I would dearly love to see it."

Jake smiled at his new friend. "There just might be a way."

* * * *

"You will go along with the shore party. The Granger Prince will stay on the ship." Pierre twirled a curved dagger with what looked like a gold nugget serving as the pommel. "If you do not return with the water party, I will remove your master's right hand."

Bart paled noticeably and licked his lips. The Anglics might believe Jake was the servant here, but Bart knew better. Jake could simply walk away and leave Bart to his fate.

The barbarian ship dropped anchor a few hundred meters from the rocky shoreline and Anglic sailors began the hurried unloading of half-a-dozen empty water barrels into a ship's launch.

"I'm sure your men can find water without my help," Jake said. In the distraction of men leaving the ship, it would be relatively easy to escape.

Pierre laughed. "I was wise to your games before your mother sold her body to your father. You will go because you can swim. The Granger will stay because he is a Granger."

Jake nodded grimly. At least it was getting late in the day. Perhaps they would still be close to shore when evening fell. In the dark, he might be able to drag Bart to shore without being impaled by barbarian arrows.

"Tie the slippery one's hands," Pierre shouted.

Andre stepped in with a rope, but Pierre paddled him out of the way. "Someone who knows true knots."

The man who tied Jake's hands definitely knew knots. He used Jake's neck as a cleat, tying his arms behind his back with his shoulders bound so he couldn't step out of the tight knots.

Pierre looked at the sun, still high in the sky but noticeably heading toward the horizon. "You have four hours. Any later and I leave without you."

The four sailors detailed to the water party took that threat seriously, hustling Jake into the launch, then rowing toward shore with all their strength.

* * * *

Jake's nonexistent tracking skills soon became the butt of jokes for the sweating sailors. They detached one of their own to look ahead for fresh water and put Jake to work hauling the barrel cart.

Although empty, the heavy oak barrels with iron bands weighed a lot. Jake was only slightly surprised that he was able to manage one. His body had responded to the high-gravity challenge and he was now stronger than he had ever been in his life. Maybe next time Manny wanted to play games with the beer barrels, Jake could play back. All of which assumed, of course, that he would make it back to Otranto City.

The scout shouted something that Jake didn't catch and the sailors hustled Jake toward a low hill.

The glade could have been one of the ancient masterpieces of 2-D painting. Earth-descended trees formed a perfect circle around a bubbling spring. White marble pillars, some still standing and others tumbled over, graced the western side, the sun's reddening rays giving the marble the look of life.

He supposed that the small building that remained could have been a home or even a shop, but Jake couldn't help believing that it had once formed a temple.

"Who built this?" he asked one of the sailors.

The sailor shrugged his shoulders, then spat on one of the pillars. "Who knows? You can see it's pagan, though."

Following the sailor's gesture, Jake noticed the carved frieze that surrounded the temple's eves. Depictions of centaurs, nymphs, and half-man-half-fish creatures cavorted among streams that were carved so skillfully that the water seemed frozen, ready to move the moment he looked away.

Under the frieze, a line of Otranto script proclaimed the area one of peace and sanctuary.

Another of the sailors shouted something and Jake heard the thrum of a bow and the wosh of an arrow, then the thin scream of a rabbit. Peace and sanctuary the temple may have served once. Today, it was part of the violence and squalor that had overtaken Arcadia in the millennia since the collapse of early human colonization.

"Enough talking," Jake's sailor said. "Fill your barrels. We need to get back to the ship before dark."

The barrels were large enough to crawl into and coated with green slime that stank so badly he wondered how anyone could survive a long distance trip on this primitive planet. From what he'd seen of the Anglian sailors, they must be incredibly brave to travel thousands of kilometers in their small vessels.

Jake had spent the past weeks cursing his lack of spacer skills. One skill that he had honed to a fair degree of expertise, however, was barrel cleaning. And if he was going to have to drink water from these barrels, they desperately needed to be cleaned.

Jake shrugged his shoulders and gathered a handful of soft white sand from the banks of the spring. He'd use the sand as an abrasive to clean the worst of the slime from the barrels.

"Anyone going to help me?" he asked. "You're going to benefit from fresh water too, you know."

The laughter that met his question died quickly when another bowstring twanged.

"Thought I saw something."

"Something like another rabbit?" one of the men asked.

"Something like a person," the scout replied. "Come on. Three of you come with me and the rest watch this Otranto heretic work."

* * * *

This would have been a good time to escape. The pirates had untied his hands and seemed more intent on sleep than on watching him.

A mental picture of Pierre lopping off Bart's hand stopped any such ideas in their tracks. Jake might not have a plan but he wasn't going to leave Bart behind him.

He knelt and crawled into the first of the barrels.

The insides were every bit as disgusting as he had thought they would be. His hands skidded across the slime-covered planks that made up the barrel and the coarse sand barely scratched the surface of this living substance.

It took fifteen minutes before Jake thought the first barrel was even close to ready. He climbed out, rolled it over to the spring, and swished out the remains of sand and slime.

"You'd better hurry," one of his captors advised. "I don't plan on being left behind. If you're not ready, I'll pay the Granger bloodprice myself on your worthless Otranto hide.

Which said something about both Granger and barbarian societies, Jake realized. Neither seemed to put much value on human life. Otranto was only slightly better, of course. But when it came to basic human dignity, even small differences can be important.

"I've got one barrel done," he answered. "If one of you would help me, I could get this clean more quickly."

His guards laughed.

Jake poured the rinse water out of the clean barrel, then filled it, resting the lid against its side. He'd seal all of them together.

Cleaning and sealing barrels was a skill he'd never imagined would come in handy when he'd been a spacer.

Jake paused in mid-scrub as his mind dealt with the words he'd just selected. *When he'd been a spacer.* Did that mean that he wasn't a spacer any more?

He scrubbed harder. Spending the rest of his life in this kind of backbreaking and positively smelly surroundings was insane. Of course he would go back to space. First, though, he had to rescue his friends.

He rinsed out the second barrel. This one hadn't taken as long. Of course it wasn't as clean either. Jake figured that he and Bart would drink from the first barrel.

The remaining two barrels, Jake paid only cursory attention to. He rolled them around, kicked the ground, and tried to sound busy while looking for something he could use as a weapon later. Pierre didn't trust them and would certainly tie them or lock them up for the night. With a knife he could cut the rope. With a piece of thin steel, he could pick any of the simple mechanical locks the Arcadians used to protect their properties or their prisoners.

Jake turned up neither.

"Time to go," his guard snapped when Jake rolled the last barrel under the trickle of water from the spring that flowed like a fountain over a sharp drop and made it possible to fill the barrels without endless stooping and filling with a bucket.

The three guards who had run after whatever ghost the scout had seen straggled back into the clearing.

"They got away," the scout said. "I think I stuck one, though."

"Yeah. If he was a tree I'd say you got him," one of the others said. "That's about all what were in danger from you. Not that there was nobody out there no-how."

"I tell you, I saw someone move."

"Maybe it was one of the spirits of this spring," Jake offered. If he could appeal to the superstitions and paranoia of these men, something good might come of it. If he could take Andre's words as the truth, the barbarians believed in demons and spirits.

"Yeah, and maybe a prisoner should keep his heretic mouth shut," the scout fired back. "Are you ready to go, or should we just slit your throat and tell the captain that you ran?"

A snappy answer jumped to Jake's lips but he cut it off there. The scout looked pissed enough to take it out on Jake. "Let me seal these barrels and I'll be ready."

He moved quickly, fastening one after another until he got to the last barrel.

The top of the barrel rested in place, ready for him to seal it. But he could swear he'd left the top leaning against the barrel, not on top of it.

Unlikely though it seemed, maybe one of the sailors had decided to help after all. Not that this had been much help. He would have rather have the cleansing light of the sun shine on the algae for a while.

He grasped the cover and tried to move it but it resisted his efforts.

"What the--"

"Shh."

Even on Arcadia, barrels didn't talk. Besides, he recognized that voice.

"What are you doing here?" he whispered back. "You'll get yourself killed."

"I snuck in while the others distracted the sailors," Castile answered from inside the barrel.

"What's the holdup?" one of the guards demanded.

"Coming." Jake toyed with the idea of dumping the barrel but he couldn't think of anything he could do that wouldn't increase the risk to Castile. He nailed the top shut.

The sailors helped Jake with the barrels on the way back to the launch. Castile hadn't emptied much of the water from hers and he hoped she'd left enough air in the barrel and that the water would cushion the sailor's rough handling.

* * * *

The sun had set into a purple twilight by the time they made it back to the ship.

Pierre cursed fluently in Otranto, Ebron, and Anglic as he had his men swing out tackle to raise the barrels from the launch and then lower them into the hold.

"I'm quite thirsty, Captain," Bart observed. "Do you think you could lower one of the barrels into my cabin?"

His cabin? It sounded like the captain was ready for Jake's escape attempt.

"You'll have it until I hear one word of complaint," Pierre answered. "Just one word and the water goes into the hold and you can either drink whiskey with the rest of us, or die for all I care."

"I am truly grateful." Bart gave a graceful bow.

"Weigh anchor and let's get out of here," Pierre shouted. "Granger and Otranto, get below where you'll be out of the way." He tasked two of his sailors to stand guard.

In every 3-D Jake had ever seen, the guards would wait peacefully outside of the prisoners' room. Pierre had evidently not seen the 3-D's and instructed his sailors to tie up Jake and Bart and to keep an eye on them the whole time.

Jake stared at the barrel in the corner of their room as their guards tightened the ropes that would keep him from freeing Castile. The air in the barrel would not last for long.

"Would you get us some water?" he asked when the barbarian had tightened the rope that fastened his wrists to an eyelet spike set into the wall.

The sailor muttered to himself, but knocked out the bung and filled a large mug which Jake swallowed with relish. He'd heard the gurgle of air entering the cask when they'd drawn the bung. If it wasn't already too late, that would give Castile a few more moments.

Bart needed little urging from Jake to follow his example and demand some water. Unlike Jake, who had been surrounded by water for hours, Bart was genuinely thirsty. Still, he gave Jake a raised eyebrow at his insistence, then a low nod. He'd figured something out, although what, Jake couldn't tell.

"I learned a game of dice when I traveled to Shara," Bart told the sailors. "If you'd reach into my pouch, you'll find the eight pair of dice you need to play it. Since we're going to be together for hours, we may as well enjoy ourselves."

The sailors looked at Bart, uncertain how to take this sudden move toward fraternization.

"Of course, if you don't gamble, I'd quite understand."

"We only have ship script," one of their guards grunted. "We exchange it for gold when we leave the ship."

That was probably a lie, Jake knew. A ship this size would have its own underground economy like those on the massive galactic trading ships he'd interned on before he'd made the biggest mistake of his life and signed on with the John Gault.

"It hardly matters," Bart said. "I am so poor at the game that I'd probably lose all of my gold if we played. I play only to escape the boredom."

The guards looked at one another, greed transparent on their faces. "On the other hand, you'll be leaving the ship shortly. You'll be able to exchange your winnings for gold when we reach Spoleta."

"So I will." Bart seemed overjoyed at the idea. "Then we must play. We'll play only low stakes, of course. Shall we say a gold piece a roll? I've got to make my gold last." He brought his bound elbow against his pouch eliciting a metallic clink. The gold Bart carried, Jake realized bitterly, had probably dragged him into the Erlang Sea in the first place.

The guards opened Bart's purse, exclaimed over the beauty of his dice, and tried not to gloat over the small hoard of gold coins he carried.

Bart was a trader, Jake reminded himself. That was why the Tiflis had sent him. Of course he would carry money. Still, Jake couldn't see how losing a small fortune was going to help them escape. Let alone escape in time to free Castile before she suffocated.

Bart launched into a complicated explanation of the game. The sailors, following Bart's instructions, each rolled two pair of dice and Bart cursed, then told them that each had won two gold coins.

"Bah. You could have won twice as much if you'd been more careful," Bart exclaimed. "When you reach Spoleta, you'll find that this game has swept the entire Granger Khanate. Skillful players can make a fortune. Most of my fellow Granger are too impatient to learn the finer points. Unfortunately, my Otranto is too poor for me to explain it to you. If only there was some way I could simply demonstrate it..."

The guards huddled briefly, then untied one of Bart's hands. "No funny business," the taller said. "We'll have to kill you if you try anything."

Bart seemed overjoyed. He picked up the dice, then proceeded to explain a poker-like game to the two men. The sailors got closer and closer to the floor where Bart rolled the dice, piles of gold coins mounting in front of each.

"Ah, no, my cursed luck," Bart exclaimed when he rolled what looked like a fairly normal pair of sixes.

"What?" the taller guard wanted to know. Both guards knelt over the dice, staring at them as if they held the secrets to the universe--or at least eternal wealth.

"This." Bart grasped the man by the hair and smacked his head against the other. Both men fell unconscious.

Bart turned to face Jake. "So, who's in the barrel?"

Chapter 14

With Bart's hand unfastened, it took Jake and Bart only a few moments to untie themselves.

Jake stumbled to the barrel, awkward in his hurry and from the circulation rushing back to his legs.

"Take time to get this top off," Bart observed.

"So start now." His hands shaking with hurry and concern, Jake yanked the stopper from the bunghole. The water seemed to gurgle out in slow motion.

He felt sick. Manny would probably kill him if Jake returned without his daughter, but that wasn't the worst of it. Castile was one of his comrades and he felt a sense of responsibility for her—a responsibility he'd failed at. Increasingly, the carefree and irresponsible life he'd enjoyed as a student and junior trader seemed alien, as if it had belonged to someone else--someone the new Jake might not even like.

"Got it," Bart growled. He threw the barrel lid to the ground and reached into the barrel dragging Castile out.

She was limp, wet and unmoving.

Despair settled over him like a night fog. "Too late."

"Better work your magic on her," Bart told him.

He glanced at Bart trying to make sense of the man's words, then remembered that basic resuscitation was one of the many skills that Arcadia had lost when early Terran civilization had collapsed.

Bart laid Castile out on the low cot and Jake hunted for her pulse.

For a long moment, he found nothing, then a painfully slow beat filled him with elation.

He pressed his lips to hers, exhaling and filling her lungs. If her heart was beating, she would live. She had to.

He kept up the pace for a good five minutes, taking short breaks to keep from hyperventilating but otherwise working steadily when Castile's eyes flickered open.

"I dreamed you were kissing me," she told him.

"Uh--"

"It was so totally gross."

Just as well. The last thing he needed was some schoolgirl with a crush.

Relief warred with anger now that he knew she was all right. "What were you thinking? Do you have any idea how close you were to dying? And now there are three of us locked up on this ship instead of just two. I have no idea--"

Castile pushed her fingers over his lips. "Do you want to yell at me or do you want to escape?"

"Hey, she's got knives in here," Bart said. "And some sort of bags."

"Pig bladders," Castile announced. "Some local villagers said they could be used for flotation."

At least they'd put some thought into this crazy escapade although Jake still didn't like it. "You could have just put those in the barrel, and not come yourself," he said.

"Right. And you would have known to get access to the barrels or guessed there was something inside?"

Jake capitulated. "Anyway, you're here. So how are we going to escape?"

Castile smiled at him, her dark eyes completely trusting. "You'll figure something out."

Even though they'd been tied up and guarded, Captain Pierre had been suspicious enough to have their cabin door solidly locked and barred from the outside. The porthole might be large enough for a rat to slide through but not even Castile could wiggle her slender frame into it. A quick examination of the floor and ceiling was no more successful. Both appeared to be major structural elements built of what looked like several inches of solid oak.

"They're going to have to change the guards sometime," Jake said. We can pretend to be tied up and capture the new guards when they arrive before they have a chance to close the door."

"That could work," Bart agreed.

"Except we'll be hours farther from the spring where the others are waiting," Castile observed. "Do you really think we can swim that far? This ship moves fast."

She was right. They had to do something soon.

"Come on, Jake." Castile looked at him with both encouragement and what appeared to be a bit of skepticism. "You're a spacer. Think of something clever."

She was right. Ships are ships and he had spent a lot more time on them than either Bart or Castile.

For lack of a better idea, Jake called up the schematic for the John Gault. For a disorienting moment, he felt overwhelmed by nostalgia for the place he had sometimes called home and often called the biggest pit in the explored Galaxy. His implant manipulating his vision to make the schematic of the space merchant ship appear to be hanging in midair before him. For long seconds, nothing dawned on him. A vague feeling of panic started deep in his stomach, trying to force itself up his spine to his brain.

He brutally forced it down, then zoomed into the schematic. Why were some of the bulkheads solid while others were dotted lines? All of the extruded aluminum plates had looked the same to him.

Then abruptly, he knew what to do.

"Check the walls," he told Bart.

Bart obliged. "Can't find any extra doors or anything."

"How do they feel? Not the one to the gangway, but the ones to the cabins on either side."

"Like wood. A little shaky, maybe, but that's all."

"That's what I thought." Jake looked at Castile who still huddled in the cot where Bart had laid her. "Are you ready to go?"

"Don't tell me you figured something out."

Jake shrugged. "Do you really want to sit here and wait for the sailors to find you?" He felt like a heel but he didn't want to have to carry Castile if he didn't have to. They were going to have enough trouble as it was.

"I'm coming." She struggled to her feet. She looked woozy and the wet fabric of her smock clung to her slender body like a second skin.

He took one of the knives Bart had fished out from the barrel, grabbed the blanket from the cot, slit a hole down its center, and tossed it to Castile. "Pull this on. You'll freeze."

"I can't swim with this."

He rubbed his hand over his face. "Just do what I tell you. Please."

"Oh, all right." She slid the impromptu poncho over her head and settled it on her shoulders. "I look like something out of a horror story."

"Bart, would you fill two of those bladders with water?"

Bart nodded.

"They're for flotation," Castile argued.

He ignored her and checked both side walls for latches. This was a merchant ship as well as a pirate vessel. Jake couldn't imagine any merchant ship designed with bulkheads that weren't collapsible to allow introduction of different cargos and different passenger configurations.

The Anglic ship was no exception to Jake's rule. Eyelets in the floor and ceiling showed where the bulkhead could be fastened in place. Except the eyelets were empty. Once again Pierre had foreseen the possibility of escape and taken steps to cut them off.

Jake was beginning to get very tired of Captain Pierre.

"I'm not seeing any great progress," Castile said.

Jake centered himself, gathering his chi, then launched a side kick against the nearer wall.

His foot met the wooden wall with a crash, but he, rather than the wall, bounced back.

He rubbed his foot. That hurt.

"Looks like you budged it," Bart admitted. "Sort of put a crack down the middle too."

Jake nodded. "All right. A couple more kicks, then."

Which was what it took.

The bulkhead crashed down under Jake's third kick and he stumbled in after. The scent of tar, paint, and turpentine hung heavy in the stale air that invaded their cabin.

"Could start a nice fire here," Bart said. "Be a distraction for our escape."

Jake started to nod, then remembered the guards they'd left unconscious in their cabin. They were just men doing their jobs and hadn't seemed like bad people. Setting a fire down here would be little short of murder.

He shook his head. "Too dangerous."

Bart gave him a look, then shook his head. "If you say so."

"I do. So let's get out of here."

Like all the doors on the ship, the storage room door was latched from the outside. Unlike their cabin door, which had been secured by a heavy bolt and a wooden slat across the entire doorway, this lock was a simple hook. Jake's kick yanked the brass screws from the oak walls and the door flew open with a crash.

"Might want to be a little quieter," Castile whispered.

Had he really been happy to see her a few minutes before? Jake growled at her. "Just follow me."

He led the way into the gangway.

Wood, paint, and gunpower make for a deadly fire danger. The Anglics minimized their risk by avoiding use of lamps below deck. The gangway was almost completely dark.

Jake headed toward the bow rather than toward the stern using the mental map his implant had constructed out of the portion of the ship he had seen. Surely a ship this large would have multiple hatches to access the deck, and the crew would probably be thickest near the ship's wheel.

Unfortunately, what little light there was faded as they proceeded until they were stumbling in complete darkness.

He shook his head at his stupidity and enhanced his infrared vision.

Just in time. They were surrounded by sleeping crew members, each hanging in a hammock that draped down from eyelets in the ship's ceiling.

He wanted to shush his comrades but even that noise would be too much. Instead, he grasped Castile's belt and signaled that she do the same for Bart, then inched his way among the sleeping forms.

There had to be at least twenty sailors, hung out in two long rows.

When he passed the last sailor, he couldn't hold back the faint sigh of relief.

Too soon. Castile's slender grace maneuvered past the last sailor, but Bart blundered into the hammock.

The sailor startled.

Go back to sleep. Jake willed the words with all the force of his soul.

"Who's there?" The words were soft but suspicious. The sailor's eyes opened wide and he reached for a long-bladed knife on his belt.

Jake reacted without thinking. He threw a hand over the sailor's mouth beat his hand to the knife, and slid the dagger between his ribs.

The sailor thrashed, then stilled. The steady drip of blood joined the faint sounds of snoring and deep breathing from the remaining sailors.

Jake grasped Castile's belt again and tugged trying to fight down the tremble in his hands.

The man hadn't done anything to him, might not have even known him, yet Jake had killed him.

It was terrible. But he would have to be sick later.

* * * *

Twenty steps further, he saw what he'd been looking for. A narrow ladder leading up to a closed hatch.

"I'll go first," he whispered to the others. "Give me thirty seconds, then follow."

"Right," Bart breathed. He looked grim.

The hatch opened soundlessly on well-greased hinges.

To Jake's dark-acclimated sight, the ship seemed to glow with light from the small moon overhead, the glittering swath of the Milky Way across the southern sky, and the faint luminescence of the water below.

A single sailor slithered down the mast and stepped toward Jake.

"What are *you* doing here?" the man demanded.

Jake whipped the dagger, underhanded, at the sailor, catching him in the throat.

The man fell, his eyes darkening and Jake moved to catch him.

One of the ship's boats was mounted over the side of the ship.

Jake weighted the risk of stealing the boat against those of swimming. They would be more visible in the boat and its loss would be noticed more quickly. If they swam, Captain Pierre would probably spend some time searching the ship before he assumed that they had left. If Bart could swim, he would have taken the chance. As it was, the boat seemed the more reasonable risk.

Castile appeared by his side. "Just the one?"

She'd seen the body and this was her only reaction? What kind of planet had he ended up on where human life was such a trivial commodity?

"So far," he answered. "Help me unlash this boat."

"I thought we were going to swim."

"Just help me."

Without his night vision, Jake wouldn't have been able to see anything. Castile, however, managed to find the lines that held the dingy to the ship and went to work with both fingers and her dagger.

Bart emerged from the hatch seconds after Castile, tripped over the body, and fell with a significant thump.

Jake grabbed him, meaning to help Bart to his feet and found himself confronting a gleaming dagger.

"It's me, you idiot," he hissed.

"Oh, sorry." Bart climbed back to his feet, then hauled up the bladders filled with fresh water. "Where's Castile?"

Jake looked around to make sure that Bart's stumble hadn't attracted any unwanted attention. If it had, evidently the sailors had assumed it was just another of the creaks and groans that made up the normal cacophony of a sailing ship.

"I've almost got it." Castile's whisper was immediately followed by the groan of wood sliding against wood and a tremendous splash as the boat fell into the water. "Oops."

No sailor could ignore that sort of noise and they didn't. Shouts were quickly followed by the sounds of running feet and the clash of steel being drawn.

"Into the water, quick," Jake shouted.

Castile slipped, otter-like, into the dark sea beneath them, not even making a splash. Bart, however, clenched a stay, his knuckles white even in the near-complete darkness.

"Come on, Bart. We've got to get off."

"I'll drown."

"I won't let you drown. Come on, they'll kill you."

"I can't."

"It's not just you. They'll murder us too. Do you really want to be responsible for getting Castile killed?"

"Go without me. I'll hold them off while you get away." He waved his dagger in the air nearly slicing Jake's throat.

Jake ducked under the dagger, grasped Bart in the neck, and squeezed his carotid artery.

Bart struggled briefly, then collapsed in Jake's arms.

Jake heaved the deadweight over his shoulder and jumped.

Unlike Castile, Jake splashed hard and sank like a stone with Bart's bulk weighing him down.

He let himself sink in the cool water, kicking away from the ship rather than toward the surface.

A popping noise and the near miss from a zinging musket ball cutting through the water near him let him know he'd made the right decision. Or at least he had if he could find Castile, their dinghy, and somehow manage to keep Bart from drowning.

Why was it that his life on Arcadia seemed to consist of jumping from one frying pan into the next?

When he could hold his breath no longer, he kicked to the surface. The ship was a couple of hundred meters away, but it yawed wildly. In minutes, Jake knew, the ship would turn back and start quartering this section of the sea looking for him, Castile, and most important, their boat.

There was still ample shouting coming from the ship and he decided to risk a call to Castile.

"Over here," she called back.

Jake tucked the still unconscious Bart under his arm making sure his mouth and nose were above the water level and sidestroked toward Castile's voice, dragging the unconscious Tiflis with him.

"What's his problem?" she asked when Jake paddled up.

"Which problem do you mean? Bart's, or Pierre's? Bart didn't want to come with us so I had to persuade him. Pierre's problem is spotting us in the dark. Unfortunately, it's a problem he'll figure out the answer to.

Jake heard a distant splash and turned to look at the ship. It had dropped a barrel holding some sort of lamp that created a little pool of light.

"Enough of those and they'll find us," Jake said. "It seems odd that they are bothering."

Castile nodded. "You'd think they had something to hide."

"Speaking of hiding, you don't think that dingy sank after you dropped it off, do you?"

"Oh. Sorry about the splash."

Well, Jake's fantasy had been of lowering the boat gently so as not to disturb anything. That sort of fantasy had been backfiring for him lately.

"Forget about that. But do you know where it is?"

Another splash indicated that another barrel with a light had been dropped.

"Uh, no."

Wonderful. "Can you hold Bart for a minute? Just try to keep his face above the water."

Castile took the Tiflis, almost sinking under the weight of his muscular body while Jake enhanced his night vision, then kicked himself up at the peak of a wave and tried to look around.

It took a couple of waves but finally he saw the boat, mostly submerged, only about a hundred meters away.

He took Bart back and started the haul.

"Look at the water." Castile's voice was filled with awe.

A faint glow of luminescence accompanied every movement they made, creating a ghostlike shimmer around them.

"It's beautiful," Castile said running her hands through the plankton-rich water to create new eddies of light.

"It's going to get us killed," Jake answered. "Come on."

The boat wasn't much of a refuge, but it was all he could think of.

Bart struggled slightly in his grasp, indicating that he was on the way toward regaining consciousness. Mostly that was good news. Except if Jake didn't have things under control by the time Bart rejoined them, they were going to have another panic attack on their hands.

The boat, when they finally reached it, was equipped with oars, a short mast and sail bags, but no water or food. It was a good thing he'd brought those bladders of water.

"Do we get in?" Castile asked.

He was tempted. They could row at least three times as fast as they could swim pulling Bart; every nerve in his body wanted to put as much distance as he could from the searching ship.

A larger wave picked up the dingy, its decking and cockpit gleaming white over its blackened bottom.

"I think I may have a better idea."

"Good, because the ship is coming this way."

He risked a look and wished he hadn't. The ship seemed to be pointing directly at them and it launched another light barrel as he watched.

"Help me flip the boat over," He said.

Castile looked like she wanted to argue but, for once, she simply did what he asked, adding her small weight to his as he rocked the boat, filling it with water.

When the boat was almost entirely under water, he shoved down hard, putting all of his weight on the gunwale and motioned for Castile to do the same.

The boat teetered, then slowly flipped, its heavy wooden frame crashing down on the water nearly taking Jake's head off.

A surge of luminescence exploded out from the boat but there was nothing Jake could do about that.

"Now what?" Castile asked. The ship was getting closer but Jake could now see that it was going to miss them.

But not by much.

"Go under the boat, inside of it."

Castile looked at him like he was crazy. "Maybe a spacer can breath under water but I can't."

He sighed. "Please just do it."

She nodded, then vanished.

Jake covered Bart's nose and mouth with his hand and followed Castile.

The boat held a large bubble of air as it floated low in the water.

Even without his night-enhanced vision, the plankton provided enough light to see. Jake saw Castile looking at him like he was some sort of miracle worker.

"How did you know this air would be here?"

"Help me drape Bart's arms over the thwart," Jake said.

"Thwart?"

"Seat."

"Oh." Jake held Bart up and slung his arms over the thwart while Castile tried to arrange them to hold him on without their constant attention. Finally she cut a bit of rope and tied his hands together.

"Won't they see us?" she asked.

Jake wondered if Castile could possibly go more than two minutes without asking a question. Then he remembered how long she'd laid, completely silent, in that water barrel. For that, he was prepared to cut her as much slack as she needed.

"Maybe they will. But the bottom of the boat is black while the top is white. We have a better chance this way."

"But we won't be able to see them."

He hated that too. Even though he knew there was nothing to do, the idea of sitting there helplessly made him feel uncomfortable.

"If they're smart, they'll quarter the area, sailing back and forth over where they saw us last, cutting larger and larger search areas. If they miss us on this sweep, we can hope that they don't come back this way."

"But they'll see us when it gets light out."

"So we'd better be long gone before then."

Bart chose that moment to regain consciousness, cursing the barbarians, the Granger, and Jake at considerable length and in painful detail.

"Quiet. The Anglics will hear us," Jake told him.

Bart laughed. "Do you have any idea how Tiflis imagine Hell? It's this. Being stuck with your head barely above water, your hands tied and helpless. So do you really think I'm afraid of the barbarians?"

"Well we are," Jake told him. "You're tied so you won't sink."

"Where are we?"

Jake explained quickly, then, once Bart assured him that he wouldn't do anything crazy, borrowed Castile's dagger and cut the rope that bound Bart to the thwart.

"I'm going to see if they're still out there," he told them.

He emerged as slowly as he could to minimize any extra plankton glow.

The barbarian ship had wandered off and was now a couple of kilometers away. A nearby light barrel sputtered, then went out.

He waited long enough to make sure that the ship was still heading away, then swum under and rejoined his friends.

The carbon dioxide level inside the air bubble had significantly increased in the few moments that he'd been on the surface. It was still safe enough, but Bart's eyes were beginning to show the first signs of a renewal of his panic. High carbon dioxide levels could make him feel like he was suffocating even if he wasn't.

"Let's flip it back over," Jake said.

The boat was heavy, but it was built to float right-side up so they didn't have much problem turning it over. They had more problems with Bart who accidentally went underwater when the boat flipped and came up shouting.

Jake had to threaten to knock him out again before he calmed down.

They managed to clamber into the boat.

It was, Jake saw, a little larger than he'd first imagined. Possibly five meters long, it had a half keel but had lost its centerboard during one of the flips. It would sail like a tank.

"Castile, you start bailing and Bart and I will row," Jake said.

"Bail with what?"

When they'd flipped the boat, they'd lost everything that hadn't been tied down and this included whatever had been intended as a bailer.

"Just use your hands," he suggested. "It's going to be hard enough for Bart and I to move this thing even if it isn't full of water."

The oars *had* been tied down, so he unshipped the two oars, settled them into their oarlocks, and signaled to Bart that he was ready for his help.

Bart stood, nearly swamped the boat, and collapsed onto the deck.

"Come on," Jake urged. "You spent the past week on a canoe. Surely you know how to move around on a small craft."

"I swear I'll never ignore my religious leaders again," Bart moaned. "If only I survive this terrible day."

"If we don't get a long ways from here by daylight, you won't have to worry about surviving," Jake told him. "Now get your butt up here and start rowing."

Bart glared at him, then laughed again. "Even if you are the devil, you are right."

Each of them took an oar and they started rowing.

After twenty minutes of bailing, Castile allowed as how she had done all she could and shipped the rudder.

"Do you think we're going to get away?" she asked. They hadn't seen the ship in some time now.

Jake shrugged. "Who knows? I don't know how fast the ship was going, or how far we are from land. No matter what we do, they'll be faster than us so they'll find us eventually unless we make it to shore first."

"Will we?"

Jake consulted the faint pulses from the GPS satellites that orbited Arcadia. "Probably not."

Chapter 15

For once, Captain Pierre seemed to have outsmarted himself. Having backtracked toward the spring where Jake had gathered water and, not so incidentally, Castile, it seemed to Jake that Pierre must have now determined that Jake and crew had headed out to sea. Although he'd come within a couple of kilometers of their boat during the night, the Anglic lookouts missed Jake's small boat in the dark.

When the sun rose, it rose to an empty sea. Neither land, nor the Anglic ship could be seen.

Once the pirate ship had passed out of sight, Jake had steeped the short mast and hoisted the two small sails that had been stored beneath one of the thwarts.

With the morning sun came a sudden shift in the wind. The jib shivered, then flopped madly. Jake sheeted it in, but the wind shift was too dramatic.

"We'll have to tack," he said.

Castile and Bart both looked at him as if he had been speaking in a foreign language.

He checked his memory but no, he'd been speaking in Otranto. "Tack," he explained. "We can't sail directly into the wind so we zig-zag across it." Evidently neither had paid much attention to the reasoning behind his navigation on the canoe. Of course when they'd still had the canoe his navigation had been a matter of convenience and speed. Now it could spell their survival.

"If we don't sail directly toward the shore, the barbarians will catch us," Bart argued.

"They can't sail directly into the wind either," Jake answered. Not that Bart didn't have a point. The larger ship would have a lot more speed than their little boat and it's full keel would let it claw far closer to the wind than would their boat's little half-keel.

The boom swung around abruptly. Both Jake and Castile ducked, but it thumped Bart in the head.

Bart collapsed to the bottom of their boat clutching his head. "I want to get back to my ponies."

If they were successful in setting up a trade route between Otranto and the Tiflis, Bart would spend most of the rest of his life on a sailing ship. Jake decided that now wasn't the time to remind him of that.

"The wind is like a steep mountain," Jake explained. "You can't climb straight up, so you use switchbacks to navigate it. We'll have to use the switchbacks and Captain Pierre will too."

"Except he's faster than us," Castile added.

"But we're ahead," Jake replied. "Let's hope that he doesn't turn around in a hurry."

An hour later, Jake spotted a line of clouds on the horizon. Half an hour after that, he saw the points of three masts and the upper sails of a large ship behind them. Pierre had realized his mistake and was after them.

The race was on.

"If we were on horses, I would drop caltrops to slow them," Bart said.

Some sort of mine would be handy, but their boat didn't turn up anything more than it had the last time he'd searched it.

"If we make it to land, we'll probably be able to outrun them," Jake told him. "We have to make it to land first."

The larger ship closed the distance fast. With every wave, Jake could see more of the huge array of sail that the ship mounted.

"Do you have any idea about their range?" Castile asked Bart. "You saw their cannons, didn't you?"

Bart shrugged. "They looked big. They were shooting at us from a long way away yesterday."

Was it only the previous day when they'd been swamped by the barbarian ship? It seemed to Jake that half of his life had passed since then.

"I think we can get to shore before them," Castile said. "But that'll still give them a long time to shoot at us."

"I suggest you start bailing," Jake told Bart. "I'll trim the sails. Castile, try to sail a little closer to the wind. We don't want to have to tack again." If they tacked, they would expose themselves to the barbarian broadside. Jake thought they might be able to avoid the larger ship's chasers since ancient-style sailing ships like this couldn't mount much weaponry on their bows. They wouldn't have a chance against even mediocre shooting from the ship's main guns. And he didn't think Captain Pierre would put up with merely mediocre.

The familiar sound of the ship's ranging shot rang out a few minutes later. The shoreline was getting close--already Jake could make out the individual trees rather than the green mass that they'd originally seen. The barbarian ship, though, had closed much of the gap.

"We could jump in and swim," Castile suggested as a cannon ball skipped closer to their boat. "We'd be harder to hit that way. Besides, it worked last time."

It had worked for Castile and the others, not for himself and Bart.

"You two save yourself," Bart said. "I'll sail on in the boat. That way, they might not even see you."

If they lived through this, Jake was going to teach Bart how to swim.

"We aren't going to abandon you," he told Bart. "Besides, we need this boat."

"We'll never get the boat away," Castile argued. "When we reach the shore, they'll either blast it or come after it. Either way, we lose it."

"Without the boat, we've got a couple of hundred kilometer walk through Granger territory. With it, we sail a couple of days. Keeping it could save our lives."

Without conscious thought, he grasped the tiller from Castile and swung it hard to the right.

The cannon ball splashed only a few meters to the right of their boat, exactly where they would have been if he hadn't reacted.

A huge wall of water splashed over the gunnels and halfway swamped their boat.

"Bail," he told both Castile and Bart. "All that water is going to slow us down and make the helm sluggish."

His enhanced eyesight could actually pick out the trajectory of the cannon shot giving them a couple of seconds to react. For now, that was enough. He veered to avoid another shot.

Again, the splash came close. And with every meter of distance that the barbarian ship gained, another fraction of a second of warning was lost. Soon, he would be unable to react.

"Should I row?" Bart asked. "Maybe it'll make us faster."

The breeze was strong if almost directly in their face. Rowing would give them the advantage of being able to move directly into the wind--something the barbarians simply couldn't match.

Rowing while the sails were up would slow them down rather than speed them up. On the other hand, they could drop the sails, unsteep the mast, and make themselves a smaller target.

Jake toyed with the temptation for a moment, avoiding another cannon shot almost automatically. The land was only a kilometer or so ahead. Already, he could see the breakers against the shore. The barbarians were even closer than that. They had two choices--hope to run their boat down, or swing around and fire a broadside. The choices, fortunately, were exclusive. If they wore ship to fire, and they missed, they wouldn't have time for a second shot nor for resuming the chase.

Jake knew that Pierre hadn't fired a broadside until now partly because he wanted to recover his boat and partly because they hadn't been close enough to make even a broadside a sure thing. Now, though, he'd had to decide. If Pierre was more concerned about the loss of the boat and his prisoners, he would fire. If he wanted to recover his boat, he would take the risk that they would get away. Jake didn't think he would care that much about the boat.

The wind picked up, making Jake glad he hadn't taken Bart up on his offer to row.

He heard his heart racing, the song of wind against rigging, and the ominous roll of breakers counterpointed by the occasional roar of the ship's bow chaser.

He avoided a shot aided as much by luck as by skill. The range was too close now for anything like even the near-instantaneous plotting of the cannonball's arc.

Bart bailed the latest surge of water out. The long swells of the sea were being transformed into a short chop that splashed over the limited decking of their boat, creating the need for continual bailing.

"Watch out," Castile screamed.

He hadn't seen the telltale puff of smoke, but he twisted the tiller anyway guessing to turn to the left because he'd turned to the right the previous two turns.

No splash sounded nearby and he glared at Castile. She'd nearly given him a heart attack.

"Rocks," she said.

A jagged rock showed itself just meters from the side of their boat, then vanished again under the waves. The white caps, whipped up by the freshening wind, and the choppy surf had conspired to hide that destructive fist of stone until almost too late.

Not that it mattered. In seconds, Captain Pierre would decide he had lost the race and turn his broadside on Jake.

Unless--acting rather than thinking, Jake pulled the dagger from his belt and slashed a long cut in the main sail.

The boat instantly slowed, plunging unsteadily into the waves.

"Are you crazy?" Castile berated him. "We were going to get away."

He ignored her outburst watching the ship behind them.

The ship's sails shivered as the men prepared to wear her around and Jake feared that Castile was right and he'd made a horrible blunder. Then it straightened and plunged ahead. With Jake's reduced rate of speed, the ship had a chance to recapture the boat and mete out a more lingering punishment to Jake and Bart. What they'd do to Castile didn't bear thinking about.

Bart pulled out his own dagger. His eyes narrowed as he glared at Jake. "I was prepared to give up my life to save yours and now you do this. Why?"

"We weren't going to escape," he explained. "They were at the point of turning their broadside on us."

"At least we would have died quickly," Bart answered. "Think what they'll do to Castile."

Obviously the less said about whatever torture they'd devise for Jake and Bart, the better.

A gust of wind completed the rip that Jake's dagger had started and the mainsail fluttered into two ineffective banners.

"Now we row."

Bart looked at him in disbelief, but moved to the forward thwart as Jake lowered the remains of the mainsail and the jib.

He yanked the pair of oars they'd converted into an impromptu centerboard from the centerboard well and handed one to Bart keeping the other to himself.

"Try to avoid any rocks," he told Castile who had taken back the tiller.

She nodded uncertainly, then something clicked and she grinned at him. "But not by too far, right?"

"Right." If Pierre's ship hit one of those rocks at full speed, it would be destroyed and a significant percentage of the sailors would be killed or injured.

The thought was vaguely sickening, but not as sickening as what they would do to Castile, Bart and himself if he failed at this crazy maneuver.

The sailing ship was close now, so close that Jake could see the individual sailors. He imagined he could make out Captain Pierre's grim expression as he commanded the ship's wheel but that might have been an overactive imagination.

Castile counted out the stroke for them and Jake put his back into the oar using every bit of the new muscle that he'd gained in his weeks on this miserable high-gravity planet.

To his dismay, their boat waddled rather than plunging ahead.

The ship sped through the sea, passing over the huge rock that had nearly gutted Jake's boat.

He almost closed his eyes at the horror that he knew would unfold.

The ship continued on. A freak wave, good luck, or possibly an alert crewman had saved it.

"They missed." He groaned the words, putting even more of his body into the rowing.

"There are other rocks," Castile reminded him.

Then, suddenly, the ship spun, one of its sails parting. Sailors swarmed up lines and rigging, cutting down the torn sail and lowering all the other sails as well.

"What are they doing?" Bart demanded. "They're practically on top of us."

Jake's initial hope that they had hit a rock faded. The ship was too organized.

"They probably realized that it would be dangerous for them to continue. But don't worry, they haven't given up on us."

As he watched, the ship's launch swung away from the ship and at least twenty armed sailors swarmed aboard.

"We'd better make it to land quickly."

Thanks to Jake's reliance on his implant for navigation, they were less than half a mile from where the Anglic sailors had landed a day earlier to take on water.

They rowed hard, beaching their boat at full speed, the rudder popping out from its mount.

The Anglic launch was still a couple of hundred meters behind--close enough that one of the sailors stood to fire a bow at them and promptly collapsed overboard when an unexpected wave hit the launch. The arrow flew straight into the air and landed only five meters from the launch.

The remaining sailors left the unlucky archer to make his own way to shore, continuing on without pause.

"Let's go." Bart gathered up his dagger and headed away from the beach.

"We've got to take the boat," Jake said. He stepped into the water and tried to lift his end.

Although it had seemed a small and insignificant vessel on the water, he could hardly budge it on land.

Castile joined him in his efforts to shove the boat the rest of the way out of the water. The gravity-enhanced weight of the boat more than offset Castile's gravity-enhanced muscle. The boat eased forward a few centimeters and ground to a halt.

Bart turned red in the face. "They're almost here. We've got to go."

Without the boat, they were as good as dead, Jake knew. They would never make it through hundreds of kilometers of hostile Granger territory. Yet, continued futile shoving at the immobilized boat would be suicidal.

"He's right," Jake told Castile. "Run."

The Anglic sailors poured off their launch by the time Jake and Castile reached the first scattered trees. A couple of arrows whizzed by them. Jake ducked and one stuck in a tree right where he had been.

Jake plunged on, keeping an eye out for Castile who needed his help about as much as Bart needed another long sea voyage.

Behind them, Anglic voices slowly faded into the distance.

Only then did he slow. Castile strode alongside him and pointed. "This way."

"Where are we going?"

"The others are waiting."

This was news to him. "Maybe we should split up. That way, at least some of us might make it out."

The curl of Castile's lip told him what she thought about that idea. "One or two people alone could never make it out of here. We've got to pull the group together."

Jake nodded. She was right. Without their Tiflis guides, none of them stood much of a chance this deep in Granger territory.

"We'll have to set some traps, try to thin out the Anglic crewmen."

Castile nodded but rolled her eyes. "What do you think Lucer and the guys have been doing for the past twenty-four hours?

He wouldn't have guessed Lucer and the guys would have expected to see himself, Castile, or Bart again. He had to hope that he'd been wrong. "Lead on," he told Castile.

She stepped onto a narrow animal trail that snaked through the dense brush.

He saw no signs of any traps and Castile didn't make any obvious efforts to avoid anything. After a few minutes, he began to wonder if she might not have exaggerated the team's preparedness for attack. Then Lucer stepped out from behind a tree. Next to him stood a stranger.

"Glad you could make it, boss," Lucer told him.

This boss thing wasn't growing on him, but Jake knew he wasn't going to shake it off now.

"I'm afraid we brought about twenty Anglic sailors on our trail," Jake told Lucer.

The stranger nodded. "My neighbors have already signaled as much. Although there may be fewer now."

"Permit me to introduce Ahmed Broussard," Lucer said. "Broussard is the headman of a local village."

For an instant, Jake nearly panicked. Twenty angry barbarians was trouble. Involvement with the Granger government would be disaster. Then he realized that the local headman was no more Granger than Jake was. Broussard looked Otranto and he probably was just that--even if he lived in a land that hadn't been ruled by the Emperor of Otranto for hundreds of years.

"I appreciate any help your villagers can offer," Jake said. "Perhaps you could lead us safely through these woods."

Lucer laughed. "Broussard would be terribly disappointed if I let him do only that. I promised him wealth for his aid."

Jake almost blurted out the minimal extent of their wealth but managed to hold his tongue. He was a trader after all, and he recognized another trader when he saw one.

"Perhaps we should talk alone."

Lucer shrugged. "Broussard knows we are carrying no great wealth with us. Yet even the boat you stole would be of considerable value in a costal village that the Granger has long ago denied ships. And pirates, as you know, generally carry their wealth on their bodies."

"You'll help us for that?" Jake asked.

Broussard nodded. "If you have other wealth, I would be happy to discuss that too."

"Exactly how many villagers do you have?" An idea was starting to percolate through Jake's mind.

"Perhaps twenty families live in my village. But there are others nearby. All within twenty miles have sent their young men to see if they could raise their fortunes and perhaps strike back at the barbarians. In all, now, there are perhaps thirty of our people, armed with bows, slings, and throwing sticks."

"No guns."

Broussard laughed. "The Granger do not allow Otranto subjects to carry guns. This morning, we had none. By this evening, I think we will have two if the reports can be believed."

"Have any of these villagers ever sailed?" It was a forlorn hope.

Broussard's eyebrow lifted. "You were right, friend Lucer. Your boss does make big plans. You think we have a chance to seize the barbarian ship itself? The wealth of that ship would make these villages the richest for hundreds of miles."

Which would mean little if the Granger decided to take that wealth, Jake knew.

"We kill all of the sailors who landed, take their boat, and row back to the sailing ship." Lucer's voice was calculating as he tried to feel out the plan. "If we wait until dusk or later, it might work."

"They'll have some sort of code," Jake said. "Their Captain Pierre is nobody's fool. Even if he believes there is little danger, he would have devised some sort of identification and he'll be suspicious if we don't know it."

"So what do you propose?"

Jake pointed at Broussard. "Starting now, you are the priest of the temple at the spring. The Granger have attacked your temple and you've hidden the gold. You take me captive and turn me over to the Anglic landing party. Tell them that if they'll help against the Granger, you'll share the temple treasure with them."

Broussard frowned. "If more sailors come, my villagers will be outnumbered. We know the countryside and many of us are hunters, but the pirates are killers. I fear they'll discover us and slaughter us."

Jake nodded. "It's a risk. Still, they'll think they're your allies. Lead them deep into the forest, litter the trail behind them with traps, and then vanish. As they return, you can whittle them down. That will give us our only chance to capture the ship. We need more of them on land."

Broussard didn't look very happy but he nodded slowly. "For the wealth of that ship's cargo, it might be worth the chance."

Jake's brain whirled with the opportunities. "That ship's cargo may be only the beginning. If we succeed in establishing a trade route between the Tiflis and Otranto, the ships will need a convenient stopping point between Umbar and Otranto city. Your villages could become rich beyond your dreams if you could supply ship supplies, food, and the fresh water of your spring."

Broussard's eyes widened as Jake described the possibilities and he nudged Lucer with his elbow more than once. As Jake wound down, though, he got a thoughtful look in his eyes. "The Granger will prevent it. They are a problem."

That was the understatement of the year. The Granger were simultaneously holding down both Otranto and Ebron cultures, stifling trade, and conducting a long-term policy of genocide against their Otranto subjects.

"They are a problem. Yet I'd give a lot for a handful of Granger warriors right now."

"What?" Broussard looked like he couldn't believe his ears. "Why?"

"It would give the barbarians something to think about."

Broussard smiled slowly. "I see. If you have two enemies, persuade them to attack one another and spend their strength. And make sure they don't find a way to join against you. You are wise as well as clever, young friend." He slapped Jake on the back practically knocking the younger man to the ground. "As it happens, there is a Granger garrison about ten kilometers from here. I could send a message that the barbarians are attacking. Our Tiflis friends speak their native tongue and could pass as former barbarian captives. If so, we could probably persuade them to help us rather than join the barbarians in the attack."

"Do it."

For the next fifteen minutes, the small clearing where Jake and Castile had met Lucer and Broussard became a command headquarters. A messenger was dispatched to summon the Granger garrison and Broussard and two other village graybeards mapped out the route they would attempt to lead the barbarians on--at least until they made contact with the Granger.

Finally the immediate orders had been issued and Broussard turned back to Jake. "All right, how do we do this?"

Ten minutes later, a badly beaten Jake sprawled into the barbarian encampment.

One of the barbarians drew his sword and lunged at Jake who narrowly avoided the thrust.

"Careful, my friends," Broussard said as he stepped from behind a tree. "Unwrap my gift only when you understand what he has to offer."

Captain Pierre hadn't come himself, but Jake recognized his first mate, Armand. The man had a scrape on his forehead and a cut in his tunic.

"And who are you to tell us what to do?" Armand demanded.

This was the key moment. If the barbarians didn't believe Broussard's story, the villagers would try to cut them down in their camp--and certainly suffer high losses even if they were successful.

"I am a poor priest," Broussard lied. "Once my temple was one of the wonders of Arcadia with its golden statues of the goddess in all of her attributes. Each year, merchants would come from all over the world to add gold to her ornamentation." He sighed slowly and a single tear, apparently unnoticed, slipped down his cheek. The man, Jake realized, was a consummate actor. Jake would have to be very careful if he ever tried to negotiate another bargain with him. Come to think of it, perhaps he had already given Broussard more than he had asked for.

"Sounds like that would be worth some money, priest," Armand said. "And what does being a priest have to do with your capturing this slave?"

"Although most of Otranto gave up the faith of the goddess hundreds of years ago, people from our village have held onto many of the old ways," Broussard went on. "For our Granger overlords, however, the old religion is to be wiped out without mercy. Of course, any treasure taken in the process is converted to Granger use."

"And the Granger are attacking?"

"Even now," Broussard agreed. "We helped the Granger party your ship had sent ashore and they learned about the temple. Now they've contacted the Granger garrison and are moving on our temple. This slave and another Granger tried to join them. The Granger got away, but I captured this one." He gave Jake a kick to the back of the kidneys. "I thought he was a real Granger in the darkness of the sacred grove, but you can tell that he is not."

"Let's just kill both of them and get on with it," one of the sailors said.

Armand flattened the offending sailor with a backfist to the nose, then turned back to his captives. "You say the Granger are on their way to steal your treasure?"

"It is even so."

"Can you give us directions to your treasure? Uh, I mean your temple?"

"Directions?" Broussard wrinkled his forehead as if contemplating a radical proposition. "Take two hundred paces in this direction," he waved vaguely, "then turn right. Or maybe just a little short of right. You'll walk until you see a lightning-struck tree—"

Ahmed shook his head. "Can you lead us?"

Broussard nodded. "Of course. Oh. My brother priests have agreed that you should have a quarter share of the temple treasures if you help us rescue them from the Granger."

One of the sailors snickered, but Armand pretended to consider the offer seriously. "How many Granger are attacking?"

Broussard waved his hands ineffectually. "It is difficult to know. Perhaps thirty. My priests know little about fighting."

"Half your treasure," Armand countered.

"But I am only authorized to offer up to a third," Broussard whined. "I could never--"

"Right. A third. And you'd better be right about the size of the gold treasure."

Not that Jake believed Armand would have any qualms about taking the entire treasure when he'd captured it.

"Right. Let's go. Jean-Claude, kill the slave and let's get some directions from the priest."

Jake barely rolled over to escape the sailor's attack.

"I'll need his help to carry my share of the treasure back to the temple," Broussard said. "Surely you can wait to kill him."

"I'll wait," Armand said. "But not for long."

Chapter 16

Armand twisted on his heels driving a fist directly into Jake's unprepared body.

"Ugh." Jake gasped for breath, cycling through his health program looking vainly for something to confront this sudden attack.

"I'll be happy to beat my new servant if he displeases you," Broussard offered.

Armand pivoted into an open-handed slap to Jake's left ear. The attack reeled Jake back on his heels. "This all seems so convenient. So I think it's time that he talks."

This attack was supposed to make Jake talk? He could hardly breath.

Armand grasped Jake by the tunic, halfway lifting him from the ground. "You escape from our ship and immediately attack these Otranto priests. Why?"

Jake might not have been prepared for the attack, but he was prepared for easy questions like this. "My master's cousin found the temple. They lost a great deal of treasure when you sunk his canoe and didn't want to arrive at Bathsheeba empty handed."

"He was looting his own countryside?"

Jake did his best to look mystified. "Of course not. He was looting Otranto priests. My master would never attack a Granger." His explanation wouldn't make any sense to anyone who didn't know the Granger. To those who did, it should be sufficient. From what Jake had seen, the Granger truly believed that their subject people were nothing but slaves serving at the humor of any Granger who might come along.

"And you just happened onto the local garrison?"

"The prince's servants who survived your attack on the canoe contacted the garrison."

Armand slapped Jake's undamaged ear. "How many in the garrison?"

Jake shrugged. "Twenty, perhaps. More than enough to handle pirates like yourself."

Armand's knee slammed into Jake's groin and Jake collapsed to the ground sucking for wind and futilely trying to bring his bound arms around to cover the damaged area.

"We are Anglic warriors, not pirates."

Jake forced himself to breath. "It is easy to beat a bound man. To beat Granger on horseback will prove a little more difficult."

Armand's face turned a rather frightening shade of purple. Jake wondered if he had gone too far this time, not that he'd had a choice. He needed to empty the Anglic ship of warriors and this was the only way he could think of to do so.

"Together, my priests and your brave warriors might have a chance against the Granger," Broussard suggested. "We could show you where to hide in ambush, taking the Granger by surprise."

Armand nodded slowly. Jake could almost read his thoughts. Together with the supposed Otranto priests, Armand's men might be able to defeat the Granger. But their losses would make it difficult for them to seize the treasure. And that supposed treasure was the only reason for Anglic interest.

"Yet we would do better with more men," Armand concluded. "Andre, take two seamen and tell Captain Pierre that we'll need another twenty warriors. And take back the slave with you. I don't want to waste men as guards."

"But I'll need him," Broussard said. "The priesthood wants to flay him for his impiety."

Armand laughed. "Oh, is that it? Well, for that, I'll make sure you get him back."

"Can't you send someone else back with him?" Andre begged. "I've never fought Granger before."

Armand frowned and shook his head. "You'll have your chance. Now move."

Jake found himself half jogging and half dragged toward the ship's launch.

The land breeze wafted the launch back to the anchored ship and Jake found himself once again below deck, this time in what must serve as the ship's brig.

At least he knew the password--Andre had shouted it out as the launch approached. But he had no way of communicating it back to his comrades.

The ship didn't empty, but the constant sound of the ship modified as many of its warriors crowded into the launch and set out to join Armand.

Five minutes after Jake heard the launch pull away, he was joined in the brig by Captain Pierre.

"So, you've returned."

"Not by choice," Jake lied.

"Is that so? It is odd that I have sailed in these waters for so many years and yet I've never heard of a great temple treasure. I would have thought the Granger would have looted it decades ago."

"Evidently the Otranto keep their secrets."

"They don't seem to have kept this one."

"Prince Bart is known to be a lucky man."

"Indeed?" Pierre smiled, his even teeth looking predatory. "I sent enough men to handle the Granger garrison even without help from the Otranto. Not that the Otranto are likely to offer anyone much help. There has never been such a degenerate race."

Jake didn't want to debate that issue. He wanted the Anglics and the Granger garrison to go after each other. Still, if the Otranto were as worthless as Pierre seemed to think, and as everyone had been telling him since he'd landed on this planet, their chances of capturing the ship were slim.

"I'm tempted to kill you now," Pierre said suddenly. "Can you offer me any reason not to do so?"

Moral arguments didn't look like they would go far. "If your warriors do lose, or even win but any are captured, you might be able to exchange me. I have proven useful to the Prince before."

Pierre looked into Jake's eyes, then nodded abruptly. "For now, at least, that is enough." He seized the oil lamp that provided the only light in the brig and vanished, leaving Jake alone in the darkness.

Jake felt each link of the chain that held him to the brig wall. Many of the links were rusty, but none yielded to his strongest twists.

The chain ended in a ring embedded in the oaken wall of the ship itself. Even planting his feet against the wall and pulling with all of his might did nothing.

Lacking a file, Jake contented himself with rubbing one link against another. Probably it would take him a year to break through this way but it gave him something to do. And he had to do something. He needed a way to get the code back to Broussard and Lucer.

Without his computer implant, he would have lost all sense of time. As it was, he calculated he was left alone for better than an hour when a sudden commotion sounded outside the ship.

Minutes later, a faint light appeared which, to his darkness acclimated eyes, was a blinding glare.

"They've met the Granger army." Andre's voice sounded excited, as if this was a 3-D video that didn't truly affect him. Jake guessed that Andre was in his late teens. Not much younger than Jake himself, and only a year or two older than Castile. Yet, Andre seemed more like the run-of-the-mill teens that Jake had met throughout the galaxy than either himself or especially Castile.

"And the Granger have sliced them to pieces?" Jake asked.

Andre frowned. "Anglic warriors are the best in the world."

"The Granger are fighting on their home territory and are all accomplished horsemen. Your Anglics don't stand a chance."

"We will win," Andre told him. "We have enough warriors to overwhelm the Granger." He paused for a moment. "They should have let me go and fight with them. I am a man, not some child to be protected."

Had Jake sounded like that, whining to Captain Trabert about how he was ready to take on more of the trading responsibilities aboard the John Gault? No wonder the man had been frustrated with him.

Jake tried to look harmless, which wasn't especially difficult given the beatings he'd recently experienced, the fact that he hadn't eaten in forever, and that he was chained in the filthiest place he could imagine. "From the start, I wondered why they treated a warrior like you as beneath them."

Armand ate it up. "Just because I am young, they keep me from joining in their battles. Yet how will I learn if I am never allowed to fight?"

"That is true," Jake sympathized. "Still, if your men somehow defeat the Granger, think of the treasure."

"Which I will never see. You think they will share with one they think too young to fight?"

"All that wealth and you'll get nothing?"

Andre clenched his teeth in a transparent and futile effort to hold back tears. "I never get anything."

Jake squelched any guilt feelings about using Andre. He had to think about saving Castile and the others, not to mention his own skin.

"I see the problem. No doubt you were left to guard me, which was just their excuse to keep you from the battle and from your share of the wealth."

"Exactly." Andre wiped the back of his hand against his eyes.

"If I was to escape, however, you could follow me to the shore. Once there, you could join in the battle."

Andre eyed him suspiciously. "How could you possibly escape?"

"Did you know that no one searched me? Would it be so odd if you returned from a call of nature only to see that I had filed through the chain? You would have to bravely follow me and, once on land, you could seize your share of the treasure."

"The captain said to hold you as hostage."

Jake laughed. "In case you are defeated. Do you really think that could happen, especially if you were in the fight? Besides, is it your fault that Armand was to busy hitting me to bother with a proper search?"

Andre paced nervously, then suddenly spun, pushing his lamp near Jake's face. "Do you really have a file?"

Jake smiled. "I don't, yet. But only the two of us have to know that."

"You want me to help you escape?" Andre sounded as if his barbarian pride had been mortally wounded.

Jake held out his chain-bound arms. "I am a slave, not a Granger warrior. Losing me would mean nothing to your captain and, frankly, holding me would mean little as well. Do you really think a Granger would stoop to ransom a slave? So, it seems like a fair deal. Great wealth for you and my life for me. It costs your captain nothing and gains you much."

"But--"

"Once you prove yourself as a warrior, they will never again be able to keep you from the battle."

For a second, Jake thought he'd pushed too hard. Then Andre nodded. "Take the file with you and throw it overboard."

"Deal." Jake stuck out his hand.

Andre looked at it, then spat on the floor. "I am doing this because I am a man. I do not strike bargains with slaves."

So much for feeling guilty about what he was going to do to the kid's reputation. Jake dropped his hand. "I forgot myself, master."

Andre grinned. "That's more like it. I'll bring you the file."

Ten minutes later, the heavy chain parted. With the ship as underpopulated as it was, Jake was able to work his way through the below-deck areas without running into any sailors. He emerged from the rear hatch just as Andre 'discovered' his escape.

"The Granger slave. Stop him."

It was too soon, of course. Fortunately, Jake hadn't depended on Andre's sense of timing. He dashed for the side of the ship, lashed his cut chains at the one sailor who managed to grab for him, and plunged over the side.

The iron chains dragged him down and Jake had to kick with all of his strength to regain the surface.

A badly aimed musket ball splashed water into his face and an arrow whizzed by. This was getting old.

He struck out for shore as best he could. Fortunately, both the ship's launch and its dinghy were ashore already. It would take some time for Andre to rig together another boat.

Swimming with his hands chained was hard. Finally Jake discovered a sort of sidestroke that let him make decent progress. He reached the shore just in time to see a small skiff set off from the Anglic ship, Andre, waving a huge barbarian sword, screamed bloody murder after him.

"Come off the beach before someone gets the idea to put a cannon ball into you," a voice called.

Jake stumbled up. A rough hand grasped him as he reached the tree line, then dragged him down into cover.

"Lucer?"

"Who did you expect? The Emperor?"

"How is the battle going?"

Lucer laughed. "Battle?" Broussard led the Anglics into the Grangers and ducked out of sight. Twenty minutes later, there were ten Anglics and no Granger left. So now the Otranto have some nice horses and nice loot, and we've got seven Anglic prisoners."

"Seven?"

"Three of them didn't think the Otranto could shoot."

"Try to capture this next boat load. The kid helped me and I owe it to him to keep him alive."

Lucer nodded slowly. "You're a strange man, boss."

"One more thing. The code word is *captive*." Jake's eyes suddenly felt incredibly heavy. He couldn't remember the last time he'd slept and just resting his eyes for a moment sounded like paradise. He started to set his computer implant to awaken him in five minutes, but he was asleep before he could do even that.

* * * *

Another foot in his ribs knocked the fatigue out of him. Jake rolled over, grabbing the offending foot, and then yanked.

Castile tumbled on top of him. Her lips only inches from his.

For a brief moment, he thought she was going to kiss him. Then she hammered a fist into his stomach. "Let me loose, you barbarian."

Jake blinked. "You kicked me."

Castile rolled back to her feet. "If I'd kicked you, you'd know it. All I did was nudge you with my foot. Harold says they need you and I was supposed to wake you up. You weren't supposed to attack me."

"Sorry."

"You should be."

He shook his head. After this was over, he was going to find somewhere and sleep for twenty-four hours straight. His internal clock told him he'd snatched an hour. All that had done was make him want more.

"You'd better hurry." Castile made pushing motions with her hands. "Harold couldn't plan his way out of an outhouse."

Harold's plan was about as bad as Castile had implied. The plan was to row out, get on the ship, capture anyone who fought, and give the rest a choice between being marooned somewhere in Granger territory or sailing for Jake. Getting *to* the ship relied on Jake's password working. Getting control of the ship relied on a whole lot of luck.

Unfortunately, Jake couldn't think of anything better although he did insist that Captain Pierre and Armand be held prisoner rather than slaughtered. He had stretched his morals to the breaking point, but he still refused to consider cold-blooded killing of prisoners.

"Then let's go," Harold said after they'd reviewed the plans a final time.

Jake's understanding of military action centered around lengthy preparation periods, complex coordination, and intricate logistical operations. After all, he'd been trained as a merchant, not a warrior. This action consisted of gathering Harold, Jake, Lucer, and the dozen Otranto youths who seemed least intimidated by their own weapons. All wore clothing that had been confiscated from the Anglic pirates. It would take a miracle for them to fool anyone for five seconds.

Jake was thankful for the dark as the Otranto war party fumbled with oars, then managed to entangle them in a pair of knots.

After the surf washed them back to the shore, Jake got out, untangled the oars, and physically shoved the launch out past the surf.

He climbed into the stern of the launch and took the tiller. "I'm going to count out the strokes. When I say stroke, you'll stroke. If you're not ready, do it anyway. We can't afford to look like a bunch of idiots who have never touched an oar before. Unless you want to eat cannonball for dinner."

The men looked intimidated, which wasn't the attitude that Jake wanted when they went to capture a ship where they were badly outnumbered. But they did pay more attention to their oars.

The ship lookout didn't spot them until they were within twenty meters.

Jake called out the word *Captive* in response to the challenge, muffling his voice so it wouldn't be recognized.

"What's been taking so long?" the watchman demanded in Anglic.

"Took a while to sort out the loot," Jake answered. "We'll bring the rest when its daylight."

"That much?"

"You won't believe your eyes."

The launch bumped up against the side of the ship and Jake motioned to his men to board.

Harold and Lucer moved at once, scaling the rope ladder that hung down to the launch. The Otranto hung back.

Jake brandished the sword he'd confiscated from Armand. "Get moving or so help me, I'll slice you myself."

More frightened by Jake than by the pirates above, the Otranto moved.

Just in time. The Anglic ship had been largely emptied by the raiding party and much of what crew was left was below decks sleeping. Still, Lucer and Harold were hard pressed when Jake finally shoved the last Otranto up the ladder and followed.

The Otranto scurried for cover as soon as they had climbed the ladder and when Jake emerged, an Anglic sailor tried to split his head with a heavy club.

Jake ducked, let the club splinter on the deck, then vaulted onto the ship in a move he would never be able to repeat if he tried a hundred times.

Another sailor swung at him with a heavy cutlass and Jake blocked.

Armand's sword rang in his hand, the vibrations almost knocking it loose as the sailor grinned, then swung his cutlass around for another blow.

This time Jake was ready. Although Jake was no swordsman, he knew the basics. He ducked the slashing blow, then hammered his hilt into the sailor's hand.

His foot connected with the sailor's groin at the same moment the cutlass hit the deck.

Jake bent down, avoiding an attack from behind, picked up the cutlass, and tossed it overboard.

Then he spun, wrapped his new assailant's blunt-ended slashing sword in his own, and twisted it free.

This time he sent the sailor rather than the sword overboard. Jake held onto the short sword.

Lucer and Harold had been shoved into a corner of the deck by six cutlass-armed sailors while another madly stuffed a bullet into a muzzle-loading musket.

Jake was still five meters away when the man shouldered the musket. Jake threw the short sword.

The sword smacked into the musket and the weapon discharged, the shot going through a sail but not hitting anyone.

The musket's roar distracted the six cutlassmen. Three spun around leaving only three to face Lucer and Harold. Harold cut his down, then disarmed one of those attacking Lucer.

An arrow lodged in the throat of one of the three coming after Jake. Three more arrows stuck in the deck near the others. The Otranto had finally gotten into the action.

The surviving Anglic sailors threw down their weapons.

"Nail the hatches shut for now," Jake ordered Lucer. "Put a couple of Otranto with bows near each and feather anyone who tries to come out."

"Right."

* * * *

Seven days later, the reunited party sailed their ship, now christened the Castile, into Otranto harbor.

Despite the Otranto flag that one of their adopted sailors had found somewhere deep in a chest, the entire city seemed to take alarm at their entrance to the harbor.

Huge cannons poked their noses from the forts that lined the narrow bay that made up Otranto's harbor.

According to *Arena of Otranto*, large ships could tether at the huge stone piers, letting longshoremen load and unload even the largest vessels efficiently. Jake wasn't ready to trust a fictional account with quite so much credibility. Instead, he anchored half a kilometer off shore and waited for a pilot boat.

It took two hours before a rickety launch poked out from one of the forts. An overdressed and hugely overweight man sat on the forward thwart glaring occasionally at Jake's ship as if he thought its mere existence an affront to Otranto's honor.

He said something to one of his oarsmen.

The oarsman shouted, "what ship are you and why do you fly the Otranto flag?"

"We are the merchant ship Castile," Jake shouted back. "We fly the Otranto flag because we sail for that nation."

The boat bumped up against the Castile and the oarsmen made it fast.

"He's Admiral Boren of Thebes," Castile whispered in his ear. "And naming the ship after me was silly."

"Admiral of what?"

"Of the Otranto navy, of course."

"Do you have a navy?"

"He's sitting in it."

Jake looked down at Boren's rowboat. One of the oarsmen was busy bailing even though the protected water of the narrow gulf was almost glass-smooth. *That* was Otranto's navy? No wonder the country lost every war it fought.

"What's he waiting for?" Jake asked.

Castile giggled. "Do you really think he could make it up that rope ladder by himself?"

Jake considered, then shook his head. "Andre."

"Yes, Captain."

"Lucer is Captain. I'm only the owner."

"Right, Captain."

He shook his head. "Do you think you could rig up some sort of block and tackle to haul that Otranto on board?"

"The overstuffed peacock? Sure you want to stretch out a perfectly good line on the likes of him, Captain?"

Since those perfectly good lines had handled tens of thousands of kilograms of thrust, the question wasn't completely serious. It wasn't completely facetious, either. Jake didn't have a lot of experience on primitive planets but he had plenty with bureaucracy and this admiral without a fleet looked to be the very definition of a bureaucrat.

"Bring him up," Jake sighed. "We'll have to deal with him sooner or later."

"Or we could just run into Erlang," Andre suggested. "It'd cut a couple of days off the trip to Umbar."

Jake had thought of that but shook his head. He'd been in denial as long as he'd been able, but he had to face reality. He was no longer a spacer. He was stuck here on Arcadia. He could either snivel and feel sorry for himself, or try to make a difference. And if he was going to make this planet his home, Otranto seemed the only possible base. Even if he had to drag it up by its bootstraps.

"Haul him up."

The 'Admiral' got right to the point. If Jake wanted to trade in Otranto, he needed official permissions. Lots of permissions.

"I'd be happy to offer my personal assistance," Boren told him. "Of course that would mean making some considerable sacrifice of my time."

Jake nodded, but was careful not to agree to anything. He'd pay bribes if he had to, but right now the ship was his major asset. Anything he paid now would cut into his ability to trade.

"I'll need to consult with my legal advisor," Jake finally told Boren when the admiral ran out of steam.

"Oh. And who might that be?"

"Princess Marie Delphonte," Jake answered.

"Ah. Well, the Princess is temporarily indisposed. You may want to consider another option, at least until she is able to resolve her difficulties."

That sounded bad. "Indisposed in what way?"

"She and her husband were accused of witchcraft. You know how seriously we have to take these accusations. With the Granger infidels to our west and the schismatic barbarians to the east, witchcraft at home could destroy us."

"Of course."

"I'd be happy to accept your note, written against the value of your ship."

"I'll certainly look forward to your support," Jake said trying to hide the sickening feeling in his gut. The longer he spent here, the more difficult everything seemed. No wonder Otranto was in trouble. "Perhaps you would dine with me tomorrow and we could discuss the details," he continued. Jake lowered his voice. "After all, we don't want everyone to know how lucrative my trading practice is likely to be."

Boren widened his eyes at the unsubtle hint, then glared at the leaking launch which had carried him out to the Castile. "Tomorrow?"

"Tomorrow would be best. It's a pity that we have to wait until then as I'd like to pull up to the quay and unload the perishable items from my cargo, but I understand the procedures are complex and the forms need to be followed."

Boren's wheels might turn slowly but even he wasn't dumb enough to miss out on the possibilities there. Once the Castile docked at a quay, it would take only a quick legal twist before it became the personal property of one Admiral Boren.

"No, no. We mustn't delay the exchange of goods between Otranto and its subject provinces. You must dock now. I'll come tomorrow evening to discuss our business arrangements more fully."

"I'll make sure I have gold on hand to deal with the necessary procedures," Jake said.

"Ah, yes. Gold." With luck, greed would make Boren hold off until he thought he could get both ship and treasure. "My launch will serve as a pilot boat for you. Follow it and you'll avoid the dangerous reefs."

"Then you'll sail with us?"

"Nothing would make me happier. I am looking forward to seeing how my--uh, I mean your ship sails."

Chapter 17

Manny Delphonte's inn still smoldered and the sweet smell of partially fermented wort filled the air like an autumn bouquet. At the small mill, the water rushed by an unmoving wheel. And huge barrels still leaked beer where they had been roughly tapped for a thirsty mob.

Castile wiped a tear from her eye, smudging a sooty trail across her cheek. "We've got to set them free."

"But they were accused of witchcraft." Harold had been around Otranto long enough to understand and fear the power of her church.

Castile's fists clenched. "I've got it. My father's apprentices will riot. In the confusion, our sailors can raid the prison and set my parents free. If we kill a few of Emperor Fernis's fat sycophants while we're at it, so much the better."

Jake considered Manny and Marie to be among the few signs that Otranto was still alive, could still offer anything to the world of Arcadia. That Otranto had turned against them was a bad sign. Still, they needed Otranto as a united and friendly base, not as a hostile and burned-out wreck. Of all of the cities they'd passed through, only Erlang offered a fraction of the potential. But Erlang's independence was a shallow fiction. It's location, weak defensive walls, and smaller size made it a poor second choice. Otranto's strategic trading location on a narrow channel separating the eastern and western continents, defensibility, culture, workforce or market size, made it the true prize of the planet.

Now that he had a ship, Jake intended to build a mercantile economy. Otranto had to be an anchor.

"There has to be a better way," Jake said.

"Well, what is it then?" Castile glared at him as if it were all his fault.

He scratched his head. How was he supposed to know? "They're accused of witchcraft. Surely we could prove them innocent at the trial?"

"Trial?" Castile laughed shortly. "For witchcraft? All it takes is an accusation and off you go."

"But--"

"Witches would use their evil magic on the judges if there was a trial," Mark explained. "It is the same everywhere, not just in Otranto."

"Hmm. So if we circulate a letter accusing the entire population of Otranto City of witchcraft, they'd all go to the stake."

"It isn't like that," Mark answered.

"What it is like," Lucer said, "is that witchcraft is a handy accusation for the powerful to use against an uppity foreigner who doesn't know his place, especially if his patron is dead."

It was a good reminder given that Castile was the only native Otranto citizen in their entire party. If they didn't walk carefully, they might be joining Manny and Marie in whatever dungeons the church used for its victims.

"It's not just foreigners," Castile reminded them. "My mother is not just an Otranto, she's a princess. They arrested her anyway."

Lucer grimaced. "So they kill two birds with one stone. First, she's a woman and Otranto has always been suspicious of women in power. Second, she married a barbarian mercenary. Given how many barbarian mercenaries have decided to become Otranto Emperors over the past thousand years, the Otranto nobility don't have to look for an excuse to turn on them. In this case, they even have evidence."

"What evidence?" Jake asked. Even if he'd believed in witchcraft, he'd never seen Manny or Marie do anything that even hinted at the occult.

"From what you've told me about his beer-making techniques, he's been doing things no one has done before. If that isn't witchcraft, it's close enough to suit their purposes."

"But what kind of idiot would want to put the man who makes cheap beer out of business?" Even as he asked the question, Jake knew the answer. Humans resist change, even change for the better. Manny's techniques would upset the few old-line brewers who refused to adopt his methods and bureaucrats who saw Manny's methods as a potential state monopoly and resented the money he made, especially because he was, as Lucer had reminded them, a foreigner.

"Panic makes people irrational," Lucer reminded him. "The Granger are moving to attack, Otranto hasn't won a war in over a hundred years and is out of provinces to give up. The people know it will take a miracle to prevent the Granger from overrunning the city this time. In this kind of environment, it doesn't take much of an excuse to get them excited about stomping out witchcraft." He walked over and kicked one of the charred support posts in what had been Manny's tavern. "I wouldn't be surprised if Otranto City didn't decimate itself between now and when the Granger take over."

Jake didn't like Lucer's assumption that the Granger would win but he couldn't argue with the logic.

"Well, forget about the big picture. Let's think about Manny and Marie. Surely there's someone, some authority, who could determine that this particular witchcraft claim is nonsense."

Lucer sat on a fencepost and stared briefly at the sky. "I suppose the Patriarch could. There are probably a few monks that are holy enough to get away with it. But why would they? The people like an occasional witch burning. Adding a beautiful princess to the fire makes it almost a holiday."

"I'll go talk to the Patriarch," Jake said.

"May I go along?" Mark was normally so quiet that Jake often forgot that he was part of their group.

No one answered him so Jake was left with the decision, again. "I'm not sure bringing someone the Patriarch will see as an infidel will help our arguments."

Mark frowned. "You may be right, of course. On the other hand, the Patriarch wrote a fascinating paper on the logic of Aristotle. He might just be amenable to the concerns of another student of philosophy."

"Or he might just throw both of you in prisons with my parents," Castile said. "I'm going too."

Lucer shook his head. "The Patriarch thinks that women are tools of the devil. If Castile goes, you'll never even get in to see him."

In a rare moment of realism, Jake decided that this was not the time to make a political statement about the role of women in modern society. It would be a long time before Otranto was anything like a modern society. That time would stretch to eternity if it didn't survive the coming Granger attack.

"Sorry, Castile. It's going to be me and Mark. We'd better get on with it before they start lighting the fires."

"If we don't hear from you in the next eight hours, boss, we're coming in after you," Harold said.

"Forget that. You and Castile should show Bart and Wart around Otranto. We need cargo for our ship--stuff the Tiflis will buy from us. Obviously it isn't going to be beer. At least not this trip."

"Eight hours," Harold repeated.

"That's the great thing about being boss. I get all the responsibility but no one listens to me when I give them directions," Jake complained.

"Oh, you're finally figuring that out?"

"Yeah. I guess it took me a while."

* * * *

The Patriarch's palace dominated the eastern side of the city, towering over the homes of the nobility and churches that seemed even more numerous than taverns.

"The Patriarch is not receiving visitors," an officious clerk told them. "See your parish priest if you have any religion questions."

"The Patriarch needs to hear us." Jake lowered rather than raising his voice going for the tone of command that his first captain had used.

"Why is it that I doubt that?" The clerk slapped his forehead in an annoying gesture. "Oh, that's right. Because you're a foreigner and that other one is a pagan."

"A pagan who once paid your gambling debts," Mark observed softly. "Haven't you come a long way, John?"

The clerk squinted. "Mark? Is it really you? When did you return to Otranto?"

The Ebron laughed. "I told you I would return. There are some books that I could only find in the Otranto libraries, so here I am."

"But the Granger--"

"The Captain here allowed me to join his party," Mark explained.

"We'll have to have a bottle of wine and talk about our school adventures." John's voice was animated for the first time. "I'll send word out to those of us who are still left. I'm afraid that the schools are rather empty these days. If you're hoping to support yourself by teaching, you will be poor indeed."

"Once, Otranto's schools of philosophy taught hundreds," Mark explained to Jake. "When I was here, there were maybe twenty new students each year. John joined, what, two years after I did?"

"Three," John corrected. "There are only eight in this year's class. The Granger have prevented any more Ebrons from joining us and the barbarians speak such bad Otranto that their students can't keep up and usually hurry back to whatever eastern pit they crawled out of."

It looked like the student reunion might go on for a while so Jake interrupted. "I wonder if you could catch up on things after Mark and I see the Patriarch. Quite simply, it is a matter of life or death."

John didn't look sympathetic. "Everyone dies sooner or later. Getting together with an old friend is special."

Jake barely fought down the urge to pull his dagger and let John consider how much more attractive *later* could be than *sooner*. The priests of Otranto were important. Together with the Imperial bureaucracy, they kept what remained of the nation running while incompetent or ineffective Emperors clawed their way to the throne.

"The Captain has ideas on how to strengthen the Otranto economy," Mark observed.

John wrinkled his nose as if he had smelled something funny. "I have studied the ancient texts on economy. The processes are like a beautiful machine. One that individual people can do nothing to alter."

"Even before I left Otranto, John was the city's leading expert on the philosophy of economics," Mark commented.

Luckily, Jake had read a few of those pre-historic economics texts, although he had found them a sure cure for insomnia. "Innovation and invention can change the nature of the economic machine, and one man can certainly introduce those."

John shook his head. "Much overrated, according to the texts."

Jake smiled. "That would depend on the texts you chose. Perhaps we can continue this discussion over a mug or two of ale." He paused meaningfully. "After we meet with the Patriarch."

"And there is no ale to be had in the entire city. No one can remember a time like this. It'll have to be wine."

"If you let me in to see the Patriarch, I'll make sure there is ale again," Jake growled.

"Is he always like this?" John asked Mark.

Mark nodded. "Always."

"Right. I'm tempted to send you away just because you are so annoying, but for my old friend Mark, I'll see what I can do." John turned and vanished down a long corridor.

"They aren't all like that," Mark observed when John had stepped beyond earshot.

"Who aren't like that? And like what?"

"Philosophers," Mark answered. "John always thought philosophy should be separate from the world. Something to divide the sophisticated from the masses."

That pretty much reflected Jake's feelings about philosophy as well, except he saw himself on the side of the masses. "I take it you don't agree?"

"If it can't explain the real world, what good is it?"

"There is that."

Jake whiled away the wait inspecting the paintings that clustered the Patriarch's hallway as thickly as wallpaper. There seemed to be three separate types. About half were portraits of grim-faced men wearing clerical garb. These were uniformly bad. Most of the remainder were ornate, gold-embossed and jewel toned icons reflecting the particular religious beliefs that the Otranto people had developed after they had been cut off from contact with the rest of humanity.

Many of these icons depicted crude and anatomically distorted views of the human form. Still, every one reflected a power of faith that Jake envied. Far down the hallway, a handful of paintings showed the use of perspective, natural colors, and a close study of the human form.

"The barbarians have adopted new realistic techniques of painting," Mark observed, pointing to the more naturalistic artwork. "Once, Otranto's art was sought by everyone, even the Ebron and the so-called schismatic barbarians. No one minded that their religions were different when the Otranto artists seemed to have a window onto the divine."

"I understand the Ebron have a different faith, but I thought the barbarians and Otranto shared the same faith."

"Before the schism," Mark corrected. "Although a humble Ebron like myself cannot tell their religions apart, I hear that the slight differences are highly important."

"There is a huge difference between the truth and error." The voice quavered, but the words were delivered with a sense of certainty, as if the speaker had looked the truth in the eye and now need never doubt again.

Jake had expected a man dressed in the overly ornate garb that adorned the hundreds of official portraits. Instead, the Patriarch wore the cassock and hood of a simple priest. A small and unadorned Cross hung from his rope belt.

Intelligent black eyes peered at Jake. Although the wrinkled face reflected age, those eyes held the power to compel.

"Thank you for seeing us, Your Holiness," Jake said.

Mark gave a stiff bow, then stepped back.

"My clerk tells me that you promised him a philosophy lesson if I spoke to you."

Oh, great. This was the man who had written the book on Aristotle. All Jake could remember about Aristotle was that he hadn't agreed with Plato. "He expressed interest in economics--a field near to my heart."

"Yes, that most mundane of philosophies appeals to some. Are you not the Captain of the merchant ship that sailed into port earlier today?"

Jake bowed. "I am its owner, at any rate."

"Oddly, I have heard of a ship whose description matches your uh, Castile. What I heard was that it was an Anglic ship licensed to trade in Otranto waters by the Emperor Fernis himself."

A bead of sweat collected on Jake's back and rolled down. He adjusted his health computer to dilate his arteries and made himself relax. "It is true that my colleagues and I were attacked by a barbarian pirate and were lucky enough to capture their ship."

"Indeed? There hasn't been an Otranto merchant ship for two hundred years. Not since the Emperor Theodore of Blessed Memory licensed the Otranto trade to the barbarians in return for their aid in the wars against the Granger."

Jake didn't like that *blessed memory* editorial. Surely Otranto couldn't be so tradition-bound that it would give up a free opportunity to develop its own mercantile fleet. Still, this was the type of problem that spacer merchants faced all the time. After all, once you got out beyond the first generation worlds where space travel had never been completely lost, spacer merchants had to fight for everything they got.

"I am certain that the Otranto bureaucracy could find a valid reason to abrogate that ancient and failed treaty."

"Abrogate a treaty entered into by a Saint?" The Patriarch's eyes blazed with barely controlled energy.

"If the Emperor Theodore was a saint, he was the only saint who signed that agreement."

The Patriarch frowned, then shook his head. "I think that you and I are going to have to continue this conversation." He turned and opened a door that had been obscured by a thick covering of paintings. "John, bring us a bottle of the red wine." He considered briefly. "Not the good red wine, the other."

Well, that told Jake where he fit on the Patriarch's priority list.

Jake followed the Patriarch into an airy room illuminated by windows holding as much glass as he had seen on all his previous journeys through Arcadia.

The Patriarch gestured for Jake and Mark to sit, then eased his ancient frame onto a straight-backed wooden chair.

John bustled in with a decanter of red wine and four ceramic mugs.

"Oh, all right. Join us," the Patriarch said.

John smiled, then flopped in a soft leather sofa. "Thank you, Your Holiness."

The Patriarch shook his head. "Once, a Patriarch could choose from a thousand educated clerks. Now, I get a choice between pig-ignorant parish priests who couldn't reason their way through a page of Aristotle's logic and so-called philosophers who study only to prove that their subjects have no relevance to this earthly world."

John poured himself a mug of wine, took a sip, then caught the Patriarch's stare and filled the other mugs as well. "Think how boring your life would be if your clerks were practical people."

The Patriarch sighed. "I suppose that is so. Now, tell me Captain of the Spacers, what do you think of Otranto?"

The Patriarch was well informed, Jake realized. And he'd asked a trick question. If Jake admired Otranto too much, he was a liar. If he told the truth, he would probably have his head cut off.

Something in the Patriarch's gaze convinced him that this was the time to tell the truth.

Jake took a sip of wine while he deliberated how to answer the Patriarch's question. For something the Patriarch referred to as 'not the best,' it was surprisingly good. He made a mental note to find out where it came from and determine whether he could trade in it.

"Everyone believes that the Granger will overrun Otranto City within the next ten years," Jake said.

"Within the next year is what I hear," the Patriarch said.

"From what I saw of the Granger, that would be a terrible loss. They care nothing for philosophy, for trading, or even for the welfare of their subject people."

"Go on."

"Yet Otranto has reacted by withdrawing into itself. You yourself told me that Otranto has not had a single merchant ship for two hundred years. Mark tells me that Otranto artists were once sought after around the world, but have now been surpassed by the barbarians. When we do discover a new art, like sophisticated beer-making, Otranto reacts in panic, accusing the brewer and his wife of witchcraft."

"Ah. The true reason for your interest emerges. You are speaking of Manny Delphonte."

"I worked with him and never saw any evidence of anything but hard work and skill. No witchcraft."

"Yet, would any witch let his witchcraft be visible?"

The conversation was starting to take on a cadence that Jake recognized, with a bit of shock, as bargaining.

"If we assume that every man who succeeds must be a witch, we have opened the doors to the Granger as surely as if we tore down the city gates. If we punish success, we will have only failure."

The Patriarch gave Jake a tired smile. "So you are a philosopher after all. But when witchcraft is claimed, any who defend the witch are automatically suspected themselves."

Jake felt the grip of a cold hand at his heart. "I am not a witch."

"Are you not? Do you know what a witch is?" The Patriarch shook his head. "But I was not thinking about the danger to you. I was thinking about myself."

"You? You are the Patriarch. The supreme leader of the church in Otranto."

Again, the humorless smile. "There are many within the clergy who feel that Otranto's doom can only be prevented by extreme piety." He shrugged. "I am not the most pious of priests. Some see my philosophies as a form of witchcraft themselves." Another shrug. "If I freed your friends, I might find myself replacing them on the stake."

This wasn't good news. Still, the Patriarch hadn't said no. That meant that they were still bargaining.

"Could the issue of a man's innocence come into the question?" Mark asked.

The Patriarch shook his head slowly. "To save Otranto, I would be willing to spend dozens of innocent lives. Do you have any idea how many would die if the Granger overran this city? Do you have any idea how many so-called witches would burn if the extremists took over the church? Should I risk these to save the life of one barbarian warrior?"

Okay, still bargaining. All Jake needed was something to exchange. Something that would be worth the Patriarch putting his own life and the survival of his city at risk.

"My first captain," Jake said slowly, "once found himself stuck in a foreign port with only enough money to buy fuel. Yet, he sold his own personal furnishings to fill up his cargo holds with a strange spice that no one on the ship had ever heard of."

"I am certain you are telling this story for a reason," the Patriarch observed. "Does it get to the point soon, or should I send out for some more refreshments?"

Jake was surprised to see that he'd finished his glass of wine without even thinking about it. The Patriarch was definitely a shrewder trader than Jake had imagined. Fortunately for Jake, his computer implant could cope with alcohol.

"It definitely has a point. I thought he was insane to buy the spices since he had no known market for them and I told him so. He told me that the ship was lost if he sailed without cargo. It was better to take the one chance at success, however slight the chance, than to accept defeat."

"I suppose that he found a huge market for the spices and became rich beyond his dreams," the Patriarch said.

Jake shrugged and shook his head. "Actually, it worked out that the ship's owners caught up with him and tossed him out. Although they eventually made money on his spices, it didn't help him much. Still, his point is a good one. If you do nothing and let Manny and Marie die, Otranto will fall. Only if you take a chance at more immediate destruction can you give Otranto that chance at success."

The Patriarch leaned forward. "And how can these two people, both accused of witchcraft, save our city?"

That was the sixty-four thousand credit question. Jake knew he'd have to wing it with his answer. Just like his old captain, he was selling a pig in a poke and had no idea what sort of market it would find. "Manny has created an entirely new trade good for the city. He's also independently rediscovered many of the techniques of mass production--techniques that could be used in many more industries."

"So we are a richer victim when the Granger invade. How does that help us?"

"Otranto depends on mercenaries. How can we hire them without money? Then too, it is sometimes possible to buy off an enemy."

The Patriarch looked disappointed. "As when we defeated the Ebron by hiring the Granger to attack them? I had hoped for more." He reached into a pocket and withdrew a string of beads, then slowly clicked through them.

Jake said nothing. He couldn't explain that a strong economy was essential to support a modern army. Otranto wasn't going to have a modern army in the next century or two. For at least the next decade, both the barbarian east and the Granger west would be militarily stronger than Otranto. The examples of the low countries on ancient Earth, and the siege of Gregorgrad three centuries ago early in the second expansion proved that merchants could stand against professional warriors, but Jake wasn't going to bet his life that Otranto could turn out a native citizen army in time to defeat the Granger.

The Patriarch met Jake's eyes, staring at him as if trying to read his soul.

Finally he nodded. "I see that you believe in the possibilities. I fear I do not. Still, your Captain's lesson is a good one. I will give you your chance."

"You're going to set the Delphontes free?" his clerk gasped. "You'll risk all of our lives on the crazy theory that a single man can transform the economy? You yourself taught me the Hegel and Marx that proves that no man can stand against the forces of history."

"Yet our faith proves that one man did," the Patriarch reproved John softly. "And Captain."

"Yes?"

"I will want to see a detailed plan on how the Otranto economy can be transformed. I want a survey of the products available to our city that could be traded on our own trading ships. I want to know what resources we have available for building additional trading ships. I want to know how many workers we have that waste their days through idleness, enjoying the bread and circuses that Fernis uses to maintain his grip on power rather than contributing to the Otranto people. You have one month."

Jake nodded his head. "I will call on you in one month, then. May I borrow some of your clerks to help me in this effort?"

For the first time, the Patriarch's smile was more than a polite mask. "I will spare you John for the next month. This will be an opportunity to see if philosophy can be practical."

"But--" Jake wasn't sure whose protest was louder, his or the clerk's.

The Patriarch shook his head. "I'm afraid that my next clerk will have to be one of the hard-headed self-flagellants if I'm to survive this decision."

He reached into his robe and pulled out a sheet of vellum, already folded over and sealed with the Patriarchal seal. "John will take you to the prisons and give this to the warden."

"You knew you were going to do this?" Jake said.

The Patriarch shook his head. "I wanted to set them free, I hoped that you could give me a better reason than you did but it was barely enough.

If you had argued your case any worse, I would have burned this letter."

Chapter 18

"We rescued a load of statues before they could be burned," Bart said. "Should be some sort of market for them in Umbar but they're too heavy to carry on our caravans. Other than that," he made a dismissive gesture with his hand. "Otranto doesn't seem to make anything."

Jake had called a council of war on his ship but no one had come up with any ideas. Bart and Wart's failure to turn up any trading goods was the biggest blow yet to his idea of building on the one thing he knew--business.

Jake gritted his teeth. This had to work. He knew less about weapons and military tactics than half the Otranto population, let alone the war-like Granger. The one advantage he had was that he'd seen the power of a mercantile civilization. He knew that Otranto could dominate the world again if it could somehow regain its control of its trade routes. But it couldn't do so as a purely passive collector of tariffs. That approach might work while Otranto still controlled the lands doing the trading. As it was, the largest city in the world should be able to produce something that people wanted. And beer alone wasn't going to do the trick.

Manny, Marie, Wart, Bart, and the others stared at him, looking for him to lead, for him to make the decisions. The Delphontes had been returned in the middle of the night by a squad of armed monks from a feared order of martial monks.

Jake caught Castile watching him too, but her look was different, speculative. He wondered whether she was just waiting for him to quit again--as he had quit every other time they'd faced a challenge up until then. Well, that was over. He would manage to build a mercantile civilization, he silently swore. Somehow, he'd find a way.

"What about the silks?" he asked. "There's got to be a market for those."

"Your spacers bought the entire stock up," Wart replied. "Price is through the roof. Besides, they don't actually produce the raw materials here. And there's a shortage of silk cocoons."

Jake rubbed his eyes. "Help us out, here, Manny," he pleaded. "What the heck are all the people who live here doing?"

"About a quarter of them are in the church," Marie answered for her husband. "They're busy with prayer and studies as well as training the next generation of priests. Then there are the government functionaries. They make up another quarter. Who knows what they do?"

Okay, Jake could understand that. Religion probably kept a trickle of wealth flowing into the city and this was the capital city. Of course it would have its share of bureaucrats. "What about the other half?"

"The rest of us mostly sell services to the priests and the government," Manny admitted. "Since we turned over our trading to the barbarians a couple of hundred years ago, we just haven't had much focus on the rest of the world."

Which might just explain why they hadn't won a war for about that long. With no martial tradition of their own and too little wealth to hire the best mercenaries, it only made sense that the Otranto regime was on its way out. The miracle was that it had survived as long as it had.

Jake had his computer implant do a quick search for any small but valuable commodities he'd either traded on his two stints as a space merchant, or read about in any of his history classes. Spices, fabrics, jewels, ultra-pure high temperature superconductors, and art works popped up.

A very small lightbulb went off in his head. "Besides praying, what do all those priests and monks do?"

Manny shrugged and Marie fluttered her hands. The church kept its mysteries even from the Otranto nobility.

To Jake's surprise, Mark broke the silence.

"They teach young students, copy and study the ancient philosophical and religious texts, and wander around the city deciding who just might be a witch."

"What about the wine that the Patriarch served us. Are the grapes grown on church land? Do they have wineries?"

Mark shrugged but this was a question that Manny could answer. "Just south of here is an island completely dedicated to monks from around the world. Each monastery has its own specialty. One of them makes wine. Others make honey, paper, or cheese."

"Those sound like tradable goods," Jake observed. Although a part of him rebelled at supporting the religiously socialistic monastery economy, he was in no a position to be fussy."

"If we could get some," Wart observed. "We didn't see any quantities of those products in the city's shops."

They were probably being traded by the barbarians, Jake realized. "All right, I'll talk to the Patriarch about that. What else?"

"People from around the world want to come here to study," Mark mentioned. "Couldn't you sell the passage?"

High-value cargo paid a lot better per square meter of space, but Jake wasn't about to say no. On the other hand, right now he was looking for exports he could ship to Umbar and he didn't think many of the Otranto City natives would have much interest in that journey. Compared to Otranto City, Umbar was an unimpressive backwater.

"What about books?" He asked. With paper and the closest thing to a global university, Otranto had to make books.

Mark shook his head. "It takes months to copy a book. Who would bother shipping such a treasure to the unlettered?"

"Surely you haven't lost printing technology? You know, movable type." Jake could see how the galactic collapse would make it impossible to preserve the highly complex technologies that few of the frontier planets had ever manufactured at home but the printing press was so basic an invention that it should have been no more lost than writing itself.

"Printing?" Mark looked baffled.

"With presses," Manny said. "Etching plates and making dozens of copies from a single impression."

Jake had been thinking even larger volumes, but Manny's explanation proved that at least the idea of the technology remained.

Mark shook his head firmly. "Who would read so many books? Even if the scribe's guild would allow it."

Jake took two quick notes. Increase literacy and find out what these guilds were about. Between his run-in with Arnie the teamster and what he was hearing now, the guilds seemed to be major foes of progress. He wondered if they might even be behind Manny's recent troubles with the church. Or could that have been the Granger ambassador?

"We could sell a few books to the Shara, maybe," Bart admitted. "Not many, though. They don't speak Otranto."

"The barbarians do, though," Mark commented. "Although their accents are so bad that they're hard to understand sometimes."

"I thought they spoke Anglic," Jake said.

Mark nodded. "The ones who still live in the north speak whatever barbarian languages they started out with. The ones who settled in Otranto lands have picked up the Otranto language as well. After half a thousand years or so, they've mostly forgotten whatever language they started out with."

After what he'd seen of Pierre, Jake wasn't sure that he'd be trading with the barbarians any time soon. They didn't seem to welcome any competition on their trading routes. Of course, one solution was to set up Otranto as a depot, the handoff point between the barbarians in the east and the Tiflis trade route to the west. With a strong manufacturing economy and the tourist economy that Mark had mentioned, he might just have something here.

"How much money can you raise?" he asked Manny.

"Enough to get my brewery back together," the man growled. "So much is destroyed."

"Okay, well we're going to need more capital, but I think we can pull this out."

Marie walked around behind him and put her hands on Jake's shoulders. "Does this mean you're going to save Otranto, or just that you're going to try and make yourself rich?"

"*I'm* not going to do anything. Together, *we're* going to do it. We're going to transform this rotten shadow of a city back to greatness. We're going to make it rich, the envy of the world. People will come from thousands of kilometers to see its wonders, study in its schools, and buy its products."

"And then the Granger will come and conquer it and spoil everything," Harold said.

Jake smiled ruefully. "Now that, I'm still working on."

* * * *

Forming a limited liability company in Otranto involved stretching the law, but it wasn't especially difficult. First, they bought a slave, gave him the legal ownership of the ship and Manny's brewery. Then they freed him. Since the law allowed multiple owners of a single slave and limited the liability of slave owners to the value of that slave, and since the law insisted that all property revert to the owners when a slave was freed, they had the legal equivalent of a corporation and had even managed a good deed out of it in the form of a freed slave and got a loyal employee.

As Manny had guessed, he'd had to call in favors to raise the money to rebuild the portions of the brewery that had been wrecked. John had laughed when Jake had suggested that the church owed him recompense for the false arrest. "Manny'll get his reward in the hereafter," was John's only comment once he'd gotten his laughter under partial control.

Although the Patriarch hadn't helped with Manny's brewery, he did allowed a small trickle of monastery goods to flow into Jake's warehouses.

Five days after they'd freed Manny and Marie, Bart and Wart, accompanied by two of Manny's brewing masters and a few of the pirate sailors sailed the Castile out toward Umbar carrying a cargo of old statues, honey, wine, and a few beautiful and ancient paintings that some of the more impoverished aristocrats offered when Marie put out the call. The ship's hold was only half full, but they needed income fast.

Once the ship had sailed, Jake and Manny sat down at Manny's reconstructed bar and put together an income statement for their combined venture.

It didn't look good.

"How can we be losing money?" Manny demanded. "I was making money from my brewery before you came. How can adding a merchant ship cost us money?"

His logic was impeccable. So was the logic of the income statement.

"We've got to sell product here too," Jake said. "Otranto can't just be a supplier. We've got to be a consumer. Otherwise, we'll just suck in gold and raise prices."

"What's so bad about having some gold?" Manny demanded. "We'll need it to pay the mercenaries."

That was the crux of the matter. So far, Jake's business was doing a lot for the Otranto economy. He'd hired longshoremen to load and unload his ship, warehousemen to store and guard the goods that Wart continued to scour Otranto for while Bart sailed the latest cargo to Umber, and priests to increase their honey and wine production. In return, he'd end up with the precious goods of the Tiflis and Shara, and nowhere to sell them.

"We need trade with the barbarians too," Jake said. "I think I'm going to let Pierre go. Maybe he'll help." Jake announced.

Manny glared at him as if he'd lost his senses. "If you let him go, he'll stab you in the back. Besides, you stole his ship."

Jake shook his head firmly. He might be making a big mistake but Otranto couldn't go this alone. With one ship, a dying town, and access to a caravan route that the Granger intended to cut, Jake needed allies, or at least acceptance from the dominant sailing powers of Arcadia.

* * * *

Lucer had lodged Pierre and his officers with a mercenary company he'd worked with half a generation before. Unlike the corrupt guards who watched over Otranto City's prisons and would set just about anyone free for the right price, Lucer trusted his fellow mercenaries--at least to be loyal to one of their own.

Jake and Lucer walked out to the guard tower where the mercenary company was stationed. When they arrived, half the company, Pierre, and Armand were crouched in a circle playing the dice game that Bart had taught the guards. Mental note--could Jake make Otranto City a gambling haven? More than one planet survived by opening its doors to this apparently universal human desire.

Pierre looked up from his dice, saw who had arrived, then pointedly ignored them, rolling the dice and collecting the pot.

Jake and Lucer waited for a break in the action, a break that finally came when one of the mercenaries stood, spat, and handed over a heavy silver belt to the merchant captain.

Pierre slung the belt over his shoulder where it looked dangerously like a weapon and turned to Jake. "Well, have you come to gloat? I, the greatest trader in Anglic history, am reduced to scrabbling in the dirt for pennies."

"Pennies?" the losing mercenary shouted. "That belt was presented by the Emperor himself after our great victory at Manzikert."

"It must have been a great victory indeed," Pierre sneered. "Which is doubtless why Otranto is so firmly in command of that city."

"We've come to discuss what to do with you," Jake explained quickly. "I doubt that these mercenaries are any happier hosting you than you are being their prisoner."

"Free my men, release my ship, and pay me damages for the men you have killed and I will consider forgiving you," Pierre said.

"I had forgotten what a jester you can be, Captain," Jake told him. "Your ship is gone, lost to you because of your pirating. The men you lost, you lost because of your greed. But if you are done with your humor, I wish to discuss your return to Anglica."

"If you expect my people to pay ransom for a captain who has lost cargo, men, and ship, you understand too little of my people."

That was part of the problem Jake wanted to resolve. Centuries of distrust between the Granger and their eastern neighbors had led to a complete lack of understanding in both directions. The barbarians thought of the Otranto as perpetually perfidious, willing to bargain with the enemy and too degenerate to stand and fight. The Otranto thought of their neighbors as primitive barbarians, even though the sailing vessel that Jake had captured showed a relatively sophisticated technology.

"You seem to me to be an intelligent man, Captain," Jake observed. "I hope that you'll listen to a business proposition."

"Perhaps." Pierre glared at him, his dark eyes untrusting. "If it is something that I could honorably consider."

"If you give me your parole, I'd like to walk with you around Otranto City and discuss possible trade between your country and ours."

Pierre must have thought Jake was going insane. "Trade? Everyone knows that Otranto makes nothing. It consumes, rather than producing."

Jake nodded calmly. "That may have been true once, when the Otranto Empire spanned the continent and when taxes from the provinces poured in. Those days have been gone for centuries."

Pierre shrugged. "You see how busy I am. Still, I would be happy to see the fabulous city of Otranto."

He was trying to sound sarcastic, but he didn't quite pull it off. Both he and Jake knew that Otranto City was still the greatest city in the world. Still a center of culture and of the faith. Still defended by some of the strongest walls in the world—walls that any barbarian would want to see first-hand. If for no other reason, on the off-chance that some day, he could lead an army to sack the fabled wealth of the city at the center of the world.

"Your parole," Jake reminded him.

"Even if I gave it to you, why should I honor it? You escaped from me."

"We never promised not to attempt escape," Jake reminded him. "And the reason I will accept your promise, captain, is the reason I am meeting with you. I think you are an honorable man."

Pierre didn't seem especially gratified by Jake's praise but he nodded sullenly. "I will not attempt to escape during our walk together."

"Or when we are standing still," Jake added. He didn't want to get caught up in technicalities.

Pierre sighed. "I won't try to escape at all today."

"Fine. Let's go."

* * * *

Touring the city with the eastern sailor let Jake see it in a new way himself. When he'd first arrived, he'd viewed it as a primitive burg on a backward planet. Compared to the world-city of Wayward, Otranto was insignificant. Since then, Jake had been too busy to truly reconsider his early impressions.

"A thousand men could guard this city against huge armies," Pierre announced as they clambered over the walls that protected the city. The land walls that sheltered the narrow isthmus rose at least twenty meters high while huge towers jutted out from the walls giving cannoneers enfilade shots at anyone rash enough to attack.

"The cannon, though, are laughable. They must be a hundred years old," Pierre commented. "If you were forced to fire them, they'd probably kill as many of mercenaries as enemies."

"And you can give us a good deal on cannons?" Jake asked. He had learned the secret of the Anglic ship. Pierre had traded in weapons of war--cannons and muskets--to the Granger in exchange for gold looted from the subject races. Pierre had helped arm the armies that would soon be beating on Otranto's walls.

Pierre laughed. "Perhaps I was transparent. Still, I meant what I said. The walls themselves are magnificent. The cannons," he made a dismissive gesture. "When the Granger attack, they will bring up modern huge cannons and knock down your walls. Even with the elevation from the towers, the Granger will have the range on you. Otranto will fall."

Jake looked at Lucer who nodded slowly. "The Emperor Julian had meant to improve the city's defenses, but he died before he could do more than repair the walls. Fernis does nothing."

Pierre crossed himself and stepped hastily past each of the multitude of churches that filled Otranto.

"Schismatic churches," he answered Jake's questioning gaze. "Otranto has stepped away from the true faith. Some say this is worse than even the infidel Granger who, at least, do not pretend to follow the truth."

Jake was happy he'd decided not to bring John on this outing. He was certain that John would have argued that the eastern barbarians had fallen from the one correct path rather than Otranto. He didn't need more arguments then.

Pierre was impressed by the scale of Manny's brewery and by the sample of Manny's beer that Jake had bought back from a tavern. He was, however, concerned about the possibility of making money carrying goods with such high weight and volume. Castile's mead met with even more interest although he envisioned relatively low quantities.

The Patriarch's wine, on the other hand, was a complete hit. Unlike beer, the barbarian princes understood the need to pay for fine wine and a strong commerce in wine already flowed between the southern, wine-producing regions and the more northerly areas where wine grapes did not grow well. The Patriarch's wine would fit into this trade instantly, taking the high end of the market from the Bourgundians.

"Price it high and make it sound like you're a real aristocrat if you drink it," Jake suggested. "Rich merchants will line up for a chance to get something they think is exclusive."

Pierre gave him a look that told him to go beyond Marketing 101. The man was a trader, after all. He knew how to merchandise his material to flatter the egos of the buyers.

"I can't sell books," he admitted when Jake and Mark took him through one of the Patriarch's libraries. "Everyone knows that the Otranto branch of the church has modified the holy word."

"What about non-religious books. Philosophy and mathematics and literature," Jake suggested.

Pierre looked at him as if he'd suddenly started speaking a foreign language. "Why would anyone buy books about that?"

Okay, the concept of books for enjoyment or personal growth had been lost in the east. They'd have to set up the schools first, then sell the books later.

In contrast, Pierre saw a huge market opportunity for the gold leaf-embossed paintings that Otranto had contributed to the artistic life of Arcadia. "Some churches go for the newfangled realistic school but there are still a lot who want the traditional look. Nobody does it better than Otranto. 'Course there are plenty of Otranto painters in the East too."

It was early to start haggling but Jake took it as a positive sign. If Pierre wasn't interested, or intended to return to piracy, he probably wouldn't bother trying to talk down the prices. He'd just take what he wanted.

"What about passengers?" Jake asked.

Pierre looked at the pair of churches they were passing, one on either side of the street. "Why would anyone want to come to Otranto? It's the grimmest city in the world and that's not even considering the Granger's about to attack it."

Given time, Jake thought he could change that. Hundreds of years earlier, Otranto City had been famous for its chariot races. In fact, they'd even been mentioned in Arena of Arcadia. With professional gambling casinos, museums, a University, and an active music life, Jake could see Otranto City becoming the next New Vegas, a destination city throughout the world.

The problem was, all of his ideas would take time and time was the one thing that Otranto did not have.

Mark noticed that Jake had hit a dry well and tried to take up the slack. "Otranto silken goods are famous throughout the world. In fact, silk is Otranto's major export to the spacers. Why don't we visit the silk works?"

The silk works would have been more interesting if the John Gault hadn't so recently picked through the best commodities they had to offer. Although the silk merchants could show a fairly wide variety of silk shirts and draperies, Jake could tell that Pierre wasn't getting excited.

"We get our silk goods directly from the Shara."

"They don't have to flow through Otranto?" Jake knew he was putting his foot in his mouth, but he needed to know the answer.

"Why would we bring them to Otranto? You'd just tax us. We collect them either from the Granger or in Tantalus across the gulf. They charge less."

Jake's computer implant contained a low definition map of Arcadia and he was able to follow Pierre's words but he felt as if the already heavy responsibilities on his back had just doubled. Tantalus was only a few kilometers away.

"Why would Tantalus charge less? Aren't they part of the Otranto empire?"

Pierre laughed. "Not hardly. The Bourgundians kept it after the Otranto recaptured their city."

Ancient history. So the barbarians had once occupied Otranto City itself? Another reason why the Otranto Empire continued as a shadow of itself.

"How well do the Anglicans get along with the Bourgundians?" Jake asked.

Pierre laughed. "As well as anyone gets along. Exactly as long as both sides can see the advantages."

They spent the rest of the day wandering through Otranto. Increasingly, Jake felt that he had taken on an impossible task. Still, there had to be some way to turn this thing around, other than by systematically looting Otranto of its ancient art works and cultural heritage, which was pretty much all that it had offered the world over the past couple of centuries.

The mercenaries actually looked glad to see Pierre when Jake, Lucer, and Mark returned him late that evening. They had gotten into a dispute over the dice game and Pierre was the acknowledged authority. No wonder he had managed to win, Jake thought.

"Well," Pierre demanded. "Was that just a walk in the park, or are we going to do business?"

"We're going to drop the piracy charges against you," Jake said. "In return, you'll drop any claims on your former ship or for restitution for the seamen you lost."

"Bull," Pierre said. "You know I can't do that."

"And also in return, we'll give you a fifty percent reduction on tariffs for the next six months."

"Import and export?"

Jake nodded. He'd talk to the patriarch and work out the legal details later. Not that anyone should object. Half of anything is better than all of nothing, which was exactly what they'd been getting lately from the barbarian traders.

"Six months isn't long enough," Pierre said. "It'll take time to seed the markets and to raise the capital to outfit a trading fleet. I need five years."

"Nine months."

They settled on two years, which was what Jake had planned on. Of course, that assumed that Otranto still existed as an independent country in two years.

"Now how are you going to get us back to Anglica?" Pierre asked. "I know Otranto doesn't have another ship."

"Walk?" Jake suggested.

Pierre spat into the fire and watched it boil. "My men are sailors, not dirt grubbers. You saw what happened to us when we tried to chase down that mythical treasure. We wouldn't last a week against the bandits out there."

"Could you build a ship?"

"If we had a year. I thought you'd want to move a little faster."

A year would definitely be too slow.

The beginnings of an idea popped into his mind. "So, how many ships would you guess they have in Tantalus right now?"

Chapter 19

"Technically we're at war with the Bourgundians," John explained. They were standing in on the highest tower on the Otranto City walls. "We have been ever since they led the supposed crusade that took over the Empire for most of a century."

Using a crude telescope John had found somewhere in the Patriarch's archives, Jake could barely see the Bourgundian occupied town of Tantalus. He offered the telescope to John who shook his head and stepped further back from the edge. His face looked a little pale.

Jake took another step closer to the edge and twisted the focus. Could he really see ships' masts or was that his imagination providing details?

"You say we're *technically* at war," he said. "But?"

"But since we drove them out of Otranto City, we've left them alone and they've left us alone. With the Granger threatening, rekindling a war that petered out two hundred years ago hardly sounds like a brilliant strategy."

Not to mention that Otranto's army was a polyglot of underpaid mercenary units or that Jake had no more right to command them than the Bourgundians did.

"And we'd probably lose," John added.

"Yes, that's a good reason to let sleeping wars lie."

Jake stared through the telescope again again. "Do you think they're as interested in forgetting about that war as we are?"

"They haven't attacked us lately, at least." John shrugged. "It's funny if you think about it. Tantalus is only fifteen kilometers away and yet I've never been there. I don't know anyone from Otranto who has. They're our nearest neighbors and yet they might as well be on the other side of the world."

"I guess we'll just have to check it out."

John shook his head violently. "Oh, no. The Patriarch asked me to help you with your accounting, that's all."

"I wonder how long it has been since a Patriarchal Legate has actually visited Tantalus?"

"I'm a clerk, not a Legate. Besides, I said I wasn't going to do it."

"I'll have Mark round up some of the young priests from the University to go with us. I think a legate needs a procession."

John was shaking his head so hard, Jake thought he would go dizzy if he didn't stop. "We're at war with them. They'll kill us."

"You're probably right. The way I look at it, either they'll kill us or they won't. If they kill us, even Fernis will have no choice but to mobilize his army and attack Tantalus. If they let us in, then we have nothing to lose."

"Counting on an incompetent like Fernis to avenge us isn't especially reassuring," John observed. "Besides, that would be a little late, don't you think?"

Jake didn't think the Bourgundians would arbitrarily kill a Patriarchal Legate. They would know Fernis would have to react. Even if they weren't worried about Fernis, they wouldn't want to upset the ethnic Otranto population whom, Jake suspected, still made up the majority of the population as they did in most of what had once been the Otranto Empire. Watching John squirm held a certain guilty pleasure, though.

"The Patriarch will never allow it." John insisted. He took another step away from the edge.

"If you're so sure about that, you won't mind if we just go and see him then."

"See the Patriarch?" John might have protested more but a sudden gust of wind picked up his hat and sent it sailing to the sea fifty meters below them. "You mean we can get down from here." He appeared to balance the two options. "We'll have to hurry," he concluded.

Jake hoped John would be this agreeable once they'd climbed down from the tower. Even if he wasn't, he was going to hold John to it. Otranto needed the barbarian trade. One way or the other, they'd have to deal with Tantalus.

* * * *

The Patriarch seemed overjoyed to see them. He queried John on the business plan, handed a thick stack of books to Mark, and told Jake that one of the monasteries had decided to plant a crop of hops as their income crop.

Since hops had been the one beer ingredient that Manny had been forced to import, this should help reduce costs and free up cargo space. Eventually.

When Jake explained the problem, the Patriarch nodded grimly. "At first, they just used Tantalus as a pilgrimage way-station. At the time, my predecessors argued that the emperors should allow them to continue in peace. Perhaps they were mistaken. Over time, the Bourgundians started to take more and more of the shipping that once used Otranto City's harbors. Now, we scarcely have a single ship call a month while I'm told that Tantalus has several each week." The Patriarch straightened the monk's cassock he wore. "Still, as John has no doubt been telling you, Fernis couldn't capture a sick sheep, let alone a well-defended city.

The patriarch clapped his hands and a young man in ornate clerical garbs appeared.

"Bring me the city plan of Tantalus," the Patriarch commanded.

"But your Grace--"

"Now."

Jake had thought his former captain could put a sting on his commands. Compared to the Patriarch, the captain had been a beginner.

"Of course, your Grace." The young priest scuttled off.

"I told you I'd be stuck with one of the conservative sycophants," the Patriarch observed. "Still, he's young enough that there's some hope of teaching him to think on his own." He paused, then smiled. "It won't be easy though. He's got a lot to unlearn."

"We can't send in the army, because Fernis has let it deteriorate to the point of worthlessness," Jake said. "But we can't just ignore Tantalus, either. Look what's happened over the past two hundred years. I think Otranto City's population has halved."

"It's actually less than a tenth of its peak population," the Patriarch corrected. "That's why I've given even a foreign pagan like you so much freedom. I know we're doomed if we don't act."

Learning what the Patriarch thought of him was a little humbling. Jake tried to make himself grateful for the Patriarch's honesty. Of course, by the Patriarch's standards, he was a foreign pagan.

The young priest hurried back into the room and rolled out a scroll on a low table. "Can I stay, your Grace?"

"What? Your masters aren't satisfied with what you've learned by pawing through my papers?"

"Your Grace."

"Don't *Grace* me. Get out."

The young priest started to back out when the Patriarch held up his hand. "Perhaps I was too hasty. Actually, I think you should stay."

Jake shot the Patriarch a startled look. He appreciated that the Patriarch was willing to take risks but letting a spy into their council might be plain foolhardy.

"The conservatives are fixated with the idea of purifying Otranto to regain our proper place as God's chosen civilization," the Patriarch explained. "I think they will appreciate what you're trying to do here."

Jake's plans had precious little to do with purifying Otranto, but he wasn't one to turn away convenient allies. He gave the young priest what he hoped was a welcoming smile.

"Anichus," the priest said. He held out his hand.

Jake shook it, bringing guffaws from both Mark and John. "He's a priest," Mark said. "You're supposed to kiss his ring."

"Spacers have strange customs," the Patriarch observed. He didn't make any move to insist that Jake kiss Anichus and Jake wasn't going to volunteer. The man didn't look like he'd bathed in a week.

"Now then," the Patriarch said. "Here is Tantalus's city plan from the days when it was an Otranto provincial town and a storm port for when ships couldn't make it to Otranto's harbors. You'll notice that it's built right into the cliffs."

The city plan was drawn with relatively crude but readable contour lines. If Jake was reading the things correctly, Tantalus was practically a mountain itself.

"Originally," the patriarch continued, "Tantalus was one of the fortresses that guarded Otranto City's eastern approaches. Fat lot of good that it did us."

"Looks like a fortress all right," Jake agreed.

"The pilgrim hospital is at the top of this cliff," the Patriarch added. "Don't let the word hospital fool you, though. It's certain to be the Bourgundian stronghold unless they've changed the city completely. I doubt that they would let any of the Otrantos anywhere near it."

"Even as servants or doctors?" Jake asked. "Surely after two centuries, they would relax some of their security concerns."

"You can never relax in the battle against evil," Anichus announced.

"Right," Jake agreed. "But we could help that evil would do a little relaxing."

"In my youth, I spent some time in the barbarian east," the Patriarch said. "They take their military preparedness very seriously."

Jake pointed at the drawing of walls surrounding the city. "How tall are these?"

"Not too tall. Perhaps ten meters. Unless they've built new walls. This plan is at least two hundred years old, after all. Either way, the main city defense is the hospital and the old keep, not the walls. The Bourgundians wouldn't spend a lot of energy trying to protect their Otranto subjects."

"Well, we'll find out what's going on," Jake said. "It's important that we make an impressive entrance. Since we can't do it with an army, I'm planning on doing it with priests. I need you to make John your Legate," Jake added. "One way or the other, we're going to have to live with the Bourgundians after we resolve this issue and I'd like as few lies as possible between us."

"Live with them? We should drive them out of our lands once and for all," Anichus intoned. "They are a blight on the land, an evil in God's sight."

"That's enough," the Patriarch cut him off. "Anichus, you may select three of your friends to accompany yourself and Legate John. John, bring half a dozen or so of your friends. And John?"

"Your Grace?"

"Even if my predecessors were wrong, we can't afford a war against the Bourgundians now. The Granger are breathing down our necks. Starting a war against the east when we're already losing the battle to the west smacks of the type of pride that Our Lord glories in smashing to the ground."

He was talking to John but Jake could see that he and Anichus were the real targets for the Patriarch's words. Yet, what alternative to war did they have if they were going to get the trade routes back under Otranto control?

"But your Grace, what are we supposed to do?" John asked.

"If I knew, I would tell you. Still, although the barbarians are schismatics, cut off from the whole truth, they are still believers. A bit of the word of the lord wouldn't hurt them any."

"I'm supposed to preach to them?" John had looked confused before. Now he looked truly unhappy. "I was the worst in my class in preaching. It's why I became a clerk."

The Patriarch frowned and shook his head. "You became a clerk because I decided you would. Just as I decided Anichus would. Both of you had something to learn. Now it's time for you to learn even more."

* * * *

Two days later, a procession of ten priests, eight soldiers from the militant order of monks that the church used to enforce its rules (provided when Fernis refused to loan them a single soldier), Mark, Harold, and Jake set off for Tantalus.

Fifteen kilometers is a short distance--less than ten miles by the old standards of measure. It shouldn't have taken more than the morning.

Indeed, the first segment of the trip flowed along one of the old stone roads that had once held Otranto together.

Three kilometers from the city wall, they reached the sea. Tantalus was on the other side of the narrow channel. Unless they wanted to take the land route two thousand kilometers around the Erlang sea and through Barbarian, Tiflis, and Granger territory, they needed to cross the narrow isthmus. If he'd thought of this before the Castile had sailed, Jake could have taken the ship. Now, he'd have to make do.

"There was a ferry just down the road last time I came this way," Mark said.

Jake felt like an idiot for not even thinking about how they'd cross. His high technology mindset gave him certain advantages, but it also blinded him to many of the risks everyone on Arcadia had to deal with. "Let's go and find out if it's still here, then," he said.

They continued along the shore of the isthmus until they spotted a decaying dock with a flat, open-decked boat precariously cleated to it.

A gray-haired man and a muscular teenaged boy who looked to be either his son or grandson emerged from a hut near the dock. "Two gold to carry the lot of you across," the man announced. His wiry muscles bunched as he held a long wooden pole that might be part of his ferry trade but also looked to be a capable weapon.

"Two gold?" That was enough to buy ten horses.

"See any other ferries around?" The old man made a pretext of shading his eyes and staring up and down the shoreline. "I don't see anyone else," he finally announced. "So I guess it's a question of taking my offer or going back to Otranto where you came from."

"Or we could cut off your head and take the ferry ourselves," Harold said. He'd insisted on joining the group and drew his sword to prove he was quite prepared to follow up on his threats.

"A fine lot of holy men that would make you," the ferryman answered. "Ferrymen stick together. I wouldn't want to die with a sin like that staining my soul."

Jake hadn't expected ancient mythology here but he recognized the reference to Charon, ferryman to the dead. "Do you get a lot of business here?" he asked.

The old man spat. "Maybe two groups a month. In my father's day, we used to get a lot of barbarian pilgrims coming to study at the University. Not so much, now."

"It must be hard to make a living," Jake observed.

"It would be easier if you'd pay your fare and let us get on with our work."

"If you had a dependable wage, you wouldn't have to charge so much from the few groups who look like they can afford it, right?"

"If I had a gold mine, I wouldn't have to work at all."

"How about this?" Jake offered. "A gold a month, guaranteed for five years. First year paid up front. I'll set the fares and you can keep ten percent of that on top of your salary. How does that sound?"

"It sounds like you've gone crazy. Twelve gold up front?"

"You maintain the ferry and the dock out of that."

"I'll need another two gold for the initial repairs."

"Done."

"And I want twenty percent of the fares. Otherwise it isn't worth my while."

"Fifteen."

"Done."

The old man spat on his hand and held it out.

Jake had been on enough trading trips to recognize the gesture. He spat on his own hand and shook.

"Pay the man, John."

"But--"

"I know the Patriarch gave you money."

"That was to bribe the bar...uh, never mind."

"Pay him."

John reluctantly handed over fourteen gold pieces.

The old man and his son watched with a glee that would have made Jake certain he'd been suckered into a bad contract.

What they didn't know was, if Jake couldn't figure out a way to make money out of Tantalus, he was already in big trouble. And no matter what happened, they'd need reliable and affordable transportation between the two cities.

"After the first year, you'll be paid every month. You may be tempted to run away with the money you have but think about your son. Think about what five years of a gold a month could mean. Think about having your grandsons visiting you in your manor house in Otranto City itself, maybe praying from your own pew at the Great Cathedral. You're on your way to being a man of importance. If you run, you're a criminal with a few gold pieces."

The old man's face screwed up in intense thought. Obviously he had been ready to run. Jake suspected he'd still want to run but that his son would think better of the idea. Fourteen gold was a small fortune, but the old man would likely squander it and the son would never find an offer this good again.

"Let's go, then," Jake said.

"Fare is two gold," the old man said. "Fifteen percent is—"

"Here's your first order. Fare for any trip is two silvers," Jake interrupted. "Pay him, John."

* * * *

Jake insisted on receiving his eighty-five percent of the take immediately and pocketed it. He'd pay back the Patriarch's bribe money eventually. Right now, he needed to start building up a stake and if the Patriarch would help with the capitalization, so much the better.

The ferryman and his son gestured Jake and his group into the ferryboat which, to Jake's surprise, held all of the men and their horses without crowding. Persuading the horses to climb down the sloping ramp to the boat was a bit of a challenge, but the ferryman had obviously done this before.

The ferryman used the long staff he'd initially threatened them with to pole his way out from the shore. The priests settled into the open cabin and started arguing theology, John's more liberal group trying to persuade Anichus's conservatives of something that Jake could only understand well enough to be certain he didn't want to understand more.

He looked around, found another long pole and joined the two ferrymen.

"You're going to lose your shirt on this business," the ferryman told him. "Leroy here is the only one of my boys who's stayed with the ferry. All the others quit when they saw that it was a dead end." His crooked grin showed broken teeth. "Not that I'm offering your money back."

Jake dug the pole into the sandy bottom and pushed, his muscles flexing as he moved the heavy ferry ahead.

"You may be right." He paused, then planted the pole again and pushed again. "But if we're going to turn this city around, we have to start somewhere. I'm starting with you."

"Then you're a fool."

He wasn't the first person to accuse Jake of that. "Probably."

The ferryman muttered to himself but kept up his poling despite the continual tirade.

The trip across the straits took a couple of hours. Jake, Mark, the ferryman and Leroy, the ferryman's son used heavy sweeps for the deepest part of the channel.

It was well past noon when they had finally disembarked and the ferryman squinted back across the water. "Guess I'll stay here and wait for you to return," he said.

"It'll be a couple of days," Jake guessed.

"I've got a house on this side too. Makes no difference to me where I am."

"Perhaps we should eat here," Anichus suggested. "That way we would not have to break bread in the home of our enemy."

John drew himself up and, to Jake's surprise, actually looked like what he imagined a Patriarchal Legate should look like. "The people of Tantalus have been denied the words of truth for too long. We will continue on our journey."

"I'll just wait here," the ferryman announced. "I've heard just about all the truth I can stand."

* * * *

Although the rest of the ride was uneventful, Jake could not shake the feeling that they were being observed. Sudden flights of sea birds and stillness from the frogs reinforced his feeling that someone, or something, was paralleling their path just beyond their eyesight.

In the old days of the Otranto Empire, the high roads had been set well back from the forests allowing the Otranto armies to march without fear of ambush. Centuries of disuse had allowed the jungle to grow back until trees arched over the stone road and vine creepers actually snaked along its crevices. If they had brought the pathetic mercenary armies of Otranto, Jake had to believe that they would be under attack now.

Fortunately, their watcher chose not to attack a band of priests.

His first close-up view of Tantalus was a bit of a disappointment to Jake. He had expected a rich trading town, vibrant with bourgeois wealth and the liberal ideas that so often come to those who spend time living among people of different cultures and lifestyles. Instead, the city consisted of gray stone buildings. Sewage ran in small streams down the center of the streets, its odor strong even before they came into sight of the city itself. The loss of basic sewage technology struck Jake as a good enough reason to label the easterners barbarians. Even though raw sewage lacked the diseases it had carried back on ancient Earth, it was still disgusting.

Dour guards greeted them at the gates, crossbows and halberds on guard and small cannons on the walls swiveled toward them.

"Who approaches Tantalus?" the guard captain demanded.

John nudged Jake. "You can be my herald."

Wonderful. Jake forced himself to ride forward into the point blank range of all those crossbows while the priests held back. The more he tried not to think about what one small twitch of a finger could do, the more he was tempted to flee. Who did he think he was? All of a sudden his great plan to build a trading nation seemed more like vainglorious bragging than a realistic goal.

"Constantin, the great Patriarch of Otranto and all the Otranto people, has seen fit to send his Legate, John, to hear the petitions of the people of Tantalus," Jake announced.

"We're Bourgundians, just in case you haven't noticed," the guard captain told him. "Why would we care what your schismatic Patriarch wants?"

"The great Patriarch believes that all men of the true faith must pull together when the true church is under attack from infidels. But even more importantly, he knows that many who live in Tantalus continue to follow the faith of their fathers."

"Yeah? Well just cool your heels and I'll send for the Baron."

Jake looked at the sun which was now well past the noon hour. "Perhaps your men would like to join us in our midday meal while we wait for your Baron's word."

He waved at John, hoping that the man would understand his signal.

Mark and John whispered for a moment, then dismounted and pulled a pair of tablecloths from a saddlebag and proceeded to lay out a picnic.

"Otranto is justly famous for the quality of its ale and wine," Jake added. "And its beautiful women, of course." Maybe he should have brought Marie on the trip.

"My men have eaten," the captain told him.

"Well, if any are still hungry, they are welcome to join us."

John and Mark encouraged the priests and their guards to dig in. Jake did so as well. From what he could see of Tantalus, he feared that this would be his last decent meal before he made it back to Otranto City.

Jake was gnawing on the rich bread Otranto baked in its hundreds of bakeries and taking a small sip of the purple wine the Patriarch was so proud of when a small door built into the Tantalus gate opened and the guard captain emerged along with a huge man wearing a heavy mail coat.

Jake stepped to his feet and, not knowing what else to do, gave a martial arts bow, his eyes continually on the man's face. This, he guessed, was the Baron the guard captain had mentioned. A Baron had to be the local equivalent of the military governor of the region.

"So Otranto has sent some of its black crows to darken my gates," the Baron observed.

"We hoped you would see it as a mark of respect," Jake answered.

"Overall, I think I'd rather be left alone."

"In this world of trouble, no man, no city, can be an island," Jake answered. "Otranto is in need of allies, but is still strong enough that it can be a useful friend."

The Baron laughed. "Otranto? Strong? You can field five thousand mercenaries. If that. I could hold off the entire Otranto army with just the men I have here. What possible help could you offer to Bourgundia?"

Mark saw Jake's signal and approached with a large silver flagon of wine. "My Lord, will you join us in a cup of welcome."

"I have my own wine."

Jake smiled. "We must have a tasting, then. We'll compare the wines of Otranto to those of Bourgundia. And do you have your own ales as well? Those of Otranto are considered to be the best in the world."

"There is no wine better than those we grow in Bourgundia," the Baron announced flatly.

"Then we must have a bet," Jake announced. "Shall we say ten gold pieces over whose wine is the best."

The baron laughed. "Make it fifty and we have a bet."

Jake hesitated. The Patriarch had pawned half of his treasures to raise that much money. Before he could respond to the Baron's escalation, John stepped in.

"You have yourself a bet, Baron. Tonight?"

"Tonight, by Our Lord," the Baron announced. "The priests and the merchants may dine with me in the keep. Your guards may stay in the barracks with my soldiers. And if you're spies sent to see how strong we are, welcome. We fear nothing Otranto can throw at us."

"You are right that you have little to fear from Otranto," Jake agreed. "But not for the reasons you think. Rather, all of our forces must face our shared enemy: the Granger Khanate. If the strong arm of Otranto fails, do you think the walls of Tantalus can keep them out?"

"If the true faith depends on the strong arm of Otranto," the Baron said barely holding back his laughter, "then it is in worse trouble than I think."

He seized the silver flagon from Mark, held it to his lips, and took a deep draught. "Hmm. Perhaps it will be a contest after all."

He signaled to the guards on the walls and the gates to the city swung open. "Look your fill. Tantalus will never fall to the arms of Otranto."

Jake nodded. Not to the arms of Otranto, for certain. But perhaps to even more persuasive arts.

Chapter 20

John paraded their group into Tantalus.

Behind them, on the walls, guards muttered about the risks of allowing their centuries-old enemies within the gates. Increasingly, however, their path filled with ordinary people dressed as servants or craftsmen. Their dark hair and olive colored skin marked them as ethnic Otranto despite their living in a Bourgundian-occupied city.

"We must go to our church to give thanks for our safe arrival," John announced when they'd all crossed under the city gates. "When should we arrive at the keep for your promised feast and for our little wager?"

Jake knew that the *little wager* constituted every last penny that the Patriarch had sent with John, but the priest was doing a good job playing his role. Jake was torn. Fifty gold would probably clean out the Baron's treasury and might even make him late in paying his soldiers. Still, Tantalus was a busy port city. Jake didn't see how winning the bet for the Patriarch's wine could really damage Tantalus or give Otranto an advantage. Of course losing was almost unthinkable. Loss of that much gold might result in the Patriarch's overthrow.

"Shall we say six hours," the Baron said. "My kitchens must have time to prepare."

"We shall look forward to the evening and to the gamble," John answered.

"Marcel will accompany you to ensure that no one troubles you," the Baron said.

John smiled. "All are welcome in the house of the lord."

Marcel looked startled. Entering a church his people thought of as schismatic could risk his soul. Still, he was a soldier first. He nodded grimly.

"Let us go and give praise," John said.

When they turned away from the Baron and rode toward the high stone church, a whisper went through the crowd that had gathered, a whisper that grew gradually until it became a cheer.

Jake kneed his horse to John's side. "Brilliant strategy to identify with the people."

John gave him a strange look. "I am a philosopher and maybe the Patriarch's Legate, but I am a priest first of all. Of course I will go to the church."

* * * *

Although they had talked to no one but the town guards and the Baron, the church was filled with dark-haired Otrantos, all apparently anxious to see the visitors from the capital--a city less than fifteen kilometers away, yet which must seem as distant to them as if it had been on an entirely different planet.

An aging priest, straightening his cassock as he scurried down the ancient marble aisle, knelt before John and kissed his ring.

John bowed deeply, then hugged his brother priest in a gesture made more touching by the obvious tears in his eyes. Even Anichus seemed moved by the meeting.

"It has been so long," the priest murmured into John's traveling robe. "So long since we have even heard from our mother church."

Two young underpriests nodded in agreement.

Anichus cleared his throat. "Our Patriarch wishes to make Otranto strong again, and the faith of our fathers to stand with pride rather than cower under the fists of the schismatic barbarians or the infidel Granger."

That might accurately represent the feelings of the Patriarch, but those were also fighting words.

The hushed murmur of voices from the Otranto parishioners swelled into a low growl. Here at least, the Otranto natives were not completely spiritless. Of course if they rioted, the Bourgundian guards would slaughter them. Perhaps this was Anichus's plan--without Otranto natives to do the manual labor, Tantalus could become untenable.

As a military strategy, it might be sound. As a practical matter, Jake couldn't stand for it. He was a merchant, not a mass murderer. If Otranto's survival depended on inciting its people into suicidal gestures, he wasn't sure it was worth protecting.

"Since we are so close, why don't you send one of your underpriests to Otranto to study theology at the University," Jake suggested, moving to defuse the tension. "What better way to protect the church than to ensure that its priests are firmly grounded in the true faith?"

The two underpriests whispered between themselves, broad smiles on their faces. To them, Otranto must have seemed a mythical place of magic and faith.

The old priest laughed bitterly. "The Bourgundians do not permit us to leave and, even if we could, the ferry costs more than any of us could afford."

"I have taken steps to reduce the price of the ferry," Jake explained. "Tonight, we will speak to the Baron about his travel policies."

The priest shook his head. "He is a hard-hearted fool. I cannot count the number of times I have told him of his errors and yet he does not listen. Surely he is doomed to the very fires of hell."

With that attitude, Jake wasn't surprised that the Baron hadn't listened. "Perhaps--"

"We will chastise him most sternly," Anichus interrupted before Jake could complete his thought.

John took Anichus's arm and half-dragged him toward the altar. "Come, father," he spoke to the priest. "The Patriarch's clerk and I wish to celebrate our safe return."

Jake watched as the three men vanished behind the screen that separated the parishioners from the altar. John's entourage shuffled their feet then followed, leaving Jake, Mark, and the underpriests as well as the still-murmuring mob of ordinary citizens.

"Tell me more of Tantalus," Jake suggested to the underpriests, "and Mark can tell you about the University in Otranto."

The priests' understanding of economics was dismal. Neither had any idea how many ships called in an average week although both thought that the four ships currently in the harbor was unusually high. The storage warehouses had overflowed onto the streets and dozens of Otranto natives had enriched themselves when guards were distracted.

According to the locals, though, Tantalus, had nothing to offer but a mediocre harbor and Bourgundian guards. If that was the case, Jake's impulse decision to buy the ferry was a frighteningly bad investment. Fourteen gold was enough that the Patriarch would take notice--and lose any faith he had in Jake's abilities.

"Perhaps we could move this discussion outside," Mark suggested. "My eyes are not used to the incense."

"Are you an infidel, then?" the younger priest asked.

Mark laughed. "Not to my way of thinking. I am an Ebron and therefore follow the faith of the one god."

The two priests murmured among themselves and stepped slightly away.

"I had the honor of attending the University at Otranto for a number of years," Mark continued.

The two priests moved back quickly, a flood of questions bursting from their mouths.

"Outside," Mark reminded them.

As they walked down the narrow, dung-ridden streets, Jake listened with half an ear and tried to find any evidence of industry.

The sound of iron ringing on iron turned out to be a Bourgundian weapon-smith. He was happy to show off his wares but, to Jake, they didn't look any better than those he'd seen in Otranto.

In answer to his questions about muskets, the weaponsmith merely shrugged. Those were forged back in Bourgundia proper, not relegated to more distant provinces.

After a few moments of uninspiring conversation, Jake, Mark, and the two underpriests continued their exploration of Tantalus.

"What are those?" Mark asked. They had reached the city walls and stepped through the narrow door at the bottom of the gates.

The priests followed his pointing finger and shrugged. "Trees."

"Indeed. But what kind of trees?"

Neither priest had any idea. Tantalus lived off the sea, not the land.

Jake followed Mark up an overgrown pathway. The remains of an old stone house crumbled in the midst of what had once been a well-ordered orchard.

"Olives," Jake breathed. In a primitive world like Arcadia, oils of any kind were rare and valuable. Olive oil made both an excellent cooking oil and an adequate lamp oil.

Mark poked at the earth underneath the trees and tugged on a few of the branches. Ripe olives glistened black and huge with oil.

"Does this help?" he asked.

Jake nodded. It could help a lot. "Who owns this land?"

Neither priest knew although they guessed that it probably belonged to the Baron since no one had worked the land for at least as long as they had been alive.

"How long do olive trees live?" he whispered to Mark.

"I think a long time. Maybe fifty years," Mark answered.

They continued their journey around Tantalus. Jake was struck by the ruins of airy homes and the small plots of subsistence farming overlaid on what had once been large plantations.

Constant warfare had destroyed not only people and equipment, but the entire way of life that had once made a comfortable lifestyle possible.

"Mulberry trees." Mark said. They'd followed one of the old stone Otranto Empire roads for about two hours, mostly through olive groves. The last of the subsistence plots was now more than an hour behind them.

Unlike many of the stone roads of Otranto, this didn't look like it had been built primarily for marching soldiers. Instead, gouges remained from where heavily loaded wagons had once carried something to the markets in Tantalus. Wagons meant merchandise and where merchandise had once existed, it might exist again.

"Keep away from those," the taller of the young priest warned. "It's covered with bugs."

Jake reached up and harvested the abandoned cocoons left behind by maturing silkworms.

"Why don't we turn around now?" he suggested.

* * * *

Although they hurried, they were nearly late for the Baron's dinner. Jake decided against wearing his spacer garments.

Anichus was in a foul mood and passed this on to Jake and Mark. "I don't know why John even invited you two, let alone allowing you to attend a formal dinner," he grumbled.

"Maybe that's why he's the Legate and you aren't," Jake fired back, then instantly wished he'd kept his mouth shut.

"For now," Anichus returned.

With that grim warning, they ascended from the Baron's guest rooms into the central keep.

Dozens of Bourgundian guards marched around the keep, manned heavy cannons, and stood at attention at various closed doors.

The display interested Jake. Maintaining a strong military force in a region unlikely to be threatened by anyone showed a combination of paranoia and the extreme value Bourgundia received from this Otranto seaport. Clearly Otranto City had a lot to gain if it could reclaim at least some of the shipping. Equally clearly, the odds of Otranto being able to effectively besiege and capture this town were so low as to be insignificant.

The Baron greeted them, asked Jake how he had enjoyed his walk through the wilderness beyond Tantalus, and inquired as to the health of the aging priest. He was, Jake saw, both remarkably well informed and going out of his way to show it.

"Wilderness indeed," he answered the Baron. "I would not be surprised to hear wolves howling tonight."

"There are some who claim that once there were vast farms spreading up the mountain," the Baron continued. A faint gleam in his eyes warned Jake that the man was already bargaining.

Jake laughed shortly. "Who would be foolish enough to farm a mountainside? The soil would run off the first time it rained leaving only rocks."

"Perhaps."

Jake mingled among the fifteen Bourgundians who were attending the dinner. Eight were captains or officers from the four ships in the harbor. The remainder consisted of senior officers from the Bourgundian occupying forces. None were local businessmen.

Better and better.

Dinner, to Jake's surprise and pleasure, consisted of huge slabs of meat served on plate-like rounds of bread. The odd onion was the only vegetable contribution to the meal. Otranto cooking, in contrast, consisted mostly of vegetables with meat served, if at all, in small chunks.

The Baron sat John on his right, one of the ships' captains on his left, and scattered the lower ranking Otrantos among the Bourgundians.

Jake found himself seated between a guard captain and one of the ship's lieutenants.

The guard was happy to talk about his training and, for a few moments he and Jake exchanged a few notes on martial arts training. He promised to teach Jake a couple of sword moves in exchange for Jake's help with some Hapkido pressure points that Jake described to him.

The lieutenant ignored their conversation until Jake mentioned that he had recently visited the Granger Khanate.

He nodded grimly. "So that's why you're here. Believe me, it won't work."

"What?" Jake asked.

"The Baron is not a free man who can offer his troops as mercenaries. You'll have to meet the Granger invasion without our help."

For a moment, Jake regretted all the rich food he'd been eating. His stomach roiled. "Invasion? You make it sound like it is coming soon."

"Indeed. As I am sure you know. The Granger have massed on the border. Why else would they have purchased an entire shipload of cannons?"

So much for any dreams of the time to build up some commercial capacity. "What else have they bought lately?"

The lieutenant shrugged. "Gunpower, of course, although they also make their own. No armor, but that's because they say ours is too heavy for them. This trip, we sold them three hundred muskets."

"So what cargo did you buy from them?"

The lieutenant's face twisted. "That's the strange thing. They paid with gold. We made a fat profit, but we are going home with gold rather than a cargo we can sell."

"Perhaps you should pick up a cargo in Otranto City."

The lieutenant laughed. "Otranto takes. It does not give. While Tantalus may be a poor port, its taxes are affordable."

"That has changed."

"Otranto always says it has changed. After a thousand years, who would believe them?"

Maybe he'd think differently after the wine tasting. Then again, maybe none of this mattered. The Granger were set to invade and all Jake had done about it was to steal a pirate ship and buy a ferry line. For the millionth time, he castigated himself for not being more heroic.

"I have a brother who might be willing to bring his band to Otranto." The guard lieutenant broke the silence that had fallen after the merchant captain's announcement. "When the king made peace with the Anglicans, my brother lost his job."

"If the captain is right, Otranto will be hiring," Jake said. Although what they would pay with was a mystery to him. He had studied enough history to know that well-paid mercenaries can be dangerous enough but unpaid mercenaries were almost always disasters worse than any defeat could be.

A small army of native Otrantos carried out the dramatically diminished platters of beef and other meats that Jake didn't recognize and then carried in wine barrels. Neither was the barrel that John had brought from the Patriarch so they'd obviously been re-casked to make identification more difficult. Jake didn't think anyone would be confused.

"The Legate and I have agreed to a wager," the Baron announced. "Both of us are proud of the great wines of our countrymen. Now we will put them to the test. To decide, each of you will be given two mugs." He reached behind his throne-like chair and pulled up one clinking bag after another until five bulging sacks sat on the table. He untied the leather string that held one shut, removed a single gold coin, flipped it, and watched it land on the table.

"The cask to the right will be shields. The cask to the left, faces."

John took up the story. "Each of you will be lent a coin from these bags. Sample your wine and vote by turning your coin to faces or shields based on your preference. The winner keeps all of these hundred gold pieces."

The wine barrels themselves had elicited smiles and a murmur of conversation. John's announcement of the size of the bet brought a moment of startled silence.

It sounded like a losing proposition to Jake. There were only ten Otrantos and fifteen Bourgundians. Surely they would all recognize the flavor of their native wines and vote for that no matter which they preferred. If he hadn't spent the afternoon wandering through the wilderness outside of Tantalus, maybe he would have been able to arrange a more equitable system.

The servants poured two large clay mugs for each of the guests, slammed them on the table, then vanishing into the woodwork. Somewhat to Jake's surprise, none of the gold coins had vanished with them.

"Otranto and Bourgundia have been at war for two hundred years," the Baron continued as he picked up one of the wine mugs set before him. "The Legate and I have agreed that our conflicts should include more civilized battles such as this."

He drank deeply, set down the mug, and then drank deeply from the second. A mystified look came to his face.

Once the barons had sampled the wine, the remainder of the guests felt free to do the same.

Even though he'd never tasted Bourgundian wine and hadn't tasted this vintage of the Otranto wine, Jake could tell the difference instantly. The Otranto wine was simply more refined. Perhaps the Bourgundians hadn't learned the art of aging their wine to allow the rich flavors to develop and to quell the harshness of a young wine.

All of the Otranto Priests quickly selected the shields sides of their coins. Neither the Legate nor the Baron moved to touch their coins, however, and the remaining Bourgundians looked as confused as their Baron.

Finally, one selected the crown side and a rush of votes took place.

Although all of the guard lieutenants selected crowns, the merchant votes were more mixed. The merchant to Jake's side selected shields.

"Perhaps we will take your suggestion and stop by Otranto," he murmured.

"You won't regret it."

With only Jake, the Baron, and John's votes left to cast, the vote stood at eleven each.

The Baron's face turned red as he turned his coin crown side up.

Jake met John's eyes, trying to send a message. The Patriarch had stripped his city to raise the money to allow even this limited expedition, but the political side of their journey could hardly be facilitated by bankrupting their host.

Jake turned his coin shield-side up, bringing the vote back to a tie. Only John's vote remained.

"As guest, I must vote for my host's selection," John quipped, turning his coin crown-side up.

The Baron breathed a huge sigh of relief, collected the coins, and slid them back into the coin sack.

"Let's have a few more casks of wine, then, shall we," he called.

Suddenly, though, Jake wasn't very thirsty.

* * * *

"Get up." John's voice sounded like it was coming through a thousand kilometers of hangover.

"Huh?"

"We're going to see the Baron. You'd better have a good reason for me to have lost that bet last night. Between your crazy ferry and that bet, all of my money is gone and I've got nothing to show for it. We could have won. The patriarch would have been rich."

Jake nodded. "Let me wash my face."

He splashed cool water over his face and ran a jolt of adrenaline through his system. It didn't help much.

"The Patriarch gave you the money to pay bribes. Who better to bribe than the Baron himself?"

"The Patriarch will be interested in more concrete results."

Jake wasn't so sure. From what he'd seen, the Patriarch could appreciate slyness. "If you'd simply tried to bribe him, he would have been insulted. Instead, you allow him to win a wager. From his perspective, you've done him a favor and taken him off the hook. Did you see the guards' faces?"

"So?"

"I suspect that the money was their pay. If he'd lost, Tantalus would have been in trouble."

"So Otranto could have recaptured it."

That had been Jake's original idea as well so he couldn't object to John sharing it. "First of all, even if we could capture it, we can't afford to garrison it against the Bourgundians. Second, these men aren't mercenaries. I don't think many of them would turn bandit just because they missed a payday."

John shook his head. "Between what he sent with me and what he's invested in your cargo, the Patriarch is broke. When they learn of this, the conservatives will oust him. And thanks to my friend Anichus, they will learn soon enough. I'm going to have to watch him constantly to make sure he doesn't send a message ahead of us."

"Then we'll have to bring the Patriarch something worth his investment. Come on and let's see the Baron."

The sun was barely over the horizon, but the Baron was in the keep's exercise yard bashing a two-handed sword against a large wooden target.

Massive muscles flared across his bare chest as he took the heavy weapon through its paces.

When he saw John, he smashed the blade into the top of the wooden target, then swept up the smaller priest into a fierce embrace, crushing him to his naked torso. "Welcome, my friend. Thank you for joining me."

"We came as quickly as we could."

The Baron led them into a brick-floored room, poured water over his body, then wiped himself with a towel which he then discarded on the floor. "Let's have a mug of wine and then discuss relations between our two cities and nations."

Wine at this hour was about as exciting to Jake as letting the Baron use him for target practice. Talking about their relationship, however, sounded like common sense.

The Baron plopped down on a bench, poured three mugs of wine, then dumped a pitcher of water over a pile of stones to the side of the room. A cloud of steam exploded up.

"No one will bother us here," he concluded.

"Are you authorized to make decisions for the Bourgundian Crown?" Jake asked cautiously.

"Are you authorized to make decisions for the Emperor?" the Baron countered. "I believe that my government will back me up and I'm prepared to believe that yours will do the same. Good enough?"

It would have to be. Jake couldn't believe he had let himself forget Emperor Fernis. He'd have to do something about that once he returned to the city. From what he'd heard of Fernis, the Emperor would need a backbone transplant before he could stand up to a Granger invasion.

"Let's start with the status of Tantalus," John said. "Clearly Otranto cannot accept Bourgundian control over a city so close to our capital."

"Ridiculous," the Baron countered. "Tantalus has been Bourgundian for two hundred years."

"Might I suggest saying that we cannot accept Bourgundian sovereignty," Jake corrected. "Control is different."

The Baron frowned. "Otranto word games. The two mean the same."

"Not at all. Bourgundia controls Tantalus, everyone knows that. Yet if this was a lease, Tantalus would remain within the Otranto Empire, yet allow Bourgundia its important trading port."

"For as long as the lease lasted."

"Shall we say ninety-nine years?" Jake suggested. "Our descendants could decide whether they wanted to renew or not."

The Baron laughed. "So we end the war for a century, at least."

"Assuming that no one else starts it," Jake added. "That no one in the east gets the idea of another crusade against the schismatics."

"I'm afraid our crusading energies are drained," the Baron said. "Yet you said a lease. I am minded that leases generally have payments associated with them."

"There are some old Otranto plantations outside of town," Jake said. "They appear to be unused, untouched for decades. I think these would be fair payment."

"For ninety-nine years rent?" John demanded. "Are you crazy?"

"It is a rent you have no power to demand," the Baron reminded him. "Yet it is a clever thought. You receive something of apparent value, but which we don't use, in exchange for giving us something with apparent value, but which you have no real control over. Both sides are left with their honor intact, yet we can end the war between us."

Jake nodded gravely. Although if his plantations turned out to have no value, he'd eat his worn spacer uniform, flexible semiconductors and all.

"As a part of Otranto territory, we would feel obliged to protect Tantalus from Granger attack," Jake continued.

The Baron's eyes goggled in amazement. He stuttered for a moment, then burst out into loud brays of laughter. "Otranto soldiers defending Bourgundians? Where did you find this jester, Legate?"

"I think my friend is suggesting that we would expect the same from you. That if the Granger were to attack Otranto, we anticipate that you would send soldiers to our defense."

The Baron considered, then shook his head slowly. "Lord knows, I hate the Granger. My Grandfather fought against them half a century ago and they sent home only his head." He picked the towel off the floor, wiped his eyes with it, then tossed it back down. "But you ask what I cannot deliver. My garrison stays to protect Tantalus."

Between the heat and John's increasing frustration, the Legate's face was growing bright red.

The Baron tossed another pitcher of water on the hot rocks and sighed as a new cloud of steam filled the room.

"I would be happy to put out the call for mercenaries, of course. Assuming that Otranto is able to pay for them."

John muttered something about what had just happened to Otranto's gold, but Jake sushed him. "We will make reasonable payments."

"Good."

"Of course we *will* count on the Bourgundians to keep the Granger out of the Tantalus straits."

The Baron started to object, then nodded. "I think that falls within my authority. Once the Granger invasion begins, I'll try to make sure that at least one armed ship is kept here always on the ready."

"I guess that wraps things up," John said. "Oh, the Patriarch sends his regards and he's also sent two embossed copies of the Holy Books. I gave one to the Otranto church. We would be happy if you'd accept the other."

"Otranto Holy Books?" The Baron looked suspicious.

John laughed. "Our paths have diverged, I'll agree, but the Holy Books are the same."

"Really? I guess I don't know that much about the schismatics."

John smiled, the angry red had faded from his face. "Otranto City is close, my lord. Perhaps you would come and visit with us. I know the Patriarch would be happy to share is beliefs with you. He, better than I, could explain the differences."

"Perhaps I will," the Baron said. "Although the ferryman makes it difficult."

"I think you'll find that problem transformed," Jake said.

"Oh, speaking of gifts," the Baron said. "I wonder if you would be interested in four dozen muskets I seized from an Anglican pirate that tried to sail through the Tantalus straits."

Jake nodded quickly. "I know the Patriarch would be overwhelmed." And four dozen muskets would arm Manny's makeshift brewers militia perfectly.

The Baron laughed. "The Faith may have all of the answers, but sometimes the truth comes from a musket, no?"

Chapter 21

"Ninety-nine years?" the Patriarch exploded. "That is as long as forever."

Jake hadn't expected to be promoted to instant sainthood. He had anticipated that the Patriarch would agree that he'd made the best bargain available to him and to Otranto.

"You don't understand," he started.

"No, *you* don't understand. We don't have enough money to bribe the Granger and the Bourgundians are draining us dry with their anchorage in Tantalus."

"One of their ships should call on Otranto this week," Jake said. "They're looking to buy wine."

"Wine to Bourgundia, now that is a switch," the Patriarch almost smiled but not quite. "One ship isn't going to do the job."

"We should be able to sell them some of Manny's ale and maybe some books and art too."

"Bah." The Patriarch waved his hand. "We're selling our precious heritage when we should be getting rich from cargo fees."

In the greater galaxy, mass manufacturing had been almost completely eliminated by the widespread use of molecular assemblers in every home. As a result, it had taken Jake a long time to see how critical large-scale manufacturing would be to Otranto's survival. He could see it now, though, and he hoped it wouldn't be too late. Otranto would become a hub for transshipment only when it also became a producer. Of course, a city used to bureaucracy and theocracy hardly seemed the most likely home to a new industrial revolution, but Jake had to try.

Jake reached into his pouch. "Also, what do you think of this?" He handed over the towel he'd taken from the Baron's sauna.

The Patriarch stroked the fine material. "Nice. It's cotton, right?"

Before he'd seen the Baron's towel, the only fabrics Jake had seen on Arcadia had been wool, silk, and a truly rough form of linen. "So, do we have any?"

"It doesn't grow here. All cotton comes from Aethier. The Ebron captured it from us five hundred years ago. And the Granger from them three hundred years ago."

"Maybe we should send a ship there."

"You didn't do well last time you tried to trade with the Granger."

"Mark seems to think that, given the right incentives, the Ebron in Aethier might be ready to revolt."

"Are the Ebron any better than the Granger?" the Patriarch demanded. "Both walk far from the true faith."

"The Ebron might not be more open to the faith, but they would be more open to trade."

The Patriarch actually managed a small smile. "Other than far-off Shara, Otranto is the center of the world's silk production. Add cotton and we become a commerce strength indeed."

Jake nodded and then reached back into his pouch. "Speaking of silk, one of the plantations we received as rent for our lease of Tantalus is covered with mulberry trees. I brought these home." He handed over the cocoons he'd stripped from those trees.

"Silk," breathed the Patriarch. "It is hard to find soil that will support the mulberry."

Jake grinned. "The other was a huge olive plantation. The trees are loaded now. We'll harvest those, bring them here for pressing, and our ferry business should really start to take off."

The Patriarch's smile was very real this time. "*Our* ferry business? It was my money that paid for it."

"If you aren't interested in a partnership, I'll pay you back for your investment and own it outright. Of course we'll need somebody to harvest the olives and to tend to the mulberry trees."

The Patriarch shrugged. "I'm not made out of monks, you know. I've already called up all of the favors I could when I raised the gold for your Tantalus mission and gathered the goods for your ship."

"I wasn't thinking of monks for this. Just some peasants."

The Patriarch rolled his eyes. "I'm not made of peasants either. Besides, it isn't that easy. How many members of the olive guild are free and available? How many members of the silk producers?"

Jake didn't like the sound of this. "The plantations are near Tantalus. Don't forget, we just signed an agreement to lease that land to Bourgundia for the next ninety-nine years. We shouldn't have to worry about Otranto's ridiculous rules."

"Whether you find them ridiculous or not, they are the law. Do you expect to unload the olives and silk in the harbor? Do you expect Otranto silk looms to weave your silk? Otranto machines to press your oil? You'd better give some thought to the guilds."

Jake sighed. "I'll handle the guilds. First, I've got to get the workers."

"Good luck," the Patriarch observed.

* * * *

Finding Otranto farmers should have been easy. For decades, the Granger had encroached on Otranto lands, sending thousands of refugees fleeing to the capital. Yet the huge city had its own attractions. Its decline in population over the centuries had left thousands of houses unoccupied and ripe for squatters. The trickle of food that the Patriarch and Emperor allowed the urban masses to prevent rioting was often better than they had known when they had supported themselves through subsistence farming. Once again, Jake needed capital and he'd already gone to the well when it came to the Patriarch.

A blaring trumpet blast nearly deafened him as he, Mark, and John left the Patriarch's palace and stepped into the broad square between the palace and the cathedral.

Dozens of soldiers marched through the crowd which, already sparse, thinned to almost nothing.

Behind the soldiers, a score of beautiful women walked, scattering flowers in their wake. Behind them, an ivory and gold-leaf litter, diaphanous silk curtains partially concealing the shape of an obese man behind them.

John sank to the ground in a low recline and, after a moment, Mark followed, tugging on Jake's arm as he did.

"Get down, idiot."

"Who is it?"

"The Emperor."

Two soldiers headed Jake's way, apparently not happy with the speed with which he went into his recline.

"Respect your emperor," the first soldier shouted while the second kicked Jake in the ribs.

"Keep your mouth shut," Mark hissed, apparently reading Jake's mind.

The whisper earned Mark a kick as well, but the Emperor's litter continued and the soldiers had to hurry to catch it as the Emperor was lifted into the great Cathedral.

"Did you see that litter?" Jake demanded. "I could retire on what that would bring from any museum in the civilized worlds."

"Somehow I don't think the emperor is going to give it to you," Mark said. "He doesn't seem to like you much."

"I think it's time to introduce Emperor Fernis to the joys of the joint stock corporation."

John shuddered. "If Fernis loses money, you're likely to lose your head."

That wasn't too different from the rules of the Commodity Police back on the so-called civilized worlds so Jake wasn't completely surprised.

"You're the accountant, aren't you? We'll just have to make sure we don't lose any money."

John shook his head firmly. "I'm a priest. I don't lie."

"So let the numbers lie and keep your mouth shut. Now how do we get in to see him?"

That, it turned out, was easier said than done. The Empire's bureaucracy was matched to the empire's once great power rather than its current limited status. As a result, Jake would have to go through dozens of political hacks, bureaucratic clerks, and current cronies before he would have a chance to meet with the Emperor himself. Worse, each of the hacks, clerks, and cronies expected a bribe. More capital that Jake simply didn't have.

"Are you sure we need the Emperor's money?" Mark demanded. They were sitting in a bar situated a couple of blocks from the cathedral drinking the first of the new batches from Manny's brewery.

"The Patriarch was right," Jake said. "It isn't just the capital. We're talking about a different way of doing things. Every time we try something new, we're going to run into the guilds and the taxmen. We need political cover. From what I've seen of Otranto, the cover doesn't get much higher than the Emperor himself."

"Fernis covers his own ass and that's about it," John observed. "Besides, you'd be asking him to rock the boat. He has everything he needs now."

"He might, but only for as long as the Granger keep their distance. From what we've been hearing, that won't last much longer. If the invasion hasn't already started."

"Well," Mark concluded, "drink up. We can't get in to see him anyway."

They made their way back toward Manny's brewery, walking through neighborhoods that had been deserted for decades, through open fields that had once been sites for huge estates and for sprawling villas, but which now served only as grazing lots for cows and goats.

"How much agriculture goes on within the city walls?" Jake asked.

"Not much," John answered.

"So, how do the people get fed?" Jake had seen the shipping that came into Otranto's beautiful harbors. There wasn't even much of a fishing fleet. And the fields that surrounded the city petered out into open forests within ten kilometers of the city limits.

John shrugged. "There is always food."

Jake wasn't so sure.

Manny's home and brewery were a hotbed of activity in the otherwise dying and rotting town. Jake intended for Manny's industry to serve as an incubator and as an example to the rest of the city. Yet, the city had its own strengths, its own way of dragging everyone down to ruin with itself.

Manny rolled a glistening barrel off the delivery wagon. It was larger than any of the ones he'd used before, representing a huge investment in the future.

"You made it back with your head still on your shoulders," he shouted when Jake turned the corner. "I would have bet that the Patriarch would throw you in his dungeons for selling Tantalus to our enemies."

Jake waved off Manny's concern. "The Patriarch can be reasoned with."

"Unlike some others," Manny observed.

An idea crossed Jake's mind. "Who grows the barley for your beer?"

"Farmers, somewhere."

"Just any farmers?"

"Well, sure. Barley is easy to grow. Malting it is only a little complicated."

"So could you get some of the farmers to work for us?"

Manny paled. "The grain guild would kill me."

"I thought you said they were just farmers."

"The people who *grow* the barley, yes. But they can't just sell it. All grains are *sold* through the grain guild. The guild is responsible for ensuring that all of the grain is top quality, and for maintaining prices that are fair to both farmers and customers."

"Does it work?"

Manny laughed shortly. "The farmers get almost nothing and the customers pay through their noses. As far as the guilds are concerned, that's wonderfully fair and it works great."

"Why not buy directly from the farmers?"

Manny rubbed his neck. "Because I value my head."

"We've got to get around them, then," Jake declared. "There's money on the table, just sitting there waiting for us to pick it up. I'm not going to let archaic and destructive rules get in our way."

"They may be old, but they're how Otranto has always done business."

"The way Otranto has always done things has cost us the empire. We've got to start doing things because they make sense, not because we always have."

"Well, good luck, then. But the guilds are almost as old as Otranto itself. Anything that old has to be strong. And they'd rather see the Granger in charge than lose one gram of their power."

"You overcame the brewers' guild."

"I *became* the brewers' guild," Manny reminded him. "And even so, I would have lost my life if you hadn't gone to the Patriarch. The only way around the guilds would be through the Emperor himself. And we all know what the odds of getting Fernis to do anything are."

Jake gritted his teeth. "Help me get in to see him."

Manny took a deep pull from a beer stein. "I could have gotten you to see Julian. Fernis would as soon kill me as listen to me."

"But--"

"But you're talking to the wrong side of the family," Manny interrupted. "Marie may have married a barbarian outsider who actually works with his hands, but she's still a princess. If anyone can get you to the other side of the pearl walls, it's her."

* * * *

"This is going to cost us," Marie announced. She had listened to Jake's needs, vanished with Castile for two days, and finally returned with three strikingly beautiful princesses.

"What is?"

Castile pulled on the sides of her mouth and stuck out her tongue. "It's completely stupid."

Jake trusted Castile's judgment as much as he would trust any sixteen year old's. On the other hand, Marie knew her way around Otranto's elite in a way that neither he nor even Castile could even begin to understand.

"Why don't you tell me what's stupid and maybe I can help make it smarter."

"Oh, yeah. Like you're some genius."

Well, that let him know where he stood with Castile. Good thing she was too young for him.

"You know what the Emperor does, don't you?" one of the women with Marie asked. She completely ignored Castile's outbreak.

"He's the ruler, right. Makes laws, commands the army, that kind of stuff."

"I suppose it might seem that way to an outsider. In fact, he's caught up in a labyrinth of ritual much of which goes back to the early days of the Empire, even before the true faith was revealed to us."

Jake made a mental note to learn more about Arcadia's different religions. They seemed to matter a lot.

"Okay. But I don't see where this is going."

"One of the reasons he is so hard to get to is that his cronies intentionally isolate him. By controlling access, they gain power."

"I understand that." That bureaucratic tendency was a constant across the galaxy.

"But the more important reason is that every hour of every day has its own rituals. Things that only the emperor can do. Things that he has to do to keep the world on its tracks. He literally has no time of his own."

Jake thought he saw where this was going. "So the best way to see him is to become a part of whatever ritual he needs to be involved in."

The woman beamed at him. "Exactly. Marie told me that you were smarter than you looked."

As compliments went, Jake could have done without that one. "So what ritual do I get included in?"

"*You* don't," the woman explained. "There is no ritual that for heathen spacer barbarians. You cannot contact him."

"So you can?" he asked Marie. He could brief her and she would be an effective ambassador.

"Not me. Castile."

Castile stuck out her tongue at him again. "This is a very bad idea."

There was no point in hiding his mystification and Jake didn't bother trying. "I have no idea what you're talking about."

"Surely even spacers have some sort of adulthood rituals," Marie suggested. "One of the Emperor's responsibilities is the welcoming of the imperial family into their coming of age."

Probably the closest Jake had experienced had been his college graduation. The ceremony had consisted of registering his retinal pattern in the University's database, but it had been something. "You're saying Castile is an adult?"

Castile met his gaze, glaring into his eyes, then stomped his foot. He was impressed. Most people would have given him at least a fraction of a second warning by shifting their eyes before striking. Castile hadn't.

"Ow."

"Oh, grow up. It didn't hurt that much." Castile hazarded a kick at his shin but this time he was ready. "Besides," she continued as if she hadn't just assaulted him, "Fernis is gross. All the girls say he paws at them. And he stinks."

"We all have to go through with it," Marie remarked unsympathetically. "You should have gone through it years ago, but I put it off to humor you." She turned her attention to Jake. "Unfortunately, what was once a sacred ritual has become a bit of a stock show. The emperor and his ministers use Otranto Princesses as rewards for whatever barbarians they can't afford to pay off with gold."

The idea of shipping Castile off to some illiterate and unappreciative boor bothered Jake more than it should have. "If she doesn't want to--"

"We all have to make sacrifices for our country," Marie stated pragmatically. "Did you think I *chose* Manny? I was just his reward. Yet he turned out to be a good catch."

"Better than I got," the youngest of the visiting princesses said. "If you marry someone in the court, it's almost impossible to get out of the Pearl Walls. And nothing ever happens there."

"Except once in a while, they murder the old emperor and replace him with a new one," the oldest of the princesses added.

"The ceremony will be held in two weeks," Marie announced. "Castile, you might as well stop complaining. For the next two weeks, you're going to live with your Grandmother inside the Pearl Walls so you might as well learn something."

"Now, let's talk about what you want out of Fernis," the older woman said.

* * * *

The two weeks flew by. Lucer returned from his first beer caravan with a little gold and a lot of merchandise including the porcelain Jake had noticed on their trip, six mules, twenty war horses, wagon-loads of wool, and a couple of extra carts.

He also brought back a small army of ex-bandits who were ready to become mercenaries again. Word was getting around that the Granger were about to attack and that Otranto was hiring.

Jake put the mercenaries to work harvesting the olives and silkworms from his plantations on the east side of the Strait of Tantalus. He hoped that Fernis would be reasonable when it came time to pay them because they charged a lot more than peasants would have and he plowed back every penny he made to build the oil presses and the looms he needed for mass production.

A few days later, The Castile docked and disgorged a motley crew of Tiflis tourists, more wool, fine silk from the Shara, pearls from no-one knew where, and almost no gold.

Even his ferry business had generated a stream of income as priests, olives, books, and beer flowed both ways over the narrow strait. Even the Bourgundian Baron dropped by, drank some of Manny's beer, and delivered another load of confiscated muskets.

Jake lowered the ferry prices twice and was carrying up to three loads a day. Within weeks, he would be able to repay the Patriarch for John's 'loan.' Of course, a considerable share of the fares were *in-kind*, and Jake now ran a substantial chicken farm, and supplied most of Otranto with its geese and ducks.

And, over the two weeks, four Bourgundian ships anchored in the Otranto harbor, released their crews to the more dubious parts of the city, and bought the Patriarch's wine, Manny's beer, and Jake's first press of olive oil. In return, they offered muskets, a few light brass cannons, gunpowder, which Jake traded to the Tiflis, and more mercenaries.

Jake's *invention* of paper money was not especially popular, especially among the mercenaries he paid with it, but he felt he had little choice. The trading missions were crippled if they had to barter for everything, yet the entire planet seemed devoid of precious metals. Even the small amount of additional commerce and production he had generated had resulted in a severe deflation with gold denominated prices falling nearly in half across the board. At least making the paper money exchangeable for Manny's beer kept the mercenaries from rioting although it didn't please Manny at all.

Naturally, non-specie money implies a bank and Jake set one of those up to control issuing of money but also to allow for the beginning of a financial sector. The Moneylenders Guild was not happy, but couldn't get the city guard to do anything given he wasn't dealing in gold and had the support of the Patriarch.

As Castile's coming out ceremony approached, Manny's home became converted into the headquarters for a growing number of women, both royal and servant, who seemed intent on sewing anything that stood still and slaughtering and cooking anything that moved.

Almost all of the pearls, much of the silk, and a significant population of pigs, ducks, and chickens went into the party preparations as well. Jake was finally forced to make his own living arrangements and, two days before Castile's event, Manny joined him.

"Could it be worth it?" Jake asked when his friend dropped, exhausted, into a narrow cot.

"As long as Fernis is Emperor? I doubt it."

"Then why are we going through with this?"

Manny looked him in the eye. "You still don't understand Otranto, do you? Why do you think we've lost so many wars? It isn't that our people are bad warriors. It's that our culture is fundamentally impractical. We have more priests than blacksmiths, more palace clerks than soldiers on our walls. We spend so much effort on *being*--being Otranto, being the center of the world, that we don't have much effort to spare for actually *doing* anything."

"*You* manage," Jake argued.

Manny shook his head. "I'm a barbarian. Even so, I nearly got myself killed. And if you don't watch out, the same thing is going to happen to you."

Jake felt a chill down his spine. "Have you heard anything?"

"Everyone knows you're my friend. I just have a feeling."

"But we're trying to save Otranto."

"That's the way we see it. Some of them don't see the Granger as such terrible enemies. After all, if Otranto fell, it would become part of the Granger Khanate. Where do you think the Granger Khan would move? Here, of course. And wouldn't they need clerks and bureaucrats to manage their affairs? Half of the city thinks that we'd be better off under the Granger than we are now. We'd have an empire again, even if it wasn't really ours."

It wasn't a completely irrational thought. Jake knew that the Mongol conquest of China had worked out like that with the Mongols taking over the imperial posts but the basic bureaucracy continuing largely unhampered. Unfortunately, the profound indifference Jake had seen among the Granger for anything smacking of civilization made him quite certain the Otrantos were living in a fool's paradise. "Maybe we should just send those bureaucrats to live with the Granger now."

Manny nodded, then took a deep swallow of his beer. "The new batches are even better than what we were making before. Anyway, the only good news is that Fernis can't think that way. Even if the bureaucrats would do fine under the Granger, Fernis wouldn't."

Jake was aware of plenty of cases in history which had pitted the powers of the leader against those of the bureaucracy. Occasionally the leader won. More often, the bureaucracy did. Nothing in Fernis's record gave Jake any confidence that this would fall into the former category.

"If it isn't going to do any good, why are Marie and the princesses so set on this ceremony?"

Manny took another drink, then laughed. "They're women and women like to party."

Jake couldn't help thinking that there was something deeper going on. Marie, at least, kept her thumb to the pulse of Otranto politics. If she hadn't thought there was a way to make this work, she wouldn't have set it up.

When the day of the ceremony finally arrived, Marie dropped off a package for Jake and Manny then vanished into the palace district.

"Clothes," Manny complained. "I'll look like a peacock."

Jake was rather pleased with his black pants, white silk shirt, and tan vest held shut with a black swordbelt. Manny, in contrast, got turquoise pants, a yellow shirt, and a deep maroon vest. A huge seal emblazoned on the back of the vest portrayed fields of barley, flowing water, and a mug of beer.

"Some idiot selected this as the dress uniform of the brewers guildmaster three hundred years ago and now I have to live with it," Manny explained. He too belted on a practical looking sword.

"Why the weapons for a coming out ceremony?" Jake asked.

"Shows our rank," Manny explained. "Ordinary people can't carry weapons. 'Course ordinary people don't have this type of ceremony either."

"Is this the apprentice brewer uniform, then?" Jake plucked at the thin silk of his shirt.

Manny slapped him on the back. "What do you think Marie has been working so hard on? You're now assistant harbormaster and knight bachelor of the empire. Cost you a pretty penny, too."

"Does this mean that I get a cut of the harbor fees?" Jake asked. There had to be a silver lining beyond looking cool in an outfit that showed off exactly what hard work on a high gravity planet did to the muscle tone.

Manny punched him on the arm, his belly rolling with laughter. "Maybe it did six hundred years ago when the post was real. It's an aristocratic post. None of the aristocratic families actually have anything to do with their ancestral functions and none, as far as I know, get any of the money out of them either."

So much for his bourgeoning mercantile empire. "Then what's the point?"

"The point is this is the only way you can get into Castile's ceremony." Manny gestured at the costume he'd put on. "Hell, this is the only way I can get in and she's my daughter."

Chapter 22

Castile's ceremony started late.

Jake and Manny arrived in time to be the first attendees. For the next two hours, Otranto functionaries and aristocrats wandered in, helped themselves to some of the food that Marie and her sisters and friends had prepared, and sat waiting.

All of the doors in Manny's house had been thrown open and Jake was surprised to see that the entire first floor opened into a single huge room. A small band played insipid music at one end of the extended hall while servants fluttered around with trays of food, cramming additional platters onto already overfilled tables.

The foreign ambassadors arrived slightly later. Unlike the natives, they avoided the rich foods Marie had set out. "They think we'd poison them," Manny whispered in Jake's ear.

"Would you?"

"Only if I thought we could get away with it. I can't even count the number of wars Otranto has avoided when the enemy king or emperor just happened to die and squabbles broke out over the succession."

"Surely poisoning an ambassador would backfire, though."

Manny grinned. "Maybe. But don't tell them that. They eat enough as it is."

A tall blond man wearing traditional dessert robes made his way over to the corner where Jake and Manny were trying to lay low. "Which of you is Jake the Spacer?" he demanded.

"Who wants to know?" Jake demanded.

"I am Daniel, Granger Ambassador to the court of our vassal, Otranto."

Jake gave the man a martial arts bow, never taking his eyes off his enemy. "Then I am Jake, a former spacer. At your service."

"I doubt that. Do you deny invading Granger territory, inciting an outbreak of violence between our Ebron and Otranto subjects. Can you justify attacking a group of Granger warriors who were patrolling Granger's highways?"

Jake bowed again. "I deny all of those accusations, of course. I am a merchant, not a bandit or a raider."

"A merchant? Yet you wear the uniform of the traditional Otranto aristocracy. An odd affectation for someone who was not even born on our planet."

"Otranto blood runs thin," Manny observed calmly. "Few who carry the old aristocratic names are truly of that blood."

"Indeed," the ambassador agreed. "Yet Granger blood is thick. Otranto would do well to look to their neighbors for fresh blood, not to the distant stars. Still, the spacer's assumed position does give him a certain, shall we say, vulnerability."

A peal of trumpets interrupted the Granger's threats and Manny's home began to fill with the immediate entourage of Fernis, dictator, general, and apostle of the Otranto people.

The Emperor was younger than Jake would have guessed possible for someone who had committed all the sins laid at his feet. He wore armor of stiffened silk, a feather-light sword, a crown that reared a full two feet over his head, and scarlet slippers adopted from ancient Earthly history.

A sigh went through the audience as Fernis stepped lightly from his sedan chair and then seated himself in a gold and pearl throne which, Jake suddenly realized, must have cost him the best part of his profits over the past two weeks. For the value of that chair, he could have hired half the mercenaries who had applied for work, and not had to dip into creative finance.

An assistant rang a small silver bell and a broad-faced and overdressed eunuch stood, bowed to the emperor, then unrolled a parchment scroll.

"Any who would be seen as princesses of the Empire should stand forth, be judged by the equal of the apostles, and stand to do his will."

He sat down abruptly.

"All that work for this?" Jake whispered.

He thought he'd spoken softly, but obviously it wasn't softly enough. Half the people in the huge banquet room stared at him. A dozen nearby women hissed him to silence.

"Never mind," he whispered.

A gaggle of priests appeared at the door to Manny's home, swinging incense burners to send pungent clouds of smoke into the crowd.

Jake kept his eye on the Granger Ambassador. The man looked like someone who would take advantage of this kind of confusion to slip a dagger into an enemy's back. For now, though, Daniel's attention was on the Emperor rather than any lesser prey.

A sigh from the assembled crowd called Jake's attention back to the business at hand.

Accompanied by at least twenty princesses of Otranto, a closely veiled female form entered the hall.

Jake recognized the coffee-brown eyes that glared at him but he couldn't reconcile his mental image of tomboy and child Castile with the definitely female form wrapped in layers of thin white silk. The rope of pearls forming Castile's belt circled an impossibly thin waist at least four times. Her hips swayed with her step. The only similarity between her narrow pace, constrained as it was by her tight silk sheath, and her normal walk was the catlike grace that she maintained no matter what the occasion.

Castile knelt before her Emperor and waited.

Fernis had chosen that moment to whisper something to one of his eunuchs. He ignored Castile until his servant had whispered back, then the two shared a laugh.

Castile, Jake knew, had to be humiliated. Still she waited patiently.

Finally, Fernis deigned to notice the kneeling girl. "You wish to be admitted to the ranks of the princesses of Otranto?" he demanded. His voice was suddenly stern, fatherly.

"It is my wish to serve my country and Emperor," she replied, her voice low and husky.

The Eunuch handed over a scroll that Fernis either read or pretended to read.

After several minutes of contemplation, Fernis nodded firmly. He gestured and his slaves raised his throne so everyone in the room could view him.

When he raised his hand, the crowd went completely silent. He addressed the hundreds of people who crowded into Manny's home with a quiet voice that still penetrated, entrancing the listener. "By blood, Castile Delphonte claims to be a princess of our Empire. She traces her ancestry to the founders of Otranto. Four emperors contributed to her line. Are there any here who would dispute her claim?"

This whole ceremony, Jake realized, was similar to an ancient Earthly wedding. For an uncomfortable moment, he cast his eyes around Manny's home looking for anyone who would stand up and deny Castile her moment.

Enough of the other guests were doing the same to let Jake realize that this was not a mere formality.

Fernis waited a good minute before nodding firmly. "None deny Castile's right by ancestry." He took a flask from his Eunuch and swallowed deeply, a single drop of red wine staining his pure white silk shirt. "In other kingdoms," Fernis announced, "mere ancestry is enough to make a princess. Otranto is different. An Otranto princess is a gift to whatever nation she may be sent. To be a princess of Otranto requires both wit, intelligence, and beauty." He paused, taking another drink. "Castile Delphonte, are you prepared for the questions?"

"I am, Protector of the Faithful."

The Emperor nodded. For the next half hour, he drilled Castile on philosophy, mathematics, history, and foreign languages. Given how Castile had avoided her tutors, Jake was surprised that Castile knew many of the answers. He was even more surprised that Fernis could conduct this type of questioning. Certainly everything he had heard about Fernis before had been negative. Could so many men whose judgment he trusted be wrong?

The audience amused themselves by nibbling on the food which had been set out, murmuring in appreciation when Fernis asked a particularly probing question or Castile gave an especially witty answer, and whispering among themselves. Few of the whispers, Jake thought, had anything to do with Castile.

Of course, neither did the event. This was supposed to be about an opportunity to confront the Emperor directly, yet everything had been open, ritualistic, and subject to the close inspection of the suspicious Granger ambassador.

That ambassador, Jake noticed, was circulating among the guild leaders, shaking hands, passing out small gifts that looked suspiciously like bribes, and generally making himself at home in Manny's house.

It would be the height of irony, Jake decided, if this hugely expensive event became merely an opportunity for the Granger to expand its influence over Otranto.

"Daniel called Otranto a vassal to the Granger," he mentioned to Manny when the man's attention momentarily strayed from his daughter's performance. "What is that about?"

Manny frowned. "When you lose wars, you agree to humiliating terms. When Julian lost the last war, he agreed to an annual tribute. It didn't seem like a lot of money at the time, but it did let the Granger claim us as a subservient state. Of course we're poorer now and the levies grow worse."

Jake glanced at the Emperor with new appreciation and, for a fraction of a second, their eyes met.

Fernis's amber eyes seemed to hold knowledge that took centuries to learn. He was not a happy man, Jake realized. Jake couldn't blame him. He stood the risk of becoming the last Emperor in Otranto's two-thousand year history. The Empire's resources had grown so thin that even Jake's modest enterprises could make a real difference in transforming the economy. What little money Otranto had to spare after supporting its bloated bureaucracy went to pay a never-ending tribute with little left over for the rapacious mercenaries who formed its precarious protection. Being Emperor was a job that Jake wouldn't want on a dare.

Abruptly, Fernis laughed and clapped his hands.

Unlike his predecessor, Julian, Fernis was not known as a warrior, but that movement displayed a fluid control that let Jake know that the man didn't lack fighting experience.

"Castile Delphonte is delightful," the Emperor announced.

From the sudden murmur, Jake determined that this must be more than the standard level of approval. Well, good for Castile, although Jake had no idea where she'd learned all of this. It certainly wasn't from hanging around with Jake's crowd.

"Every princess must be flawless in body," the Emperor announced, returning to his stately form of address as if that brief surge of humanity had been a mistake. "Only her immediate family may attend this test."

The Emperor's eunuchs cleared a space around the emperor and Castile, moving both Castile's companion-princesses and anyone else out of the way.

"That's my call," Manny announced heading toward the emperor.

The Granger Ambassador strode toward the Emperor's throne only to be blocked by a fat, yet strong eunuch guard. "Only the immediate family," the guard insisted.

Daniel drew himself up. "I am the representative of the Khan of Granger himself."

The eunuch shrugged. "Are you saying that the Khan is bidding for marriage? If so, of course you will be entitled to prove the princess's flawlessness. I have heard no such bid, seen no treasure as brideprice."

Daniel spun away, brushing against Jake who had been listening to the encounter.

"You dare attack me, sir?" the Ambassador demanded.

"I believe you walked into me," Jake answered.

"And now you are calling me a liar. My friends will call on your friends."

From Daniel's assurance, and from the sudden silence around them, Jake realized this was no idle threat. In addition to words and gold, Daniel apparently relied on more direct measures to eliminate anyone he judged as a threat to Granger interests.

Jake knew he should keep his mouth shut. Unfortunately, sometimes knowing something just isn't enough. "Should you be able to find a friend, I'm sure my friends would be delighted to entertain so openminded a creature."

Daniel's tanned face turned deathly pale. "You dare."

"You've threatened me already. Go and pay someone to become your friend. I'm quite certain you were never invited to this home."

The Granger stomped away. It wasn't a fatal blow to the party. Jake was more interested in any who followed him.

To Jake's dismay, two guild masters and three mercenary captains chose to depart within the next several minutes. If Granger bribes and threats had penetrated that deeply into the very heart of Otranto City, perhaps things had gone beyond any hope.

The Eunuch guards pulled curtains and doors shut, enclosing the Emperor, Manny and Marie, Castile, and a number of Eunuch officials within an enclosed area.

The musicians, on some cue that Jake couldn't hear, began playing a slow and eerie song.

It sounded like nothing Jake had heard in his weeks on Arcadia but it was obviously familiar to the rest of the excluded audience. Several of the men grinned and a couple of the younger women moved their hips in a sensual beat in time with the music.

A surge of anger swept over Jake and he stepped toward the curtains that cut Castile off from his view.

"Don't." One of the princesses he'd met when they began this charade clutched his arm.

"This is ridiculous. He's a dirty old man."

The princess laughed. "He's the emperor. Do you think he has to go out of his way to find bedmates? Or that he would invite the girl's parents to watch if he did?" She shook her head. "This is an ancient ritual, from the days when Arcadia was not fully terraformed and when mutation was still a major problem."

"Oh. Well, I still don't like it."

The princess smiled, then shook her head. "No, I suspect you do not like it. Perhaps you will like it even less when Castile is sent to marry into some foreign court in return for a few dozen mercenaries or a year of peace on the borders."

Jake essayed a laugh but didn't even convince himself. "She's much too young for marriage."

"She's sixteen. I married when I was fourteen."

Jake assured himself that he wasn't interested in Castile that way. Still, the idea of any other man fondling her, taking advantage of her energy, grit, and good spirts sickened him.

"How long does it last?" he asked.

"Marriage," the princess giggled, "or the proving?"

He gritted his teeth. "The proving."

"Not as long as it seems. Not as long as I wish it could. Remember, this is the moment you have made all these sacrifices for."

Jake barely resisted smacking himself in the forehead. Of course. Castile and Marie finally had Fernis alone, except for a few of his Eunuch guards.

* * * *

Too much wine mixed with too much beer and too much food left Jake feeling lethargic and stupid. And too lazy even to turn up his metabolism to deal with it.

Daniel had been good for his word. His seconds had called on Manny and Mark. After a bit of negotiation during which Daniel's seconds rejected Jake's suggestion that they settle the argument with wooden staffs, they agreed on pistols. Daniel was too well known as a swordsman for Jake to stand a chance with any bladed weapon. Daniel was also well known as a crack shot with the pistol, but Jake suspected that it would be quicker to pick up the pistol than a sword.

A heavy fog had descended over the city and a light rain fell through it giving Otranto an unearthly feel. Castile hadn't been able to read Fernis's reaction to her words when she'd told him about the Granger threat, Jake's need to uproot the Guild system that held Otranto in check, or Jake's plans to strengthen the city. For all Jake knew, he might have simply marked himself as a threat to the throne rather than as a potential ally.

He and Mark were stumbling back to the old warehouse he'd converted into his Otranto headquarters when two men stepped out from a narrow alleyway.

"Come with us," the first man growled.

"Why? Can't the Granger Ambassador wait until the time we agreed on?"

"This isn't about Daniel."

They weren't casual footpads. At least Jake hoped that common thieves wouldn't be on a first name basis with the Granger ambassador. On second thought, though, maybe Daniel had his fingers as deeply in the Otranto underworld as he did in the guild halls and mercenary companies.

A closer look at the men's cloaks told Jake that these men weren't common anything. The wool weave was so tight that they seemed to repel the rain. Gold-hilted swords glistened where they peeked out from under the cloaks.

"Are we under arrest?"

The first man shook his head. "We don't have much time. Follow us, please."

Jake nodded to Mark. "They could have slit our throats if they'd wanted to. Let's see what this is about."

"Shh," the first man whispered.

They followed the two men through several alleys, finally ending up at a closed tavern.

"Go in," the speaker said.

"It's closed."

A long suffering sigh. "Just go in. You have my word that no one will attack you."

The man thought his word was worth something. For Jake, that made it worth investigating.

He nodded, seized the door, which proved to be unbolted, and pushed his way into the unlit room.

Fernis, Emperor of the Otranto, Equal to the Apostles, Theoretical Prince of countless provinces lost from the Otranto Empire for the past thousand years, sat, hunched over a earthenware mug of beer. His black wool cape hid most of his body and a broad rimmed cap substituted for a crown and obscured his face.

"So, you expect great things of me," the Emperor demanded.

The man who had led Jake into the tavern discretely disappeared leaving them alone.

"You don't trust your guards, yet you trust me?"

"An Emperor learns never to trust anyone," Fernis replied, his quick smile showing even teeth. "But one does not become Emperor without learning to take chances and to judge when a chance is worth taking." He paused, refilling his mug, then poured one for Jake as well. "I've been watching you."

"I see." Considering that Jake hadn't decided whether Fernis would be an impediment to be removed or a helper, this wasn't an especially comforting feeling.

"At first, I thought you might be trying to win the loyalty of the mob and the army. It has been done, you know."

Jake had studied enough history for that. "That isn't unique to this planet."

Fernis smiled again. "I imagine not. Yet you are hiring mercenaries. You own a ship that was once a pirate but we now are supposed to think a merchant. You have purchased the ferry that connects our eastern Empire to the western-- the route that the barbarians took last time they invaded. And you have entered into negotiations with both the Bourgundians and the Anglicans. Quite a feat for a man who has been here for only a few months and who claimed only to wish to return home."

Jake stared at the emperor whom everyone believed to be a weak fool. He might be a number of things, but he was neither weak, nor a fool.

Time, Jake decided, to tell the truth.

"I realized that Otranto was the best hope for this planet. The barbarians lack scientific curiosity or a unified government. The Granger are worse."

Fernis nodded. "I have met with a number of spacers, both before and after I became emperor. None of them had hired bands of mercenaries. They claim that their governments are responsible for their wars."

"Not quite," Jake corrected. "Or rather, outside the narrow boundaries of each planet, the merchants are the government."

Fernis nodded slowly. "And you see yourself outside these narrow boundaries now."

Anger might be a terrible mistake, yet Jake had drunk too much and slept too little to care. He slammed a fist down on the wooden table. "The Otranto government has been responsible for losing every war it's fought over the past two hundred years. Don't you think it's time to try something else?"

Fernis waved away the head that popped around the corner of the tavern when Jake raised his voice. "My friend is merely making a point," he told the guard.

"I had hoped you would help," Jake concluded a little weakly. "I need more money, more information about the Granger plans, more soldiers, and more ships."

"If I had money, ships, or soldiers, Otranto wouldn't have the problems it has."

That wasn't strictly true, Jake knew. Otranto's problems came less from a lack of wealth and more from its bureaucratic ineptitude. An ineptitude that his difficulties in arranging a meeting with the Emperor and the past two weeks of preparation for what was essentially a debutante party, made completely evident. He told Fernis exactly that. "The guilds are a fist clamped around Otranto's heart," he concluded.

The Emperor pressed his hands together, fingers to fingers, palm to palm. "You're quite right. Every war we fight, win or lose, we pay a price. For each moment of barbarian support, we give up the rights to trade in certain areas. For each peace treaty with the Granger, we surrender tax-paying territory. As a result less money flows in and we become less able to fight and less able to pay off the Granger. So, a noble raises a force of mercenaries that the government could not afford and his family is given freedom from taxes. A corrupt Emperor has a bastard and the mother's family is granted the revenues from one of the few provinces remaining to the empire. Each is a drop, but combined, tax revenues flood away and never return."

"It is a common problem," Jake replied.

Fernis laughed. "The barbarian kingdoms deal with it by invasion. The new rulers toss out all of the old and corrupt and start over. The things you claim to admire about Otranto are the things that prevent us from acting."

"Couldn't you declare an emergency and revoke these old and corrupt practices?" Jake plucked at his uniform. "Make the Harbormaster either go to work mastering the harbor or give up his post to one who would do so."

Fernis shook his head slowly. "Theoretically the Emperor has vast powers. In practice…" he paused briefly. "In practice, the Emperor is a prisoner of his role. I march in ceremonies, greet girls who think they should be women, and join the Patriarch in praying for rain for the farmers."

"And lead the military," Jake added.

"In times of war, yes," Fernis agreed. "With what little money the Senate coughs up to fund it."

"And the Senate?" Everything Jake had heard about the Otranto Senate had led him to believe that it was a figurehead organization rather than the practical parliament Fernis seemed to be claiming.

"They protect the entrenched interests. I could, of course, overawe them and get them to agree with whatever I proposed, but the instant I left the city, they would revoke the regulations and probably proclaim a new emperor. That's one reason we so rarely win wars, you know. Successful emperors are deposed so they can't come back and try to exert real control."

"Is that what happened to Julian?"

Fernis nodded. "For a while, it looked like he might actually throw the Granger back and recapture several of the provinces his predecessors had lost. But he ran roughshod over traditional privileges. The Senate invited barbarian mercenaries into the city and declared him deposed. Hence, me."

"You didn't have anything to do with tossing him?"

Fernis took another swallow from his mug. "Hell, yes, I did. I saw what was happening and decided to make my move. If I hadn't, the Senate would have picked someone else. Worse, they would have sent their army to attack Julian's from behind while the Granger attacked from the front. I stopped their pay and Julian's mercenaries melted away."

Jake wasn't particularly impressed. Surely there should have been some way that Fernis could have helped Julian against the Granger and the Senate rather than conspiring to depose him. He would have to watch this man if they allied. On the other hand, Otranto was incredibly weak. Maybe they needed a scheming bastard more than an honorable warrior.

"I have a plan," Jake admitted. It wasn't really a plan, yet, but he did have the beginnings of one.

"I'd love to hear it. You don't think I want to be known as the last Emperor of Otranto, do you?"

It might have been the truth, or Fernis might still be acting.

"Haven't there been Emperors who shook up the nation and gave it new life?"

"Hundreds of years ago."

"Then maybe it's time for another."

Chapter 23

"I think we're ready to hear your plan," Fernis stated. They had entered the Imperial palace and sat in a dark library surrounded by maps and scrolls that depicted the current, sorry state of the Otranto military.

Fernis had invited only two men to join them. Christopher Plum was a small man with a pock-marked face, a slightly unctuous air, and a bald head that glistened with balls of sweat even in the cool air of the Imperial library. He was also Fernis's spymaster. Osiris was a barbarian whose calculating gaze reminded Jake of Lucer. At two meters in height, Osiris towered over the others and had to weigh well over a hundred and twenty kilos. Despite a scarred face that would have looked more at home in an arena than in a boardroom, he was the head of Fernis's military. He might be a mercenary, but he had fought Otranto's wars under three emperors, and seemed willing to continue to fight what could only be seen as a losing, or rather long-lost, battle.

"Otranto is the barrier behind which the new civilization shelters," he told Jake when pressed for an explanation of why he didn't simply return to his Bourgundian homeland with the golden rewards of his long service. "Perhaps two more generations and the east will be able to stand on its own. Now," he shook his head ruefully, "now we would be overrun, disunited and played against each other like children squabbling over a sweet."

"Even my generals do not believe that we can restore the luster of the Empire," Fernis commented. "So we fight the losing battle. Or rather, the barbarian mercenaries fight and Otranto pays first in gold, then in the suffering of her people when the mercenaries fail."

"Civilizations don't rise or fall by themselves," Jake said trying not to sound like one of his stuffy professors but, he feared, failing. "It's up to us to decide whether Otranto will stand strong, or fail."

"Perhaps." Fernis unrolled a map depicting what had once been the western half of the Otranto Empire but which was now mostly Granger territory. "I hope your plan isn't to strike first and take the fight to the Granger," he told Jake. "That plan has been tried. One reason the Granger turn rich farmland into desert is that the Otranto armies can be surrounded, cut off from supplies, and gradually starved. How often has that happened over the past two hundred years, Osiris?"

"Seven times," the general replied. "The Granger light cavalry cut off scavenging parties and garrison the cities. Even if we capture one of their cities, they destroy all of the food and simply leave us with more mouths to feed."

"We've tried to arrange popular uprisings among people of Otranto descent," the spymaster added shaking his head. "The Granger allow the Ebron to slaughter them for a while. Their subject people kill each other and the Granger can still devote all of their attention to us."

"What about the Ebron?" Jake asked. "Haven't they ever revolted?"

Plum nodded grimly. "Of course. When they do, the Granger encourage the Otrantos to slaughter the Ebron. Either way, the Granger win. The Granger didn't create the mistrust between Otranto and Ebron, but they use it brilliantly."

"So we bring in barbarian mercenaries, defend what land we can, and gradually lose everything," Fernis concluded. "But we've never had access to Spacer weapons before. With those, perhaps we could wipe out the attacking Granger, level their city walls, and reestablish borders that could be sustained."

"I don't have any spacer weapons," Jake admitted.

"We know we've lost much of the knowledge our ancestors brought from the stars," Plum said. "Even if they aren't modern spacer weapons, you could share these with us. We've read about rapid-fire self-propelled artillery, smokeless powder, subspace missile attacks, weaponized biochemical agents, or thermonuclear devices. All sound like they would be useful. Unfortunately, we have no idea how to create any of these weapons."

"I don't either," Jake said. "I was an ancient literature major before I got my business degree."

Fernis slumped in his chair pressing his face into his hands. "When your little princess told me about you, I had imagined that you would be able to offer more, that maybe there would be something we could do."

All of this defeatism was starting to piss Jake off. "I told you I have a plan. Don't you even want to hear it?"

"Oh, yes, by all means," Osiris said without a great deal of conviction.

"We don't have the men to defend Otranto's borders but Otranto City is strong. We could hold it for months against even a huge Granger army."

"Only if we were willing to give up the rest of the Empire," Fernis noted.

"Which is what? Barely a hundred kilometers in any direction from the city. If we could smash the Granger army, we would take it back--and more. Without their field army, they would hardly be in a position to adopt their normal tactics."

"It would never work," Plum declared. "First, the people would riot. Second, the Granger would starve us out. Third, the mercenaries would desert once they realized they were bottled up, and fourth, if we had the ability to smash the Otranto army, we could do it at the borders without having to retreat to the city."

"You may be right about the first one, but you're wrong about the others," Jake declared. "You're still thinking about Otranto City as the administrative center of an empire."

"What else could it be?" Fernis demanded.

"Tell me what Empire it administers to? I took a caravan through the towns surrounding Otranto. Do you know what I found? Starving peasants, broken-spirited merchants, and bandits. That's your empire."

"It's all we have," Osiris pointed out.

"But it isn't. You have Otranto City. It's still the largest city in the world."

"What possible good is a city without the countryside?" Fernis demanded. "Cities survive off of the bounty of the countryside. Their farms feed our people. Their excess sons fill our armies and our priesthood. Their taxes pay for the layers of bureaucrats that weigh on all of us like leaden blankets."

"Wrong," Jake countered. "Or rather, it doesn't have to be that way. A city can support itself. Food can be brought in by ship. Soldiers can be trained from the population of the city or brought in from the east."

"Food costs money. Soldiers cost money. Weapons cost money. Even my spies cost money," Plum said. "With the few kilometers of land we receive taxes from, we already fall deeply into debt. Surely you don't think that you could make enough charging mercenaries to cross on your ferry to pay for them. Or will you pay whole armies only with beer?"

Jake had to give Fernis and his spymaster credit. They knew what he had been up to. They might even know what the Granger were up to. Unfortunately, that didn't help them with a solution. Of all of the men in the room, he alone knew the economic power that a manufacturing city could bring to bear. If Otranto City could only transform itself from an administrative center with nothing to administer into an industrial center like those in long-ago nineteenth century Earth, it might be able to put up a credible defense. Hell, give him a couple of years it should be able to dominate the planet. On Earth, England had ruled the planet without much in the way of land or natural resources. Earlier, Venice had controlled the Mediterranean with its trading ships and mercenary armies from a single city. Hong Kong, Singapore, and New Baltimore had done the same a little later in history. With the largest city on the planet, couldn't Otranto do the same?

He outlined his plan quickly. The city could free up eighteen layers of bureaucracy that supposedly administered to regions of the empire lost decades or centuries before. Its university would become the intellectual center for the planet, bringing in gold and spreading Otranto culture. The trade routes that had been cut off by the Granger and lost to Tantalus would be re-opened with the help of his one-ship fleet, his one boat ferry service, and his Tiflis allies. Over time, the fleet could be expanded using the forests near Ahmed Broussard's village to build shipyards. Finally, and most importantly, he and Manny would introduce modern manufacturing techniques--or at least techniques that were more modern that what Otranto was used to. He might not be able to recreate high technology weapons from his nonexistent knowledge of modern warfare, but he could certainly help Otranto turn out more beer, better wine, steam-driven textile looms, and maybe even standardized versions of the weapons they already had.

He didn't expect applause, but he did expect more than the bemused headshakes of the three men.

"What?" he demanded. "Look what we've already done. Otranto hasn't had a navy or merchant fleet in two hundred years and we have one now. Manny's beer and the Patriarch's wine are being exported throughout the world, and with the Bourgundian ships calling, we've even gotten a start on building a marine services business."

"This is a long term plan," Plum said. "My spies tell me that the Granger were set to invade six weeks ago when you somehow threw off their plans. At least I assume it was you?"

"Yeah, it might have been," Jake admitted. "With a lot of help from the Tiflis."

"Well, you gave us that much more warning. We've been hiring mercenaries as fast as we could find them, but the Granger army crossed the border yesterday morning. The invasion is already on. We don't need a long-term plan, we need to survive tomorrow."

"Not to mention we don't have the mercenaries to smash their armies, either at the borders or at the city walls," Osiris added. "We're down to hoping that the Khan of the Granger will suddenly die or something. It isn't the most brilliant military strategy."

"Are you fighting them?" Jake demanded.

"Oh, yes," Osiris admitted. "We even won the only battle of the war so far. 'Course it didn't matter since the Granger light cavalry ended up surrounding our troops after our victory and we barely managed to fight our way out."

"Have the troops fight a delaying action, burn the bridges, burn the farms, and bring the people to the city," Jake urged. "We need more workers if we're going to do this."

"Haven't you heard what we're saying?" Fernis demanded. "We don't have time."

Jake tried to rein his temper but failed. "How much time do you think you need? Otranto has had a thousand years to learn to fight and all it's learned was how to lose. Even if we don't finish, we can start."

Fernis ignored Jake's outburst and unrolled another scroll, this one ornate with wax seals and gold leaf. "The Granger have made us an offer."

"What offer?"

"If we give up the city, they'll let us continue to rule over the remainder of our territory. We'll be technical vassals, but in reality completely independent."

"That's ridiculous," Jake argued. "You'd be baring your own throats. I saw how they treat the Otranto in their territory. It's slow murder."

"Not always so slow," Osiris added. "Are you considering this offer, my Emperor?"

Fernis re-rolled his scroll. "If Otranto is lost, it is my duty to do what I can for her people. The church fathers have urged me to forge an agreement."

"The Patriarch wants to surrender?" Jake had been sure that the Patriarch was a fighter.

"The former Patriarch has been removed from office," Plum said. "Our sources within the church hierarchy tell us that the Granger promised the church religious authority over all the Otranto natives living everywhere within Granger territory, and over the schismatics when the Granger conquer the eastern barbarians."

"If I don't agree to this," the Emperor concluded, "the priests will preach rebellion. We'll have nothing."

Jake shook his head numbly. He needed time, and he needed the active support of both the Patriarch and the Emperor.

"The Granger Ambassador has also been busy with his bribes," Plum added. "Half the guilds in the city are calling for surrender." He gave Jake the mere beginnings of a smile. "The Brewer's Guild was not in that number."

"So, we're deserted by church and by the very industry that you count on to protect us." Fernis slumped in his chair. "Earlier this evening, after your Princess's party, I invoked emergency powers and called on the church to turn over all of its gold and silver ornaments to be used to pay the mercenaries. This has been done eight times in history. The previous seven time, the church complied. For the first time in history, the church has refused. We now lack the funds to pay our existing mercenaries, let alone any new forces which might be foolish enough to flock to a doomed city."

"We have enough soldiers in the city to enforce your decree," Osiris urged. "The church fathers are not known for their martial prowess and the martial monks are relatively few."

"I don't know what to do about this," Jake admitted, "but sending schismatic mercenary soldiers to loot the church's treasures would be insane. The people would riot and the Granger would just walk into the city."

"The spacer is correct," Plum admitted. "It seems to me that we have no alternative, then."

"No surrender," Osiris growled.

Plum's grin widened into something completely evil. "Oh, no. I think we're going to have to try the Spacer's plan."

"But--" Fernis grasped the table, his fingers turning white. "We're all agreed that the Spacer's plan cannot work."

Plum drew a small knife of the type a scholar might use to trim his quill pens and plunged it into the table. "Otranto must not surrender. The spacer is right. For at least two hundred years, the city has been the empire, my lord. Between us, the spacer and I will find a way to handle the church and guilds. I suggest that Osiris head for the front and urge our few rural citizens to abandon their farms and come to the city with whatever livestock and crops they can bring.

If you join him, you can later blame the spacer and myself for anything that happened while you were gone."

Fernis stared at the quivering blade. "Perhaps you are right. The battle is hopeless, but better a hopeless battle than surrender."

It was a heroic attitude. One that Jake didn't share. Somehow, he intended to pull this thing off. Better yet, he intended to make a profit on it.

* * * *

Jake didn't make it home until after four in the morning and collapsed into bed without even undressing.

He was only twenty-one but he was too old for the combination of late night partying and even later night plotting.

He woke up when the sun peeked through the narrow windows of his chamber but buried his heads under the covers. How had Arcadia possibly lost the science of coffee making? Without a welcome shot of caffeine, he was completely sure he couldn't face the day.

His eyes had barely shut when he heard the faint brush of his door against the floor. Someone had entered his room.

All thought of sleep fled. Memories of the Granger Ambassador flooded back to him. What if the man had decided not to wait for a formal duel where Jake just might have the chance to get lucky?

He forced himself to relax, continue breathing slowly, and listen to the faint whisper of feet against his silk carpet.

From his breathing, Jake judged the assassin to be small. The better to sneak into closed rooms. Unless Jake was very lucky he'd probably had no direct contact with the Ambassador.

When the footsteps neared Jake's bed, they quickened.

Jake relied on his martial arts training to envision the assassin, dagger drawn, moving in for the kill.

He timed his reaction knowing that he would have only one chance, then exploded from the covers, grappling with his assailant, one arm reaching for his knife hand, the other for his throat.

Uh, *her* throat. The struggling figure he grasped was definitely female.

Since both of his hands were fully engaged, it took Jake a moment to free his head from the covers.

"What are you doing here?" he demanded.

"Let me go," Castile shouted, wiggling away from his grasp. "What kind of barbarian are you anyway?"

"Sorry. After what happened with the Ambassador, I'm a little nervous."

Castile's face paled. "Do you mean the Granger Ambassador? What happened?"

After seeing Castile in the Princess ceremony the previous day, Jake would never again be able to think of her as an androgynous child. She was all female, all curves and slender muscle.

He pushed the inappropriate thoughts from his mind. She was five years younger than he. Now if she had an older sister--but she didn't.

He realized that his untoward thoughts had completely driven whatever she'd been saying out of his mind. "Huh?"

"The Ambassador. What did he do?"

"He challenged me to a duel."

232

"Oh, no." She ran one hand down his chest sending a small shiver down his spine. "He'll kill you."

"I don't know. If I was that easy to kill, I'd be dead by now." It wasn't just braggadocio, either. During the past few months, he'd been in danger more often than he'd been safe.

"Hun-uh. He is a professional killer," Castile whispered. "If you agree with him, he pays you. If you disagree, he has you killed. If you're important, he kills you himself."

That didn't sound very encouraging. It did sound like an intelligent strategy for undermining your enemies, however. Unfortunately for Jake, he was one of those enemies now.

"Well, he hasn't killed me yet," Jake said trying to sound upbeat. Even to himself, it didn't work. "But anyway, that isn't why you came here. I would have thought you'd be off doing princess things now that you've had your ceremony."

Castile put her hands on her hips and glared at him. "I did princess things for two weeks to get ready for that dreadful party. All so that you could meet with Fernis. So, instead you get drunk, don't even look at the Emperor, and have a fight with an assassin. You are such an idiot."

Jake wouldn't argue that point. "I met with Fernis last night," he told her. "After your party."

She sat on the bed uncomfortably close to him. Jake was glad he hadn't gone to sleep naked as he normally did. "Really? Cool. So, what did you say?"

"I told him our plan."

She punched him on the arm. "Don't drag it out. I need to know."

"The Granger have invaded and our armies can't hold them back. We're retreating to the city whether we want to or not. It's our only chance to make a stand. I just hope that the army doesn't get cut off before it retreats behind the city walls."

Castile nodded slowly. "I thought I could feel something in the air on my way here. There are more soldiers than normal wandering around the streets. The ones I saw looked a little nervous and they've started drinking earlier than usual."

Since the soldiers generally started their days with a half-liter of ale, starting to drink earlier could be serious. Drunk soldiers could panic and panicked mercenaries generally loot before they run.

He groaned. "Things just don't get easier, do they?"

"I told Harold to circulate around and let all the soldiers know that you have things under control."

"*I* have things? Fernis is the Emperor."

"And the soldiers trust him as far as they can throw him. He's never led an army."

"Neither have I."

"Yeah, but that hasn't been your job. Not until now, anyway. Besides, nobody has mentioned that to them. And everyone knew you were backing up the beer money."

If he had anything to say about it, things would stay that way. Jake didn't want to be Emperor and he definitely didn't want to be a general. "I'm going to need help," he told her.

Castile grinned at him. "Well, at least you're finally admitting it."

"This isn't a joke and you aren't going to like it. I need you and your mother to help with the Aristocracy. We need gold and silver. We need soldiers. We need doctors for the hospitals. And we need people who can write and do numbers to help run the businesses we are going to create."

Castile wrinkled her nose. "You're right. I don't like it. Aristocrats are useless parasites."

"Look at you," he reminded her. "You're a princess and you're not a parasite. Or worthless," he quickly added. "And don't tell me that's because you're half barbarian. Your mother isn't worthless either."

Castile stood and paced across the room for a good thirty seconds before stopping and whirling toward him. "I'll do it, but on one condition."

"What?"

"I want to run the steel business."

He wouldn't have guessed anything like that if he'd had all day to guess. He remembered Castile's early fascination with the blacksmith's trade and guessed it made some sense. There was one slight problem, however. "We don't have a steel business."

Castile snorted. "This morning we don't. Do you seriously think we have a chance to win the war if we don't change that? Somebody has to make steel for the cannons and for the muskets and for the swords and for the wheelbarrows. There's money to be made and I want to make some of it."

Back on Wayward, that kind of attitude would have been labeled profiteering. Maybe that was why Wayward was an overpopulated planet used as a dumping ground for inferior merchandise from the rest of the galactic trading republic. "Wheelbarrows?"

"We're going to have an extra fifty thousand peasants and all of their farm animals in the city, aren't we? They're going to need something to haul around their produce and their waste. Trust me, we need wheelbarrows."

They also needed coal, iron ore, and capital equipment he couldn't afford. He could explain that to Castile, argue with her until he was blue in the face, or he could give in and let her learn her own lesson.

"Please," she added.

"All right, you get the steel business, if you can handle it. How do you propose starting?" He felt like a heel. The one thing all of his business instructors had agreed upon was never set up a subordinate to fail. Yet he couldn't see any way out of this. Besides, Castile was right about one thing. Otranto did need an indigenous source of steel for weapons and for the industrial base he intended to construct.

Castile pulled a scroll of parchment from her tunic and thrust it at him.

He took it gingerly. It was still warm from where it had nestled between her breasts and the memory of perfume clung to it like a ghost.

"What's this?"

"Read it. It's my plan."

The *plan* consisted of a detailed work breakdown for reopening an open pit mine near Tantalus that had been closed when the Bourgundians had seized that city and sending a small army of charcoalers into the forests nearby.

"We'll need to switch to coal if we want to expand our production," Jake told her. He was impressed by the detail she'd put into the plan. Obviously she'd put some of the time she'd spent in learning to practical use.

"Eventually we'll do that," she agreed. "It isn't like we don't know how to make steel. We just have to make do with the resources we have available."

If they followed Castile's plan, they would have steel although at a hideous price in terms of labor.

"Most of the forests the charcoalers will be clearing were farms a couple of hundred years ago," Castile added. "Once we've cleared the woods off, we could introduce sheep or move some of the peasants out of the city and reestablish the farms. As long as you or the Bourgundians control the straits, farms there would be safe from the Granger. They can't walk across a mile of ocean."

Jake shook his head. Castile had leapfrogged him in this area. It was even possible that she wouldn't fail, that they'd be able to pull off some sort of indigenous steel industry. It might not be efficient, but enough steel for a few thousand more muskets and a couple of dozen heavy cannons could help when it came time to smash the Granger armies back from Otranto's walls--assuming that they still held those walls by the time Castile had brought her steel business on line.

"This is really quite good," he admitted.

"I thought you'd like it. My mother wants the ordinance business."

"But we don't have--"

Castile cut off his protest with a quick brush of her lips against his, then stood and headed for the door.

When she reached it, she turned and looked at him. "Poor Jake. You just don't understand women, do you?"

Jake shook his head trying to clear up the temporary dizziness that had come over him when Castile had kissed him. She was long gone before he could think of any clever comeback.

Chapter 24

"You can't fight him." Fernis's spymaster had arrived so shortly after Castile had departed that Jake wondered if they had set up some sort of relay.

"You mean Daniel?"

"Of course I mean the Granger Ambassador. We're expelling him from the city. If you manage to lay low for the next forty-eight hours, he'll be gone."

Jake had no particular deathwish; avoiding Arcadia's most deadly duelist didn't sound like an especially bad idea. Laying low for forty-eight hours would be harder, though. "I've got things to do," he argued. "Can't you just confine him to his quarters?"

Plum muttered something.

"What?"

"We don't know exactly where he is. He slipped the men I had watching the embassy."

Jake slammed a fist into the stone wall of his chamber. "So he could be stalking me?"

"We think he's activating his operatives through the city."

"But--"

The strident if distant sound of bells ringing cut Jake off.

"It's the alarm bell," Plum said. "The Granger can't be here already."

Jake changed his tunic quickly and followed the spymaster out of his headquarters. Several men looked up as he passed. One poured a bushel of olives into a press and slowly cranked down on the screw that squeezed the oil from the fruits. Another threw one narrow ceramic amphora after another on a potter's wheel, quickly adding to a pallet of finished and drying containers.

"Your businesses seem active," Plum said.

Jake nodded. "Active but primitive." He had counted on more time. Time to evacuate the remainder of the Otranto population into the city. Time to plant some rather nasty surprises for the invading Granger army. Time to work with Osiris and Harold to find a way to transform a number of half-bandit mercenary units into a disciplined and effective army. And most of all, time to create an industrial economy along the model of nineteenth century Britain. From the alarm bells, now sounding from every church, time was something they had just run out of.

A heavy cloud of black smoke rose from several kilometers away near the land wall that separated the city from the surrounding country.

As he left his warehouse, he called to the potter to raise the Brewers' Guild militia and send it to the walls. If it was a false alarm, he and Manny would lose a day's production they could ill afford, given that Manny's beer was the only thing that kept the mercenaries paid. Jake was prepared to take that chance.

"Don't you think you're overreacting?" Plum asked. "It looks like it's just a fire."

Jake wasn't so confident. Otranto City was built largely of stone and tile. Although he was sure there were plenty of fires in the city, there hadn't been any major fires since he'd been here. Sabotage seemed at least conceivable, especially with the Granger Ambassador gone missing just when he should be looking for Jake for a duel. And the most effective time to employ sabotage was when the distraction would most effectively prevent the city from defending itself.

"I'm heading for the land walls," he said.

"Let the firefighter's guild handle this. We need to decide what to do about Daniel." The spymaster plucked at Jake's sleeve making him feel like a chicken being prepared for Sunday dinner.

"If this is what I think it is, I suspect we'll find Daniel near the walls," Jake replied.

The spymaster started like he'd walked on a pin then nodded. "There would be no point in setting a fire if he didn't believe that he had the forces to exploit it."

"So he got the forces from somewhere." Jake broke into a jog, his muscles, now toned and accustomed to the higher Arcadian gravity, responding with an energy that reminded him that he needed to make sure he got his exercise even as he focused on building his mercantile empire.

After a moment's hesitation, Plum joined him, his strides matching Jake's. "Osiris is a capable general," he observed. "If any significant Otranto force had broken through his lines, he would have let us know. At a minimum, he would have called out the guild militia to reinforce the walls."

Jake considered that. "Maybe it isn't a breakthrough, then."

"What else? They couldn't have flown here."

"They could have sailed. A strike force could have landed a few kilometers up the coast. They could hope to seize the city while the army is in the field."

Plum nodded grimly. "Possibly. Yet the Granger have no navy, no ships larger than a canoe. They would need at least a thousand men to have a chance of taking the city. It doesn't seem possible."

"Unless they had allies." Allies like the Anglics. Maybe letting Pierre go free had been a blunder rather than a stroke of trading genius. The Anglics had certainly implied that they had a special relationship with the Granger, although it hadn't stopped them from fighting when both sides thought that a treasure could be at stake.

"Damned heretical barbarians," Plum breathed. "If the barbarians and the Granger have united against Otranto, we are lost."

"The barbarians aren't united over this," Jake reminded the spymaster. "The Bourgundians have pledged to keep the straits free of enemy forces."

"*Promises* have never been the problem," Plum answered. "It's in the delivery that the barbarians fall short." He nodded toward the walls. "Hurry."

Castile had been right about one thing. There were a number of soldiers on the streets, most of them drinking heavily. Jake shouted orders to every soldier he saw telling most to meet at the land walls but detailing some to the sea walls as well. The Anglics and Grangers were smart enough to use more than one feint. If they had the ships to land a Granger army, the Anglics might just attempt a marine assault as well.

As they neared the walls, the smoke got thicker, the acidic fumes making Jake's eyes sting and throat tickle. Flames burst from an entire block of stone buildings. Wisps of straw curled in the windows and floated up into the sky threatening to spread the firestorm further.

A haphazard group of men were still trying to create a bucket brigade, the uniform leather buckets in their hands indicating that this was the volunteer fire guild that did what it could to keep Otranto safe from the occasional outbreak of fire.

"My daddy is in there," a young child wailed as she clutched at Jake's trousers. "Can't you please help?"

She was a girl, Jake guessed. The child couldn't have been more than five. Or maybe a little older on this primitive world where even the minimum guidelines for nutrition were rarely met.

He hesitated for a moment, stutterstepping in his run.

"We're needed at the gate," Plum reminded him.

"But--"

"What do you think will happen to her if the Granger break in?"

Jake could imagine that all too well. He'd seen Granger indifference to people and read about the sack of great cities of the past. He gritted his teeth and continued his run knowing that his nightmares would hold the Otranto girl's face for the rest of his life.

He grabbed a staff from a man who appeared to be a newly arrived peasant as he ran past.

"Hey."

"Help this girl find her father," he shouted.

Jake was beyond the man's reach before he could react.

The gates to the city were wide open as Jake and Plum arrived, breathing hard but still fresh from their run through the city. A bustle of peasants chatted amongst themselves as they rolled a heavy wagon into the city.

"Looks like a false alarm," Plum said indicating the peaceful scene.

Or was it? One of the guards lolled against a dark stain on the city wall. Jake zoomed his vision. Something didn't feel right. Was the guard breathing?

Jake motioned for silence, then listened.

Without his enhanced hearing, he would never have been able to make out the peasant's voice. Even with it, he couldn't understand the words. But he recognized the language.

"Grangers," he shouted. "The peasants are Granger in disguise."

Without taking a moment to consider how absolutely insane he was being, he launched himself at the infiltrating army.

Even Otranto mercenary guards wouldn't have been oblivious enough to let obviously armed men through the city gates without question, so Jake's attack wasn't instant suicide. He spun his staff like a molecular saw, knocking away knives as soon as they appeared, brushing away a dagger thrown at his head, and clipping knees, elbows, and heads.

"Otranto," he shouted. If this city couldn't pull together to save itself, maybe it didn't deserve to survive. Of course that left the little matter of his own survival.

A startled spymaster and, moments later, a couple of volunteer firemen with arms like blacksmiths' joined him.

Ten seconds of furious attack left five Granger infiltrators on the ground. The remainder tried to back out of his range.

Jake considered pressing his attack, but a shower of rocks warned him that he no longer held the element of surprise. He stood at the gates of the city, forcing himself to breath deeply. Running five kilometers hadn't winded him nearly as much as these few seconds of battle.

"Close the gates," he yelled to the watchtowers overhead. "We can cut them off from reinforcements." Why hadn't the guards already done so? Where was Plum in all of this?

"He's a madman," one of the Granger infiltrators called out. "We're just Otranto scum fleeing from the Granger army."

The soldier should have kept his mouth shut. Both his word choice and his accent gave away his Granger background. Not that the guard shouldn't have at least questioned supposed peasants with the typical Granger blond hair. An angry murmur went up from the small crowd at the gate.

"Cavalry approaching," someone shouted from the guard tower overlooking the gate. "Doesn't look like ours."

Seconds later a bell sounded in the tower.

The bell was a signal that should have been echoed by churches throughout the city as Otranto pulled itself together for the final fight. Instead, it was met only by silence.

It rang a second time, sounding more desperate. Again nothing.

Plum joined Jake, his thin sword glinting in the cool sunlight. "I told Fernis that the church was rotten."

Jake nodded. "Looks like someone bought off the city guard too." Despite the alarm bell, the city gates remained wide open. The Granger who weren't unconscious began pulling swords and crossbows out of the farm wagon.

Jake looked at the staff he carried. It was already a little battered. He had trained to use the staff against the sword but it wasn't an even battle. Against a crossbow bolt, he could do nothing but duck and pray.

"Should we charge them again?" Plum asked.

Jake shook his head. "If we couldn't stop them when they were unarmed, we certainly couldn't do much against them now. Why don't you see what you can do about raising some of the militia and getting the gates closed? And find out where the brewers are. They should be here by now."

Plum shook his head. "It's only been a few minutes. They'll need time to organize."

Jake still couldn't see the Granger cavalry from street level but he knew they had to be getting closer. "If we don't get the gate closed, we're out of time." One of the Granger had obviously had a brainstorm. If they could capture Otranto City, the Otranto army would collapse, certain they'd never see a paycheck. The Granger main force would arrive unopposed.

"We don't need a lot of people, but we need something better than a couple of staffs," Jake admitted.

Jake glared at the Granger infiltrators. They, along with their bought mercenaries, had retreated into the two guard houses that protected the gear mechanism that would swing the huge wood and iron city gates closed.

A crossbow bolt brushed by Jake, coming close enough that he felt the wind from its passage. He ducked instinctively, but ineffectively. The second bolt caught him in the upper arm neatly slicing through muscle and exiting.

Involuntarily his grip on the staff loosened.

Cursing his inability to afford a first-rate medical implant, Jake sent a surge of dopamine through his system. It didn't take away the pain, but it let him at least control his body and reduced his blood pressure enough that he wouldn't instantly bleed to death. It was a stopgap measure, but then again, everything he'd done since arriving on Arcadia had been stopgap.

A clash of steel against steel gave him a momentary hope that reinforcements had arrived.

At least the Granger hadn't bribed everyone. Some of the guards had descended from the watch tower. They were attacked, however, by the five mercenaries who had let the Granger enter. It made sense, Jake realized. After taking the Granger money, they were committed.

For the moment, at least, the Granger crossbowmen shifted targets, picking off the Otranto guard. One of the bribed mercenaries also fell with a bolt through his back. One less bribe to pay, Jake guessed.

He wondered if he could hear the hoofbeats of the rapidly approaching Granger force, or if the sound was only his heart. The portion of the Otranto guard that hadn't been bribed was dying fast. Obviously they wouldn't be able to break through and close the gates. On the other hand, they had distracted the Granger guarding the gate.

"I'll charge them. You follow me and close the gates," he told Plum.

"But you're wounded."

Not much of a newsflash. "Now, while they're still distracted by the guards."

He rushed forward, the dopamine in his system making every step feel like one of those dreams where you couldn't get traction and ran without making any progress.

Then he was among the Granger. Amazingly, no one had shot him when he'd charged.

He swung the staff, smacking a crossbowman as he aimed at one of the Otranto guards. The bolt whined off into space but the collapsing Otranto got off enough of a warning shout to awaken the others to their danger.

Suddenly, Jake was surrounded by swordsmen.

He parried the first two thrusts before he saw his first opportunity. One of the swordsmen looked behind him. There was no doubt now that the Granger cavalry was arriving.

Jake jabbed, taking the swordsman in the throat.

His staff, soaked with the blood from his arm, slipped from his grip.

An Otranto boot caught him from behind and Jake plunged to the ground.

He tried to turn, but he had lost all strength in his arm.

He was, quite literally, saved by the cavalry. A Granger horse leapt over his prone body while the infiltrators danced out of the way. Their task was complete now that their cavalry had arrived.

The whole thing was simply distressing, Jake decided. He managed to press his left hand against his right arm, slowing the flow of blood from his wound and cranked up his body's resistance to shock. That much was basic, although, even as he was doing it, Jake wondered why he bothered. Wouldn't a relatively painless death here be better than whatever the Granger had in mind?

Granger war cries indicated that the battle had moved away from the gates, sweeping away the handful of soldiers who had descended from the guard tower. Every second that passed, more cavalry poured through the open gate. With Otranto's army still in the field, even a fully mobilized city guard would be ineffective against these numbers.

The sudden roar of a musket salvo broke into Jake's muddled thoughts.

Granger shouts were joined by screams.

Had the Granger brought dragoons among their cavalry? Jake's curiosity got the better of his common sense. Rather than let himself suffer in peace, he forced himself to roll over, then dragged his body to a wall where he could pull himself partway up.

A heavy weight dropped on his arm just as he gained his vantage point.

He screamed in pain as the man slammed into his wound.

The Granger cavalryman stared at him with glassy blue eyes. A huge exit wound opened like a crater across the man's back.

Another salvo of musket fire sounded. Then a third.

The Granger cavalry reversed direction, their momentum lost as half their number were cut down.

Slowly, the city gates swung closed.

Jake seemed to see the entire scene with perfect clarity. In his doped up state, time seemed to have lost meaning. Events occurred instantly, or with painful slowness, all jumbled together like an amateur 3-D.

The Granger cavalry officer stared at the closing gate, his mind obviously torn between the need to keep his mounted forces mobile and the realization that he could reopen the gates if only he could clear the pesky musketmen from the Otranto streets.

His indecision lasted only seconds--or at least Jake imagined it was seconds. It was, at any rate, long enough for the Otranto musketmen to loose another volley.

Jake had to give the cavalry captain credit. The man was hardly older than Jake himself. No one would have blamed him if he had retreated and saved his men from being cut to pieces by the heavy bullets of the Otranto musketmen.

Despite the gaps the latest musket volley had put in his numbers, the officer put two fingers in his mouth and gave out a piercing whistle, then gestured with his saber pointing directly at the thin line of Otranto musketmen.

Behind him, the Granger formed up, then charged.

The musketmen wavered.

The brewers militia had arrived. Jake hadn't had time to watch them practice, but Manny had given him regular reports. From Manny's viewpoint, they were virtually worthless despite the beautiful muskets that Jake had given him. Right then, Jake hoped that Manny's standards were high because a group of brewers were the only thing standing between Otranto and destruction.

The Granger pressed forward. A few fired pistols into the tight mass of brewers who blocked their way to a victory that would rank among the most glorious in Granger history.

Jake hadn't really taken a good look at Manny lately and was surprised to see that the man had slimmed down. He was still strong and powerful, but he sat on his horse with his back straight and a deadly looking saber held in his hands. This, Jake realized, was the real Manny--the Manny who had fought for the Empire and won himself a Princess. No wonder he had managed to make something of the force of Brewers that Jake, and the rest of Otranto, had considered a joke.

Manny got most of his musketeers ready in time to get two more ragged volleys off just as the cavalry line reached the infantry.

Horses and humans screamed as the heavy musket balls scythed through the cavalry ranks.

Jake crossed his fingers as the young Granger officer, somehow unhurt by the musket shot, pressed ahead. The young man kicked his spurred heels into his horse's flanks and slashed his saber at a bayoneted musket.

And that, Jake realized, would end it. Infantry stood a chance against cavalry only so long as they stayed organized, providing an effective front. Once the Granger burst into their midst, the slaughter would turn around.

The Granger had won his bet.

The officer smiled as his steel saber sliced off the end of the musket's iron barrel, the bayonet clashing as it hit the ground.

From nowhere, a small figure appeared, pressing a bayonet through the officer's thigh and into the horse.

The animal reared, then collapsed onto its side.

Castile, for it was she who had wielded that fatal bayonet thrust, advanced at the remaining cavalry, death in her eyes.

The Granger pulled on their reins wheeling away to regroup, then turned back in time to see the brewers redressing their lines.

Behind them, Plum and the firemen had finished shutting the gate.

The Granger glared at the musketeers and Jake thought they would charge again but then one threw down his saber. The same panic which had nearly destroyed the brewers only moments before went through the Granger ranks as the line of bayonet-bearing brewers closed. The cobblestones rang with the sound of weapons being thrown down.

They'd survived the first attack—by the skin of their teeth.

* * * *

Castile ignored the surrendering soldiers and ran to Jake.

"You're wounded."

It was such an obvious statement that Jake laughed despite himself. "I'm dying."

Anger warred with concern in Castile's eyes. Warred and won. "That's the most ridiculous thing I've ever heard. You're shot in the arm, not the heart."

"I've lost a lot of blood." His sensors could have told him exactly how much, but that didn't really matter.

"Then we'd better stop it, hadn't we?"

Castile used the sharp blade of her bayonet to rip a seam from her skirt, then tore a long bandage from it. "Give me your arm," she demanded.

Jake obeyed. Despite himself, his eyes were drawn to her legs. They were slender, but they weren't child legs. Instead, Arcadia's high gravity, or maybe just extremely lucky genes, had given Castile's legs a firm muscular shape that speeded his heartbeat.

"Stop it," she hissed at him.

"What?" It was a futile attempt to hide the truth.

"I don't mind you looking at me, but try to keep your heartrate under control." She pressed harder against his wound.

"I wasn't looking," he lied.

"Just shut up," she told him. "Do you have any idea what would happen to me if you died?"

He shook his head. He didn't have a clue how to answer that question.

"Well, it would be terrible. I'd never get to run the steel business, and I'd probably be packed off to marry some Granger baron. Fernis was already talking about that, you know."

Jake felt a surge of totally irrational anger against Fernis. How could the emperor think about marrying off a child like Castile? How could he even consider a Granger?

"There." Castile tied the makeshift bandage around his arm. "If it doesn't get infected, you'll live."

Jake might have bought the cheapest medical implant he could find, but it wasn't so primitive it would actually allow bacteria to attack him. Besides, Arcadia's terraforming had left behind the worst of the pathogens that made ancient Earth such a hell-hole.

"Thanks."

"Oh, Jake. You can't help being such an idiot, can you?" For the second time that day, she brushed her lips against his. "I'm going up to the guard tower now. Time to shoot some Granger."

"Wait. We've got to decide what to do next. There have to be more Granger out there."

"Later." Castile's face was deadly serious. "I'll see if we can whittle them down a little for you. I need to pay back those bastards for killing Clovis." She gave him a tired smile. "After that, I'll come back and get you. I'm going to need your help."

"Doing what?" Castile seemed perfectly capable of doing just about anything she put her mind to.

"Killing some of our own people. It should never have been this close."

Jake watched Castile disappear, then looked around at the scene of destruction. The corpses of at least fifty horses and even more men lay littered around the square that served as the portal into the city of Otranto.

Otranto had barely survived the first attack. Yet, what had it really done other than show how painfully unprepared it was for a real battle against a force that would number in the tens or even hundreds of thousand?

* * * *

Fernis took a deep draught of wine, then slammed his fist against the table. "What possible good can your mercantile empire do us now? The Granger are at the walls and our own army is cut off."

He and Osiris had taken Jake's ferry back into the city, sneaking past Anglic ships in the night. The army remained in the field where it had been driven from its prepared defensive line. Several thousand Granger cavalry camped between it and the relative safety of the city's walls.

"Paying for the war will be difficult," Jake agreed. "It certainly reduces our flexibility to profit from trade."

"Which is your main goal, of course."

Jake just nodded. He didn't think Fernis would understand or believe him if Jake told the Emperor that his objectives were simply to preserve a civilization that might have something to offer the rest of the galaxy. After all, he hadn't quite been able to convince himself.

"Well, Osiris, how do you explain this military disaster?"

Osiris shook his head. "As always, the Granger prisoners say nothing. The mercenaries who betrayed us are certainly willing to talk, but they simply claim that an Otranto native gave them gold to let the peasants in, unquestioned."

"Which you believe?"

"We have the gold."

Fernis waved away that comment. "But who did it? And why? The Deity knows I'm not universally loved, but even I have to be better than a week of Granger plundering and a lifetime of slavery."

"I've seized the guildmasters from the guilds that opposed our defense efforts," Plum said. "No one who knows anything has broken so far, but my men will continue working on it."

"That cursed Granger Ambassador has his golden fingers everywhere," Fernis said. "At least this means you won't have to face him, spacer."

Jake nodded. His plan was to die of old age somewhere on the far side of two hundred, not to be shot down in a duel on a backward planet. "Not in a legal duel, anyway. Now all I have to worry about is him hunting me down."

Osiris looked puzzled. "Surely now that the war is on, he'll have more attractive targets. Men like me, for example. Who cares about a merchant once blows have been struck?"

Jake hoped that the Granger would share that attitude and misunderstanding of the role that the economy played in building a powerful military force. Maybe their rulers did, but he didn't think the Granger ambassador shared that weakness.

"It seems to me that the Granger have the military situation fairly well in hand."

Osiris nodded, his face a mask of anger. "They could never have snuck that force behind my lines if it weren't for the cursed barbarians." He turned to face the emperor. "Sire, unfortunately the spacer is correct. My men are outnumbered by the attacking Granger and by now they know that the road to Otranto city is blocked by a covering force. Within a few days, they'll realize that they're lost all chance of being paid. When that happens, they'll head for their homes and leave us unprotected. Any plans of getting the peasants into the city are also hopeless."

Jake resisted saying he'd told them so. Even if Osiris and Fernis had reacted instantly the previous evening, they wouldn't have had time to bring the soldiers home before this disaster struck. And it was a disaster despite their narrow victory at the city gates. An army of at least a couple of thousand Granger now sat outside the city walls, digging in and daring the unorganized militia and civic guard within the city walls to come out and fight.

Fernis took another drink. "What do you propose?"

Jake ran down the list of plans that he'd made, strategies that he'd considered. They could involve the Tiflis, attacking the Granger from the rear. They could incite a revolt among the Ebron, drawing Granger from the battle as well. And eventually, given time, Otranto's own industry could start to turn out the weapons and wealth that would allow them to pay more mercenaries, equip them, and send them out against the Granger horde. All of those plans required maintaining Otranto as a base, and an effective army either in the field or within the city walls.

Osiris slowly removed the heavy belt from around his waist and then withdrew his two-handed sword. "Perhaps it is time to admit that we have lost. We could use the spacer's ship, as well as the ships of our friendly Bourgundians and evacuate much of the population."

"To go where?" Fernis demanded.

"Although no eastern city would wish to be overwhelmed, I think most cities would take a few of you. Otranto is still known for its art, literature, and science. What city wouldn't welcome such an addition?"

Jake wanted to speak out against this surrender but found he could not. Fundamentally, this was an Otranto battle and an Otranto decision.

Fernis stared at his general, then shook his head. "If the Otranto Empire is destined to fail, it will fail through battle, rather than through surrender. We shall fight."

Chapter 25

"Half the members of the brewers guild are standing guard at the city walls," Manny complained. "Including almost all who work for me. I have orders I can't fill."

Considering that Manny's ale was the only real value behind their currency, the matter was more serious than it sounded. Although the other guilds were supposed to provide trained militia, only Manny had made more than a pretense at doing so. Neither Jake nor the Emperor had a lot of confidence in the mercenaries within the city. The best were with the main army. Those that remained were the dregs of the bunch. No one knew who else among them might have been corrupted by Granger gold.

"Raid the Granger Ambassador's house," Marie suggested. "He's been doling out money all over the city. There may be some left there."

This was the third council of war that Jake had attended in the past twenty-four hours and the first where he thought they might actually make progress. In addition to Manny, Marie, and the inevitable Castile, Lucer and Harold had made it back to town. Harold had sailed with their ship, bringing back a small cadre of Tiflis warriors, and word that Broussard had his men at work gathering naval supplies. How long the Granger would leave them alone was another question.

"Plum beat us to the ambassador's house," Jake admitted. "If he found any money, he hasn't mentioned it." Not that even the ambassador would have enough gold to fund the entire mercenary force. Bribing a selected few takes a lot less gold than making regular payments to thousands of soldiers.

"Plum probably kept the money for himself," Castile muttered.

She might be right. Jake would prefer to believe that Plum would use it to pay his own bribes.

"We need to get more Otranto natives into the army," Jake commented. "Even without much training, they should be able to man the walls. That would free up the mercenaries to act as the reserve and as a mobile strike force."

Manny shook his head. "I can barely persuade my own guild to help and a lot of the brewers are first or second generation barbarians. As for the other guilds..." he let his voice trail off.

"Don't they realize what will happen if the Granger win?"

Marie put her hand on Jake's arm. "Of course they do. But they see it as inevitable. So they simply decide to enjoy life as best they can while they still can."

"We've got to get the army back," Harold stated bluntly. "If we lose them, we're lost."

"And we've got to get more workers into the city," Castile added. "Do you know how many people I've found for my ironworks so far? Seven. I need seven hundred."

"Right," Jake said. "We need more soldiers and more workers. There are plenty of both outside the city in the runt of the Otranto Empire, except that the Granger have cut off the route home. So what are we going to do about it?"

"We could send out the ship," Lucer suggested. "If you crammed it full, you could probably get two hundred soldiers on it. Maybe two-fifty."

For a moment, Jake felt optimism try to lift its head. Even a couple of hundred veteran soldiers could make a huge difference in Otranto City.

"Wouldn't work," Manny said. "Even if the Granger were stupid and didn't attack while you were loading, which they would, you'd start a civil war among the mercenaries when they saw that you were abandoning most of them to the Granger."

"A few hundred soldiers won't matter anyway," Castile added. "We aren't talking about holding out for a month or two. If you're going to make Otranto thrive, we need the workers. Already, you need more workers for your olive orchards. Not to mention to help harvest the silk worms, to spin the silk, and to weave it into cloth. And did I bring up my steel works?"

"And I need more brewers," Manny added.

"Give me some of that ale," Jake demanded. He took a deep drink and wished that he could drown out his problems.

He wasn't ready for this. A year before, he'd been a student. If he'd stayed in the civilized galaxy, he wouldn't have had a chance to run a business for another hundred years, at least. His total experience in generalship had been blundering around in the desert until the Tiflis had rescued him.

"All right, so we need to get the entire army and let all the refugees in. Anyone have any ideas?"

"You've got to wipe out the Granger holding force," Castile said. "If they were gone, the army could protect the peasants and shepherd them into the city."

Jake had an uncomfortable feeling that Castile was right. The two thousand Granger outside Otranto's land wall were more than a threat to the city, they were a nail in the coffin of all of his plans.

"Anybody disagree?"

"No," Harold said. "But if the army tried to clear them out, the Granger would attack them from behind. They'd be smashed between hammer and anvil.

He'd known that, although the mental picture made it worse. They'd have to take care of the Granger force with what they could scrape together in Otranto City.

"Counting your brewmasters, how many soldiers have we got?" Jake asked Manny.

"If you're including the city guard, maybe two hundred. Fifty of us. One-fifty of them."

"And the Granger have two thousand?"

"At least," Manny admitted.

"So all we have to do is wipe out a force that outnumbers us ten to one, then get the army and refugees in before the main Granger army arrives. Anything else?"

Nobody had any answers and the meeting broke up.

* * * *

"Get up, you're in trouble." A hard boot in Jake's ribs brought him to a semblance of life.

Instinctively he grappled his assailant, pulling the man down on his bed as he reached for the dagger under his pillow.

"I'm trying to help you, idiot."

Belatedly, he recognized the voice. It was John, the ex-clerk and ex-legate of the ex-patriarch. "Huh? What are you doing here?"

"I'm trying to save your life." John rubbed his nose, which Jake's elbow had somehow connected to. "For all the thanks I get."

Jake was instantly fully awake. "Have the Granger breached the city walls?"

John shook his head. "Not their army, anyway. Today is Sunday."

Jake didn't follow the non sequitur. "They won't attack on Sunday?"

John hissed. "Stop talking and listen to me. The false patriarch has required all churches to preach that the Granger invasion is a punishment for our steps away from the truth. Your agreement with the Bourgundian schismatics is labeled as a primary heresy. So is our reliance on the barbarians for mercenaries. We're supposed to shut them out of the city and rely on prayer to save us. Also, the witchcraft charges against Manny and Marie Delphonte have been reinstated."

"That's absurd. Manny and his brewers saved the city yesterday. They're heroes."

"What's absurd is that we're sitting here talking when there's a mob gathering at every church just aching to tear your warehouses apart. There are rumors that you have entire chambers filled with gold coins, bales of silk, and barrels of ale. The priests have even been showing pails of gold coins that they say were taken from your home."

As if Jake would have reverted to paper currency if he'd had that much gold. "The Patriarch nearly bankrupted himself to equip you with a hundred or so gold a few weeks ago. So, where did they get buckets of gold?"

John shrugged. "Why are you worrying about that when we've got to save your life? Someone got the word to the Castile and it's pulled out of the harbor but you could probably take your ferry to Tantalus."

Belatedly, Jake started moving. His body was even sorer now than it had been when he'd been injured and his wounded arm screamed in pain. He reached for his staff, then dropped it when his right hand refused to close around the weapon.

"Oh, Merciful Heavens. I hadn't realized you were injured," John told him.

"I'll live," Jake told him.

John gave him a funny look. "All right, come on then. There's a mercenary detachment down at the ferry dock."

Despite John's hurry, Jake insisted on rousting some of his workers and moving the beer kegs to the front of the warehouse. He could replace beer a lot more easily than he could the bales of silk or barrels of olive oil at the back of the warehouse. The thick sheaf of paper currency he'd just received from his printer, he covered with olive oil, then thrust into the fire. He could print more money later but he didn't want to risk debasing his currency.

As John has promised, a mercenary party of about twenty soldiers guarded the ferry. The ferryman gave Jake a rueful grin. "Once I brought back the Emperor, I decided to stay in the city. The channel may be a little wider here, but it's a lot safer considering the Granger control my usual dock. 'Course those Anglic ships can still shoot me up if they see me."

Jake shook the man's hand. While John had been hurrying him along, he'd had a chance to think. Running now wasn't the answer, at least not for him. "Any of you who want to flee may do so. You took the Emperor's coin with the understanding that he would support you, yet he has been unable to do so. I, however, intend to stay here in Otranto."

"But they'll kill you," John shouted, frustration written across his face. "They'll kill all of you because they think that'll make the Granger go easier on them once the city falls."

"He's probably right," Jake admitted. "Any of you who stay with me are taking a long chance."

"I take it you aren't just planning on staying and getting captured," a grizzled mercenary sergeant growled. "What's the plan?"

"And what's the pay?" a muscular youth added.

"I don't have a plan yet," Jake admitted. "But I know what we need to do. First, we need to put the real Patriarch back in control of the church and get rid of the anti-patriarch who is stirring up so much trouble. Second, we need to mobilize the church and the people against the real enemy. Third..." his voice trailed off. "Uh, well, I don't really have a third yet. We'd be doing pretty well if we get the first two done."

"You'll be doing pretty well if you're still alive in an hour," John told him. "They have the Patriarch locked up in the dungeon under the cathedral. Even I couldn't get in to see him."

"What sort of guards do they have?" Jake asked.

"Martial monks. All of them. They've called up the entire monastery."

"We can take a bunch of priests," the muscular young soldier said.

"Shut up, Norbert," the Sergeant growled. He slammed a palm into the man's temple for good measure. "We slice up a bunch of priests and even the true Patriarch won't be able to stop the mob."

"How many martial monks are there?" Jake was starting to get an idea.

"Maybe a couple of hundred." John scratched his partially shaven scalp. "In the thousand years since they were created, they've never been assembled in one place before. Normally they're used to keep the passes between the monasteries free of bandits and for escort duty like when we went to Tantulus." So they would have experience dealing with men like Norbert was the unspoken subtext.

"Surely the patriarch has some support among the clergy," Jake suggested to John. "How many monks and priests could you get outside the cathedral to protest the patriarch's unlawful ousting?"

John wrinkled his forehead. "I'm not sure it was unlawful. The synod of the church met and voted for his removal."

"The synod was bought by the Granger."

"Even so."

"Are you saying you couldn't get a single priest to protest?" Jake let frustration creep into his voice. He needed some support now and intended to find it.

"Oh, no. The patriarch definitely had his fans. I might be able to get fifty today, two hundred by tomorrow afternoon. But they'd be mobbed once the new Patriarch gets word out to the churches."

Jake sniffed the air. The faint odor of burning might just have been someone's cooking fire, but it wouldn't be long before half the city was ablaze. "Then we'd better act quickly."

"If I take fifty priests to the cathedral, we'll be excommunicated and then slaughtered," John protested. "If these mercenaries tried to protect us, everyone would think we'd joined the schismatics. Without the mercenaries, they would never even let us get a hearing."

"I've got another use for the soldiers," Jake said.

"The martial monks are disciplined," John added. His eyes flashed white with fear. "Not that I wouldn't give up my life for the patriarch and my faith, but if you're thinking of a distraction, it wouldn't bring them out from the dungeons if that's where they were ordered to guard."

"That's what I'm counting on. Can you still move freely?"

John pulled up the cowl to his habit. "I'm just one priest among thousands."

"I need you to go to the brewers. Pull them off the city walls and have them form a guard for you and the rest of the priests. That should be safer for you than using the mercenaries. You've got two hours to put together a demonstration outside the cathedral."

"Should we try to capture it?"

Jake considered briefly. The Otranto Cathedral was the center of the state religion. As long as it remained in the conservative clergy's hands, they would maintain a false grasp on legitimacy. It was tempting to tell John to go ahead and grab the church and declare the new Patriarch a fraud. Tempting, but Jake couldn't afford a bloodbath. He needed those martial monks once the true patriarch had been restored to his throne. A couple of hundred trained soldiers more than doubled the city's strike capabilities.

He shook his head. "Just stay in the courtyard outside and shout down the false patriarch. Don't let them move you off, but don't attack them. Tell Angbert and Theo not to shoot unless the monks shoot first."

John shook his head. "I thought I was sticking my neck out just rescuing you. Now you're sending me to certain death and weakening the city walls to do it."

Jake grasped John by both shoulders. "The true patriarch named you as his legate. Until he rescinds that, or until he dies, you have a responsibility to him and to the church. If you let the Granger conquer Otranto, you will have failed both of those responsibilities."

"But I don't know what's right," John almost whined. "Since I found my vocation, I've learned to take orders and this violates every order I've received."

John's problems sounded distressingly similar to Jake's own. Well, tough. They'd both have to make do. "A legate must give orders as well as take them. Believe me, John, we won't leave you out there for long."

"But what are you going to do?"

"I told you. We're going to rescue the true patriarch."

"And I told you that was impossible."

For a moment, John looked like he was battling back tears. Then he took a sobbing breath and rubbed any moisture out of his eyes. "The ancient philosophers speak of the leap of faith, depending on God when logic fails. I will do that now. If I don't see you again, may God bless your efforts."

John seized Jake's shoulders and kissed him on each cheek, then turned and marched away. As he reached the corner, he flipped up his hood and vanished.

Jake turned to his small band of mercenaries. All looked frightened. None looked ready to take the leap of faith that John had mentioned and commit themselves to any impossible task.

"Like the man said, we can't rescue the patriarch without fighting a bunch of priests," the sergeant told Jake. "Even if we won, they'd just kill the patriarch when we got close."

Jake sagged against the stone sea wall. "That's why we won't go into the dungeon. I'm going to need both you and the martial monks if we're going to clean out that mess of Granger outside the city."

"Too bad we're not on the same side, then." The sergeant spat onto the cobblestone road. "If the Otranto heretics would just return to the true faith, all of this conflict could be taken care of. As it is, maybe the new patriarch is right. Better the Granger than heretics. At least you know your enemy. The Granger will attack you from the front. The Otranto will stick a knife in your back."

If Jake understood Arcadia history, the schism between eastern and Otranto churches had occurred more than five hundred years earlier. He wasn't going to cure that breach today, or ever. Trying would earn him the enmity of both groups.

"Preach your faith on your own time, soldier," Jake commented. "Right now, I need a decision from all of you. You can take the ferry over to Tantalus. From there, you'll eventually be able to catch a ship home. Or you can stay here and fight with me. I can't guarantee results, but I will say that anyone who joins this group has a good chance of rising fast in the Otranto army. We're going to be hiring a lot of mercenaries and they're going to need experienced NCOs and officers."

The sergeant nodded slowly. "I've always fancied the title General Adrican."

"Well, General, how about it?"

"Guess I'll stay." Adrican pulled out a thick wad of paper—his currency, Jake noticed. "Don't suspect any of this would do me much good if I got sent back to Bourgundia."

"Hey, that's right," Norbert said as if the thought had never crossed his mind. "If this city isn't here, all the money I've made wouldn't be worth wiping my butt with."

"An unfortunate expression but the right attitude," Jake said. "So here's the plan."

* * * *

The soldiers' biggest complaint about wearing Otranto priest garb wasn't that their weapons would be hard to reach. It was a concern that their souls might somehow be damned if God mistook them for real heretics. This theological debate threatened to scuttle the entire expedition until *General* Adrican took matters into his own hands and started thumping heads.

"God's good. He'll sort things out," was his final comment.

They infiltrated the mob which had gathered in the courtyard between the patriarch's palace and the cathedral. Martial monks would occasionally crack the head of an unruly rioter and a stream of loud-voiced priests climbed onto a makeshift stage and lectured anyone who could hear on the perfidy of the barbarian schismatics, the evils of Jake's attempts to make peace with the Bourgundians at the cost of giving up Otranto territory--never mind that the territory in question hadn't actually been controlled by Otranto for two hundred years--and on how only reliance on faith could prevent the city from being overrun by the Granger horde nestled outside the city.

"Traitor." A high-pitched voice screamed the word overwhelming the ongoing growl of the crowd and the tired drone of the priests. "The false patriarch and his priests have been bought by Granger gold."

That started a hubbub, especially when the speaker climbed up on a rock, showing himself to be a young priest.

Two older priests stepped toward the protestor, one smacking a heavy walking stick against his palm but found their way blocked by taciturn men wearing the symbol of the brewers guild.

John's promised fifty priests were on the scene.

Jake waited until a group of martial monks marched out from the patriarch's palace. As he'd expected, none emerged from the dungeons under the cathedral. As long as they kept the true patriarch under their control, the protests could never amount to much.

The martial monks shoved their way into the crowd and at least some of the crowd shoved back.

When the rioting started, Jake signaled to his mercenaries, along with one loyal priest as guide, to move in.

Allowing soldiers to alternate between periods of service and periods of brigandage might be the worst possible means of defending a nation but it did prepare her soldiers to be versatile. One of the mercenaries picked the lock to a servant's entryway and the soldiers, accompanied by one of John's fellow clerks as a guide, poured into the palace.

They moved quickly and silently. Even with the distraction outside, they would be outnumbered within the palace. By keeping his forces concentrated, Jake believed he could have the advantage in any battle, as long as he ended it quickly.

For the first two levels, they met only servants who scuttled away as quickly as they could go when Jake warned them to vanish for an hour. Sooner or later one of them would run into one of the false Patriarch's priests or a band of martial monks and Jake would lose the element of surprise. Still, he couldn't bring himself to slaughter the innocent servants.

The ex-patriarch had generally worked in his library and the clerk led Jake and his mercenaries to that large chamber. Four martial monks guarded the doorway, but four arrows cut them down before they could make a sound.

Jake's bile rose as they stepped over the bloody corpses and walked into the ancient library. He was slaughtering the very people he intended to protect and it didn't feel good.

Tomes stretched from floor to ceiling, pressed closely together in a wealth of literature, philosophy, and history that would give hundreds of spacer graduate students new material for their Ph.D. dissertations.

Another business opportunity. Graduate students were notoriously impoverished, but even a poor spacer was wealthy by the standards of Arcadia. And graduate students would kill to have access to a library unknown in the rest of the galaxy.

Unfortunately, besides the corpses outside the library and the mercenaries, and the valuable books, the library was unoccupied.

"There's nobody here," Adircan told him.

"I see." So, killing the four monks had been useless. Worse than useless, actually. Jake needed those monks at the city walls, not lying dead in the patriarch's palace.

He suppressed his feelings of revulsion knowing that he'd pay for it in nightmares for months to come. Marching around a gradually awakening palace seemed like a recipe for failure. "The false patriarch is no scholar. Any suggestions?"

The babble that met his question boiled down to nothing.

"Right. Does he have a throne room?"

Their guide explained that thrones were reserved to the Emperor and to God alone. The patriarch did have a formal receiving room, but it would be blasphemous even to compare the two.

"Lead the way," Jake ordered.

He scooped a crossbow from one of the dead monks and ordered that their bodies be dragged into the library although he could do nothing about the bloodstains that remained on the whitewashed walls. Time was definitely running out.

The formal receiving room was up two flights of stairs and on the opposite wing of the large palace.

They ran, sacrificing stealth to speed.

By the time they reached their destination, they'd run into and killed an additional eight monks. Worse, Jake could almost feel the palace awakening to his presence.

The group outside the receiving room outnumbered Jake's small mercenary force by at least four to one. Fortunately, they were mostly unarmed priests rather than martial monks. While they were perfectly capable of breaking the head of an aging opponent, they couldn't and wouldn't stand against a trained military unit.

Jake didn't wait for his light-fingered mercenaries to pick this lock. He seized a heavy chair and flung it into the double-door.

The door burst open and Jake strode in, his crossbow pointed directly at the heart of the false patriarch.

"I warned you that the priests outside were a mere diversion," a cold voice commented.

It took Jake only a second to place that voice--the Granger ambassador.

"Take the ambassador into custody," Jake snapped at Adircan, who'd entered the receiving room after him.

"The ambassador is under my protection," the false patriarch said. "And all of you are risking your immortal souls by supporting this spacer."

"He's playing for time," Jake snapped. "Secure the area."

His mercenaries looked around, uncertain exactly how to go about securing what looked very much like a throne room, then hustled off whatever priests had been calling on the patriarch leaving only the patriarch and the ambassador.

"I suppose you want safe passage out of the city," the ambassador said. "Something like that could be arranged. Perhaps with a bonus for this group of mercenaries."

The Granger Ambassador had bribed at least one group of mercenaries before now. If he bribed Jake's soldiers, all of Jake's work would be for nothing.

"We'll deal with you later, Mr. Ambassador, Jake sneered. He put as much contempt as he could into his voice hoping that the mercenaries would get the message. "Right now, we're trying to save the so-called patriarch's life."

The false patriarch's eyes bulged. "What? The only danger I'm in is from you."

"You're hardly in danger from them," the ambassador commented. "If they kill you, they'll never make it out of your palace alive."

The false patriarch drew himself erect. "Quite right. Thank you for pointing it out."

"Are you truly certain you want to thank him?" Jake lowered his aim and pulled the trigger. The bolt shuddered through the air into the patriarch's foot.

The man screamed in pain, writhing around the iron missile that pinned his foot to the solid oak floor.

"Don't let him fall," Jake advised Adircan. "That might damage him."

The Ambassador smiled coldly. "Assaulting a priest is a capital crime in Otranto. You seem to be digging yourself quite a hole."

Jake nodded. "Next time I talk to the Emperor, I'll definitely have to beg for an official pardoning. He is equal to the apostles, after all, so that should be within his power. In the meantime, perhaps you'll understand my rudeness. We do have a civilization to save." He paused for only a moment. "Gag the Ambassador. His threats are starting to annoy me and I don't really want to kill him before turning him over to the Emperor's torturers."

Some of the mercenaries looked reluctant, but they followed Jake's order under the glaring eyes of their sergeant--uh, General.

Jake turned his attention back to the false patriarch. "Now, reverend sir, I suggest that we go down and free the true patriarch."

"Why should I help you?" the patriarch demanded. His eyes glowed with pain, but the ambassador's words had apparently rekindled his hopes.

"Right now, we think you are a good man who was lied to and misled by the Granger Ambassador," Jake said. "Once you've done a nominal penance, I'm certain that you would be welcomed back to your former church offices."

"But I'm the patriarch."

"Deposing the true patriarch was illegal," Jake's pet clerk stated. "Making your election null and void."

"Both null and void makes a strong combination," Jake commented wondering why legal language got so stale in just about every culture.

"I'll guarantee the Ambassador's offer of safe conduct and full pay to your soldiers," the false patriarch offered. His face dripped with sweat, but his eyes looked calculating.

"You know, I'm afraid you'll always walk with a limp," Jake said. He borrowed a second crossbow from one of his mercenaries. "At least you still have one good leg. It would be a shame if something happened to it."

"You wouldn't dare."

Jake laughed. After what he'd been through since he'd arrived in Arcadia, he would dare just about anything.

For a moment, the false patriarch met his eyes, glaring at him, trying to read whether he would go through with his threats. Jake put every ounce of his energy into the truth. He would do anything it took to free Otranto from the Granger grip. Making the patriarch pay wouldn't even be high on his list of regrets.

"All right. What do you want?"

* * * *

The pot of Granger gold, the newly freed patriarch, and the haggard deposed false patriarch told the story in a way that the Otranto mob could understand.

After a brief address, the true patriarch marched triumphantly into the cathedral, still dressed in his prison rags and covered in mud, feces, and straw from his cell. Under the urging of John's priests and the watchful eyes of the brewer militia, thousands of citizens shouted out their support for holy war against the Grangers who had tried to subvert the true way. Schismatic barbarians were at least temporarily forgotten.

"We could send the mob against the Granger outside the wall," Adircan suggested. They were standing near the back of the huge cathedral as the patriarch pulled out the emotional stops. "Wouldn't bother me none if the Granger and these nuts both sliced each other up and left me alone."

Jake shook his head. He'd taken a lot of chances to get here and didn't intend to blow the opportunity by sending untrained citizens against ordered military units.

"Getting half the city killed isn't going to win this war for us. I've got a better idea."

The true patriarch had given his rival far better accommodations than he'd received himself, but the man was definitely in a cell when Jake went to see him.

"He's badly hurt," a nun told Jake when he entered the cell. "I'm not sure he's strong enough to talk."

"He'll want to talk to me," Jake said. He sat down next to the failed priest.

"He doesn't look like it." The ex-patriarch was thrashing in the bed like he'd been stimulated by electric shock treatment.

"Perhaps you'll leave us for a moment, sister," Jake suggested.

"But--"

"I'm here as his confessor."

"Oh." The fact that Jake was no priest didn't seem to register as the woman fled.

"Haven't you done enough? You told me I'd be returned to all of my previous positions."

"I said you would have to do penance first. And I'm here to offer you a chance to start on that."

"I'm already suffering. I think that heaven will take that into account."

Jake nodded. "No doubt. But your church will require more. Even you can see that."

The false patriarch sighed. He suddenly looked old and worn. Perhaps, Jake thought, the man was not evil himself. Perhaps he was simply clueless about political realities.

"What do you want me to do?"

Chapter 26

It took two days of solid effort, but the stonemason's guild, prompted by a substantial percentage of the captured Granger gold, had done its work.

Jake walked around the newly enclosed courtyard and nodded. This would have to do.

"I'm ready." John was white with fear. Despite his heavy priestly robes, he trembled with cold and fright.

"Are you sure you want to do this?" Jake asked.

"It has to be a priest."

"But does it have to be you? You've already done a lot, taken a lot of risks."

John forced the mere beginnings of a smile. "It doesn't work like that in the world of faith, my friend. The Granger are likely to have followers of the false patriarch with them. If we sent one of their own, how could we be assured of his loyalty?"

"But they know you're loyal to the true patriarch?"

John laughed bitterly. "Everyone was loyal to the true patriarch when he was in power. When he fell, most of them switched to the false patriarch. Only you and a few others know the role I played. Switching over to the winning side is a longstanding Otranto tradition. Besides, if anyone suspects my loyalties, they'll know that the false patriarch wouldn't have any problems risking my life."

Jake shook his head but he knew he couldn't win this argument. If he kept on trying, he'd only undermine his friend's confidence and he'd need every bit of that to survive the coming night.

"Try not to get hurt, then." He shook the man's hand.

"Be careful." Castile reached up, brushed back the hood to John's cassock, and kissed the priest on his lips. "I'll pray for you."

John blushed enough to put a little color back in his cheeks. "One can never have too many prayers."

Jake handed him the note he and the false patriarch had spent hours crafting, and then the Granger Ambassador's heavy seal ring. "I hope this isn't overkill."

John gave him a twisted smile. "You and me both." He turned toward the city gate.

"Open it," Jake commanded.

Adircan opened the small door at the base of the great gate and the priest slipped out.

No sound of gunfire or slap of a bowstring sounded. At least John had survived the first test.

"You know what to do here," Jake told Osiris. Despite the ten feet of stone wall between himself and the Granger force camped outside, Jake kept his voice soft.

"Don't worry about us."

"Yeah, right."

The general clasped him on both shoulders. "I wish I were thirty years younger. Hell, ten years younger. I'd join your group in a heartbeat."

"You're needed here," Jake reminded him. "Keep the Emperor from getting killed."

"That's the problem, isn't it," Osiris told him.

"Only one of them."

* * * *

Jake's ferry could hold thirty armed warriors. The reinstated Patriarch had insisted that Jake take twenty-nine of his martial monks to let them work off the stigma of having imprisoned the rightful Patriarch. If they had time, a second boat would arrive with reinforcements. Jake didn't think they'd have time. They would win or lose with the thirty, including himself. It was an incredibly small force to set up against an army of thousands.

* * * *

Even after months of living on Arcadia, Jake had still not gotten accustomed to the absolute darkness of the nights when Arcadia's small moon was out of the sky. His vision enhancement allowed him to see into the infrared range, but the cloaks that the monks wore seemed to block that infrared too, and they quickly blended into the background. Only the monk assigned to stay with Jake and serve as his relay remained visible.

"You know the plan," Jake whispered. They'd walked for two miles from where the ferry had dropped them and were now close to the Granger forces.

An owl hoot was the only response that got, but it was enough to bring the monks to absolute stillness.

Jake burrowed into the underbrush. They had allowed time for problems and, uniquely for Jake's time on Arcadia, they hadn't had any. It would be two hours before dawn. Two hours before the Granger would attack--if John's scam had worked. If it didn't, his band of thirty monks would face an undamaged cavalry force of two thousand men. Now that wasn't a reassuring thought.

Despite his almost uncontrollable adrenaline surge and the dull throb in his arm, Jake actually managed to doze underneath the thick black silk cloak his workers had made for him. The tight woven fabric would actually absorb a blow, or so they'd promised him.

To his surprise, his reminder implant informed him that he had been asleep for an hour and a half when his liaison monk put his hand over Jake's mouth.

Jake suppressed his moment of panic. If the monk meant to kill him, he wouldn't have to bother to keep Jake silent.

The priest gestured at the eastern horizon, which might possibly have been slightly lighter than it had been in the complete darkness of night.

"Soon," the man breathed.

"Is everyone ready?"

Jake kept his voice to an absolute dead quiet, but even that breath seemed too much for the monk. "Of course."

Although the monk's woolen robes partially hid them from his vision, the Granger soldiers increasingly stood out as the planet's sun made its way toward the horizon. They were moving about purposefully, silently, preparing for something.

"John's letter must have convinced them," Jake whispered.

"Quiet."

Jake shook his head, but shut his mouth. This was his plan, yet the priests treated him like he was some sort of barely tolerated trained weasel, useful against the rodents, perhaps, but not properly a part of the family.

Which was, he realized, exactly what he was. He wasn't of their faith, or of any faith. He'd adopted Otranto because it seemed to offer the most hope to the world, and because it met his own commercial goals. Why should a group of martial monks see him as anything but another foreign mercenary?

A group of unmounted Granger soldiers crept closer to the Otranto City walls, heavy shields held over their heads. They might believe John's letter, but they weren't taking unnecessary chances.

When they reached the city gates, they stopped, gathered together, and then shoved them open.

A single shout went up from somewhere in the massed Granger cavalry--a shout that ended abruptly in the solid clunk of a saber hilt slamming into a helmet.

The offending Granger soldier crumpled to the ground and the remainder of the cavalry moved forward toward the open gates.

"Now?" The monk's voice was pressing, demanding.

"Wait."

"But--"

"Wait." Whatever their training, he didn't want the monks to be heroes. In fact, he would have preferred well-trained mercenaries. They, at least, would have some respect for their own lives. Allying with religious fanatics who believed that they would be accepted into heaven if only they managed to die in battle didn't give Jake the greatest confidence that he'd be safe himself.

There were more Granger than Jake had supposed. More shiploads of soldiers must have landed while he'd been busy rescuing the Patriarch. His eyes widened as he increased his estimate of the enemy force from two thousand to at least four thousand.

At this point, though, they had no choice but to follow the plan. The gates to the city were already open and the first wave of Granger horsemen were already reaching the walls.

"All right. Now," he said. He didn't have to lower his voice any longer. The undulating battle cry of the Granger forces ripped through the air like a weapon.

Jake didn't want to think about the number of Otranto armies and Otranto cities that had fallen into panic under that battle cry and been overrun. That was history. If they survived the day, the Otranto forces would begin to build a new sense of self-confidence that no screaming nomadic warrior could undermine.

It was a big if.

The monks moved out of their hiding places. Each strung a long bow and planted a quiver of arrows in the earth before them.

Jake waited until the second line of Granger cavalry reached the city walls and poured into the open gates, then nodded. "Begin."

The arrows didn't cut into the mob of Granger troops. Instead, it ripped through the guards left behind in the Granger encampment.

If there were any screams, they were drowned out by the battle cries, shouts, and bellows coming from the direction of the open city.

"Move up. And keep your eyes open for the patriarch's Legate."

"Don't tell us how to do our jobs," Jake's liaison monk sneered.

Jake realized that he had just been standing there, crossbow in hand, while the monks had cleared the palisade of all visible sentries.

"Right."

He ignored the monk's attempts to persuade him to stay behind the line of black-cloaked monks as they made their way toward the Granger encampment.

Six sentries slumped near the main gate, long black arrows protruding from eyes, throats, or narrow slits in their armor. Jake clambered over the earth and wooden walls.

Two of the monks took the obvious entryway through the gates and quickly ran into an ambush.

Jake watched helplessly as a dozen men swarmed toward the two priests. He didn't trust his aim with the crossbow enough to shoot at the Granger without the risk of hitting one of the monks instead.

The remaining twenty-seven monks had no such scruples. They rained a shower of black arrows into the Granger guard. The last Granger ended his charge with a warrior monk's mace imbedded in his forehead and another's arrow in his back.

"Leave five to search the camp, ten to guard the palisade, and take the remaining fourteen to cut off any Granger stragglers," Jake ordered.

The monk nodded abruptly and Jake realized that the man had heard the plan so many times he hardly needed Jake's instructions. Still, it helped Jake to think that he was involved.

With their camp intact, even if they lost their effort to capture the city, the Granger would simply regroup and remain as an active force to prevent the Otranto army from gaining access to the city. With an effective Otranto force in the camp, they, rather than the Otranto army, would be the force surrounded by their enemies as Otranto's army closed the distance to its city.

Jake should have gone with the monks cutting off the stragglers. They'd done what they needed to do here in the Granger camp and any time he wasted here could hurt their chances. Still, he needed to find John and make sure the priest was safe. He owed him that much, at least. When he saw the Patriarch again, Jake intended to be able to tell him that his brave legate was alive and well.

Inside the rough palisade, the Granger had erected the same kind of tents their ancestors had used in the deserts for hundreds of years before they had become a conquering and imperial people.

Jake calculated that John would be held in the largest of the tents and strode toward it.

The faintest hint of movement stopped him just before he threw open the flap and entered.

It might have been only the wind moving the tent's silken fabric, but Jake was already taking plenty of chances that day.

He stepped a third of the way around the tent, drew his knife, ripped a long tear through the tent fabric and followed the knife with his body, diving through the hole, rolling forward using his arms, back, and hip to break the fall, then regaining his feet.

His injured arm screamed a protest and he upped his endorphin supply—again.

Two Granger soldiers turned toward him moving in what felt like slow motion. Each held long swords in their hands.

Jake pointed his crossbow and pulled the trigger.

The man he'd aimed at flinched, then laughed to find himself alive when he hadn't expected to be.

Jake's crossbow bolt lay on the carpeted floor of the tent where it had fallen when Jake had rolled.

He threw the heavy bow at one of the soldiers and pulled his knife. A knife against two trained swordsmen didn't give Jake any sense of confidence.

"Come to visit your friend?" one of the Granger demanded in an accented Otranto.

Did he mean John? Jake could hardly take the time to look around the room but if John was there and unbound, he would have joined Jake by now. Either he wasn't there, or the Granger had tied him up.

"Haven't you heard?" he taunted. "Otranto finally realized they'd been making a mistake hiring soldiers to fight with the Granger. They decided to hire rat catchers when they became aware that the Granger are rodents rather than human."

It wasn't much of a taunt, but it was the best he could come up with offhand. He needed to end this foolishness, find his friend John, and then get into Otranto and make sure that the trap had truly sprung and that the Granger hadn't overrun the traps and new interior walls they'd built to protect the Otranto militia, mob, and the few guards they'd been able to find.

"Rodents?" The first Granger flung himself at Jake like a madman, swirling his sword over his head, through his legs, and around his body.

He was showing off, trying to intimidate Jake with his sword skill while not really caring about any defenses that Jake might mount. Why should he, after all. A twelve centimeter knife against a one meter sword is going to end up the same way every time. With the knifeman dead.

Jake waited until the Granger was almost on top of him, then threw his knife.

It wasn't the approved technique to deal with a swordsman and it shouldn't have worked. The Granger *should* simply have batted the flung knife from the air. Because he was intent on the attack, however, the Granger already had his saber out in a long thrust. The knife buried itself in his eye before he could react.

Jake didn't stay to watch the results. He dove backward through the hole he'd cut in the tent.

It wasn't nearly as successful a dive this time. He landed hard on his shoulder and stayed on his back, his wind knocked from his lungs.

He was still struggling to his feet when the second Granger charged him.

Jake grasped dirt and threw it at the man's eyes, but missed.

The Granger laughed, extended his saber, then jerked hard. He opened his mouth and a trickle of dark blood emerged.

He tumbled slowly forward, a black arrow protruding between his shoulder blades.

"Did you find the Legate?" Jake hadn't even seen the black-clad monk until he spoke.

"Not yet."

"He's got to be in that tent. We've searched everyplace else."

"Anybody hurt?"

The monk nodded. "Most of us, at least some. We lost two dead. The Granger like to play the ambush game."

They'd counted on losing at least half their numbers on the assault on the camp, but still Jake shuddered. He was responsible for two more deaths of people who'd relied on him, plus who-knew how many Granger soldiers who were just doing their jobs.

"I'm going back in," Jake said. "I don't think there are any more Granger soldiers in there, but why don't you follow and cover me?"

"Why don't you take his sword?"

Jake shook his head. "If I need it, it's too late for me. They've got to know we're out here."

The monk met his gaze for a moment, appearing to look inside Jake's mind. Finally he nodded. "Right. I'll be behind you."

Rolling into the last tent hadn't worked especially well but Jake couldn't think of a better alternative. Sticking his head in and asking for it to be chopped off didn't appeal.

The tent's opening hadn't been securely fastened so at least he didn't have to warn whoever was inside by slicing the tent's side this time. Jake simply dove through the tent's opening and rolled forward, slapping the ground to break his fall.

Or rather, he meant to slap the ground. What he actually slapped felt uncomfortably like human flesh.

Before the other could react, Jake grabbed what could only be a foot, twisted it, and pulled hard using the leverage of his planted feet and hips to give him added strength.

The man's foot moved easily, as if it held no weight, but he didn't tumble to the ground which had been Jake's intent. Instead, he swung in the tent. Perhaps, Jake thought, he was hanging from the tent's support beams although why anyone would do that was beyond his befuddled imagination.

Although his mind might not be working at full speed, his underdeveloped psychic senses screamed that something was wrong. The sense of wrongness was compounded by a familiar but unrecognized scent that lingered in the tent's air like a bad perfume. "I need a light," Jake shouted in the direction of the opening.

Moments later, a lit lamp, held at the end of a long staff, protruded into the tent.

Jake had thought he was ready for anything. The brutal lamplight proved to him just how wrong he had been.

Suspended from the tent's wooden framework, his body pierced with dozens of shallow knife wounds, John's corpse swayed slowly.

Around him, crude instruments of torture lay scattered as if they had stopped their work suddenly when it was time to attack Otranto--as if they had tortured John not until they were convinced he was telling the truth, but until they ran out of time to change their decision.

"The legate is a martyr to the cause." The warrior monk had entered the tent and stood beside Jake.

Jake struggled for words, but found nothing. Arcadia's history was full of martyrs to one cause or another. Indeed, dead martyrs seemed to constitute much of human history everywhere. And for what? Everything that Jake did, all of his efforts to help evolve an industrial economy and preserve the intellectual heritage of Otranto simply meant that more people were dying.

"Help me cut him down," Jake ordered.

"There is a battle to fight. A fetish over his body would merely risk our loss of momentum."

"Then stop arguing and help me," Jake shouted. He yanked out his knife and started sawing at the rawhide straps that held his friend in place.

After a moment's contemplation, the monk moved to assist him, holding John's bloody body to give Jake easier access to the ties.

It took only a few moments to cut John down. Gently, the two men laid the corpse on a pile of carpets.

Jake fumbled for a pulse hopelessly. He knew his friend was dead but didn't want to accept that reality.

"No one could survive those wounds," the monk told him.

Despair gripped him like an icy hand at his heart. "It isn't worth it."

"He was your friend," the monk told him. "It is natural that you feel the sense of loss. But if he had not taken the message, four thousand men of the Otranto army would have perished within the week. More, Otranto City would have fallen and countless thousands of civilians and priests would have been raped and murdered. He knew the risks when he volunteered."

"So I'm supposed to feel good about this?"

The monk shook his head slowly. "Our faith teaches that life is a precious gift. Sacrificing that gift should never be done rashly, yet there are times when even that gift must be returned. Surely this was such a time."

Jake wanted to argue, to prove to himself and the other that this was different. It wasn't too late. He could run from Otranto now, take his ferry to Tantalus and catch a ship to one of the Bourgundian cities where he could wait for the eventual arrival of a galactic trading ship.

"Would running have avoided this death?" the monk asked him.

Pure shock filled him. Jake had to manually override his systems to turn down the flow of adrenaline that surged through his body. "How did you know what I was thinking?"

The monk shrugged. "I have been teaching young monks for twenty years. Do you really think, just because we have a calling, that we are different from you? All men seek to escape from their destiny."

Jake nodded grimly. Maybe he would try to escape his destiny, but not now, not today. Right now, he had to finish what he'd started, finish what John had given his life to secure. "Let's go."

The Granger had left a rear guard to hold the gate when they'd charged inside. The martial monks and the Granger rear guard exchanged occasional arrows with neither side able to gain the advantage.

One of the monks approached Jake and the monk who'd helped him with John. "We've lost three more, Captain."

"How many do they have in their rear guard?" the monk demanded.

"Probably a hundred."

"Too many to rush, then."

"People are dying in Otranto now," Jake urged. "If the Granger knew that their escape route was in danger, they would panic. We could save lives."

The monk shook his head. "Your friend's death was a sacrifice. Asking my men to rush the enemy would be vainglorious stupidity. We would die and the Granger force would be able to recover this camp. Everything we've done would be for nothing. If we keep them trapped, eventually the forces inside the city will prevail. Or we will all lose."

Jake knew the monk was right. He also knew that Manny and the brewers guild, Mark and the rough force of students he'd pulled together, and Harold and the few mercenaries within the city were at risk, were dying, pitted against a

Granger army that might be outnumbered but that lived for battle in a way that the civilized militia of Otranto city never would.

He toyed with the idea of charging the Granger rearguard singlehandedly. With the covering arrows of the martial monks, he might actually be able to get into the midst of the Granger force. Once there, though, he would be a sitting duck.

Jake was depressed about the loss of his friend but he wasn't suicidal.

At least his brain seemed to be working a little bit again. He'd seen a pair of heavy although small gage cannons at the gate to the Granger stockade. "Let's blast them out."

"Cannons are used against buildings, not people," the monk protested.

"Is that a religious rule or just practical tactics?"

"It only makes sense," the monk replied. "What idiot would stand still if you pointed a cannon at him. Fortifications have to sit still."

"Well, I don't think the Granger rear guard is going anywhere. And if they decide to move because they see the cannon, that's got to be better than what we have now."

"We don't have oxen to haul the cannon around," the monk said. He examined the palisade wall to the camp's stockade. "If we tore down that corner of the stockade, though, we could aim the guns at the rear guard without moving them."

It would be a longer shot than Jake had wanted. He had envisioned filling the barrel with musket balls and crossbow bolts and hurling a wave of death at the unlucky Granger. Still, the monk's suggestions and objections had merit. "Let's do it."

"We'll be weakening our defenses when the Granger come out, you know," the monk reminded Jake.

"So we take the battle to them."

The monk nodded slowly and a hint of a smile crossed his face before he regained his peaceful equanimity. "I like the way you think."

Ten of the monks kept a slow stream of black arrows in the direction of the Granger rear guard while the remaining fifteen of Jake's surviving monks started tearing down the stockade.

Jake watched for a moment, then called for them to stop. "This is taking too long."

"The cannon were your idea," the monk reminded him.

"So let's use them. If they can't blow a hole through the stockade, they aren't going to do much good against the Granger, are they? And you did say these things are good against buildings."

The monk looked at him. "It'll be dangerous but it's worth a try."

Rather than waste time on fruitless hacking at the wall, Jake had the monks swivel the two cannon around until they were facing in the general direction of Otranto's gate.

It took a good ten minutes to load the first cannon. Jake was tempted to double-shot the weapon, but remembered, at the last minute, how unreliable Arcadian alloys were. Getting his monks killed wouldn't bring John back to life.

Loading the cannon consisted of shoving a bag of gunpowder into the barrel, wrapping an iron cannonball in a leather rag and shoving it down after the powder, then piercing the gunpowder bag with a thin flute of gunpowder through a touch hole, and finally lighting the flute.

On the monk captain's orders, the monks withdrew from the cannon when Jake was ready to fire. "Drop to the ground as soon as you light it," his monk told him.

"What about you?"

"I'll be there too."

Jake touched a lamp flame to the gunpowder flute, then followed the monk's advice being careful to roll away from the weapon. After all he'd been through, he didn't intend to be killed by letting a cannon recoil crush him.

He lay on the ground for what seemed an interminable time. "Misfire," he guessed out loud.

The cannon's roar cut off the last part of his guess.

The heavy iron ball smashed into the stockade wall and sent wooden splinters flying like shrapnel from an antipersonnel weapon.

One of his monks screamed out in pain--a shrill cry that Jake heard even over the deafening roar of the cannon shot.

"Help Maurice," the monk captain ordered two of his men. "The rest of you, let's get this thing reloaded.

The stockade wall had been designed to withstand musket shot. The blow from the inside of the hastily constructed walls, at a range of perhaps three meters, went beyond anything that the Granger had expected. It opened a hole two meters wide, with bits of lumber drooping off the sides. Many of the timbers that had gone into constructing the wall appeared to have evaporated although more were littered on both sides of the original wall in a web of destruction.

Unfortunately, the shrapnel seemed to end up far short of the Granger guarding Otranto's city gates. The cannon shot appeared to have gone straight through the open city gates where, Jake hoped, it might have plowed into the backs of some of the invading Granger.

From the rear-guard, at least, came the sound of derisive laughter.

"We might as well shoot at them with arrows," the monk-captain told Jake. "We'd be more accurate, at any rate. With them spread out like that, we wouldn't be able to hit more than one or two at a time and it takes forever to load."

Jake had seen that. He had also seen the devastating impact of cannon shot against the palisade wall.

"Aim high."

"I beg your pardon."

"Aim at the wall rather than at the soldiers. We'll rely on the shrapnel to drive them out."

The monk nodded briskly. "Of course."

It took longer than Jake would have imagined to clean any lingering residue of gunpower and sparks out of the fired cannon, shove another bag of gunpowder down its maw, and fit an iron ball into the mouth. While he worked on the cannon that had fired the initial shot, the Monk captain worked on the second.

"Both together, you think?" he asked when they'd finally completed their efforts. He was getting increasingly nervous over the battle for the city. Surely the Granger would realize by now that their retreat had been cut off and that they had no choice but to win the city themselves or face extermination.

The monk considered, then shook his head. "First yours, then we'll aim for any groups that remain."

Mindful of the previous bloody effort (Maurice was alive, but definitely out of the battle with a foot-long sliver through his calf), the monks moved well clear before Jake fired the primer and dropped to the ground.

He covered his ears and waited for the cannon roar.

It came, but this time was accompanied by a metallic tearing sound.

Almost simultaneous with the crash of cannon fire came the smashing sound of the iron ball crushing masonry and sending rock bits like bullets through the Granger rear guard.

"That cannon is out of action," the monk captain told him.

The touch-hold appeared to have given way and bright bronze showed a tear about six inches long in the cannon's barrel.

"We'll be able to use the bronze, anyway," the monk continued. "Now let's get the other cannon aimed."

Chapter 27

The ricochet hadn't disabled too many of the Granger but it looked like most of them had suffered at least minor injuries. Jake didn't think they'd stand for too much more pounding before reacting.

"Have your archers ready," he told the monk captain. "I think they'll be coming out."

The monk nodded gravely. "You'd be right on that. Another two blasts, maybe."

The Granger would be better off if their rearguard attacked now, before more of them got killed or injured, but Jake hoped that they would try to get orders from the main Granger force before they reacted. In the meantime, he helped swab out the remaining cannon, getting it ready for the next shot.

Rather than simply smashing cannon balls into the masonry walls, this time Jake suggested aiming at a marble frieze over the gate commemorating some thousand-year old Otranto victory. Ruining valuable artwork assaulted Jake's mercantile sensibilities, but he and his friends needed to be alive. Those who were left.

His tactic was even more successful than he'd imagined. The friezework exploded off the wall, shattering into razor sharp, fist-sized chunks of death that rattled through the Granger rear-guard.

A moan made up of both anger and pain came from the Granger troops.

"Load it with these," the monk captain told him.

Jake looked at the assortment of chain links, arrowheads, and pike points the captain dumped on the ground. "Won't work," he said. "The range is too long for antipersonnel weaponry."

"The range is about to get a lot shorter. I suggest you hurry."

Either the Granger needed to psych themselves up, or Jake's shots had killed enough officers to make them indecisive because it took several minutes of shouting and organizing before the first Granger stuck his head above the makeshift fortification they hid behind.

A black arrow buzzed by that Granger and he pulled back.

"Hold your fire," the captain growled. "Do you want them to retreat inside the gates?"

Jake's four man cannon crew had finished swabbing the cannon and stuffing down the next bag of gunpowder when he heard the screaming Granger warcry and the deep-throated snap of Granger muskets.

One of the monks on his crew coughed, then settled to the ground. Blood gushed from his chest.

The other two monks working with Jake dropped to the ground to help their friend.

"Get back to work," he shouted, madly shoveling in the assortment of ironwork the captain had given him.

"But he's dying."

"Pray for him later, unless you want to join him now."

They reluctantly returned to their work, but Jake could see he hadn't made any new friends.

They didn't have time to aim. A hundred screaming Granger warriors were almost on top of them by the time they had nearly completed loading.

The panicking monk lit the touchhole as Jake was stuffing in the last of the iron bits. Instinctively, Jake dropped to the ground and clasped his ears.

The cannon roar felt like an earthquake.

Jake looked up, but could see only the blinding black smoke of the cannon's discharge.

That was bad. The badly outnumbered monks needed to use their bows rather than attempt hand-to-hand combat against the well trained Granger forces.

He realized he could no longer hear the Granger warcries.

For an instant, he let himself hope that they'd killed the entire lot. Then he realized he couldn't hear anything. The cannon, firing so close to his head, had deafened him, possibly blowing out his augmentation as well.

He struggled to his feet and found a javelin he could use as a proxy for a staff, then turned to face the Granger attack.

They should have been there by now, he realized. Again, he let himself hope that his cannon shot had done its job.

* * * *

Then the Granger were everywhere.

Jake gave himself everything his augmentation had left, trying to blur into action and to ignore his growing sense of dread and the residual effect of his crossbow wound. It had seemed like such a sensible plan when he'd laid it out.

He was fighting on his own. He wouldn't have guessed that the monks would run but wherever they were, they weren't anywhere in his sight.

He jabbed with the javelin, then whipped it around to strike with the shaft reversing the point to stab at the Granger coming up behind him.

He blocked a descending war ax reflexively, and watched as the javelin disintegrated in his hands.

Jake threw the remains at one of the Granger, did a one-armed cartwheel over the man he'd stabbed and spun to face his attackers disarmed but as ready as he was going to get.

They were screaming something, probably encouraging each other to go and get the unarmed idiot who wouldn't run away, but Jake still couldn't hear anything.

They started to advance on him, moving slowly now as if afraid he'd pull something else from his bag of tricks. Then, as if by magic, they started to collapse, long black arrows protruding from their bodies.

When three of their captains fell with black arrows in their throats, the remainder turned and headed back toward the walls. Few made it.

The captain and nine other monks surrounded Jake, their mouths moving a mile a minute.

"I can't hear," Jake said. He tried to control his volume but, from the winces on the faces before him, he realized he'd failed at that.

The captain shrugged, then pointed in the direction of the Otranto city walls.

Well, Jake could understand that at least.

"Absolutely. Let's go and see what help we can offer our friends."

* * * *

The battle inside Otranto should have been a slaughter. The stonemasons had constructed a set of breastworks and high walls that would crowd the attacking Granger, direct their flow, and allow Otranto's mercenaries to slice them to pieces. The guild forces were available as reserves, while the mob could throw rocks and pull down any Granger foolish enough to get separated from their formation. Plenty of traps should have slowed their rush, killed many of them, and made the rest careful in what they approached.

Things hadn't worked out quite so well. Despite firm orders from Fernis and the Patriarch, the Otranto mob had initially attacked, confusing the mercenaries' aim, then turned in panic and run, sweeping away many of the guild reserves and tripping some of the traps in the process. As a result, the Granger had managed to establish themselves, taking control of several segments of the temporary wall that had been designed to be used against them.

The second group of thirty martial monks finally arrived and Jake, with his small band, reached the city gates just in time to send a few flights of arrows into the backs of a Granger force huddled under the protection of one of those walls.

In itself, killing a dozen Granger shouldn't have mattered in a battle like this. In the event, however, the Granger force, which already felt surrounded and hard-pressed, simply collapsed, throwing down their weapons and looking for someone to surrender to.

Jake shouted to his monks and pointed hoping that they'd get the idea and accept the surrenders before the mob attacked and the Granger picked their weapons back up and fought to the death.

It was a victory. His plan had worked and Otranto would survive for another week, at least. Yet, John's death weighed on Jake. He felt no elation, only a fatigue so heavy that it held him almost immobile. From everywhere, he could hear only silence.

* * * *

Jake stumbled through Otranto City's open gates when he felt a sharp tug on his tunic.

Panic. Could a Granger have hidden among the dead, waiting for a chance to exact revenge?

Jake spun around.

Castile looked more like the imp she'd been when he first met her than the stunning young princess she'd turned into. She had a pair of long-barreled pistols tucked into a black belt and a Granger cavalry saber hanging naked down her back. Black smudges across her face and a sliced gash across her tunic directly below her breasts made it clear that she wasn't just wearing a costume. She'd been fighting.

Her lips moved, so Jake was certain Castile was saying something. He still couldn't hear a sound.

"I'm deaf," he told her.

She winced and stepped backward, so he knew he must have shouted.

Castile wrinkled her nose, then turned and ran down the cobblestone road.

He considered following her, then shrugged. He had more Granger prisoners to protect. Why hadn't he planned for prisoners? Any merchant who set off on a trading expedition with as little preparation as Jake had entered into the military field could expect to lose his shirt.

Although the sun told him that it was only mid-afternoon, Jake's body could barely hold him erect as he shoved the last of the Granger prisoners into the makeshift POW camp he'd had constructed in an abandoned section of Otranto. Mercenary forces guarded the Granger from mob attack as much as they kept the Granger from escaping.

Manny and the Brewers Guild militia marched around looking official and keeping the mob from looting while the Patriarch himself took command of the martial monks and the prisoners. He kept Mark with him, Jake noticed, and the two seemed to be arguing philosophy.

Jake used his command of the Granger language to try and persuade the few surviving Granger officers that they and their men were better off accepting protection from the mercenaries than they would be if they attempted to escape into the roused city. Since most of them had surrendered to get away from the mob, they didn't take much convincing. Which was lucky since Jake wasn't up to much convincing given that he couldn't hear a word anyone said to him.

Even Harold and Lucer showed up, passing out free beer to the more peaceful of the mob members and smacking the more violent over the head.

Everything seemed under control. Jake felt suddenly useless. He'd put in place institutions that might give Otranto a chance. What he needed, he decided, was sleep.

Castile reappeared, a long scroll of parchment in her hand and a fusty looking priest by her side.

Jake let himself collapse onto the stoop of an abandoned marble palace and let the priest, who must also be a doctor, poke at his body, prod his ears, and look down his throat.

Castile scribbled on her scroll. "Have you eaten anything?"

He shook his head. "Not since last night."

She wordlessly handed him a leather flask filled with a rich red wine.

Jake drank deeply, coughing at the burn of alcohol against a throat made raw by hours of fighting and then more hours of shouting warnings to those who wanted to kill the prisoners.

"Do you know anything about cannons?" Castile wrote. "I want the ones you fired outside the walls."

She wanted a lot, Jake realized. She also got what she wanted more often than not.

Jake shrugged, then winced at the discovery of a new wound. When had he been struck in the shoulder?

The priest prodded at him a little more, then stood and delivered his report to Castile.

Jake's attempts to read lips were completely unsuccessful. Castile's face looked grave as she turned back to him.

"Well?"

"He says you'll live," she wrote.

"What about my hearing?"

Castile shrugged.

"Has anyone gotten word to the army?" Jake asked. "And we need to prepare room for the peasants who'll be retreating with them."

Castile brushed a tear from her eyes, then turned her attention toward her scroll.

"All that is done. You aren't the only one who can remember to do their job."

He'd made her angry, although he hadn't wanted to.

"Do you think it will be enough?" she wrote.

Jake shrugged. With Bourgundian help, he could keep the straits open and develop a steady flow of food and trade goods between Tantalus and Otranto city. Silk and olive oil, together with Castile's iron works, Mark's university, Manny's brewery, and the Patriarch's winery and textiles industries could form the basis for an industrial city--a city that supported itself rather than being an administrative drain on the countryside around it. Given a year, Otranto would be unstoppable. But no one would give them a year. Long before that, the main Granger army would arrive. Their Anglic allies might be strong enough to beat off the Bourgundians, and were certainly enough to force Otranto to guard the sea walls as well as the land wall.

All in all, Otranto's survival would have to be called a long shot. Which was considerably better than it had been twenty-four hours earlier.

"We have a chance," he said.

"We didn't until you came along," she wrote.

He shrugged again, embarrassed. Unlike John, Jake was no hero. He was just a merchant who happened into a business opportunity. He told her that.

She shook her head, then bent and wrote quickly.

"You could kiss me, you know."

He froze. Not that Castile wasn't attractive. When she was dressed in her Otranto Princess mode, she would turn heads even on planets where beauty augmentation was universal. And Arcadia customs were different from those of the civilized galaxy. Still, he couldn't overcome his scruples. Castile was a child.

Castile frowned, then pulled one of her pistols from her belt.

He almost panicked. Teenage suicide was one disease that even modern galactic medicine hadn't completely eliminated. It could be much worse here.

He reached for the gun but Castile slapped away his hand and stepped back.

Jake was almost relieved when she pointed the weapon at him. How crazy did that make him?

She wrote, not looking at the scroll, then shoved it at him.

"Is there another woman?"

Jake laughed. "When have I had time for a woman? You're just too young for me."

Castile nodded slowly, then gestured for him to return her pad.

He started to stand, but she cocked her pistol and he sat back down on his stoop, then pushed the pad back.

"You're five years older than me," she wrote. "That isn't a big difference. How old do Spacer women have to be to get married?"

"The law says eighteen," he told her. "But most wait until they're in their thirties or even fifties."

Castile shook her head and gestured for the pad back.

"Eighteen," she wrote. "I guess we have to win this war."

He guessed she was right. Of course, by that time she would have gotten over this crush and found someone more suitable.

The small twinge of sadness at that thought didn't make any sense at all.

"Let's go have something to eat," he suggested.

Castile uncocked her pistol and thrust it back into her belt.

Her arm felt good against him as he struggled down the Otranto street returning to what had become his home.

The End

We hope you have enjoyed MERCHANT PRINCE OF ARCADIA by Rob Preece. Please visit www.BooksForABuck.com to see the latest in affordable electronic fiction.

www.ingramcontent.com/pod-product-compliance
Lightning Source LLC
Chambersburg PA
CBHW070851250626
47159CB00003B/1027